MAXIM ULTRA

J. DOUGLAS SIMPSON

EDEN'S HOLLOW PRESS

Eden's Hollow Press

www.jdouglassimpson.com

Cover Image courtesy of NASA

For Jim and Gwen

AUTHOR'S NOTE

1998. That's the year I came up with the character Maxim Ultra. Originally, he was conceived as a tough, mysterious bounty hunter-type, which is cool and all, but I felt he would work better if readers actually, you know, *liked* him. So, I started thinking of him as more of a regular guy. He's from Earth—which is extremely rare in this universe—and has gone into the family business, so to speak, following in the footsteps of his deceased father.

I had all sorts of story ideas for Max's first adventure—some of which you'll actually read someday—but couldn't decide with which one to open the series. I had an idea for a really great story that mostly introduced Litning—and yes, his name is spelled correctly throughout the novel, don't worry—but ultimately, I knew I had to really introduce Max to the audience. It is, after all, his book series. So I rummaged through my copious writing notes and found a MacGuffin that I had planned to use in a comic story submission for a very famous superhero that I never got around to writing. It worked perfectly as the introduction to Max and his world.

So, I kept writing notes and creating characters and tried to figure out how all the pieces fit together, inadvertently plotting out future novels in the series in the process. I finally took the plunge on writing the novel after I had finished up the first *Great Big World*—yes, the second is coming—and the result after procrastinating on making the final edits is the tome you hold in your hands now.

I love writing these characters and I hope you'll enjoy reading them just as much. Thank you so much for stepping into Max's world with me.

If you'd like to keep up with me online and want to ask questions or just chat about the book, you can find me at the following places:

www.jdouglassimpson.com
Twitter: @maximultra
facebook.com/jdouglassimpson
doug@jdouglassimpson.com

Thanks again for reading. I hope you enjoy the adventure!

-   J. Douglas Simpson
    March 2019

MAXIM ULTRA

CHAPTER I

He had her cornered. After chasing Sierra through the streets of Tonicen, not to mention all over the neighboring star systems, Maxim Ultra finally had her cornered.

The final leg of the chase had been a footrace leading to Tonicen's disused industrial district. The area, populated with dilapidated gray warehouses, was completely self-contained—the perfect place for her to ambush him. Bending at the waist, he sucked wind. His legs and chest burned like blast furnaces. Blood pounded in his temples. As he maintained cover behind a broken wall, he watched her scurry into the maze of buildings.

Max could have called the local authorities, but they were just as likely to haul him away as to help. Besides, this was something he had to do alone. He'd thrown in with Sierra, Kalen, and their crew for a big score that would have settled his debts, but they'd crossed a line. Now, he was trying to make things right. If he found a way out of his predicament, so much the better, but he liked to think he was being more noble than selfish. Only time would tell which was true.

From his black leather jacket, he produced a handheld that had once been an old smartphone and caught his reflection in the screen. His soft blue eyes appeared black in the dark mirrored surface and his generally disheveled look was completed with messy short brown hair and several days' worth of stubble. In short, he'd looked better. A few swipes of his finger brought up a tracking program. It amazed him at how his robot pal, Roeger, could upgrade his outclassed Earth tech, but still make it look normal enough for him to use back home without awkward stares.

He'd slipped a tracer into Sierra's boot back during the job and was glad that she didn't change shoes every five minutes. The blinking blue dot on his screen told him she was definitely in the warehouse thirty yards ahead. He wouldn't have put it past her to shed her boots and run around the cold concrete barefoot, though, just to make his life difficult.

A thick layer of dust from the crumbling structures coated the ground, but Sierra's footprints were barely visible as the sun dipped behind the buildings, shrouding the area in shadow. There could have been anything waiting for him in the industrial park. Vagrants and low-end criminals were known to dwell in the ruinous structures. The vagrants had nowhere else to go, but the criminals were the lowest of the low. Powerful syndicates controlled the crime in Tonicen—a kind of silent agreement with the heavy-handed police—but their fraternity frequented the glittering towers of the city proper. Only those criminals too dumb—or too broke—to worm their way into the real action operated here.

Max drew his fully-charged pistol. Peering past his cover one last time, he started toward the building he'd targeted. Movement to his left caused him to spin that way, leveling his weapon at a different building. He held his position, his aim never wavering.

Just your imagination, Max.

2

Lingering for one last moment, he resumed his original path. A two-story warehouse loomed ahead of him. The scene was strangely beautiful, with the setting sun's amber rays streaking across the sky, throwing the dark building into stark contrast.

The doorway, a black hole of mystery, had no door—not uncommon for the area. Those holed up in the buildings usually removed the doors in order to keep watch for any intruders. Max felt their eyes on him.

Sierra would be on the second floor in the offices above the warehouse. At least she'd be there if she wanted a tactical advantage. The encroaching darkness made it impossible to see inside through the windows, so for all he knew, she was lining him up in a sniper's scope while he gaped up at the building like an amateur.

Dashing over to the warehouse, he flattened himself against the wall on the left side of the open door. Slowly, he poked his head inside. Burning trashcans scattered about the warehouse cast a dim light around the cavernous room. The ceiling wasn't very high, but as he'd seen from the outside, the building stretched back about a hundred-fifty yards. To the left, a metal staircase led to the second level. Debris and garbage littered every inch of the warehouse floor and Max gagged at the unmistakable odor of shit permeating the area.

The building appeared deserted. He was about to call out to Sierra when he saw two human-sized figures moving toward his position. One was much more solidly built than the other—a male and a female, perhaps? It was too dark to see their features.

Max ducked down, slinking over to a support beam for cover. As he peered between his column and the one adjacent, he saw tight, thin, translucent strands crisscrossing between the two. The strands were connected to a pack of explosives above his head.

Je-sus fuck.

It was definitely Sierra's work—not enough to bring the building down, but it would most certainly ruin his day. The warehouse wasn't a random sanctuary for her—it was a trap for him.

"I saw her run through here, up the stairs," the male said in a low voice.

"Then, let's see if she wants to play," the female responded.

Max didn't like the sound of that. He wanted to bring Sierra in, not see her violated, or whatever these two had planned for her. Sighing inwardly, he raised his pistol, tensed for action.

As they moved closer, Max could see that the two were not entirely human. They both wore frayed and tattered cloaks, but the male had his hood down, revealing a smooth head with baseball-sized orbs for eyes.

A Wrenkar.

Wrenkars were scaly humanoids known to dwell in low-light environments. The warehouse was perfect for this one. Max drew back a bit, ensuring he was out of sight of the Wrenkar's navy blue eyes.

The female's face was hidden by her hood, but the long, furry tail peeking out the back of her cloak at least gave Max a clue. There were several cat-like races across the galaxy, but only a Briff would be in league with a Wrenkar. The other cat races were far more insular.

The pair moved toward the staircase.

Holstering his pistol, Max picked up a small rock. He tossed it between the columns, but under the wires. The stone clattered to the floor, causing the Wrenkar and Briff to spin in Max's direction. Purposely keeping the toe of his boot in view, he pulled it back with a scrape on the concrete floor.

"There!" the Wrenkar cried in his raspy voice.

The Briff hissed, leaping high in the air toward Max.

He raced out the door, turning back in time to see the cat-lady connect with the wires. The resulting explosion consumed her in a shrieking ball of flames.

Max's smile vanished instantly when the Wrenkar launched himself out of the smoke-filled doorway. The hissing and spitting alien came at Max, knocking him to the ground. Max's head dashed against the street. As stars danced in his eyes, he tried to pull his pistol, but his introduction to the concrete left him groggy and slow.

The Wrenkar pounced, lifting Max off the ground by his collar. "You killed Ladra!"

"Now, technically, she killed herself," Max said, still trying to draw his weapon.

The move wasn't subtle enough to escape the Wrenkar's attention. He slammed Max against a wall before tossing him back inside the building.

Skidding across the floor, Max regained control of his momentum just fast enough to avoid one of the small fires that had sprung up as a result of the explosion. In-between the two support columns laid the charred remains of Ladra. Max wrinkled his nose against the smell of burnt fur.

He didn't have time to worry about it as the Wrenkar rushed at him. Finally freeing his pistol, Max snapped off two laser bolts, but the alien was incredibly fast, and Max's aim was shit.

"So, the blast didn't get you too, huh?" Max asked as the Wrenkar batted his pistol away.

"I have very thick skin, human." The alien delivered a vicious shot to the side of Max's head. "We'll see if yours is just as thick."

Max reached for a pouch on his belt, but the Wrenkar wasn't having any of that. He knocked the wind out of Max with a swift blow to his stomach before dragging him toward the staircase.

"As I took cover from the explosion, I saw this little contraption on the floor nearby. Let's see what this does, hmm?"

Sure enough, positioned near the stairs was a metal disc about two inches thick. Max knew what it was and wasn't at all interested in seeing it work. The Wrenkar appeared to have different ideas. He gripped the side of Max's head, pushing it closer and closer to the disc.

The tendons in Max's neck strained as he fought. His hands clawed at the alien's wrists, but to no avail. The trap was centimeters from Max's face when he gave a final, powerful twist of his body that kicked the Wrenkar's legs out from under him. He released Max's head as he tried to catch himself, but it was no good. As Max rolled away, the Wrenkar fell onto the disc and screamed as the whip blade did its work.

From the disc, six sharpened tentacles sprang up, slicing and dicing the Wrenkar, flaying his flesh. A horrific sight, but the Wrenkar's screams were worse as they cut straight into the pit of Max's stomach. He picked up his pistol, taking careful aim, and put the alien out of his misery. He doubted the Wrenkar would have shown him such mercy.

Finally, once the pieces of the Wrenkar's lifeless body were no longer in contact with the disc, the tentacles, slick with blood, returned to their housing. The way up the stairs was clear, but Max took a moment to compose himself. Already roughed up, he needed to be on top of his game against Sierra.

"Hey Sierra!" he called out, hoping his voice would find her. "Why don't you just come down here and talk to me?"

Predictably, no answer came.

Maybe she fell on one of her booby traps. "All right, I'm coming up. Don't fucking shoot me."

Stepping carefully over the diced Wrenkar, Max mounted the stairs to the second floor, switching his pistol to stun as he went. He found a long hallway with windows along the left wall and a doorway on the right that probably led to the interior offices. The only light came from whatever spare rays the setting sun could provide. He advanced carefully, eyes darting around for any potential traps.

The door on the right was locked, so he proceeded down the hall. He wasn't thrilled about letting Sierra funnel him where she wanted, but didn't seem to have much of a choice.

Walking made him wince. His lower back felt like someone sticking a twelve-inch spike into it. Sciatic pain shot down his leg with each step. It felt like he'd re-aggravated the injury he'd picked up a few years previously after a run-in with some errant grandings. He'd taken a near-fatal spill chasing after the little purple bastards for a client and his back hadn't been completely right since. Stopping, he leaned against the inner wall and popped two pain pills from his belt.

He peeked around the corner, but pulled back quickly upon seeing Sierra standing by a window, gazing out at the landscape.

"Didn't you hear me downstairs?" he called out to her.

"I heard you, Maxim. I just wanted to see if you had the stones to come up here."

"Ouch." Despite her taunts, Sierra's voice still melted him into a powerless goo. *Stay on point, Max.* "Come on Sierra, you know you love me chasing after you like this."

"A little, yeah." He could hear the smile in her voice. "I kind of hoped that someday I'd make your list. The only problem here is, someone should be chasing after *both* of us, Max—maybe Alesha."

Her mention of Alesha cut him deep, as she probably knew it would.

Alesha.

Their romance had always been more of a "friends with benefits" relationship, but more often than not, they were together. He'd let her down by running off with Sierra and didn't know if she'd ever forgive him. That went for his whole crew too, dumping them for a new one. He had a lot of apologies to make. Bringing Sierra in was the start of his road back.

"I'm sorry, *lover*." Her tone went from flirty to nasty. "Did I hit a nerve? Are you still there?"

"I'm still here, Sierra. I'm not leaving without you."

"That's adorable, but you helped us steal that artifact, Max."

"You killed a guard. More than one."

"No, that was Kalen and he's been captured. You knew how unstable he was—you signed up for it."

"I didn't sign up for murder."

"Stop it. You sound like a child. Do you remember when we first met? I hired you to help me find my brother's killers." She breathed deeply. "You were so cool and on point. Now...you're a joke."

He winced. How had he let this woman talk him into joining her? *Oh yeah, the massive payday I was promised.*

There was a moment of silence. She sighed. "Are we doing this or not?"

Again, he peeked down the hallway. Though she'd already drawn her pistol, she kept her stance nonchalant. She could have been the harbinger of his death, but he couldn't tear his eyes off her. About half a foot shorter than him and poured into a black cat suit that accentuated her ample curves, she had her auburn hair pulled back into a ponytail that glowed in the fading sunlight.

She smiled at him. That damn smile—lately, it had gotten him to do a lot of things he shouldn't have. As entrancing as she was, the spell was broken as soon as she fired the first blast from her pistol.

Max ducked back behind cover as the laser bolts burned into the wall behind him. Switching to his off-hand, he snapped off a couple of shots down the hall. No return fire came his way. He didn't hear her hit the floor, so he knew his aim was off. *What else is new?*

Stepping around the corner, he was greeted with Sierra's boot connecting with his face. She staggered him, keeping the pressure up with a kick to his side. He fired his pistol, but the blast impacted harmlessly on the floor as her next kick knocked his aim off. Dropping his weapon to free his hands, he grabbed her leg and flipped her onto her back.

She wasted no time in tossing three small daggers at him. Two missed him completely, while the third made him thankful for his leather jacket—the dagger merely sliced the thick sleeve, sparing his arm. He moved to rush her, but stopped short as a blade popped out of the sole of her boot. Another step would have impaled him. She forced him away with two quick kicks and then got back to her feet.

They both breathed heavily, but if he was honest with himself, she handled it a lot better. His back tortured him and the Wrenkar fight had left him sluggish. He decided to stall for time, retrieving and holstering his pistol.

"Sierra, don't do this."

"What? Kick your ass? I'm not letting you trade me for a pardon, if that's what you're after."

She didn't even let him get a response in before she was on him again with a flurry of kicks, this time without the blade. He feinted, drawing her in closer. Wrapping his arms around her, he forced her to the ground. As he fell on top of her, she grunted.

"I am *so* hot right now," she said before licking his face.

Violence wasn't a turn on for him, but he had to admit that his close proximity to her was distracting. Even after all this, a part of him still wanted her.

She squirmed in his grasp as he tried to pull a tranquillizing dart out of his belt. When he finally thought he had one, she flipped him flat onto his back. The crash to the floor sent waves of pain through him. In an instant, Sierra's boot blade headed for his face. He instinctively threw his hands up to protect himself and the knife punched through his left palm as he caught her foot.

The inhuman scream that erupted from him reverberated throughout the hall. His hand felt like it had exploded as the protruding blade dripped blood on his face. Convulsions hit his body. His breathing quickened as tears leaked out of the corners of his eyes. *Don't go into shock—not now.*

Sierra's expression became one of malevolent joy as she began to twist her foot and, in turn, the blade. He knew then that she was serious about not being taken alive.

"No, no, no…" he pleaded.

"Sorry," she whispered back with a shrug.

She jerked her foot. The blade twisted inside Max's hand, tearing through muscle and sinew. He screamed again, but drew his pistol and fired wildly up at Sierra. His desperate attack forced her to pull back, freeing the knife from his hand, which was now a contorted, bloody mess. Just looking at it brought bile to the edge of his throat.

Sierra didn't wait around. She took aim at him with her own pistol, but Max was faster, hitting her squarely with two shots that brought her to the ground in a heap.

He needed her alive, but how he'd get her back to his ship with one good hand was another matter entirely. Holstering his weapon, he reached into his belt and pulled out an antibiotic spray. He closed his eyes as he sprayed his injured hand, gambling it would be enough to fight off infection before he could properly treat it on the ship. He just hoped he'd be able to use it again.

Using his good hand to lean on the wall, he pulled himself to his feet, stumbling toward Sierra's motionless body. She was definitely breathing—it looked like the stun setting had done its job. He crouched beside her, taking her wrist in his hand to bind her.

Her arm stiffened.

In a flash, she sat up and thrust one of her daggers into his thigh with a wild grin. He fell back from her, trying to maintain his balance and draw his pistol at the same time. *How is she not unconscious?*

She laughed.

He managed to get to his feet, but it was useless as Sierra's next kick connected with his chest.

Max crashed through the second floor window onto the grime-covered street. Luckily, the fall hadn't been enough to pulverize his bones. His body throbbed like a giant abscess and the growing patch of blood through his jeans was disconcerting. His ruined hand moved down on his list of concerns.

As he attempted to get up, his leg gave out. His back started to lock up as his knees scraped against the street. More than likely, he had a broken rib or two to go with his injured leg, mutilated hand, and swollen jaw. He retched up blood-tinged sputum.

I am not having a good day.

"Max? Honey? You okay?" Sierra's muffled voice echoed from the broken window.

All he could do was groan.

"I'm coming down."

His body seized at her threat. He drew his pistol, attempting to aim at the second floor. Stabbing pain doubled him over. She was already gone anyway.

He holstered his weapon, searching frantically for a means of escape. Lucky him—he was in an alley. Instinctively, he reached for his handheld, but remembered he was alone this time. No one would be coming to help him.

Maybe getting involved with Sierra and Kalen wasn't such a good idea. It had only been about the billionth time he'd had that thought.

He managed to drag himself to the end of the alley, trying to ignore the blood trail in his wake. Taking up a position against the concrete wall, he charged his pistol and waited. This time, he set it to kill. *To hell with bringing her in alive.*

"*Maaaaxim…. Maaaaxim….*"

He tensed as her sing-song voice floated down the alley.

She poked her head around the corner and gasped. "Why, Mr. Ultra, are you going to shoot me with your big, hard gun?"

"Come down here and find out."

Again, her demeanor shifted to steely cool. "I really don't want to hurt you any more than I already have, Max. Put it away."

He had no cover, no means of escape, and could see her own pistol trained on him. Who knew? Maybe she'd even show some mercy and take him to a medical center. *Yeah right.*

She'd beaten him. He powered down and tossed the pistol aside.

"That's better." She stepped out from behind the building. "Remember, I know all about your holdouts too—no funny business."

"How are you still walking around?" It hurt to breathe.

"The suit absorbs a lot of what you threw at me. You should have shot me a couple more times—it might have overloaded it." She ran a gloved hand up her thigh seductively.

Christ, even when I'm bleeding out, she's flirting with me.

She sauntered down the alley, her ponytail swaying with each step. Her girlish giggle didn't jibe with the sexy persona she currently displayed. In the time he'd known her, she'd proven to be quite unhinged. "Maxim Ultra, I do believe this is going to negatively impact your professional reputation. I was really expecting more from you."

"Sorry," he croaked as his voice caught in his throat. He gazed at her and closed his eyes in pain—pain he told himself was from his body.

"What did you say?"

"I said, 'sorry to disappoint you.' You didn't have to kick me out the window, Sierra. You know about my bad back."

"It never affected you in other activities. And don't forget, you started this. I would have been perfectly happy to split the take with you."

"Hah! I'll bet. Where's the artifact?"

She flashed a broad smile. "I don't know. I've misplaced it."

"Yeah, right. Just as I thought."

Her brow furrowed, but then he thought he saw a hint of compassion behind her jade eyes. She reached into a pouch on her utility belt and put a pair of goggles on. He was touched—it *was* compassion.

The lenses rotated through a rainbow of colors before settling on a dark green hue. The reverse side of the lenses lit up, illuminating Sierra's eyes.

"No real serious damage. That leg isn't doing you any favors." She paused. "I'm sorry about your hand."

"No you're not."

She took the goggles off and tucked them away. "You're trying to take me in, Max. What did you expect? I'd come quietly?"

"Sure, we could've tried that." He paused, fatigue gripping him. "So, how much did your buyers pay for the statue?"

Her eyes narrowed. "Nice try."

"Better have a smarter answer if you see Kalen again."

"Kalen's a psychotic. He got what he deserved."

"I hate to break it to you, sweetheart, but that's what's in store for all of us."

"And I guess that's why you've had a change of heart?"

He shrugged. "Just doing what comes naturally, I guess."

"Yes, saving your own skin."

"No. Correcting a mistake."

She raised her eyebrows. "A mistake, hm?"

"Well...not *all* of it was bad."

She took a hesitant step before finally crossing to him, kissing him deeply. "Goodbye, Max."

"Wait, you're just going to leave me here?"

"I'll call someone to assist you—once I'm well off-planet."

"I might bleed out by then."

She paused. "It's a chance I'm willing to take."

That hurt him, but he hid it well. "You *do* know where the artifact is, don't you?"

Again, that smile. "Goodbye, Ma—"

The laser bolt came out of nowhere, striking Sierra in the back. She crumpled to the ground, still—too still to be just unconscious.

"*Sierra!*" He tried to move to her, but only managed to slump forward. Dragging himself back against the wall, he reached into his jacket for another weapon. He stopped. A red laser dot moved across his chest.

Sniper.

Max pulled his hand away slowly and the dot danced around his chest a few more agonizing moments before finally disappearing.

He waited a few beats, looking up the alley and beyond to see where the shot had come from. The laser sight seemed to be gone, so he reached again and it reappeared. It bounced on his chest, as if the person controlling it was mobile.

Looking up, he saw a figure approaching from a building about two hundred yards away. As the person got closer, he saw it was a stocky man of better than average height with an easy gait that Max was all too familiar with.

Merthane.

Max looked at Sierra. She didn't appear to be breathing as blood trickled from her mouth. He couldn't make a play with Merthane still so far away, so he waited for him to get a little closer as he worked on marshaling his strength. The wait was torture.

"This is, perhaps, the most touching display I've seen in all my long years." A smug Talon Merthane smiled. He always did that when he had one up on Max. The breeze tousled his short, salt and pepper hair. His obsidian eyes glinted as he started to chuckle. "Maxim, my boy, what have you gotten yourself into this time?"

Max attempted to clear the lump in his throat, but couldn't swallow his rage. "I needed her alive, you fu—"

"Ah, ah, ah, watch your language, Maxim. I still haven't decided what to do with you yet. You don't want to say anything to…set me off." His taunting voice was as gravelly as Max remembered.

Merthane cut an imposing figure, his gray fatigues blending with the scenery. In his right hand, he held a large pistol that, like the rifle slung over his shoulder, was outfitted with laser optics. He knelt down next to Sierra. "You wanted her alive so she could get you out of trouble. Why would I want that?"

"Don't touch her."

"Please, stow the heroic drivel. This girl was going to leave you for dead here, so don't get all misty." Merthane touched Sierra's chin and turned her head from side to side. "Oh, she *is* quite a looker. You do know how to pick 'em, my boy. By the way, how's Alesha?"

Max didn't answer. Merthane grinned.

"It was you I saw earlier, wasn't it?"

Merthane's grin only widened.

"I thought it was a vagrant."

"You're losing your touch, my boy. No one in this area could move with such stealth and grace as myself. People like this girl aren't the type you—what's the Earth term? Fuck with? You need to stick to what you know best."

"That's what I was trying to do here."

"Sure, after you failed at playing bandit."

"What do you care?"

"Maxim, you wound me. I greatly enjoy these little conversations we have."

"Well, are you going to stand there and gloat all day, or are you going to shove off? I mean, we both know you're not going to kill me. You live to make my life miserable."

Merthane chuckled. "Right you are, my boy."

"Yeah, why is that, I wonder?"

A wistful expression took hold of Merthane. "Any number of things. Call it professional jealousy. Maybe it's my intense, undying dislike for your father." He paused, looking directly at Max. "*Gage.*"

"God damn it, Merthane, Gage wasn't my fault! How many times do I have to tell you?"

"Never enough for me to believe you." He stayed silent for a moment, possibly reminiscing about his son. "Or, maybe I just want to get you before you get me."

"Well, here's your chance, big man."

"Maxim, what you've never learned," Merthane began, looking up at the sound of distant sirens, "is that I don't have to kill you in order to get you. Now, I have to take my prize and be going. Those," he pointed to the sky, "are sirens and the Tonicen Police are on their way to collect you. Someone must have tipped them off that you're wanted on Aval. It seems they don't take too kindly to murder there."

"That was Kalen. I didn't murder anyone."

"Maybe not, but you're the one holding the bag. Oh wait, no, that's gone too apparently."

Max gritted his teeth as Merthane moved to scoop up Sierra's limp body. His eyes flicked to his discarded pistol—no time for that. His body tensed and he launched himself at Merthane, who hopped back a step, firing a shot into Max's good leg.

"Agh!" Max fell back against the wall and slid down into a sitting position.

Merthane kept his weapon trained and held Sierra up by her utility belt with his free hand. Her glazed, lifeless eyes stared into Max's.

He gripped his leg, focusing on that pain.

"Don't do that again, Maxim." The sirens drew closer. "Say hello to your mother for me—if you ever see her again, that is."

CHAPTER 2

Maxim's eyes fluttered open. He was in his bed on Modan, a single beam of sunlight stabbing him in the eye. *Why are the sliding shutters open?* The other side of the bed was empty aside from a darkened data pad on top of the rumpled gray sheets.

"Morning, Earth Boy."

Alesha stood in the doorway, wearing a T-shirt and nothing else, cradling a cup of tea in her hands. Flicking her dark eyes up at him, she gave him a lopsided smile.

"That's Earth *Man*, thank you very much." His eyes traveled up her tan legs. The shirt's hem barely concealed her ass.

"Sorry, but you'll always be my Earth Boy. Should have met me when you were a little older," she said, crossing over to the bed.

"We're the same age. And it's not my fault my father dragged me into space as a teenager."

"I seriously doubt he had to drag you, Max." She got back into bed, the shirt creeping up as she sat down, giving him a nice little show. When she caught him looking, she arched her eyebrow. That expression always sent a thrill through him.

She laughed at his subsequent wink—an inside joke between them from when they'd first met. He'd been trying to be a cool tough guy, failing miserably.

He couldn't take his eyes off her. She was absolutely beautiful. He'd always thought so. Her brown, almost black hair was worn in a loose, curly bob—her current style, as she liked to change things up frequently. She could subdue him with just a look, but her eyes, while warm, were always intense, like there was an endless hunger behind them—a hunger for life that continually drew him to her through all their ups and downs. Those eyes stayed trained on him as she sipped her tea.

He walked his fingers across the bed to caress her thigh, slowly sliding his hand to more sensitive areas of her body.

She inhaled sharply, closing her eyes as she set her cup on the nightstand. Her shirt came off, revealing the rest of her tanned body. On Earth, women might've killed to have a body like Alesha's, but it didn't seem to matter to her. She was who she was. Of course, she constantly told him that she was perfect anyway.

He embraced her, kissing her neck as she ran her fingers through his hair.

"Tell me how much you missed me," she whispered, softly biting his ear.

"I'm sorry I left. It won't happen again."

"Why did you let me die?" a familiar voice asked over his shoulder.

"*What?*"

He turned, only to see the lifeless Sierra lying on the other side of the bed. Fear coursed through him as her dead eyes stared back, almost accusatory. Alesha and his bedroom on Modan vanished, replaced by the industrial park on Tonicen, night falling quickly.

His attention was wrenched away by the man standing off to one side. It was Max's father, disappointment etched on every part of his face.

Suddenly, Sierra sprang to life, rotting skin falling off her face. She lunged at him. "You killed me, Max!"

He woke with a start, heart pounding as he glanced around wildly. For a moment, he couldn't even register where he was—his mind seized with panic. As his breathing slowed and his senses came back to him, his surroundings became clear, telling him only one thing.

Yep, still in prison. He couldn't tell if the breath he let out was from relief or not.

Closing his eyes, the trailing wisps of his nightmare came back to him. Two and a half years later, remembering Sierra's fate still twisted his stomach like a rag being wrung out, but the utter disappointment in his father's eyes lingered the longest. He'd been visiting Max a lot in his dreams, always expressing his disapproval in some way.

The recurring dream always started with Alesha, though he considered that the ultimate torture. Calling her back to mind resulted in a bittersweet smile. His prison sentence ensured he'd never see her again, but she was all that kept him going, or at least stopped him from sticking a spoon through his eye—one of the very few ways he could kill himself here.

The walls of his cell were smooth steel with a light greenish tint. A paint store probably would have called the color *sea mist*, or something similar. The cell was small—just big enough for his bed and a toilet in the corner. Though the prisons on Aval may not have looked like crumbling dungeons with rusted-over bars, they still weren't big on amenities. The bed was really just a padded bench jutting out of the wall, while the climate-controlled cells made sheets and blankets unnecessary.

Max had plenty of time to think in his cell. He ran over the scenario again and again, wondering if he could've done something different on Tonicen—if there had been a way to prevent Sierra's murder. Unfortunately, it hadn't been up to him. Talon Merthane was always very good at getting what he wanted.

Despite the fact she'd tried to kill him, Max still had fond memories of Sierra. He hadn't been in love with her, but they'd definitely shared something. Their affair had been more lust than love.

Any thoughts of love only brought him back to Alesha and how he'd betrayed her trust. It was a vicious cycle—think about the woman who died right in front of him or think about the one who'd been the best thing that had ever happened to him only for him to throw it all away.

Of course, he could've put himself through the ringer even more and thought about his mother back on Earth who had no clue where he was or what'd happened to him. Maybe Alesha or Roeger had gotten word to her. He hoped so. He only had the rest of his life to dwell on all his failings. Alone.

The muffled, droning voices outside his cell told him it was time to start the day. He wasn't much interested in doing that. His cell door beeped before sliding open.

"MAXIM ULTRA—RISE." The guard's voice was loud and authoritarian—just the kind of voice Max liked to ignore. He stayed on his bed.

"MAXIM ULTRA—RISE."

The spartan nature of the prison extended to the guards as well. They looked like men, aside from the fact that their heads were completely white—opaque and blank, like a light bulb—and they had speaker boxes for mouths. The speakers relayed messages from overseers who were too important and, quite frankly, too smart to get on the ground level with the general population. Max assumed the guards were automatons of some kind, due to both their looks and their complete lack of emotion, but Roeger, his best friend since he was twelve, was a robot and he had feelings, so who knew?

"Not today, Sparky. I'm not in the mood."

"All prisoners must submit to cleaning." The change in voice told Max that he was now talking to the people running the prison, but that was just a theory. All issued commands came in the stilted, robotic voice, while more nuanced explanations sounded like a person speaking through an intercom. "RISE."

"Pass. Sorry buddy." Two and a half years later and he still didn't know who he was talking to. "My back's killing me." That wasn't exactly the truth. The injury had hung around like a specter, but two and a half years of essentially sleeping on a board had straightened him out. He also had other ways of keeping any potential relapses at bay.

"We can fix that for you Maxim. We have some of the most skilled surgeons on staff. They did an excellent job in repairing your other injuries when you arrived."

That was a fact. Max's palm had looked like a handful of shredded pork and now all he had was a dull ache from time to time and a wicked scar. *So much for visiting palm readers.* Still, he wasn't going to pat his jailors on the back. "You also have some of the most *un*skilled surgeons locked up here, Boss. *Next.*"

A brief pause. "MAXIM ULTRA—RISE."

They're not going to leave me alone today, are they?

Max got off his bed with a groan, almost losing his balance as the metal slab slid back into the wall. His legs felt wobbly and he knew it wasn't from his phantom back injury. Sweat broke out on his upper lip as he leaned against the wall for support. He needed some more "help," and in order to get it, he needed out his cell.

"DISROBE FOR CLEANING."

Ooh, my favorite part of the day.

The black prison uniform was similar to hospital scrubs and such a deep black that he wondered how they kept it from fading. He felt like an interstellar mental patient. A small drawer for his dirty clothes emerged from the wall to his right. He looked at the faceless guard disgustedly.

The guard stepped into the doorway. "DISROBE FOR CLEANING."

Max rolled his eyes and did what he was told. They went through this practically every day. It was losing its appeal. He stripped off his clothing—no shoes, though. He guessed the jailors wouldn't have cared if a prisoner sliced a foot open. Of course, they *did* have some of the most skilled surgeons on staff, or at least that's what he'd heard.

As soon as he put his clothes in the drawer, it snapped shut. Slats opened above the door and on the side walls, revealing small hoses. Before he could make another smart comment, they doused him with soapy water, causing him to yelp in shock. Apparently, his jailors didn't understand the concept of hot water. He stepped into the center of the room, spitting a mouthful of water into the drain that opened up beneath him. All the while, the guard stood in the door, blocking the way.

"Are you going to watch me jerk off too?"

The guard didn't acknowledge him.

"Can you at least turn around?"

No comment.

"Perv."

Max washed up as fast as possible. After a few minutes, the hoses were replaced with vents that blasted warm air at him. *What do these people have against towels?* Within moments, he was dry and another drawer slid out from the wall with a fresh set of prison clothes.

Once he dressed, the guard ushered Max out of the cell, where he was joined by the rest of his cellblock's inmates. Several towers made up Aval's prison complex—he didn't know the exact number. It seemed like they were always building a new one. Each floor above the fifteenth was a cellblock holding thirty or so prisoners and some of the towers were fifty floors high. The worst of the worst were kept on the top floors with their own personal guards. Max, being incarcerated for a single murder, lived somewhere in the middle of his tower. Protestations of his innocence were generally ignored.

As the guards herded the prisoners toward the cargo elevator that would take them all down to the dining hall, Max peered around for Gelf. He couldn't see him, which wasn't unusual—Gelf was rather short. Generally, though, the little guy would be right by Max's cell when he emerged. His eyes darted around—nothing. Sweat beaded on his forehead as his body went hot. He flexed his hand, which had started to tremor.

Where is he?

The crowd around him became a blur as his heart hammered. He breathed heavily. The shaking in his hand had moved throughout his body.

Where is he?

He felt something slip into his left hand, which he closed fast. The haze of panic lifted. Looking over, he saw Gelf walking beside him. The little humanoid had yellow skin, but never really told Max where he came from. All he'd told Max was that he'd been living on Aval for several years prior to getting arrested. Max didn't pry—everyone was entitled to their secrets.

"What took you so long?" Max asked, glancing at the small vial in his hand. It held four small sticks of rimi.

"Me? You were late. The guards will only let me hang around just so long before they start getting handsy," Gelf replied. *At best* Gelf was four-foot-four, so it was easier for him to get around the guards, especially in bigger crowds and especially when delivering a package. Max never asked about Gelf's supply, but was grateful for it. The four sticks would get him through the next several days. He used to be able to stretch one over a week.

"Thanks…for this," Max said with a sidelong glance at one of the nearby guards.

"You're welcome, Boss. I don't know why you don't just see a doctor about that."

Max didn't know or care if Gelf knew his back was no longer an issue. It made him feel better to continue the ruse. "It's a long story." He snuck a stick into his mouth, grimacing against the bitter taste.

"If you say so," Gelf said with a shrug, rubbing a hand over his shaved, yellow head. "But I figure we've got all the time in the universe."

Max ignored him. As soon as he bit down on the rimi, his senses sharpened and the dull ache through his body faded. He could smell the sweat on the prisoners mixed with the antiseptic soap the prison used. Whatever he looked at seemed like it was a shade or two brighter and everything around him seemed to be moving at three-quarter speed. A rush flowed through his body that ended in his tingling extremities. Despite his heightened perception, he felt thoroughly relaxed. He was sure there was a complicated medical explanation for what was happening to him, but all he knew was, he needed that feeling. That need forced him to ignore the physical risks of rimi—seizures, hallucinations, insanity, and, eventually, death. He tried to control his usage to stave off these effects, but it was getting more and more difficult not to succumb to the drug's pleasures. Besides the conscious high it gave him, the rimi also enhanced his nighttime fantasies of Alesha. The fact that his dreams consistently morphed into nightmares escaped his concern.

This wasn't his first go-around with the drug. Several years previously, he and Alesha had been trapped by a rimi supplier and her private army. In order to escape, the pair had to use the drug. It gave them the edge to fight and survive against such overwhelming odds. But their escape came with a price. The supplier, Swann Nestive, had the purest product Max had ever encountered. Although their exposure had been brief, the rimi still got its claws into Max and Alesha, transforming them into hopeless addicts. After months of wallowing in their addiction, the two of them made the effort to get clean. Eventually, they succeeded, the process bonding them forever. That was the bond he'd broken by running off with Sierra in the pursuit of fabled wealth. Facing a life sentence, he happily turned back to rimi to make him forget all of his shame and regrets.

As the rimi's effects washed over him, he couldn't help turning his dreamy smile to Gelf, who shook his head and muttered something. They'd met during Max's first few weeks in prison when, for reasons Max had never fully sorted out, Gelf had run afoul of some of the rougher inmates. Max hadn't planned on getting involved, but he'd always been a sucker for a person in need, and Gelf had certainly been in need. Though he'd won a trip to the infirmary and hadn't done his back any favors, Max managed to break one attacker's knee with a well-placed kick.

Ever since that episode, Gelf had become something of a sidekick. The fact that he was able to provide the rimi was only *one* of the reasons Max kept him around. Everyone needed a friend in prison, otherwise the isolation would be maddening.

For Max, allies were few and far between. Gelf was the first inmate he'd jumped to defend, but not the last. The other inmates had saddled Max with the moniker, "The Helper." Not exactly the superhero name he'd shot for when he was a kid, but it was an accurate description, he supposed. He'd also developed a bit of a bad reputation among the less savory prisoners. It didn't help that his father might have been responsible for putting some of them away. In short, Max was *real* popular. Being a target wasn't enough to make him stop sticking up for the underdog, though. He never wanted prison to change who he was, but the vial from Gelf told him it already had.

The prisoners packed onto the cargo elevator, a sturdy metal platform with a control panel that would ferry them down to the dining hall. Max figured that the elevator, with the prisoners in such close proximity to one another, would be the perfect place for an ambush, so he always kept his head on a swivel. Either that or the rimi made him paranoid—a possible side effect to be sure.

"I heard Elkeith might be looking for you," Gelf mentioned over the sound of rushing air.

"When *isn't* Elkeith looking for me?"

"Just a friendly warning."

The lift delivered the inmates into the massive dining hall. Though all the tower's convicts couldn't fit in the room, it could hold a great many. Max hoped to get lost in the crowd—avoid Elkeith, and a fight, altogether. They always found him, though. Whoever they were, they always found him.

Gelf and Max moved into line to be served by the cook, Gerry. Gerry was a Glutob, a sentient, friendly, blob-like creature with multiple tentacles. At that moment, he had a ladle gripped in each one. His formless body had an orange tint to it to it with two white eyes at the top and a large mouth about twelve inches below that.

"*Chutho*, Maxim. Chutho, Gelf," Gerry greeted them as he slapped some watery, orange protein paste on their trays. Max found the similarity in color and texture between Gerry and the food disconcerting. As the dining hall cook, Gerry was probably about as popular as Max with the majority of inmates, but he could only work with the ingredients the prison provided him.

I'll try to pretend they're sweet potatoes. "How's tricks, Gerry?"

"Maxim, I told Elkeith what you wanted me to. He…did not take it well." Gerry's gurgling voice quavered.

"I'll handle it, Gerry. No one in this place should be paying protection to that fat shit. In fac—" A rough hand yanked Max into the air. His body slammed onto a nearby table, ruining everybody's breakfast. Groaning, his hand instinctively went to his lower back, but even if there had been pain, the rimi kept it in check. "Hey fellas, sorry to disturb your meal."

The aliens glared at him through the protein paste that covered their faces. One of them, a crimson-skinned humanoid with four arms, grabbed him with all four hands and pushed him back toward Elkeith, an especially ugly Inwain with a bulbous, piggish nose. Max managed to stop his momentum before running into his assailant.

"Why are you butting into my business, Ultra?" Elkeith asked in his deep, burbling voice.

"Y'know, just trying to clean up the neighborhood."

"Am I going to have to send you back to the infirmary?"

Max smiled. "I could ask you the same thing." Elkeith owned the knee Max had busted upon meeting Gelf. Despite his trip to infirmary after that encounter, their initial run-in had made Max a little cocky. Also, the rimi was *really* kicking in.

Elkeith, who *was* a fat shit, growled, lunging at Max, but to no avail. The Inwain's lingering limp allowed Max to easily sidestep the attack, propelling his opponent into another nearby table.

"Grab him!" Elkeith called out.

Max tried to move, but the four-armed brute grabbed him from behind, holding him fast while Elkeith collected himself. Max struggled in the strongman's grip, but in this case, four really was better than two. Max wasn't going anywhere. His pulse started to race.

This could pose a problem.

About a head taller than Max, Elkeith limped toward him. Thanks to a patchwork of stubble, his mouth, which hid a couple of rows of needlelike teeth, looked like it had been sewn onto his face crookedly, while his beady, orange eyes peered out from under a curtain of eyebrows that was easily three inches in length. His mottled purple and gray skin made him look like a walking bruise. Elkeith was also a fan of the comb-over to try and hide his naked dome.

His two compatriots, much thinner than their boss, stood silently with dead-eyed stares from their piercing emerald eyes. Max could have sworn they were zombies of some kind. Their dark orange skin made them look like they'd been accosted by rogue spray-tanners. Since Elkeith went through flunkies like tissues, Max couldn't place their species, but they creeped him out.

"Who are these two, the makings of your boy band?"

Elkeith's face twisted. "What?"

Max shook his head. "Sorry, Earth joke."

"Well, I *hate* Earth jokes!"

Max was pretty sure that wasn't all Elkeith hated, but he couldn't vocalize his suspicions before his tubby opponent punched him square in the face. His face went numb, but soon enough, the pain kicked in. The Inwain punched him twice more, making his head feel like it was five sizes bigger than normal.

So much for the rimi.

The other inmates stood and took notice, but the guards didn't seem too concerned with Maxim's status as a punching bag, despite Gelf trying to rally them.

Max fought to break away, but Four Arms held him tight. He went to old reliable, kicking his foot back into Four Arms' knee. The popping sound was sickening, but the subsequent scream was worth it. The shrieking Four Arms released Max in time for him to duck Elkeith's next punch, which smacked Four Arms instead. Before Max could counter, though, Elkeith's henchmen were on him, snapping and biting.

I knew it—zombies.

He tried to feint away, but they were quick. One grabbed his arm, about to take a bite out of it until Max punched him in the side of the head. The first zombie released him, but the second was there to jump on Max's back. Frantically trying to dislodge his attacker, Max threw backwards punches and elbows. The zombie's ragged and phlegmy breath was hot against his ear.

Elkeith moved in, but Max managed to jump at him, launching the crown of the zombie's head into the fat ass' jaw. The now unconscious zombie slipped off his back while Elkeith staggered backwards, stunned. Max didn't let up, punching his adversary in the nose with a loud crunching of bone. The sight of the Inwain's blood was satisfying.

Elkeith howled, covering his broken nose with his hands as he wheeled away, but the first zombie had recovered and swiped at Max, drawing blood.

Max yanked his wounded arm away, dodging the next attack.

The zombie's speed won out again as he tackled Max onto a table. Right in his face, the zombie was all teeth and spit as Max tried to hold him back with his injured arm. His good arm grasped for anything he could use as a weapon. He wasn't sure what the alien had done to him when he'd scratched him, but Max felt his arm weakening. The freak closed in on his neck for an after-breakfast snack.

This is a shitty way to go out.

Finally, his fingers connected with a spoon. He gripped it tightly and jammed it into the zombie's eye—handle first—with all the strength he could muster. The hot fetid breathing ceased as the alien slumped on top of Max, dead. He pushed the creature off of him before getting off the table on rubbery legs. His arm burned like fire. Dizzy and lightheaded, he didn't have a moment to savor his victory before the floor rushed up to meet his face.

CHAPTER 3

Max came around slowly. He sat in a chair, though propped up would probably have been a more accurate description. His scratched arm had been bandaged and his forehead was damp, like he'd been feverish. The room was pitch-black, save for the light generated by the holo-pad on the table in front of him. From the spill off of light, he could just make out a tall, bald, dark-skinned man in a black suit in the corner, watching him.

Creep show.

He turned back to the holo-pad to sort out what exactly the video playing in front of him showed. It looked like a chaotic clip playing on a loop. His body stiffened when he saw Kalen tearing through a contingent of prison guards. To look at him, there was nothing out of the ordinary about Kalen, but hidden in his wiry frame was a skilled and ruthless killer waiting to get out.

"That fucker put me in here," Max said, almost forgetting he wasn't alone.

According to the video evidence, the tower guards definitely had some cybernetic properties, but weren't totally automatons. It got worse when fully flesh and blood security personnel got involved. Blood flowed like someone had turned on a tap as Kalen used whatever he could get his hands on to break, maim, cut, and kill whoever and whatever got in his way.

Kalen had been imprisoned in one of the other towers on Aval. The way Max had heard it, he was at the very top of that tower, what with all the wanton death and destruction he was so fond of—death and destruction that played out on the recording.

The guy could win a fight with anything. He'd find a way to murder someone with baby food if given the opportunity. His complete lack of a moral compass made him an effective killer—not very efficient, though, as he was perfectly willing to slash through an army to get to one person. He'd killed several people during the job, which is what landed Max in prison in the first place, though he was thankful he'd only been charged with *one* of Kalen's murders. Kalen's methods turned Max's stomach, but Sierra had been right, he knew what he'd signed up for—or at least *who* he'd signed up *with*.

The last part of the recording took place in the office of the tower's overseer. It appeared that Kalen had been in the clear, but decided to make a special pit-stop to crush the man's skull with his bare hands. It should have made Max queasy, but whatever drugs the infirmary doctors had given him, combined with the rimi, left him feeling like a million bucks.

The recording looped back around to the beginning. Before he had to watch Kalen murder a bunch of people again, it stopped. The lights came on in the room. The lanky man in the corner approached the table with an easy gait, like he wanted people to know he was in charge. He looked like he scowled a lot—which he did at that very moment—while his eyes drilled into Max's. His whole demeanor screamed law enforcement.

"What did you think?" the dark-skinned man asked with a voice that sounded much older than he looked.

"It was certainly…eye-popping."

The man winced. "That was in poor taste."

"What do you want me to say? That I can't believe Kalen did all that, even though I know he's certainly capable of it? He got out and is much, much farther away from me now. I'd say it's a relief, actually."

"Actually, he tried to break in *here* to get to *you*."

That was sobering. "What?"

"Oh, have I got your attention now? Ten days ago, Kalen Vandeir escaped from *his* prison and then attempted to break into *your* prison to try and kill you. All evidence leads me to believe that he would have succeeded had the outer defenses not turned him away."

"Hey…I can…fight," he said the last part with a little less confidence.

"A lucky shot against a fat tub like Elkeith, maybe, but a weapon like that? I highly doubt it Mr. Ultra."

"Who the hell are you, then? The guy they send in to make me feel worse about myself?"

"My name is Matthias Glintock. I'm with the GAC and I'm your best shot at getting out of here before they take you out on a slab."

Max paused. *What is this guy talking about?*

The GAC or Galactic Authority Commission—formerly Corps, but the agency wanted to downplay its militaristic origins—was the organization that held the loose Galactic Union of Planets together. All the worlds governed themselves, but the GAC was tasked with maintaining peace and order throughout. It was the FBI, CIA, and United Nations all rolled into one powerful entity.

Earth, of course, wasn't in the Galactic Union. With all the countries squabbling amongst themselves, the GAC wouldn't make the overtures until a single world government was in place—it was difficult to maintain law and order when each country had its own rules. Max was one of the rare Earth-born humans running around the galaxy, which also contributed a bit to his reputation, good or bad.

The GAC was a powerful player in the galaxy, but could they really get the Avalian government to release him? Would they interfere that much in local politics?

Glintock's story must be good. "All right Glintock, you've got my attention. Let's hear it."

"That's Agent Glintock."

Max folded his arms with a slight wince. "Whenever you're ready."

Glintock sighed, but moved closer to loom over Max. "This Vandeir situation is a problem for us…and you."

"How is it a problem for me? I'm in *prison*, for *life*."

"You don't think outside the box very much, do you Mr. Ultra?"

"I *live* in a box, asshole." He could've argued that in his former line of work, all he *did* was think outside the box, but he knew Glintock was playing the old legal game of only asking questions he knew the answers to. Plus, his mind was a little foggy after the fight in the dining hall. At least that's what he told himself.

"Why do you think that man tried to break in here to kill you?"

"Oh, I thought you were just saying that to scare me."

"I was, but it doesn't make it any less true." Glintock produced a small control stick from his pocket. He clicked a button and a new image beamed out of the holo-pad. It was a bloody, disfigured face that somehow looked familiar to Max. "Recognize him?" He didn't wait for an answer. "That's Dolby—the information broker that recruited Sierra Numani's team. This mess was discovered four days after Vandeir's escape."

"Oh no…." A dull ache settled in his chest. Max hadn't wanted anyone he knew involved in the job, but Sierra hadn't gotten that memo. Dolby had worked with his father a lot. Max had known him since he was in his teens. "Why'd he kill Dolby?"

Glintock didn't answer. He clicked his button again. The next image was of a woman who had been separated from her head, which was in the corner of the scorched room in the image. Glintock zoomed in for a close-up of the head. He rotated the view for a look at the dead woman's face, but the green scaled hands were a dead giveaway for Max. It was Braneith, a highly skilled thief Dolby had found for Sierra.

"Is the picture becoming clearer for you?"

Max glared at the agent.

"Brancith Cclral," Glintock stated. "Her information led Vandeir to Dolby. Our theory was that Vandeir was picking off every person who had knowledge of your robbery or even a passing hint of it."

"Why?"

"Maybe he thinks someone sold the team out. You know his profile—he'll kill anyone he has to in order to find out who. If no one tells him anything, then he cleans up any possible future leaks."

Max swallowed hard. There were a few other people who knew about the job—his old crew. Of course, they didn't have any *real* knowledge. "Wait, what do you mean that *was* your theory?"

Glintock didn't reply. He simply clicked his button again.

The image on the holo-pad switched to a video feed. Max heard dripping as the camera panned slowly to the right. A boot scraped on the floor as dim lighting filled the frame. Max's stomach dropped.

Large humanoid bodies lined the bottom of the picture as the camera continued to pan. The floor glistened with the blood of the dead, their vital fluids congealing into a brown sludge. Despite the blood coating the floor, Max could make out the tile pattern and he knew from where the video feed came and who the bodies had been.

Max's heart shot into his throat as the camera finally focused on the center of the room. Hanging from the wall, beaten and bloody, was Carfen, the fence that had pointed him to the statue. More importantly, she was one of Alesha's closest associates and friends. Max had royally fucked up the whole "don't use people I know" plan, but all his other options had been exhausted before he'd taken Sierra and her gang to Carfen. He'd had no choice.

No, I had a choice, I could have walked away. His eyes welled up.

The sorrow and guilt he felt quickly became white hot rage as Kalen stepped into frame. Carfen had always protected herself with state-of-the-art defenses—the dead bodies were cloned bodyguards—but apparently, the completely unscathed Kalen had had an easy time of it.

The killer's body looked as though he'd dipped himself in a vat of blood. Even with his gory veneer, he still demonstrated grace and agility in his movements.

Carfen stirred, her chains jangling.

"*What was that, darling?*" Kalen's condescending tone came through the video loud and clear.

Carfen only sobbed and moaned in response.

"*You must be exhausted. I'll repeat my question: Where is the statue? You told Ultra where it was and I can only assume he gave it to you after he double-crossed us. So, where is it now?*"

"*I...I don't know. I haven't seen Maxim since the day he brought you all here.*"

Kalen's insincere smile said he didn't believe her. "*All right, let's suppose you're telling me the truth. He could have passed it off to any of his friends, but there's really only one other person Ultra would trust with such a prize.*" Kalen turned his back to the camera. "*Where is Alesha Cabal?*"

Max's eyes bulged in his head as his breathing quickened.

"*I don't know where Alesha is. I haven't spoken to her in ages.*"

Kalen let out a nasty laugh. "*I know you're definitely lying now. Ultra told us how close the two of you were—that's how he knew we could trust you. I'll ask again: Where is Alesha Cabal?*"

"*I told you...I don't kn—*"

Max cried out as he watched Kalen swipe a dagger across Carfen's belly, spilling her entrails out onto the floor. His stomach roiled as he turned away from the holo-pad. *This is my fault. I killed her.* A beeping sound emitting from the machine drew his attention back to the pad.

Kalen had taken out a communication device. He wore a confused expression as he looked at the communicator, but that melted into a satisfied grin. "*It's all right, Carfen. I know exactly where she is—Modan. I'll be sure to send Alesha your regards.*" With that, Kalen walked out of frame and the clip ended.

"This was discovered two days ago," Glintock said. "I said it *was* our theory, because Kalen's mindset is pretty clear here."

"He thinks I betrayed them and is coming after me and my old crew, starting with Alesha." Just saying the words made his chest seize. The only thing keeping him in his chair and not throwing himself at the prison gates to escape was the fact that Alesha could handle herself if Kalen found her. She wouldn't win in a fight, but she could sure as hell hide from him. He'd been dreaming of getting back to her for two and a half years and now, because of his greed and stupidity, he might have gotten her killed.

If Glintock saw the concern in Max's eyes he didn't say anything. "Well, he's not going to find the artifact that way."

"What happened to it?" Max asked absently, his mind focused on Alesha.

Glintock grimaced. "After your little incident on Tonicen, we received an anonymous tip about the location of the statue. Turns out, it was in a safe house frequented by Numani. We took possession and put it on a research vessel in deep space." He clicked his remote control and a visual of a large spaceship beamed out of the holo-pad. "This was taken from a long range satellite. The audio is a transmission we received from the ship."

For a few moments, there was only the image of the ship. The space around it was filled with the light of thousands of stars— mere pinpricks in the infinite darkness. He hadn't seen the night sky since Tonicen. A lump formed in his throat.

A voice cut through the silence—a voice marked by an excited tremor. *"This is Research Vessel 5-7-2-1. Dr. Heksrun reporting on Project Alpha Twelve. We've begun the standard battery of tests an—"*

A muffled voice interrupted Heksrun. *"Doctor, come quickly! The statue is—"*

Max jumped in his seat as the vessel exploded in a brilliant starburst of turquoise light and orange flames that were quickly extinguished once the oxygen in the ship burned up. A gnawing hollowness ate at his stomach. He had no idea how many people had been on the ship, but to see their lives snuffed out so suddenly was chilling.

"We sent a recovery ship out to investigate," Glintock said in a steady tone. "Would you like to know what they found?"

Max was pretty sure he didn't.

"A sea of wreckage, littered with bodies," Glintock said. "And in the middle of it all, completely undamaged, was the statue. Just floating there, as if the whole ship hadn't been ripped apart. Now do you understand why I'm here?"

Max took a moment to absorb everything Glintock had told him. "Where's the artifact now?"

"It's in a secure GAC facility. We've given up studying it, obviously. It's just there for safe-keeping until we can figure out what to do with the damn thing."

Max nodded. He wasn't sure that would stop Kalen. "That thing was supposed to lead us to Dalian's Bounty—that's the only reason I got involved."

"That's an old space tale, but somehow it always lures us adventurers in."

Max's brow creased. "You went after the Bounty?"

"Sure. I was young and stupid once too and I wasn't *always* a lawman." Glintock paused for a moment. "We know you were just in the wrong place at the wrong time, Mr. Ultra, but do you…know who the buyer was?"

He shook his head. "No. Sierra handled all of that. She said the buyer brought Kalen in, so he probably knows, but I have zero clue if that was true or not." Max took a second to let it all sink in. "So, you know he's after my crew and you're sitting here with me? Get out there and warn them! You're wasting time!"

"I can't have the GAC protecting every person who might have knowledge of the crime. But you…you worked with this man, you may be able to track him, figure out his next moves."

Max shook his head. "I didn't work with him long. Honestly, I kept my distance—he made me uneasy."

Glintock looked away from him, as if gathering himself for one last pitch. "I'm going to be frank with you, Maxim—I need you for whatever knowledge you can provide, but I'm really here for your father."

"You're a little late for that, Agent."

"About thirteen years late—in Earth time, of course—if I'm not mistaken. Your father was one of the greatest man hunters in the galaxy. Your resume is a bit more…*diverse* than his ever was, but what's that Earth expression about apples and trees?"

Maxim closed his eyes. He hadn't been measuring up to his father's legacy for some time, and why should he really? It was his life, but that life had been a disappointment—not to his father, but to himself. He'd never reach the high bar set by his father, but if he at least forged a path in that direction, maybe he could live with himself again.

"I need your help, Mr. Ultra. We're constantly two steps behind this man. You might be the edge I need."

Max's mind pivoted back to the video that had been playing when he'd regained consciousness. Kalen went to an awful lot of trouble to escape and if what Glintock said about him trying to break *back in* to get at Max was true…. The pieces clicked into place and he looked up at Glintock with a narrowed gaze. "You need me as bait."

Glintock's eyebrows rose. "Excuse me?"

"You just said that you can't protect my friends, which if you sat on them with some agents, eventually you'd catch Kalen. But, if you trot me around the galaxy, that might draw his attention."

Glintock almost looked embarrassed.

"Now who can't think outside the box?"

"Very good, Mr. Ultra. It's good to see that prison hasn't dulled your sharpness, no matter how hard you've been trying."

It was Max's turn to look embarrassed.

"You're right," Glintock continued. "I hoped that by involving you, that might lure Vandeir to us as opposed to waiting for the bodies of your friends to pile up."

"But you also had no qualms about letting that happen if need be."

"Yes and no. You're not seeing the whole picture here. Vandeir didn't escape all by his lonesome, not with the security they had on him. He had to have had help."

"From whom?"

"My theory? Someone from inside the GAC. We're the only agency that would have had the resources to make Vandeir's escape manageable."

"What about a third party?"

"Unlikely. There are a lot of former agents out there who might be disgruntled, but no one with enough reach to help an inmate out of a maximum security prison."

"Okay, so you want to dangle me out there like a carrot for our boy to follow. What do I get out of this aside from a probable quick death?"

"For one, you may save your friends' lives. For another, your freedom."

"Yeah, how exactly are you going to swing that?"

Glintock paused, glancing at his data pad. "You're thirty-two years old." He looked back up at Max. "How'd you like spending your thirtieth in prison? I can ensure you never have to spend another birthday in here. Just leave it to me, Mr. Ultra." He was dodging the question.

"Just to be clear—this is a full pardon, right?"

"I *said* I'd handle it."

Max wasn't so sure. "Apparently the GAC *doesn't* have unlimited reach and resources. Look I get your plan, Glintock, but I don't know you, and a guy like me is usually the last person the GAC wants to deal with. I *know* you're not telling me everything." He studied the agent carefully, but the man revealed nothing. Glintock was offering him a ticket out of prison. He'd be a fool not to agree, but he wasn't thrilled at being bait for a psychopath. If the deal wasn't on the level, he was getting something else out of it. "All right, I have two stipulations."

"Name them."

"Gelf and Gerry, the dining hall cook—they come with me."

Glintock shook his head with a bemused look. "I tell you your friends are in danger, offer you your freedom, and your first thought is to stick your neck out for a shifty narcotics dealer and a mess hall cook?"

"They won't last five minutes in here without me and they're only here on minor offenses. Plus, I need a good cook on my ship." He left out what he needed from Gelf, but was pretty sure Glintock had an idea. It was just as essential to Max as food.

"Fine. What's the other demand?"

"I work alone."

"Negative. That will *not* be happening. Let me be clear on something, your freedom is contingent upon your cooperation. I'm not letting you out of here so that you can gallivant around the galaxy and get nothing done. I'll be there to keep you on track. The target is Kalen Vandeir. Letting you warn your friends is just a courtesy."

"And if Kalen tries to hit them while we're warning them, so much the better, right?"

"Do we have a deal, Mr. Ultra?"

Max made him wait for a moment. *Of course we have a deal—the sooner I get out of this shithole the better.* He stuck his hand out. "Call me Max."

They shook on it. "And you can call me Agent Glintock."

CHAPTER 4

What am I doing?

Matthias Glintock had asked himself that question several times on this trip. Now, as he stood in the prison's processing center waiting for his unauthorized prisoner release to happen, he was sure he'd ask it again. The situation was critical, but at least the statue was safe. If anyone could break into the facility in Equor, though, it was Kalen Vandeir. Matthias *needed* Ultra to track him down or at least draw him out.

Despite the kid's complete lack of discipline, he'd picked up enough of his father's skills to make Matthias a believer. That was, of course, if his file could be believed. The world of independent contractors like Ultra was full of half-truths and exaggerations. Matthias just hoped he wasn't making a mistake by putting all his hopes into the Maxim Ultra plan.

What am I doing?

His communicator buzzed in his jacket pocket. He pulled it out, looking at the screen. "*Nakra.*" It was Brynden Brontin. *This can't be good.* He answered the call. "This is Glintock."

"*What are you doing?*" Brontin's tone bordered on incredulous. He knew exactly what Matthias was doing. Now he was going to make his life a living hell, but only if Matthias let him.

"I'm pursuing the Vandeir case. Why, what do you think I'm doing?"

Two of the guards brought Ultra, Gelf, and the Glutob into the processing area.

"*Really? I hadn't realized that the investigation had led back to Aval,*" Brontin said.

"Well, this *is* where he escaped from."

"*Yes, but not in the tower I'm currently reading you in.*"

Nakra. "What do you want, Brontin?"

The processing agent in the blast-protected booth was a pretty young woman with lavender skin. Ultra leaned on the counter.

Is he flirting with her?

Brontin continued rambling. "*I think you're trying to follow up on that absurd Maxim Ultra idea you brought up.*"

"It's a good plan. The kid has a nose for these things and he worked with Vandeir for the better part of a year. Plus, all the intel shows Vandeir holds Ultra responsible for his imprisonment and Sierra Numani's death. We may be able to lure him to us."

"*Yes, as you've beaten to death in your reports.*"

"Well, I'm nothing if not persistent," Matthias said.

The processor handed Ultra a plastic tub with his belongings, finishing their transaction with a sweet smile. The Glutob, Gerry, shuffled up to the window.

"*Persistent? That's one way of putting it, Glintock. In fact, your persistence is what made me curious.*"

Matthias froze. "Curious about what?"

Brontin continued. *"Well, I knew you'd never let this Maxim Ultra thing g—"*

"I'm telling you—" Matthias tried to stall him.

"My point exactly. I get it. You have a hang up about his old man and you think he's going to stop being such a screw-up and finally measure up. Meanwhile, we have a galaxy-spanning law force at our disposal and that's not good enough for you?"

"Vandeir isn't going to be brought in by a wide-cast net like the GAC. Catching him requires a certain set of skills—skills that Ultra possesses."

"Or so you think. You can't even fully vouch for this guy."

"I—"

"Don't try to deny it. I've read the reports. 'Though the possibilities of abject failure and an uncooperative subject exist, due to his familiarity with the target, Maxim Ultra is the best chance we have to apprehend Kalen Vandeir.' Not a very good sales pitch, Glintock. The Director didn't think so either."

Truthfully, the Director's comments had stung Matthias when he'd heard them. Relying on a man incarcerated for murder on one of the GAC's member planets was a black eye the agency wanted to avoid. Of course, the fact that Ultra hadn't murdered anyone and was simply being punished for Vandeir's crimes was apparently irrelevant. Disobeying the Director's specific orders would negatively impact Matthias' career for sure—unless it worked.

"So, why are you calling me, Brontin?"

The processor waved Matthias over to take custody of the three prisoners.

"Just wanted to let you know that I'm onto your little scheme and that I'll be putting a stop to it. The GAC is nothing if its agents can't follow orders."

The processor indicated on the data pad where she needed Matthias' approval. He stared at the screen, hesitating.

"*Watch your back, Glintock*," Brontin said. "*And your clearances.*"

Matthias terminated the call and signed off on the release. Three prisoners that he had zero authorization to free were now in his custody. He wondered how long it would take for the operation to blow up in his face.

The double doors leading back into the tower opened and his heart skipped a beat. His brow wrinkled in confusion when he saw three guards—*organic* guards—approaching with a hooded and chained Elkeith in tow.

"What the hell is this all about?" he asked.

Ultra turned from a quiet conversation with Gelf. When he saw what was coming, he grinned devilishly. Walking toward the quartet, he shook his finger at the smiling guard at the front of the group. "You...you..."

"Just a little going away present, Max," the lead guard said. "Thanks for all your help with...with everything."

"No problem Bradley, just be mindful of where you...handle business."

"Is that Ultra?" Elkeith asked from under his hood.

"That's right, Elkeith, you stupid fuck." Ultra reached up and plucked the hood off the Inwain's head.

Elkeith's beady orange eyes squinted against the processing center's harsh lights. Looking around, realization slowly dawned on his face. "They're...releasing you?"

"That's right, fucko. I'm outta here, and I wanted you to be here to watch me walk out the door before they drag your motherfuckin' ass back into that tower to rot until the end of time. How d'ya like that, fuckface?"

Matthias glared at the two of them. *Really? We're doing this now? Maybe Brontin's right.*

Elkeith's lip twitched as his jaw clenched. "What does 'fuck' mean?"

"I'm glad you asked, buddy. The equivalent out here would be *veck*. As in, the first thing I'm going to do when I get out of here is veck your mother—provided she's not as ugly as you."

That got a rise out of Elkeith. Lunging at Ultra, he pulled his chains tight, jerking his guards forward.

Ultra jumped back a step, but regained his swagger once it was clear the guards had everything under control. "Well, gotta be going, Elkeith. Don't drop the soap."

Fuming, Matthias exhaled loudly through his nose.

"Is that another Earth joke?" Elkeith growled.

Ultra's expression became thoughtful. "Yeah, I guess that wouldn't really work here. Well, you can do the math. So long, asshole." Ultra turned his back on Elkeith.

As the guards led him away, the Inwain stopped them short, turning back around. "*ULTRA!*"

Ultra made a slow turn on his heel. "Yes…?"

Elkeith's wicked smile was disturbing. "I'm going to use your broken bones to pick your flesh from my teeth."

Ultra seemed to let that sink in for a moment. "Well, it's good to have goals."

Again, the guards began to lead Elkeith back to the tower. "I'll be seeing you, Ultra—sooner than you think."

As the door to the tower slammed shut, Matthias let loose the frustration he'd been holding back. "Are we done here?! Can we leave now? Or are there any other useless vecking errands you need to complete before I kindly get you out of prison?"

Ultra seemed taken aback. Gelf, on the other hand, wasn't intimidated in the slightest. "Agent, that piece of nakra tortured us for almost three years. I say, let Max have his fun."

"Oh really, Mister…Gelf—if that's even your real name? Is that your expert appraisal of the situation? Because, your release is contingent upon Ultra helping *me* get done what *I* need accomplished." It was official: Brontin had gotten under his skin.

Ultra looked at him, eyes narrowed in suspicion. "Yeah, I was just having some fun. What's got your panties in a bunch?"

Matthias wasn't interested in sharing with him. Maybe on the ship he'd entertain the notion. "Let's go."

He led the way to the hangar, which was lined with a number of security hover vehicles. At the end of the line sat his GAC-issued shuttle. It was small, but comfortable, and sturdy if trouble came up. The main exit was open, protected from external threats by a force field.

Ultra started in again. "Seriously, what's your problem?"

Matthias increased his speed. "It's nothing. We just have to get a move on."

"Nah, nah, nah, something crawled up your butt. If we're going to work together, we need honesty, trust."

That clinched it. He rounded on Ultra. "Honesty? Trust? How can I trust you to do what needs to be done when you're wasting time bringing a powder keg like Elkeith into the open just to taunt him? When we've got a psychopath on the loose? When your friends are in danger?" He didn't wait for a response, continuing toward the shuttle and glancing around. There seemed to be more guards in the hangar than mechanics.

"Look, we're not going to find Kalen *today*. And the ship isn't leaving without us."

More guards filtered into the hangar. He might have been too obvious in looking around, because he heard Ultra's footsteps cease.

"Is this all on the up and up?" Ultra asked.

Matthias cringed before turning to face him. "We can discuss it on the ship, but right now we have to get the hell out of here."

Ultra folded his arms, resolute.

Matthias sighed. "*Fine.* I had to pull some strings—a *lot* of strings to make this happen. My ass is on the line for this now and I really don't feel like spending the rest of my days here with *you*, so can we *please* leave?"

Ultra took a moment. "I'm not really a free man, am I?"

"You will be once we get on the vecking ship!"

"I'll be a fugitive. What kind of life is that?"

"This is the only way, Ultra. You're the answer to this. I'm staking my career on it. But, a lot of people who are higher up the food chain didn't want to free a convicted murderer to catch another convicted murderer. If you want out of here, I'm your only shot."

Ultra appeared skeptical, the other two, jumpy. Gelf's eyes wandered the hangar, taking everything in, while the Glutob turned this way and that, glancing all around. He couldn't have looked more suspicious if he'd tried.

Matthias paused, glancing around. *No one moving toward us— yet.* "Walk with me, Maxim."

"Not until yo—"

"Boy, we may not have a chance to get any closer to the ship. Walk with me." He continued on—about fifty meters more to go. Ultra and his friends fell in beside him. "You may not believe me, Maxim, you may not even like me very much."

"What gave it away?"

"But I saw your face when I showed you the video of Carfen. You know what's headed for Alesha, but you're wasting time here."

"She…she can handle herself."

"You keep telling yourself that. Vandeir has a two-day head start on us. If you want to help her or any other of your friends, I'm your only hope. And after what I've put on the line, you're mine. Do I make myself clear?"

"Crystal, but I still don't trust you."

"Fair enough. Now, can we get the hell ou—"

"Agent Glintock!" At the other end of the hangar, the warden approached with a group of ten guards.

"Get to the ship!" Matthias hissed.

Ultra spotted the advancing guards. "Boys, time to *run!*" He dashed toward the shuttle with Gelf hot on his heels. The Glutob literally transformed the lower portion of his body into four legs and galloped ahead of the other two, leaving Matthias dumbstruck.

How did I get left out here?

"Stop! Stop those men!" the warden called out as his entourage of guards left the portly man in their wake.

Matthias ran at top speed for the ship's boarding ramp, which his three charges had already cleared. His long strides carried him up the ramp and he slammed the release button to close the hatch.

The shuttle had enough room for about six to travel comfortably. The Glutob and Gelf strapped in in the passenger hold, while Matthias heard Ultra cursing in the cockpit.

"What's your security code to unlock the controls?" Ultra asked.

"Do you really think I'm going to let you pilot a GAC shuttle? Move over." The pinging of laser fire against the ship's hull filled the cockpit.

"Are you kidding me? They're shooting at us!"

"I'm responsible for this vehicle! What if y—"

"Glintock, you're already vecked. Me denting this ship isn't going to make it worse." The laser fire outside intensified. "I can do this."

Sincerity shone in his eyes. Matthias had read the file—Ultra was definitely a better pilot—but still he resisted. Putting his life in Ultra's hands meant fully embracing his plan. Once they flew out of the hangar, Matthias was *committed*. Even with the warden's guards shooting at them on the landing deck, he still might have been able to talk his way out of it.

The ship rocked with heavier laser fire. Matthias nodded, punching in his code and then sliding into the co-pilot's seat.

Ultra returned his nod and took the controls. The ship shuddered as he activated the thrusters and steered it toward the hangar's exit. The view from the shuttle's rear camera showed Matthias that some of the guards were piling into the prison hover cars to pursue them.

"What kind of weapons do I have on this thing?" Ultra asked.

"None. Or at least nothing substantial."

Ultra gave him a look.

"Well, I wasn't planning on shooting my way out of here."

"Why *are* we shooting our way out?" Gelf asked from the hold.

Matthias' frown deepened. "Because a piece of nakra named Brontin gave us no other choice."

Ultra said nothing as he piloted the ship out of the hangar and away from the rocky terrain below. Breaking through the force field, they were immediately pounded by laser cannon fire from the tower's defense grid.

"How are the shields?" Ultra asked without looking at Matthias. His intense concentration on piloting stood in direct contradiction to the man Matthias had met thus far.

"Impeccable. It's a transport shuttle—usually for dignitaries—so, the defenses are strong."

"I'm going to push the engines as hard as I can to break out of the atmosphere as fast as possible, so I need you to monitor everything."

"Of course." Matthias studied the console in front of him, checking the ship's systems. A panel started beeping. "You've got—"

"I see them."

Two ships swooped out of the afternoon sky, taking up positions flanking the shuttle. A crystal-clear *ding* filled the cockpit before a stern voice sounded over the communications unit. "*This is Avalian Air Defense. Land your vehicle immediately.*"

Ultra smirked. "The military? I'm honored."

Matthias keyed the communicator. "This is Agent Matthias Glintock of the Galactic Authority Commission on official business. What's the meaning of this?"

"*You're aiding and abetting the escape of convicted criminals, Agent,*" the stern voice replied. "*Land and this doesn't have to get messy.*"

"Fuck that," Ultra said as he banked the shuttle to the left, nearly colliding with one of their pursuers. He hit the throttle and the ship surged forward. "Good pickup."

"These shuttles were designed explicitly for situations like this. Not all dignitaries are popular," Matthias said.

Ultra gave him a sidelong glance. "Yeah, you didn't think this would happen at all."

He shrugged. "Be prepared for anything, I guess."

"We've got some new friends," Ultra said as he pushed the throttle faster.

Two hover vehicles from the prison had joined the pursuit. The laser fire from their dual-mounted cannons sliced through the air.

Warning shots. Matthias had a hunch the next attack wouldn't be off-target. He was right. Within moments, the shuttle shook violently as laser blasts pummeled it. The Air Defense crafts peeled off. "I can't see them!"

"Those look like cloud-hoppers," Ultra explained. "They can be equipped with shielding to hide themselves from scanners. Tricky little bastards. Nice to see the Avalians aren't cheap." The shuttle rocked again. "What's our rear deflector shield look like?"

"Hey, you want to watch where you're flying?" Gelf called from the back. "We're trying to sleep back here!"

"Down to seventy percent," Matthias replied, ignoring the little man.

"Dial up the Cardon Lane coordinates for Modan."

"You can't enter the lanes while in the atmosphere."

"Oh *really?* I didn't know that, *thanks*," Ultra responded. "Just dial it up!"

The shuttle rocked from successive volleys. The two Air Defense crafts crossed paths in front of the ship as they looped around for another pass. For extra measure, the hover cars behind them unleashed another torrent of lasers that peppered the shuttle's shields.

"Mr. Ultra, I'll remind you that the name of the game is *avoiding* the laser fire."

"I'll remember that. Shields?"

Matthias scanned the screen. "Rear shields at fifty percent. Port and starboard at…forty."

"Yeah, these guys have a little punch. Are the coordinates set?"

"Yes, but—"

"Good."

Ultra immediately cut the throttle and thrusters, letting the shuttle go into free fall. Through the viewport, Matthias watched as the pursuing ships conducted a series of complicated maneuvers to avoid colliding with one another. Ultra looked disinterested as he glanced at the confusion overhead and then reactivated his thrusters, pushing the throttle to full. He pulled out of his controlled fall, streaking into the sky, soon breaking out of the atmosphere and into space.

Matthias fell back into the co-pilot's seat, heaving a relieved sigh. "Unbelievable."

Ultra rose from the pilot's chair, making a move to the back.

"Where are you going?" Matthias asked.

"Coordinates are set, right? It's all yours. I'm going to be in back, enjoying not being in prison."

"Yes, but y " An urgent beeping from Matthias' communicator interrupted him. He pulled it out of his jacket and read the emergency message scrolling across his screen. His eyes bulged before a feeling of hopelessness fell over him. "Dammit to hell," he whispered.

"What's wrong?" Ultra asked, trying to peek at the message.

"Emergency communique from headquarters—we have a problem."

CHAPTER 5

As usual, the weather in the Equor province of Modan was less than ideal. At least that was the way Litning understood it. It was his first time on the planet. Windswept rain lashed the walls of the GAC facility situated on the Busci Cliffs. Word had it that the facility had been constructed there so that the GAC could dump the whole complex into the ocean in the event of a massive security breach. As he scaled the outer wall, Litning prayed to all the gods in Thollavar that that particular plan of action would not be implemented at that very moment.

Memta awaited rescue inside. According to Mondo, the infiltration would be simple. Easy for him to say—he was not hanging off the side of a building in a gale. Litning was grateful for the weather-proof coverall he wore, though he felt like a stick of beef, sealed in his own juices. A skin-tight mask covered his head leaving only his eyes exposed. Large goggles meant to protect them were not worth a damn in the rain. He constantly wiped the fogging lenses so he could see what he was doing. The mask was not exactly comfortable either as it pinned his large ears to his head.

It was uncommon for a Revash to wear much clothing—certainly nothing as complicated as his current accoutrements—but in the years since his exile from his home world of Revjekt, Litning had adapted to the habits of other species. Generally, he had taken quite a liking to clothing. One might even say he was a regular fashion maven—when he could find things that fit, of course. At his size—over two meters with thick muscles—it was difficult to find anything that was not a smock. He was sure he had popped a couple of seams in his cover-all already.

The wind buffeted him as he dangled from his gravity hooks—another gift from Mondo. The hooks created low-level force fields that allowed him to cling to the facility's wall, as long as he did not lose his grip on the hooks themselves. His claws probably would have been enough to scale the structure, but it was not a theory he wanted to test some-sixty meters above the jagged rocks below.

Breaking into a GAC facility was the last thing he would have been involved with in his younger days. Not because of the GAC—Revjekt was not a member planet, so he did not recognize their authority—but simply because it was not right. Back on Revjekt, there had been little Litning had done wrong in his life. He generally obeyed his settlement's laws and customs and had even entertained the notion of becoming a member of the Meshmark—a leader in his community. After his fateful confrontation with Raork, though, none of that had been possible. He had been banished, never to return—never to see Avala again. His heart ached at the thought of her.

After a period of self-destruction, his entire reason for being was to return home. He longed to stalk the snowy plains of Revjekt again, hunting for game—catching the scent of his prey an instant before hearing its footsteps echo across the silent field in the crunching snow. He regretted many of the things he had done in order to make his return a reality. Tonight would be no different.

Once inside the facility, he would receive help in penetrating its defenses. Part of that help would come from the satchel he had slung across his body—a bag of tricks provided by Mondo. He hated relying on others, but if he ever hoped to return to Revjekt, he would have to do just that. The vision of home drove him on.

He paused once he was a hand's length from the roof's ledge. Bracing himself against the wall with his feet, he let go of one of the gravity hooks to retrieve a device from his satchel. His hand closed over the sphere. Clicking the activation switch, he tossed it over the ledge onto the roof. The storm made it impossible to hear where the device had landed, but then an unmistakable electronic *whomp* cut through nature's fury.

Immediately, his gravity hooks lost traction with the wall. A momentary flash of panic seized him before he reached up to grab onto the ledge. The gravity hooks fell away into the crashing waves below.

Those could have brought a good price. He lamented the potential traveling money that had literally slipped through his fingers. Gripping the ledge, he hoisted himself over and onto the facility's roof, landing with a thud. He froze at the sight of a surveillance bot guarding the ledge.

The bipedal robot was dark in color, standing about one and a half meters tall. It stood motionless in the pouring rain, its camera-lens eyes lifeless. The laser rifle in its hands did not rise in Litning's direction. As Mondo had promised, the sphere had knocked out all active electronics, which was why the other devices in his bag stayed powered down.

To his left, another disabled bot that had been in mid-step toppled over in a clanging heap. Dozens of the bots littered the rooftop. Their presence, along with the security cameras had necessitated his dangerous stunt. No sense in getting all the way up to the roof only to be discovered. He hoped that the bots had been mere drones with no personality programming. To others, robots were merely complex tools, but to his people, intelligence, artificial or not, was evidence of a *nepast*, and all nepasts deserved respect.

Retrieving the spent sphere—Mondo had warned him to leave as little evidence as possible—he moved to the sealed door that would get him inside the building and out of the wretched rain. The control panel was dark. The sphere had done its work very well.

Though the door was slick with rain, his gloves gave him the traction he needed to get a grip on the smooth metal surface. Placing his palms on the door, he exerted his considerable strength to slide it open. The shrill grating sound of metal sliding across metal set his teeth on edge. Finally, creating enough space for his burly frame, he entered the facility, sliding the door shut behind him.

He headed down the nearby staircase. At the bottom, a door snapped open, revealing his human contact, just as Mondo had planned. Mondo also had not exaggerated the sphere's short range.

"Whoa, you *are* a big one. Our friend wasn't kidding. I'm—"

"No names," Litning growled, his voice muffled by the mask. He did not want the interior cameras recording his face, so he left the mask on. His size was already a dead giveaway, but every little bit helped.

The human only nodded. Armed with a pistol and baton, he wore a bluish-gray security uniform. "Fair enough. I'm not gonna lie, this probably won't be as easy as our friend advertised."

"Just get me to the vault." Litning patted the satchel. "This will do the rest."

"As long as the pulse didn't knock out anything else we'll need."

Before Litning could respond, the man's radio on his hip beeped. *"Perimeter breach from roof access. All available officers converge on that area."*

Litning's stomach dropped and the man gave him a withering look. "You didn't close the vecking door?" He clicked his radio. "This is Twenty-Five, I'm in the area, but I don't see anything. Moving to secure the door now."

"Copy that, Twenty-Five. Unit Four, proceed to that sector." Then the radio buzzed. *"Twenty-Five, we had some anomalies in your sector and on the roof. We're sending additional officers to you."*

"Uh, okay, thanks." Once he ended his transmission, he swore. "Nakra! This is not good."

"I closed the door behind me."

"Clearly not all the way. This complicates things."

"Do you have the device to blind the cameras?"

"Yeah, but I can't shut them off now that they're on their way."

"Then we will need a distraction for your comrades."

"What kind of—?"

Without warning, Litning smacked Twenty-Five in the chest with the flat of his palm, sending him sprawling across the hall. As the human writhed on the floor, groaning, Litning inched up the stairs, hoping the darkness would conceal him. He soon heard the clattering of approaching boots.

"Twenty-Five, what happened?" A stern voice echoed up the stairwell.

"He-he came out of nowhere, knocked me out." Twenty-Five certainly sounded convincing. "I think he went that way."

A disconcerting silence followed. The only sounds came from the clanking equipment of the idle security officers. Litning held his breath, trying to stay perfectly still.

"All right," the stern voice sounded again. "Seventeen, stay here with Twenty-Five. The intruder may double back. The rest of you, on me."

The sound of the security forces departing sent a wave of relief through Litning. He maintained his position, though, listening for clues on how to proceed next.

A new voice sounded, presumably Seventeen's. "You all right? You don't look so good."

"Just winded," Twenty-Five responded. "Bastard packs a wallop. I'll be fine in a minute. Why don't you take a position down the hall in case he comes back?"

"Yeah, as soon as I clear this open door up here."

Litning froze as Seventeen's footsteps approached. A confrontation was imminent. He silently prayed that his nepast would remain whole. Liberating Memta was too important for a single man to stop him, though.

A shadow appeared in the stairwell doorway. Litning pounced, grabbing the man roughly by the front of his uniform, while knocking his pistol away with his free hand.

Terrified, Seventeen's hands flew up to grasp at Litning's.

Growling deep in his throat, he pulled the guard into the stairwell and delivered a blow to his forehead with the heel of his palm. The attack snapped Seventeen's head back, leaving him unconscious as Litning lowered him gently to the floor.

"Is he dead?" Twenty-Five asked, picking himself up off the floor.

Litning paused, studying Seventeen's chest. "No, he is still alive."

"Too bad, that guy's a real veck."

Litning let the vulgar term slide off his back. He closed his eyes for a moment, thankful his blow was not fatal. Of course, that also meant the security officer could awaken and cause problems. He reached into his satchel while Twenty-Five went to secure the door.

Mondo had briefed him on the items in the bag and their functions. He removed one of several metal discs with three notches on the bottom, set up in a triangle pattern. Placing the disc on Seventeen's chest, he hit the black button on the device's face. The notches extended, burning through Seventeen's uniform until they made contact with his skin. A jolt of electricity shot through the guard, causing his body to jump. The only physical evidence that something was amiss came in the form of periodic twitches from Seventeen.

"What'd you do to him?" Twenty-Five asked, moving to touch the unconscious officer.

Litning grabbed his wrist. "Do not touch him, unless you want to end up the same way. The disc puts a constant current through him, keeping him incapacitated."

"Nice. Let's get going." Twenty-Five rubbed the area where Litning had struck him. "Oh, and the next time you need to cave my chest in, just warn me first."

"With pleasure."

Twenty-Five retrieved both his and Seventeen's pistols, handing them over to Litning. "Here."

"What should I do with these?" he asked, demonstrating that his hands were too big to properly use the pistols.

"I'm your hostage, get it? Don't you have a weapon in that goodie bag?"

"My strength is my weapon."

Twenty-Five balked. "That's a little melodramatic, isn't it? Also, it's not going to help you when the other officers start shooting."

Beneath his mask, Litning grinned. "When that happens, my hostage will serve as a shield."

"With that mask on, I can't tell if you're kidding or not. Stow the weapons in your bag and make it look like you've got a gun in my back."

"Will you not be disabling the cameras?"

From his back pocket, Twenty-Five produced a long, thin, metal cylinder with a lens on its tip. The item bent awkwardly in the middle. "I didn't expect to get slammed to the floor by my partner."

Litning winced. "My apologies. I reacted to the situation at hand."

"Yeah, well no more rookie mistakes. Let's go."

With Twenty-Five leading the way, they ventured into the facility. The building was a maze of interconnecting hallways that all looked the same to Litning. The walls and floors were a glossy, steel blue, matching the security uniforms. Bright lights built into the high ceiling illuminated the halls. Every door they passed was closed to them, but Litning was really only concerned with one.

As soon as the first active security camera spied them, Twenty-Five's radio beeped. *"Intruder spotted on Level Five. He has a hostage. Repeat, we have a hostage situation."*

The radio beeped again and another, more commanding voice spoke. *"This is Security Prime—Unit Four, converge on Level Five. All other units, fall back to Vector."*

"What does any of that mean?" Litning asked as he tensed for the impending conflict.

"Those guys I sent away? They're on their way back here. Security Prime is the Head of Security for the facility. And Vector? That's the vault."

Litning grimaced. A fight was imminent. He had been hoping to avoid one altogether. Also, his victory was not assured. A few guards could be incapacitated, but an entire guard force?

"We gotta figure something ou—" Twenty-Five was cut off by a buzzing from his radio.

Security Prime's voice sounded through the unit. "*This message is for the rather large intruder I'm looking at right now. You cannot win this. You're not the first intruder we've repelled from this facility, you will not be the last.*"

Litning's mind rattled off all the ways he could handle his predicament. "Tell him that unless your comrades stand down, I will kill you."

Twenty-Five shrugged. "He probably won't care, but all right." He clicked his radio. "Sir, this is Twenty-Five. The intruder tells me that unless you call for a general stand down, he'll kill me."

"*Well, I'm sorry about that, Twenty-Five, but I can't allow this person to further breach security. I do hope you'll understand. Mr. Intruder? The offer to surrender is due to expire...now.*"

An electronic bell sounded from down the hall.

"Nakra!" Twenty-Five swore. "I'll probably need those guns back."

"Yes, our ruse is seemingly at an end." He handed Twenty-Five back the pistols before removing his gloves, revealing his fur-covered hands and claws. The men coming for them would show no mercy, but he had to be better than them. He glanced at Twenty-Five. "What is it?"

The human gawked at his gray fur. "Uh, no offense, but what *are* you?"

Since the two of them might be dead in a matter of minutes, he settled on the truth. "A Revash."

Twenty-Five seemed to consider the revelation. "Never seen a Revash before."

"Few have." He pulled three small spheres from his satchel. "Shoot out the lights and only fire again if they are on you." Twenty-Five hesitated as the bell sounded again and the lift doors at the end of the hall opened. "*NOW!*"

His cry shook Twenty-Five out of his trance. The security officer fired both pistols up at the lights, raining darkness and shards of glass down on them.

Litning tossed the three spheres down the hall.

The first ball hit the floor as the initial security guard stepped off the lift. The ball, like the other two that followed it, exploded, releasing a thick white smoke that, combined with the darkness, brought visibility to nearly zero. Litning heard the cries of confusion down the hall as he walked toward the lift. As the smoke enveloped him, he removed his mask, his nostrils filling with the musky scent of his own sweat-drenched fur. The climate-controlled cool of the facility felt refreshing after wearing the mask for so long. He would have been fine stripping off the rest of the cover-all, but he still had need of it. He tucked the mask and goggles into a pouch built into the front of his suit.

Who needs sight when I can track them by scent? He dropped his satchel by the wall as he hunched over. *Brothers and sisters, forgive me.* With a single menacing growl, he bounded deeper into the smoke on all fours.

"Hold it!" he heard the stern officer call out to his men. Without the mask pinning his ears down any longer, Litning's hearing sharpened significantly. He heard the distinctive sound of a man urinating in his pants. Then, he picked up the scent—his first target.

There were only seven of them. Bowling into one, he knocked the guard to the floor. He punched the man in the head before jumping back to his feet and slashing out at another target to his left. Feeling his claws tear through the guard's uniform and connect with flesh sent a jolt through him. The warm spray of blood over his hand pulled him closer to the violent haze that threatened to cloud his mind. Blood pounded in his head, while his mouth practically salivated at the thought of crushing these humans' bones. He tried to shake the thoughts from his mind. Picking up another officer, Litning slammed him into the one he had cut, knocking them both out of the fight.

The hallway filled with screams and stray laser fire. One bolt sizzled past his head only to strike one of the other security officers. The close call left a burning smell in the air. Litning snarled, pouncing on a guard attempting to flee the pervasive smoke.

"Please! Don't kill me!" the guard pleaded.

Litning said nothing. He picked the guard up and swung him by his legs, connecting with two bodies before tossing him down the hall toward Twenty-Five.

The battle lasted all of two minutes—its end signaled by the *whoosh* of the ventilation system finally kicking on to disperse the smoke. Litning made sure to pull his hated mask and goggles back on as the smoke cleared. His chest heaved, but more importantly, the chests of all the guards still moved as well. He had beaten back the bloodlust and won. Pride swelled in his chest. *Perhaps there is still a way through this.*

Despite the blood making it look worse than it was, Litning's opponents were all unconscious, save for one who sat dazed on the floor. He looked as though he could not process what he was seeing. Once his eyes settled on Litning, they widened. He scrambled for his pistol, but Litning was on him instantly, stripping the weapon away. As the pistol clattered to the floor, he picked the guard up by his collar, hoisting him effortlessly.

"Look at your comrades. Do you want to join them?"

The guard glanced over at the others. His face twisting in anger, he spat at Litning.

The glob of saliva landed on Litning's mask. He slammed the guard into the wall, claws ready to strike when a laser blast struck the man in the head.

Beneath the mask, Litning's face contorted in rage. "I told yo—"

"He was Unit Four's commander. He wasn't going to give us anything." Twenty-Five approached slowly, gesturing around at the fight's aftermath. "If I had known you were going to be such a pussycat, I would have used this earlier. Leaving these guys alive does nothing for us."

"But they are your comrades."

"Hah! You've got a lot to learn out here, my Revash friend. This is just a job. A joyless, soul-crushing job and these poor vecks mean nothing to me. Our mutual friend made me a better offer. Money is a powerful motivator and I want a new life. Plus, you heard Prime on the radio. How can a man who would callously sacrifice his own men endear any loyalty or respect?" He aimed his weapon at the unconscious guards.

Litning dropped the lifeless body in his hand and knocked Twenty-Five's aim off with a blow across his arm. "Stop! No more killing. There is no need."

"The enemies you don't kill will come back to haunt you."

"There is always another way."

Twenty-Five holstered his pistol. "Yeah, you keep telling yourself that once we reach the vault." He moved past Litning down the hall toward a marked stairwell.

"That area will be heavily defended."

"Yeah, whose fault is that?" Twenty-Five snorted.

"I am not sure a direct attack is the correct approach."

"Well thank you, Mr. Expert. Prime is going to keep throwing guards at us until we're dead. If we manage to get through that, we still have to break into the vault anyway. Might as well go there now."

Litning eyed Twenty-Five with suspicion. The man was his only ally in the facility, but the ease with which he threw away his loyalty did not endear him to Litning. He did not trust Twenty-Five. *But who would trust either of us? We are both criminals.* Having no other choice, he followed Twenty-Five to the stairwell.

As soon as the stairway door closed behind them, Twenty-Five's radio buzzed. *"Where do you two think you're going?"* Prime's voice sounded over the radio. *"And yes, I clearly saw how you treated Commander Four on the camera, Twenty-Five."*

Twenty-Five swiped his radio from his belt and held it close to his mouth as he ground out his words. "You're lucky it wasn't you up here, Prime. I would have made sure to shoot you a few times more."

"Such bravado. Consider me duly intimidated. Your friend doesn't do much talking, though. I'd like to know where he's from so I know where to send the GAC agents to pick him up if we don't capture or kill you first."

"That goes both ways, Prime. Only we're not looking to capture you."

"Surely you can't be headed to Vector. I have thirty men down there waiting for you."

Before Twenty-Five could attempt another smart reply, Litning took the radio from him. He pressed the button to transmit. "No. We are coming for you." He handed the radio back to Twenty-Five, who looked on, dumbfounded. "This Prime seems like the type of person who believes in self-preservation. Perhaps he will divert some of his resources from the vault."

"We're about to find out," Twenty-Five replied as they reached the bottom of the staircase.

Twenty-Five opened the door into a wide corridor. To the left, the hall turned a corner, while to the right stood a set of double doors.

"Which way?" Litning asked. His blood pumped with the anticipation of another battle.

"First thing's first," Twenty-Five responded as he leveled his pistol at a small ceiling camera tucked into the corner. He fired once, destroying the unit in a shower of sparks. "That'll keep Prime confused a little longer. We go through the double doors. Follow me."

A thrill rippled through Litning's body. *Soon Memta, soon you will be free.*

With Twenty-Five leading the way, they passed through the double doors and ducked into another stairwell that Litning hoped would take them to the vault.

Twenty-Five's radio beeped again. "*S-Prime to Vector, we believe the intruder's headed your way. Be on alert.*"

"How?" Litning asked.

Twenty-Five shrugged. "The cameras see everything. I just take comfort in that your threat to Prime probably made him drop a nakra in his pants."

Litning could not suppress his grin at the joke.

The stairwell terminated around the corner from the large open area housing the vault. Litning took a moment to check the lay of the land. As Prime had promised, there had to be thirty or more guards milling around. Some looked alert, but most appeared relaxed, clearly confident in their numbers. *Mistake number one.*

Twenty-Five snorted. "Their boss just said we might be headed this way and these guys couldn't care less. Contract security for you, I guess. I hope you're going to drop your whole no killing policy here. There's no way we get through all these guys without *one* of them ending up dead."

"Let me worry about that."

"I'm not thinking of you, I'm thinking of me."

"Switch your pistols off."

"You think I'm going into this fight defenseless? You're out of your vecking mind."

Litning glared at the man. "Turn them off." He growled a bit to hammer the command home.

Twenty-Five resisted for another moment before finally shaking his head and switching the pistols off. "Happy?"

"No, but you will be." Litning took his final electronic disrupter from his satchel. As he had done on the roof, he switched the device on and tossed it into the crowd of security officers. The electronic *whomp* sounded and Litning nodded at Twenty-Five. "Wait here." Tightening the strap on his satchel, he strolled nonchalantly around the corner.

The officers guarding the vault immediately took aim at him. "Stop!" one called out.

Litning ignored him, continuing his approach.

"Fire!"

The clicking of thirty or so useless triggers tickled Litning's ears. The sphere had rendered their rifles useless. Again and again the officers tried with the same result. A few in front charged Litning, batons held high.

Litning charged right back at them with a loud roar. He felt his inner warrior taking over his consciousness, pushing his rational mind to the background, but he held fast to his convictions. He did not want to kill these men. They were only armed with batons. He could take their abuse without resorting to killing.

He caught the first officer with a shot to the throat that left him choking for air. The next, he picked up and tossed back into his comrades, sending several of them sprawling. He slammed another into a wall. The officer slid to the floor, looking lifeless. A pang of regret cut through the violent fog that encroached on his mind. He hoped the man was only unconscious.

Baton strikes rained down on him as he waded into another group of guards. Each blow chipped away at his resolve, but he gritted his teeth and continued to keep his attacks as non-lethal as possible. He tried to focus on Avala. His memory of her burned in his mind like a beacon keeping him on course.

Lasers lanced out from behind him, striking some of the guards around him—Twenty-Five had reactivated his pistols. The fact that the man spat in the face of Litning's wishes angered him, but he was more concerned with the fact that the lasers came increasingly closer to hitting him than he was comfortable with.

The distraction of Twenty-Five proved costly. One of the guards lashed out with a knife that cut across Litning's arm. Another strike dug into his side and the light Avala's memory provided was instantly snuffed out, consumed by a crimson haze that craved retribution and blood.

The mob of officers hit Litning like a wave, but he held his ground, thrashing those who attacked him. With every strike, he felt his mind slipping further into the haze. Worries about keeping his nepast intact faded. He just wanted to hurt these men. One tried calling for help on his radio, but found the device inert. Another jumped on Litning's back, managing to peel off his mask and goggles.

He roared, palming the guard's head. Feeling his claws sink into the man's flesh, he reveled in the sensation, ignoring the guard's screams. Ripping the man off his back, he whipped him around by the head until he felt the bones snap in his neck. Litning tossed the lifeless body into another surge of approaching guards.

Becoming a whirlwind of claws and fangs, he completely lost himself to the bloodlust. He shredded faces, tore out throats with his teeth, and broke bodies, feeding the ancient hunger that had taken hold. Finally, some of the men started to flee.

He wanted to pursue them, but the massive silver door beside him held his gaze like a star guiding him home. His chest heaved. The fog in his mind had not completely lifted yet, but he tried to slow his breathing to help clear his head. He surveyed the carnage. Centuries of Revash evolution, wiped away in an instant. He could feel the pieces of his nepast breaking off like embers and ash, but the screams would live within him forever. His senses slowly returned. Blood coated him. He spat on the floor, but the metallic taste of his victims' blood remained. He doubted he would ever be able to properly wash it out. Immediately, he lamented the death and destruction he had caused. His hands trembled.

A biometrics scanner protected the vault. Mondo had briefed him on their operation, but with no power, the scanner remained dark. *It also does not help that I have killed everyone here who might be able to open it.*

Similar to a lift's doors, the vault had two halves that met in the middle. Only, these doors were much, much larger than a lift's—easily a meter taller than he. Reaching out, he worked his claws into the seam where the doors met. They parted just a bit for his fingers to get in, but the heavy slabs of steel fought against him.

Once he had a good grip, he took a deep breath and whispered a prayer. "For Revjekt."

He exerted all his strength, shaking with the effort. The doors opened a crack. He could see inside the vault. It felt as though his muscles might tear apart as he tried to force the doors open further. His body screamed in pain. Then he realized he was the one screaming.

The door opened enough for him to squeeze inside, but how would he get out? He had to get them open completely. With a final, bloodcurdling howl, he pushed his strength to its absolute limit and pried the doors apart.

He collapsed to the floor, panting. Securing his prize and escaping the facility were faraway dreams. He simply wanted to sleep.

"Y-you did it," Twenty-Five said with no shortage of awe. "Let's get in there before your little ball wears off."

"No. I must go in alone. Make sure our escape is secure and then return here."

"Hey, who put you in char—?"

A single menacing look from Litning cut Twenty-Five off.

"All right, all right, I'll go check on the skiff." After a moment's hesitation, Twenty-Five departed.

With a groan, Litning dragged himself to his feet and into the vault. The room was large and sterile white. Its stark beauty made Litning grimace at the blood he tracked inside. The vault was sectioned off into cubes along the walls, each holding some artifact or object in a stasis beam of blue light. He had no interest in any of the others, just what he had come for.

Scanning the room, he found Memta in the back corner. A grayish-green statue rotated silently, peacefully, with no hint of what it contained. When the face of Memta came into view, Litning dropped to his knees, bowing his head.

"Great and powerful Memta, allow this humble servant to guide you home," he murmured. A quick moment of silence and he rose. He stared at the statue for a few seconds more as he pulled his gloves back on. The smooth stone had a monstrous face carved into the top of it with intricate markings along the bottom edge and on the base.

Reaching into the cylinder of light, he took hold of the artifact. Even through his gloves, it was warm to the touch, but only briefly. It quickly became cold in his hand like ordinary rock. Removing a brown cloth from his satchel, he wrapped the statue.

Placing his prize in the bag, he turned to see a short man with receding black hair and a goatee entering the vault. He had a gun pointed at Litning. "I'm afraid I can't let you leave with that statue or *any* of these artifacts." The man's voice identified him as Prime.

"You do not know what this statue really is," Litning said.

"No, but I know what it's capable of, just like everything else in this vault. We're protecting the galaxy with this facility. By keeping these things locked up, people of all races and species are *safe*. I won't allow you to le—ugh!" Prime was cut off by a laser bolt to his back. The security head crumpled to the floor and Twenty-Five emerged to shoot him a few more times.

"That's for deeming me expendable," Twenty-Five said as he spat on Prime's corpse. Instantly, his demeanor changed to wonderment as he gazed around at the inside of the vault. "Look at all this stuff. Do you know what we could get for this on the black market?"

"We are only here for the statue," Litning reminded him.

"Yeah, about that...." Twenty-Five turned his weapon on Litning. "I'm going to need you to turn that over to me too—boss' orders."

Litning shook his head. "So you *were* trying to shoot me during the fight?"

Twenty-Five shrugged. "Figured it would've been easier that way. I could've worked out a way into the vault, but I needed those guards gone. Now, go ahead and hand over that statue. My ride's waiting."

Security Prime's voice echoed through the facility. "*Failsafe activated. Five minutes to evacuate.*"

Litning looked at Twenty-Five with wide, panicked eyes. "What was that?"

The security guard shrugged. "That was a recording, obviously. The failsafe is tied to Prime's bio-functions. With him dead...."

"You fool."

"We can both get out of here, but I need the statue. Not a lot of time to debate here."

Litning sighed, weary. He only wanted to leave the facility and continue on his journey. In spite of Twenty-Five's duplicity, Litning hoped to not lose any more of his nepast with this final encounter, but there did not seem to be any way around it. He threw the satchel at Twenty-Five and charged after it, barreling into the man.

Twenty-Five hit the floor and his pistol skittered away from him. He clambered after it, but Litning grabbed his leg, bringing him to a stop.

Litning dug his claws into Twenty-Five's flesh, finding grim amusement in the man's screams. "Where is the escape craft?"

"I'm supposed to *kill* you! You think I'm going to give you a way out?"

"We are both dead if you do not! Mondo is not the trusting type it seems—he wanted you out of the way too. You know how I feel about that. Do not make me kill you."

Twenty-Five stopped struggling and gripped the satchel in his hands. "All right, follow me."

"Three minutes. Three minutes to evacuate."

As they exited the vault, Litning heard the whirring of the nearby cameras.

So much for no evidence.

They scrambled down to a vehicle bay that could launch both ground and sea transport. A hydrofoil was already set to leave.

"Has the vehicle's tracking device been disabled?" Litning asked.

"Yes." Twenty-Five glared at him.

"Give me the satchel. You will pilot."

"Sure," Twenty-Five responded, sticking his hand into the bag.

"What are you doing?" Litning asked as he pulled the satchel away from Twenty-Five, who came away with Memta in his gloved hand.

"I'm getting the veck out of here!" Twenty-Five cried as he quickly turned to the hydrofoil.

Litning reached out and grabbed the guard's sleeve, but Twenty-Five pulled away violently, tearing the uniform and stumbling back into the hydrofoil. As Twenty-Five contorted his body to break his fall, Memta brushed his bare cheek.

A dazzling turquoise flash filled the vehicle bay as a subsequent shockwave knocked Litning to the ground. After a stunned moment, he looked into the hydrofoil. Twenty-Five laid on the deck, unbreathing—his eyes fixed open.

An explosion rocked the facility. Litning leaped into the hydrofoil. He said a silent prayer before dumping Twenty-Five's body into the water and carefully scooping Memta back into the satchel.

Concrete and rock fell around him as he piloted the hydrofoil out of the bay and onto the open sea. Just as the boat cleared the depot, a large chunk of the cliff side dropped into the sea behind him, narrowly missing the back end of the vessel.

Litning pushed the throttle to full and blinked against the driving rain as he turned to watch a series of explosions separate the cliff from the rest of the land. The facility plummeted into the ocean with a deafening roar. The resulting waves battered Litning's craft, tossing him around thoroughly, but he remained afloat, the satchel clutched to his chest. His thoughts, however, remained inside the doomed building.

He had done his best to mitigate the damage to his nepast, but his best had not been nearly good enough. His actions left him hollow inside. Hopefully, Memta would be enough to fill the void. He had escaped with what he needed, though he was sure Mondo would not be happy with his own plans for the statue.

He was returning to Revjekt.

CHAPTER 6

"The statue is gone."

That's what Glintock said when he received his fateful message as they escaped Aval. Now, they had *two* jobs: find Kalen *and* find the guy who stole the statue. However, at that moment, Max and Gelf stood in one of the many corridors of the Marina Spaceport, waiting for Glintock and Gerry to finish squaring away the GAC shuttle.

The Marina Spaceport was a giant tower built on a dried up lake. When the port was first constructed, it was a sprawling complex that allowed the one-time vacation destination of Marina to become a thriving city that drew more and more residents every year. To keep up with the population and economic explosion, the spaceport had to build skyward. The tower's base was three miles wide, matching the width of the lake bed. From the outside, the Marina Spaceport was a technological wonder, but in the hallway Max and Gelf occupied, it simply looked like a sleek, futuristic building. The gun metal gray walls and floors housed interactive screens to keep patrons moving to the center of the spaceport—a city in its own right. The spaceport's core was commerce, residential, and entertainment all in one package. The sheer enormity of it was staggering.

Max chose to focus on his current whereabouts in order to ignore his handheld communicator that he flipped over and over in his hand.

"You talk to your mother yet?" Gelf asked, forcing Max to deal with what was really on his mind.

Max sighed. "No. Not yet."

"It's been, what, three years since you talked to her?"

"Sounds about right."

"Don't you want to let her know where you are? Where you've been?"

"I was hoping Alesha or Roeger told her. Aval didn't exactly have the one phone call law."

"Huh?"

"It-it's an Earth thing." He gazed at his communicator. "I really want to hear her voice and let her know I'm all right, but I'm not sure I want to call her now with what we're about to do. With Kalen on the loose, do I really want to get her hopes up that she'll be seeing me soon?" Max suddenly felt very tired. "I could be dead at the end of the week."

"You know," Gelf said, "we *could* make a run for it."

Max tucked the communicator back in his jacket. "We can't. I gave Glintock my word."

"*So, what?* Let's go to your house, get Alesha, and get the hell out of here."

"You didn't see the video I saw, Gelf. We *have* to get that statue back."

"Are you going soft on me, Boss?"

Max sighed again. "No, just trying to be the man I should be instead of the screw up I've been of late." Part of fulfilling that promise was making amends with Alesha.

Glintock had covered their tracks as best he could, but the GAC was sure to be poking around the area looking for them. Max thought the agent was going to have a stroke when he received that communiqué about the statue.

"Where to after this?" Gelf asked.

"Well, Glintock is hot to go to Equor to gather clues, but we made a deal that we'd assemble the crew first. So, from here we go to Apex to pick up Roeger and Robert."

"Your old pilot? What do we need him for? You did fine flying us out of Aval."

"Thanks, buddy. But, I need Robert. On most jobs, I'm out in the field and I need a good getaway driver. That's Robert."

"Not that I care what that *petch* Glintock wants, but if the statue is as dangerous as you say, do we really have the time for this?" Gelf questioned.

"Probably not, but the GAC has bulletins out for the guy who stole the statue. Apparently, he's *massive*. He won't be able to go much of anywhere without drawing attention. I just hope getting Alesha won't turn into a long, drawn-out fight."

Sure it won't.

"I just can't believe you're not running into this docking pod and taking off in your ship. What's it called again?"

Max looked at the pod doors fondly. "*Hunter II.*"

"No offense, but that's a terrible name."

"My father's ship was the *Hunter*. So, it's a tribute to him. I actually prefer my nickname for her, the *Sequel*."

"Better, I guess. And why aren't we saving time and checking it all out now?"

"Because, I made Glin—"

"You made Glintock a promise. You gotta cut that nakra out, Boss. Because, when it all comes down to it, he's going to sell you out faster than you can say, 'I made Glintock a promise.' Mark my words."

"Duly noted, but the guy got you out of prison too, Gelf."

"No, *you* got me out of prison. And I believe I'm paying that debt."

Max grimaced. "Yeah, don't mention that around Alesha, please."

"Will do."

"And as for why we don't just blast off out of here, I'm pretty sure Glintock has some kind of tracer on me at the very least."

"You're right, I do," Glintock said as he and Gerry approached. "You actually waited. I'm impressed."

"Thanks a lot."

Glintock glanced at the sealed bay doors. "Docking Pod 101—any significance?"

Max walked over to the pod's access panel. "Nothing I'm going to tell you about."

"I deserved that, I guess."

Max swiped his hand in front of the access panel to activate the touchscreen. A flutter of excitement passed through him as he punched in his access code. The excitement only intensified as the pod doors unsealed and slid open, revealing the *Sequel*.

She was considered a medium-sized freighter, but on the smaller side of medium. Max had never needed anything more. According to Glintock, Roeger had salvaged her before taking off for Apex. Considering the type of work Max was in, he willingly sacrificed speed for armament, but the *Sequel* wasn't so loaded down that she couldn't maneuver efficiently out of tight spots.

Robert's motto had always been: "She's a great getaway vehicle, but she won't win any races." She was fast enough. When chasing down a treasure or a target, Max needed every little bit of speed he could muster, but the guns ensured that he'd be able to look forward to further adventures when the engines decided to take a dump.

He pulled his jacket sleeve back to reveal a wide black leather band around his left wrist with a keypad built into the top. The device was kind of a universal remote control, but the catch was, the owner could assign the buttons any way he or she liked, making it useless to thieves unless they knew the programmed layout. For two and a half years, it had been sitting in a bin with the rest of his possessions on Aval. Putting it back on had felt like he'd restored a missing part of his arm.

After studying the device for a moment to make sure its layout was straight in his memory, Max hit a button in the corner. A *whoosh* of decompressing air from the *Sequel*'s underside filled the pod as one of the ship's two elevators descended to the deck.

"All aboard," Max said with a smile.

The four of them loaded onto the lift, which had a waist-high metal barrier, and Max hit the "up" button. The elevator delivered them into a cage housed in the *Sequel*'s galley/common area, situated in the middle of the ship. The other elevator led to the cargo hold, but the galley elevator was used for quick getaways and Max didn't want to wait another minute to see his ship.

He stepped out of the cage and into a memory. Everything was as he remembered it. He half-expected to find the fossilized remains of his last meal on the table bolted to the deck, but Roeger appeared to have taken care of it when he rescued the ship from Aval.

Wandering away from the others, Max passed through the ship's corridors without a thought about Glintock's mission or the stolen statue or any of it. Instead, he thought about his old crew and the good times they'd had, even when times were lean. He didn't know how they'd react to seeing him again. He'd hurt all of them, even though someone like Robert probably wouldn't admit that. Even Roeger might hold that back, and he was an open book.

Christi, the *Sequel*'s artificial intelligence, hadn't greeted him when he stepped on board, so he figured that Roeger had her with him. There was a slight possibility Alesha had her, but the two of them never totally got along, so it was unlikely.

He entered the cockpit. Looking out the viewport, he was sorely tempted to hop behind the controls and just take off, despite what he'd told Gelf. But he had to see Alesha. He couldn't move on without seeing her. No matter what happened, though, he was home.

"Ultra?" Glintock called out as he stepped into the cockpit. "You ready? Time isn't on our side."

"Yeah, I was just reminiscing."

"Plenty of time for that later."

"Right."

Glintock's communicator began chirping. The two of them exchanged a wary look. Glintock checked his screen and his face fell.

"Shit, what now?" Max asked.

Glintock looked up slowly. "Three bodies found. All signs point to Kalen Vandeir. Ultra, he's on Modan."

A nervous sweat broke out over Max's body. "But not in Marina, right?"

"No. This happened in Guarong."

"Not far enough away. Let's move." They returned to the common area, where Gelf and Gerry waited. Max tried to push the looming Kalen out of his mind. "Gelf, you've got the list on how to bring the ship up to speed?"

Gelf patted his shirt pocket. "Right here, Boss."

"Gerry, the kitchen's yours. Head to the market area, specifically the *Con-3*. Ask for Pepper. Tell him I sent you and he'll get you sorted with everything we need."

"Of course, Maxim. And let me thank you again for the hospitality and the job."

"Please, you're doing *me* a favor—I hate to cook. Hopefully we'll be back in an hour or two."

With that, Max and Glintock departed the spaceport to walk the streets of Marina. Despite the early morning hour, people already jammed the city streets and it was beastly hot outside. None of it fazed Max. He was free. Outside of prisons, ships, and spaceports with the sun shining on his face. Hell, just wearing his own clothes again was reason to celebrate. He'd wanted to take care of his prison haircut that made him look like the Incredible Hulk from the old seventies TV show and his itchy beard before seeing Alesha, but there hadn't been time. Glintock's most recent update quickened his step even more.

He breathed in the fresh air deeply, trying to cleanse the worry from his mind. It was the first time he'd been outside in two and a half years. He tried to enjoy the walk even if a serial killer was on his trail and it was bound to end in a fight with Alesha.

All the buildings in Marina were one-story affairs, which had been in line with the original spaceport design. Now, with the tower, it looked like a giant spaceship had landed in the middle of the city and flattened all the surrounding buildings.

"It's not too far," Max said as the two of them worked their way through the crowds.

"Was that by design?"

He nodded. "Never know when you may need to make a quick getaway."

"Doesn't the design of the port make that more than a little difficult?"

Max winked. "I know a guy."

"What are we expecting to encounter at the house?"

"Yeah, I'm going to reiterate that I should probably do this by myself."

Glintock chuckled. "Do you think I got you out of prison so that you could traipse all over the galaxy unfettered? No, I'll join you."

He shrugged. "Your funeral."

"Do you really think it'll be that bad?"

"Have you ever dated a Valian woman, Agent?"

"Can't say that I have. I'm happily married to my work."

"That figures," he muttered.

"What was that?"

"I said, 'That's interesting.'"

"I won't apologize for my responsibilities. Not all of us are as carefree as you, Mr. Ultra."

Carefree? Yeah, right. "Was there *ever* anyone?"

Glintock went quiet for a few moments. "Yes. Once."

"See? We're making progress."

"Since we're getting personal, then, what's the situation with Gelf?"

Max bristled. It wasn't a topic he wanted to discuss, especially with Glintock, whom he was sure was going to judge him. "He helped me out in prison. I owe him."

"I think I know how he helped you."

"Look, don't start. You don't know me."

"No, not really, but I know the type of inmate Gelf is. Be careful. I need you straight to get this done—not strung out on whatever he's feeding you with."

Max's face went hot. "Duly noted." *Who the fuck is this guy to question me? The guy who got you out of prison, stupid.* He and Gelf would have to watch themselves around Glintock. That notion came with a pang of guilt. Somewhere in his heart, he knew Glintock had a point.

Max froze. His head whipped around. A woman had passed by them. Her gait, height, and hair all screamed, *Sierra.* He closed his eyes and took a deep breath. *She's dead. It's not her.* For a long time after she'd been murdered, Max saw her all over the place on Aval, but eventually, his mind stopped playing tricks on him. He did *not* want a repeat of that now that he was out.

Glintock gave him a dubious look. "You all right?"

"Yeah…I…thought I saw someone I knew." *It could be the rimi*, he thought with a shiver. One of rimi's side effects was potential madness. Max thought he'd been controlling his usage, but seeing a dead woman walking around was a bad sign. "Look, I'd appreciate it if you'd keep your suspicions about my alleged drug use to yourself when we're around Alesha."

"She's not going to be too happy about that?"

"Not exactly, no."

"Anything to do with your previous run-in with the Rimi Queen, Swann Nestive?"

Max's mouth dropped open. "Those…are some pretty detailed files you've got."

"They are. Still, I was extremely impressed with your flying back on Aval," Glintock said, changing the subject. "Those were military pilots you outwitted—no small feat."

"Thanks. We survived, that's all that matters."

"Modesty—something I never expected from you. Had you ever flown a ship like that before?"

Though grateful for the praise, Max wondered why Glintock started getting so chummy. "It's not that different from ship to ship."

"And nonchalant as well."

"Agent, I've been piloting ships since I was a teenager. It's second nature." He hid it well, but the escape from Aval had actually scared the shit out of him. He'd felt a little rusty and was trying to escape going back to prison for the rest of his life. It was more than a little nerve-wracking.

Finally, after a hot, sweaty walk, they arrived at Max's house. Its red stone exterior looked pretty much the same as he'd left it. There was the expected wear and tear from the elements, but all in all, it looked all right. He stopped Glintock at the door.

"Look, you got me here and I appreciate all you've done, but I really need to go in alone first."

Glintock's eyes narrowed as he folded his arms.

"I'm not escaping in my own house, Glintock. It's just…this'll be hard enough without you in there too."

"All right, but don't take too long. We need to get moving. There's no telling where the thief has gotten to and we need to find him."

"What about Kalen?"

"Him too, but the statue is priority number one. Hopefully, we'll be able to snag them both at the same time."

"Let's hope so. I need to get back to my life." He walked up to the front door and the handprint scanner that would unlock it for him. *Hope she didn't erase me from the system.* Placing his palm on the pad, he waited a few tense moments before the door unlocked and opened. Stepping inside, he threw Glintock a nervous smile.

The door snapped shut, leaving his eyes to adjust to the dimly lit interior. She had the shutters closed, so the only light came from a lone lamp in the living room, which looked like a disaster area. Some shirts as well as a few pairs of panties were strewn about. A toppled stack of data pads lay on the glass coffee table. The kitchen, which branched off the living room, was no better with dishes clogging the sink and counter space.

The house was small, but the furnishings bordered on posh, complete with extensive audio/visual equipment that made anything Max had owned on Earth look like Tinker Toys. Before the fateful job with Sierra and Kalen, he'd made a decent living, but wasn't much of a saver. His father's illness and subsequent death when Max was nineteen had taught him the valuable lesson that you couldn't take it with you. He'd had a nice nest egg as a result of his father's death, but had been swindled out of most of it prior to going to prison. The job with Sierra was meant to get him back to even. *Boy, did I fuck that up.*

A loud *thump* ended his reverie. The noise came from the master bedroom, and was followed by low moaning. His pulse quickened as his eyes darted around, taking in the details that had been lost in the general mess: a turned-over end table, a crack in the wall leading into the hallway, pictures that once hung in the hallway now laid on the carpet. The image of a disemboweled Carfen played in his mind on repeat. Another moan escaped the bedroom. Was he too late? Was Kalen actually in Marina?

Regretting that Glintock hadn't seen fit to give him back his pistol, Max scooped a fallen sculpture off the floor, hefting the heavy metal in his hand. The bedroom door was off its track, as if someone had been thrown into it. Gripping the statue, he raced down the hallway as quickly and quietly as he could before bursting into the room.

"Get away from h—*what the fuck?*"

"*Max?!*"

Alesha was definitely in danger—*of getting pregnant*. She was naked in bed—*his* bed—on top of Riodor, one of her mimbos that she always had stowed away in case of emergency horniness.

"Hello Maxim, good to see you my friend," Riodor said good-naturedly, his white teeth standing out against his blue skin. He was humanoid, but Max wasn't sure where he was from.

Planet of the Douchebags, probably. "Yeah, hi Rio."

"When did you get out?"

"I'm sorry Rio, love to continue chatting, but we'll have to pick this up when you're *not* fucking Alesha—in *my* bed." He bolted from the room, dumping the sculpture back to the floor.

"Max, wait!" she called after him.

Turning back around, he saw her coming down the hall, pulling on a sheer robe that did nothing to conceal her nakedness. Her dark hair was much longer than he'd dreamed while on Aval. Her eyes were filled with concern and a hint of—

SLAP!

"You come back here after the way you left and don't even tell me you're out?" she asked as she pushed past him.

He rubbed his face where she'd slapped him. "This *is* telling you I'm out. I was trying to surprise you."

"Well, consider me surprised." She stalked into the kitchen. "Lights!" The overhead lamps turned on and she started banging around to prepare her morning tea. At least some things hadn't changed.

"What's Mr. Suave doing fucking you in *my* bed?"

"It's my bed now, Max," she said. "This is *my* house."

He caught himself. "Come again?"

Sighing, she explained. "You went to prison. The lenders weren't going to let you keep the house out of the kindness of their hearts. So, the house went up for auction, I won it, I own it. The house is mine."

His head spun. He wasn't sure what he'd expected upon returning home, but Alesha owning his house wasn't it. "Is this your way of asking me to leave?"

"Max, if I wanted you to leave, I wouldn't have left your handprint in the house's database. If you must stay, you can take the spare bedroom."

Though he knew dreams were never a suitable reality, he couldn't have imagined *this* outcome. "I thought about you every day in prison—dreamed about coming home to you."

She set her mug on the kitchen counter a little forcefully before pouring her tea. "Where was that sentiment before you went gallivanting off with Sierra? Whatever happened to that *horvorka* anyway? I sure hope you killed her."

Bringing up Sierra was inevitable, but just the mention of her name sent him back to Tonicen. He flinched as he saw her murdered in front of him—again. "No, Merthane took care of that."

"Well, remind me to thank him."

His face twitched.

Her expression softened as she looked at him. "How's your back?"

"Sleeping on a steel slab for two and a half years does wonders. Thanks."

She shook her head slowly. "You really fucked up, Max."

"I know, sweetheart. I know. I'm sorry." Despite the circumstances, he loved when she used the four-letter Earth words he'd taught her.

"The others are gone. I'm the only one left here."

"I know. I came to see you first."

She arched her eyebrow. "And I'm sure this has nothing to do with the fact that your ship is still docked here. I kept up with those payments too—you're welcome."

"Thanks, but no. It's like I said, I came back for you. You're all I thought about in prison." He walked across the room to her. "How I'd hurt you. How much I regretted that. How much I wanted to make it up to you." He moved behind her.

She tensed as he gripped her shoulders, but didn't pull away.

His hands trembled as he turned her to face him. This was all he'd wanted—to hold her again. Aside from her longer hair, she was exactly as he'd remembered in his dreams. He pulled her closer, her breasts brushing against his chest. Her breathing quickened as he gently touched her face.

She turned her head away. "No." She pulled away from him, retrieving her tea as she retreated to the living room.

"I thought you'd be happy to see me, 'Lesha."

"I *am* happy to see you, Max, but…." She looked away for a moment, taking a deep breath. "But when I look at you, all I see is Sierra and how you left, and I get angry with you all over again. Things are different now. I have my own crew. I'm doing…really well for myself."

"Is Rio in your crew?" He couldn't help sneering.

"Yes he is, as a matter of fact. I've got a good team."

"*We* were a good team."

"You walked out on us—on me—and I don't need you anymore, Max."

She might as well have punched him in the balls. "I was trying to protect you."

"I don't need protection. We could have found another way."

At what had to be the worst possible moment for Max, Rio emerged from the bedroom—clothed, thankfully. "Sorry to interrupt. Sweet Baby, I'm going to go."

Sweet Baby? Fucking loser.

"Okay Rio."

"Max, glad to see you are a free man, my friend," Rio said with a sincere smile.

Max offered him a phony one. "Hey Rio, no offense, but go fuck yourself."

Rio's smile just got bigger. "What is this 'fuck?' Alesha says it all the time when we are making love. She keeps chanting, 'Fuck, fuck, fuck.' I am not understanding this word."

"Okay! Thanks Rio! See you later!" Alesha said, completely mortified.

"All right, see you!"

Rio made for the door. As it opened for him, Glintock stepped into the house.

"Who the veck are you? Get out of my house!" Alesha cried, pulling her robe closed in a vain attempt to cover herself.

"Agent Matthias Glintock, GAC." He pointed at Max. "We have to talk."

"I told you, I've got this!"

"Max, who is this vecking guy? Is he with you?" Alesha asked.

Rio grabbed Glintock's arm. "My friend, where do you think you are going?"

Glintock wrenched his arm away, grabbed Rio's wrist, pinned his arm behind his back, and throttled him into the street all in one fluid motion. He hit the release on the wall, shutting the door. As Alesha looked on in disbelief, Glintock marched over to Max.

"I told you—let me handle this," Max said.

"No, you need to stay on script."

"How did you hear me anyway?"

"I took the liberty of wiring up your clothes." His tone was matter-of-fact, as though the answer was completely obvious.

"What? Oh, you son of a bitch!"

"How else am I going to keep you on task when you're out on your own?"

"I was working up to it!"

"By trying to fornicate with your old girlfriend?"

"You're a real romantic, Glintock. I can see why there's only been one woman in your past."

Glintock stopped, jaw clenched as if Max had slapped him. "Don't. You. Dare."

"What the veck is a GAC agent doing in my house, Max?" Alesha asked, marching over to them.

"Kalen escaped from prison," Max explained as he glared at Glintock. "Agent Glintock here thinks that he's coming after everyone and everything I love. That includes you, Roeger, and Robert. I came to warn you, but I want you to come with me too."

She shook her head, her expression incredulous. "Come with you to do what?"

"To put the crew back together. I know I messed up. I'm trying to fix it."

She stayed quiet for several moments. He'd dropped too much on her at once and she clearly had to process it. Then, she closed her eyes, shaking her head. "No."

"What do you mean, 'no?'"

"I mean that I have a life now, Max, and it doesn't include you. You can stay here when you need to, but I'm not going to change my life to accommodate you." She bit her lip. "You can show yourselves out." She headed back to the bedroom, leaving a crushing silence in her wake.

"'Lesha?" he called out to her, but knew she wasn't coming back. His head swam. The elation he'd felt from finally gaining his freedom had evaporated. He felt dead inside. "Is it possible I'm not as charming as I thought?"

"Possible?" Glintock replied. "I'd say it's a definite. We have to go."

He shook his head. "But, she said no."

"You've warned her, she opted out—we're done here. Let's move onto the next one."

"This isn't a shopping list, Agent. This is my life!"

"And she clearly doesn't want to be a part of it. Let me remind you of the conditions of your release—"

"No need—I know my responsibilities. And I'll remind *you* that it's *my* ass hanging out here for Kalen to find. I'm not leaving without Alesha. I need her."

Glintock folded his arms. "What does she even bring to the table?"

"She's my partner. We're a team. *I need her.*"

"Like you needed her on Tonicen?"

"You know what, Glintock? I was actually beginning to like you." Turning his back on the agent, he marched back toward the master bedroom. The door was still off its track. He slid into the room.

Alesha stood by one of the dressers, turned away from the open door.

"I'm guessing you heard all that," he said.

"He's right," she said in a choked voice. She faced him, eyes red. "Why *wasn't* I with you on Tonicen?"

"I didn't want you involved. Any of you, but you especially."

"Why, so you could fuck Sierra?"

His head dropped. "Is that what this is? Jealousy?"

Her eyes narrowed. "*That's* what you think of me? That I was jealous of that…whore? It's like you said to that GAC flunky out there, we were partners, Max. I don't care about who you sleep with, but we were a team, and you chucked me out at a moment's notice."

"They were bad people, 'Lesha. I was trying to protect you."

"Not letting me know where you were? Letting me think you were dead? *That's* protecting me? When we finally found out what had happened, I was relieved that you were in prison, because that meant you were still alive."

"And I bet you were glad I was there, at least at first."

The corners of her mouth ticked up a bit. "At first, yes. But then I wondered if I'd ever see you again and after crying for about half a year, I realized I had to move on with my life. I have."

"You left out what I said to Glintock."

"What's that?"

"That I need you. And God, do I need you. I know you think they're just words, but you kept me going in prison, even though I knew the odds of seeing you again were remote. And now that I'm here, I just want to be with you. Not in that way—well sure, if you want to—but I just want to be around you. I missed you, plain and simple. I went away and learned that I couldn't live without you— didn't *want* to live without you."

She didn't say anything, which might have been more crushing than outright rejection.

Her silence was his answer. "I understand." He had one last card to play, but hated himself for doing it. Glintock was right, though, they were running out of time and Max knew Alesha was better off with him than fending for herself. "I didn't want to tell you like this, but I guess it's better coming from me than you hearing it secondhand."

"What?" The dread was audible in her voice.

He looked her right in the eye. "Carfen's dead."

She gasped, but then gave him a confused look. "No, that's impossible. I talked to her just a few days ago."

"That was before Kalen Vandeir paid her a visit. Glintock showed me the video. I'm sorry, I know she wa—"

"*No!* Why are you saying these things?"

"Because they're true." He crossed over to her, but she turned her back to him. "I wanted to spare you this, but you were going to find out eventually and I preferred it not to be while Kalen was holding a knife to your throat."

"Why would he kill Carfen?" Her voice was barely a whisper.

He closed his eyes. What he said next might push her away forever. "Carfen…Carfen helped me out on the Sierra job. Kalen got it into his head that the two of us wer—"

"*No!*" she cried, pushing him away violently. "You vecking petch! This is your fault!" She hit him about his chest and arms, tears streaming down her face. "*Why?* Why did you involve her?" She turned away from him.

"I was out of options! I was desperate! If I could take it back, I would, but I can't. What's done is done and I'll spend the rest of my life wishing I could have taken her place. I'm sorry I did this to you, but I can guarantee your anger will never outweigh my guilt." He let the silence hang between them to give her a moment to process what he'd told her. "If you're not coming with us, then please get the hell out of here and don't tell anyone where you're going. Once we stop him, I'll let you know and you can go back to your life." He reached out to touch her shoulder, but staid his hand. "I think you're safer with us, though." He moved to exit.

"Stop."

He turned around.

Her expression was neutral; cheeks stained with tears. "Do you really think I'd prefer you dead instead of Carfen?"

"I'm just trying to tell you how sorry I am. I love you, Alesha. The last thing I wanted to do was hurt you."

"Well, you really vecked that up, Max. On all counts." She drew a shuddering breath. "I'll come with you. Just let me grab a few things and get cleaned up." She moved toward the bathroom.

"You're sure?"

She looked over her shoulder. "You said it yourself, you need me. And I need you."

Max didn't let the hope he felt show on his face.

Sure enough, Alesha clarified her meaning. "If Kalen is after you now, I want to be there when he finds you, so I can kill him myself."

CHAPTER 7

Tonicen. The city's name brought warm, fuzzy feelings to Talon Merthane. He wasn't particularly fond of the place—in all honesty, it was a cesspool of corruption—but it *was* the place where he'd put Maxim Ultra in prison.

Talon tried to take the personal element out of it, telling himself that putting Maxim away had just been eliminating the competition from the field. He knew better, though. He'd relished the opportunity to rid himself of Maxim Ultra. The boy had always been a thorn in his side. Next to himself, Maxim had probably been the most talented man hunter in the galaxy. That made sense. James had taught Maxim everything he knew and Talon had taught James. James Thompson—every time he looked at Maxim, he saw his old friend…and enemy.

Unfortunately, Maxim spent too much time helping people and forgetting to get paid. He took on bounty hunting almost as a last resort, which Talon saw as a complete waste of talent. If James hadn't betrayed him, Talon could have taught the boy some of the more questionable tricks of the trade—tricks that might have stopped Maxim from throwing in with people like Sierra Numani and Kalen Vandeir in the first place.

Prison was a fitting end for Maxim, especially in light of what had happened to Talon's son, Gage. He'd wanted to kill Maxim when he found out his only son had died on a job Maxim had put together. Death was a part of the life they'd all chosen, but Talon had warned Gage about James Thompson's son. That family couldn't be trusted. Now, Gage was dead and Talon only had a massive hole in his heart. Yes, prison was a fitting end for Maxim Ultra.

Talon shook his head, scattering the memories. No time for remembrances—he was on a job. His current target, Willsub Wayams, was a real winner. It turned out that Mr. Wayams was heavily connected to the Tonicen crime syndicates. Though he'd been tried for multiple crimes, including murder, Wayams always slithered out of convictions. Tonicen law enforcement had no power or sway over the man—he did exactly as he pleased.

Though a powerful criminal, Wayams was local. Thanks to the toothless nature of the Tonicen cops, the prosecutor decided to go a different way. Enter Talon and his unique set of skills. Other bounty hunters had tried their luck, which explained Wayams' overblown security detail, but Talon was the best.

In fact, the numerous security flunkies actually made his job a little easier. It was difficult to track just Wayams, but a roving gaggle of nattering nannies? That was much simpler. Then it was just a matter of observing the group to figure out who was the most valuable to Wayams. *That* was the person on whom Talon planted his tracer and at that moment, she stood beside Wayams in the Nebula Suite at the top of the Vesnap Hotel.

Wayams' trusted companion was named Diak. Talon didn't have a clue if it was a first or last name, but either way, it wasn't a very pretty name for such a pretty woman. Her features were sharp and angular as she kept watch for her boss. She dressed rather conservatively in black pants and a black dinner jacket. It didn't seem like the right outfit to wear when the job called for possibly getting into a fight, but after several days of observation, Talon knew better. She wouldn't go down easy.

Just *looking* at a member of the opposite sex invariably led to thoughts of Dayna, though she looked nothing like Diak. Dayna was soft, warm, but tough as nails. Talon had known her for the better part of twenty years—professionally at first, but the sparks between them couldn't be denied and a more intimate relationship developed quickly. She was his inside woman at the prison on Aval. Tied into a network of prisons on dozens of worlds, Dayna advised Talon of any prison breaks or recently released cons that would almost certainly be headed for trouble again. She made many of his jobs a lot easier. He hadn't seen her in several weeks and missed her, more than he would ever admit.

Of course, any thoughts of Dayna usually led to Alexis. His protégé had been furious that he'd left her behind. She wasn't ready yet, though she was getting there. His pride and joy—she was his greatest student—better even than Jimmy. Once he unleashed her on the galaxy, he'd probably have to retire—there wouldn't be any targets left for anyone else.

He closed his eyes. *Letting your mind wander like a doddering old man, Merthane.*

Using the zoom feature on his goggles, he not only scouted his target, but also re-focused his mind. Wayams was throwing a party with a guest list featuring the best and brightest of the Tonicen underworld.

Guess I'll have to crash.

From the rooftop across the street, Talon had an unimpeded view and an easy way into the hotel suite. Of course, with Wayams parading around in front of such a large and welcoming window, it had to be reinforced.

Reaching into his belt, he pulled out two small cylinders that looked like frosted glass. Leaning over the ledge, he placed the cylinders against the side of the building, about three feet apart. Once he had them where he wanted, he twisted them. Both units shot out white beams of light, quickly forming a clear, but solid walkway between the two buildings.

The only way to travel—as long as a hover car doesn't smash into it.

Planting his feet on the shimmering catwalk, he began the journey across the dizzying chasm at an easy jog, his eyes darting around for any lurking danger. He groaned as the buzzing of his communication earpiece interrupted his concentration.

He touched his ear. "This is Merthane, go."

There was a long pause before a cultured, but nasal voice sounded. "*Hello? Mr. Merthane? Do I have the correct contact frequency? Hello?*"

"Who is this? I'm standing between two skyscrapers, so make it fast."

"*Ah yes, Mr. Merthane, this is Agent Brynden Brontin with the GAC.*"

Fantastic.

"*Uh, Mr. Merthane?*"

"I'm working, Brontin. What do you want?"

"*Ah yes. That's* Agent *Brontin, sir.*"

"Goodbye, Brontin."

"*Wait, it's about Maxim Ultra!*"

Talon was poised to cancel the call, but Brontin's exclamation stayed his hand. He didn't say anything for several moments, standing between the two buildings like a lost tightrope walker.

"*Mr. Merthane, are you still there?*"

"Did it sound like I hung up?"

"*I figured that would get your attention.*"

He continued his trek across the expanse. "What happened? Did he get his throat cut in prison?"

"*Actually, that's why I'm calling you—he's out.*"

That nearly made him fall from the catwalk. "*What?* Did he escape?"

"*In a manner of speaking. One of our own agents, Matthias Glintock—*"

"Glintock—I know that name."

"*Yes, well he's gone a bit off–script, shall we say. He believes Ultra is the only way to help him apprehend Kalen Vandeir. H—*"

"What, did you idiots let Vandeir out too?"

"*No. He escaped.*"

"You can't hold onto anyone, can you?"

"*Well, I'll point out that they were both held at a local facility on Aval and that the GAC really had nothing to do with their incarceration in the first place.*"

As Brontin prattled on, Talon finished his journey to the Vesnap Hotel. Glancing down at the flexible monitor screen covering his wrist to halfway up his forearm, he could see that his target, or at least the bodyguard, was still in place.

"*But, that's where you come into play, Mr. Merthane.*"

"Hah. I bet." He was half-listening to Brontin.

After a few keystrokes on the computer, the cylinders burned out and the walkway disappeared.

"*I need you to bring both Mr. Ultra and Agent Glintock into custody.*"

"A rogue GAC agent and a wanted fugitive I have personal history with? Sounds intriguing, but why don't you guys at the GAC take care of it?" When no answer was immediately forthcoming from Brontin, Talon put it together. "Oh…I get it now. This little hunt of yours sounds suspiciously like a side project, Brontin. What's the matter—Glintock too big of a star for you? You want some of the spotlight?"

While he let Brontin figure out how to talk his way out of that one, he pulled up the hotel's schematics, overlaying them onto his tracking program. The computer then projected a holographic map of the building, showing him the way to the roof access stairwell.

"*It's nothing as petty as jealousy, Mr. Merthane. Agent Glintock is breaking the law. Ultra wasn't given a pardon. Glintock is harboring a fugitive.*"

"Okay, you're a stickler, so I'll ask again, why not have some of your GAC flunkies handle it?"

"*The GAC isn't very keen on hunting down one of their own unless the evidence is airtight. Agent Glintock has been very good at covering his tracks. I've put in several grievances with my superiors, but to no avail. I fear the glacial movement of bureaucracy will be the death of this organization.*"

That was why Talon worked as a freelancer—the red tape would strangle him. "All right, well what's in it for me?"

He accessed the door he needed, taking the stairwell down to the hotel's top floor.

"*Well, I would have thought that the opportunity to bring Mr. Ultra in would provide all the incentive you needed.*"

"Yes, but I already did that nearly three years ago. It doesn't hold as much appeal the second time around." That was a lie. Talon would have liked nothing more than to snatch Maxim's ill-gotten freedom from him just as he was beginning to enjoy it, but he wasn't about to tell Brontin that.

"*You would be handsomely compensated, of course.*"

"Yes, but how much, Brontin? Clearly this isn't a job that's on the books, so to speak."

The stairwell opened into a long burgundy-colored hallway with gold accents. Plush red carpet covered the floor. It was all very old fashioned for such a modern structure. At the end of the hall stood two well-dressed, but beefy gentlemen that he recognized as part of Wayams' security detail.

He spoke into his communicator. "You know what, Brontin? Hold that thought. I have something to take care of here." Without waiting for an answer from the agent, he marched down the hall toward the two security guards. On the way, he slipped a piece of rimi in his mouth. No matter how illegal an item was, it could always be found in Low City in Apex. As he bit into the small, gnarled, brown rectangle, he felt a rush through his veins.

The two guards started as Talon approached. Apparently, they hadn't seen him walk out of the wall at the end of the hallway. He couldn't tell the two apart and was fairly convinced they were clones.

"How'd you get up here, old man? This floor is restricted," the one on the left asked.

Talon's senses sharpened, everything became much clearer.

The guard on the right stepped up to him, open hand out. "Okay friend, time to go."

He grabbed the security guard's wrist, quickly twisting it behind his back. Then he wrenched it some more until he heard a satisfying snap. As the guard howled in pain, Talon pushed him into his counterpart, who reached for something in his jacket pocket. A canister fell to the floor, but Talon scooped it up, spraying the chemical agent in the guards' eyes while putting his goggles in place to protect his own.

Both security guards crumpled to the floor, screaming and desperately swiping their sleeves across their affected eyes.

Talon swooped in, grabbing the two by their oily hair. He smashed their heads together again and again until unconsciousness embraced them. Dropping the two men on the floor, he took a step back, breathing heavily. His attack left gashes on each of their foreheads, blood streaming down their faces, pooling in their open mouths.

His hands shook as he admired his work. Rimi always did the job, but as he got older, the side effects got worse. In his younger days, he could eat a stick whenever he wanted and barely get the shakes. Now, he'd be lucky if he didn't shit his pants in an hour. It was like a thrill ride—pure adrenaline—but the crashes got worse and worse. When he died of a heart attack one day, everyone would be surprised except him.

He only used the drug when he felt he needed it, which wasn't that often, but Wayams had a lot of security goons. Part of it had to do with the fact that rimi was highly addictive. Talon wasn't interested in becoming a slave to anything, much less a narcotic. Also, the possibility of eventually going insane wasn't high on his list of things to try. In the future, when she was ready, Alexis would be the edge that he needed.

The sole of his boot crashed into the suite doors, busting them open. One at a time, he hurled the unconscious security guards into the suite, the blood from their wounds spattering against the walls. The opulent suite was packed with guests. Those closest to the entrance all turned to watch Talon enter, a supremely confident smile on his face.

Four more security men charged at him.

His smile widened. They didn't waste any time, all attacking him at once. It wasn't an issue as the rimi coursed through his veins. He felt almost telepathic, anticipating their attacks. The *whoosh* of a leg cutting through the air signaled a kick, while their punches appeared to be moving in slow motion. He deflected their blows with ease. Conducting a symphony of snaps, cracks, and screams, he freed the guards of the use of their extremities.

The guests scattered in a chorus of screams and curses once the guards hit the floor. More guards ran in to take their place as the party guests backed away. It looked like the high-end criminals wanted the men lower on the ladder to do their fighting for them. Through the crowd, he saw his target cowering behind Diak. Four more hired guns approached him slowly, all wearing confident sneers.

They actually think they have a shot here. Apparently I'm not as famous as I like to think.

He snatched one up by the belt, tossing him into the bar with a crescendo of breaking glass. The second received a fist to the mouth before Talon threw him into a wall, his back cracking against the sharp corner.

The third and fourth guards kept their distance.

Weak-kneed funtras. He hit a key on his wrist computer, launching a hail of needle-thin darts from his flak jacket. The two guards fell to the floor in a heap as did a few of the guests caught in the spray. Out of the corner of his eye, he saw Wayams trying to make a run for it.

Pulling a long-range bolo from his belt, he keyed it to track his target and let it fly. The bolo homed in on the escaping criminal like an attack animal, wrapping him up in a high-tension cord.

That's when Diak decided to show her skills. She flew in from the side, leading with a kick that caught Talon in the jaw.

He'd feel it later, but the rimi kept him lucid and upright.

She came at him with a flurry of kicks, a few of which connected.

Torva, she's fast! He staggered back, wondering if she'd taken some rimi herself. He caught her foot and pushed her away from him before hurling a dagger in her direction.

She caught the blade in-between her hands and tossed it to the ground before charging right back at Talon. Her speed was considerable, but he was able to deflect the majority of her blows. She attacked with punches, kicks, and swipes at his face with her nails, which had been filed to razor tips.

He recognized the fighting styles she employed, so as she backed him up across the room, he kept a mental count of her moves, waiting for his moment to unravel her attack.

A punch went astray and he caught her wrist. He bent her arm the wrong way, dislocating her elbow. To her credit, she didn't scream. She actually kept the attack up. Her kicks kept him at bay, but when she attempted a punch with her uninjured arm, he dodged and brought his boot down on her exposed knee, busting her leg.

This time, she howled.

She collapsed to the floor, a wailing mess. The harsh language that erupted from her mouth was enough to make Talon blush. However, her screams grated on his nerves like a needle scratching metal. A swift kick to her head stopped that. With Diak unconscious, the suite went quiet. The other security Talon had disabled had all passed out and the guests who were smart enough to stay out of his way had fled. Only Wayams' wracking sobs echoed through the room.

Talon walked over to his target deliberately. The sniveling gangster was curled in a ball, or at least as far as the cord wrapped around him would allow. As Talon approached, he scooped up an errant pistol from one of the security guards. Once he reached Wayams, he turned him over with his boot.

"You've been a very bad boy, Willsub."

"Wh-who are you?"

"I thought that would have been obvious—I'm the guy who's bringing you in. But, if you want to get specific about it, I'm Talon Merthane."

"What are you, some kind of bounty hunter?"

"Son, I'm *the* bounty hunter."

"Then you're in it for the money? I've got lots of that. Name your price and you can just pretend that you never found me. How about it?"

Talon's cold stare remained on Wayams for several moments until the man began to squirm. "Every bounty hunter I've ever met has their own reasons for taking on the trade. Some are washed up law enforcement or military, others are fortune seekers looking to make a big payday and retire, while others are just straight up thrill-seekers looking for their next adrenaline high. I've been at this for many, many years. If you think I do it solely for the money, you're wrong, dead wrong. Come to think of it, I'm fairly certain your order was alive...or dead."

"No, please no!" Wayams' body began to shake.

"The last conviction you wormed out of was a charge of arson. That particular crime led to the deaths of seven children. You're scum and you don't deserve to live. Of course, it doesn't matter to me, though."

"I-it doesn't?"

"No. I get paid either way." Talon fired the pistol straight at Wayams' head, carving a small, clean hole right through his brain with the laser. He lamented the fact that now he had to lug the body to his ship, but he was grimly satisfied with the conclusion.

"Are you still there, Brontin?" he said into his communicator.

"*Y-yes. That was…quite harrowing.*"

It might have been the rimi, but his speech to Wayams had left Talon feeling a little nostalgic. Maxim was now a fugitive. If Talon had meant anything he'd just said, there was only one answer he could give Brontin. "I'll do it."

"*Excellent! I believe they were headed back to Mod—*"

"I know exactly where they're going, pimp. I know that boy even better than he knows himself."

CHAPTER 8

Huddled against a nearby building, Litning stood at the edge of the Apex Spaceport. Hundreds of beings of various alien origins, hurrying to their myriad of destinations, flowed through the massive archway that led into the port. He watched them all through a much different haze than the one that had overcome him at the GAC facility. A pair of humans dressed in security uniforms looked his way a little longer than he liked. Pulling the hood of his tattered cloak a little lower, he pushed himself up off the wall with a groan, stumbling away from the port back down to the bowels of Low City.

Divided into two sections, Apex was a city of dichotomy. In Peak City, the sparkling spires reached for the heavens, while in the underground Low City, Litning's darkest desires could be fulfilled, turning his convictions to dust. Shortly after arriving in Apex, he found that escaping to Revjekt would not be as easy as he had envisioned. Revjekt was too remote a planet for any pilot to make the trip and make it worth their while. He barely had any currency to pay for transportation anyhow and his large frame made him a less than perfect stowaway. Home was farther away than ever. The realization, and his despair that followed, led him to Low City, where he indulged in some past indiscretions with abandon.

Not long after arriving in Apex, Litning began surrendering to his old demons. The events at the GAC facility and his actions specifically had left him shattered. Yes, he had escaped with Memta, but not only had he completely botched the burglary, he had also failed himself. Losing control at the vault was not something he could take back, nor could he redeem himself for what had happened to Twenty-Five. True, it was the human's own greed and obstinacy that had ultimately led to his death, but Litning felt he could have prevented it if he had not panicked in the face of the facility's demise. Somewhere in the back of his mind, a voice awakened by his constant intoxication blamed Twenty-Five for everything that had gone wrong at the facility. Wallowing in misery and blaming others for his actions—it was as if he were reliving the start of his exile all over again.

Guided by the neon allure of Low City, he stumbled into *Fantan's*, the drinking establishment in which he had set up semi-permanent residence. *Fantan's* felt as though it tried to be aggressively *un*modern. It had a lived-in feel to it that other bars did not. Everything was made of wood, not the plastic and metal sheen that Litning would find in Peak City. There was also no neon in sight, which was out of character for a Low City business. There was a naturalistic aura that comforted him. Or he was simply enamored of the warm feeling the alcohol provided.

He pulled up a stool to the corner of the bar top closest to the front door—his usual spot. A slight motion to the bartender resulted in a large mug of Tickto Ale appearing in front of him. He might not have had enough money to book passage to Revjekt, but he certainly had enough scrounged together to feed his demons.

After he had consumed a few rounds, an attractive human female with blonde hair appeared on the holo-screen above the bar—about the only modern accent in the entire establishment. *"The search continues for a dangerous criminal that broke into and destroyed a GAC facility in the Equor province."*

Litning stiffened at the report of the break-in, despite the fact that it had already been blasted all over the planet-wide news services.

"Authorities wouldn't comment on the nature of the facility or why the perpetrator may have targeted it, but they are seeking the large, hulking biped, who should be considered armed and extremely dangerous."

"Large and hulking are the same thing," Litning muttered into his drink before taking a long pull. If the authorities in Apex rounded up every being fitting the vague description, they would be processing suspects until the end of his natural life. Still, he made sure to glance over his shoulder at the other patrons to make sure no one looked his way. The public might not have been aware of his existence, but he was sure the GAC had a more detailed profile. The cameras at the facility would have seen to that. In all honesty, though, he was more afraid of running into Mondo than of the GAC ensnaring him.

His former benefactor had tried to contact him several times before Litning got smart and threw his communicator into the sea. He knew that probably would not deter Mondo, but he had hoped it would buy him some time.

"You're not that big bad man they're talking about on the holo-reports, are you?" a sultry, feminine voice sounded behind him as a hand ruffled the exposed fur on his arm. It was Greva, his new friend.

Greva was an attractive human with bright purple hair and ample curves. The dark circles under her eyes as well as the slightly sagging skin indicated that she was closer to middle age than not. She had locked onto him from the first moment he had stepped into *Fantan's*. After observing her interactions with both men and women in the establishment, he had made it clear to her that he was a pauper—something he thought would have been obvious based on the shabby robes he wore. Still though, she stuck by him whenever he frequented *Fantan's*. He imagined she stayed by him to ward off any potential attackers. Regardless, he enjoyed her attention.

"Of course they are talking about me," he said with a grin. "Where else would I want to spend my riches after destroying such a target than here?"

"Well, I don't know. You still won't show me what you've got in that bag of yours."

He glanced at the red nylon bag that hung from his waist. Memta hid inside and he was not planning on showing her to anyone. "It is an old family heirloom I keep with me for luck."

"Sweetheart, look around at the clientele here tonight. I could definitely use a little luck. Can't I just have a peek?"

"I am afraid not."

She sighed and slumped down beside him. "Did you have any luck at the spaceport?"

He grimaced. "Sadly, no."

"So you're stuck here."

His eyes narrowed as his mood darkened. "For the time being, yes."

"That's fine," she said. "I like having you around."

"You make staying a more pleasurable experience, Greva," he said with a tight smile.

"I'm just sad you're having such a hard time getting home." She sighed again. "I hate to say it, but if the thing in that bag brings you luck, I'd hate to see something that brings you misfortune." Her hand moved to his thigh. "How about I rub it and see if it works any better for me?"

"That would not be a good idea." Litning had seen for himself what the statue did to males, but the legends of what happened to females were far worse. By keeping Memta tucked away, he was doing everyone in the bar a service.

"Oh come on, what could a measly statue do?"

He paused in mid-sip. "I do not recall telling you it was a statue."

"Well, sure you did," Greva said with a slight tremor in her voice.

The ale fogged his mind. *Had* he told her that? Thanks to his perpetual drunkenness, he could not even be sure what day it was— they had all blurred together since his arrival in Apex.

Her hand rested on his stomach and started snaking around his waist.

He jerked away from her, falling off his stool with a loud crash. Every patron in the bar looked in his direction as he rose on wobbly legs. Greva stared at him with a kind of half-smile.

Litning did not give her a chance to say anything. His hand instinctively flew to his waist to ensure his bag was still there and he bolted out the door. Careening out of the bar, he barreled into a group of pedestrians that pushed him out into the street. He blamed his inebriated condition as the reason he tumbled to the filthy concrete.

Scrambling back to his feet, he fled down the road, knocking passersby out of his way as he ran away from *Fantan's*. After several minutes, he brought his stride from a stumbling run to a more controlled walk, keeping one eye over his shoulder. *It had not been my imagination—she tried to take Memta*. He shook his head, trying to clear the spirits from it. Had it been possible that Greva was just being playful? In his state, he was not sure he could completely trust his instincts.

Ducking into a grime-covered alley, he collapsed to his knees. All hope had been lost of becoming the Revash he wished to be. He had wanted to rebuild his life, start anew, but the struggle was great. Low City's allure called to him. After his actions at the facility, the infection in his nepast had festered. All his plans had been washed away in waves of Tickto Ale.

Despair overwhelmed him. His mournful howl became a roar that reverberated up and down the alley. He dropped his head, staring at his hands. The answers he sought could only be found if he looked inward, though. Eventually, exhaustion overtook him and he fell into a slumber in the alley. Not the safest of options, but he was confident his physical gifts would protect him.

He had no idea what hour of the night it was when he felt the bag cradled in his arms shift in his grasp. His eyes shot open in a bleary-eyed stare. A thin man stood over him, attempting to wrest Memta away. Litning felt he had seen him before, perhaps at *Fantan's*, but the fog in his mind left him disoriented and unsure. He slapped at the man's hands weakly as his senses slowly returned to him.

The thief worked more diligently. As the bag came undone, the statue's head peeked out. The thief reached out with his bare hand and brushed the stone as Litning yanked it away.

A brilliant turquoise flash illuminated the alley. Litning fell back against the alley wall as the thief was propelled against the opposite wall.

Litning gaped at the fallen thief for several moments before finally pulling the bag back over the statue and making his way over to the man. The empty streets meant that dawn was a ways off. At that moment, that fact felt like the only thing that had gone right for Litning since the start of the Memta ordeal. With the streets clear, no one could see the dead man.

Litning looked at the artifact with wary eyes. The authorities would certainly believe the statue killed the man once they laid hands on it themselves, but until that time, Litning's impaired state would guarantee incarceration. Memta would be confiscated. It would have all been for nothing.

He thought about how far he had fallen since the facility. *A pitiful excuse.* His heart craved the pleasures and vices he wallowed in. It really *was* the beginning of his exile all over again. He could be better. He *had* to be better. Filled with regret, he prayed to the Revash gods for deliverance. A soft white light washed over him.

On a video billboard above him, a human male with a tanned look and graying hair appeared. His broad smile matched his off-white suit and when he spoke, Litning felt he was speaking directly to him. "Hi friends, Baron Zeth here. I've worked hard to amass my fortune and it has taken me from one end of this galaxy to the other. I want to share that experience with you. There's no better way to sail the stars than on a Zeth Luxury Cruise. Our rates are affordable and my staff makes sure that you'll want for nothing on your voyage. Can't afford one of our stellar packages, but still want to see the galaxy? Want to earn an honest wage while doing so? Then join the crew of my flagship, the *Galactic Dream*!"

Zeth's voice echoed in his mind. Images flashed on the screen, showing the route that the *Dream* took. It did not go to Revjekt, but passed fairly close to it. Close enough to find willing transport.

It would do.

The address to the recruiting office appeared on the screen. He committed it to memory and made his way through the deserted streets with only one thought propelling him. *I am going home. I am going home.*

CHAPTER 9

Apex reminded Max of New York City, only about five times the size. Obviously, the technology was well beyond the tech in New York, but there was something else about it—probably the piss smell that permeated Low City.

Though it was night, Apex was lit up like a beacon. Even in the murk of Low City, neon colors cut through the shadows, creating a kaleidoscopic tunnel effect. Gazing into the gloom, Max repressed a shudder. He liked the energy of big cities. *But, would it kill them to clean it up a little bit? Wait, I* am *thinking of New York.*

Having docked the *Sequel*, the crew stood at the edge of the spaceport, which teemed with different species of aliens, all hustling and bustling to get somewhere they thought was important. To Max, all that was important now was his friends. Yes, if they managed to stop Kalen and recover the statue, all well and good, but the fact that his actions had put his friends in danger ate away at him. He flicked his eyes to Alesha. His body buzzed at just the sight of her.

Her eyes met his and he smiled. She wore a look of indifference.

She's coming around.

He figured she was still coping with the loss of Carfen. While onboard the *Sequel*, she begged Glintock to see the video he'd shown Max. She spent the rest of the trip in her quarters.

Max felt like an asshole, worrying about if Alesha would take him back while she dealt with her grief. He'd help her through it— if she'd let him—just like she'd helped him after his father died. Carfen hadn't been Alesha's mother, but she'd looked out for her like one.

He looked down at his communicator. According to the device, the tracer installed in Roeger put him somewhere in Low City. The only question was, who was coming on the expedition?

"Hey," he said to Glintock. "I think Alesha and I can handle this one on our own."

"You can't be serious," Glintock responded.

"Come on man, I need to talk to her." He gave her a glance. "Privately."

"I'm good at keeping my mouth shut. Besides, the last time I let you do something alone, I had to rush in to keep you on point."

"Yes, and thanks again for that. I'm sure it won't put a wrinkle in my relationship with Alesha whatsoever."

"Unfortunately, I can't trust you to stay on task. We're losing time."

"We are. So, why don't you go book us on Robert's ship and Alesha and I will go get Roeger?"

"I've already got that in motion. Brontin hasn't completely vecked me yet. It's the *Galactic Dream*, right?"

"That sounds right. 'Lesha?"

She sighed. "Yes, *Galactic Dream*. Can we get on with this? I have a life to get back to."

Ouch. That hurt. "Well, Gerry's on the *Sequel*—what about you, Gelf? Wanna tag along?"

Gelf looked like a hobo as he stood apart from the others. His wistful gaze into the crowd around them made it look like he was considering Max's offer. "Love to, Boss, but I've got some people to see now that I'm out. I'll meet you back here after you get the bot."

"Roeger," Alesha said with an edge. "His name is Roeger."

"Right, sister. Whatever."

She glared after Gelf as he turned to walk away.

Glintock chuckled grimly. "That's funny."

Gelf turned back with a sigh. "What's funny, Glintock?"

"It's funny that you think I'm going to let you traipse all over this city alone when I won't let Ultra do the same." Glintock smiled thinly. "Fall in. You're coming with us."

Gelf balked at Max. "Boss?"

Max shrugged. "He's in charge here, buddy."

Alesha snorted as Gelf stomped over to join the group.

Glintock leaned toward Max. "It seems your girlfriend and I agree on a few things."

"I'm not his girlfriend. Where are we going?"

"Low City," Max said gloomily. She'd taken the wind out of his sails.

Glintock grinned at him. "You sure you want to talk to her privately?"

"I think you need to shut the hell up." He trotted over to Alesha, who had already set off toward Low City. Despite its reputation, the majority of beings leaving the spaceport were heading down into the dark to get their kicks. "You'll need this to find Roeger," he said, gesturing to his communicator.

"Low City is Low City. I don't need to be told where to go every step of the way."

"What's the problem?"

"The problem is that I don't trust your new crew," she said, glancing behind them at Glintock and Gelf. "Well, maybe the Glutob's all right, but these other two can rot for all I care."

"Well, Glintock I can underst—"

She rounded on him. "Do you know what that petch said to me on the ship?"

"I told her I could run her in on a dozen warrants without a magistrate even blinking," Glintock answered as he strolled up behind them.

"What happened to being good at keeping your mouth shut?" Max asked, turning back to Alesha. "Is that why you're bent out of shape? I figured it was about Carfen."

"Oh, don't worry, that's still very much on my mind."

He couldn't be sure if that had been directed at him or not. "Look, Glintock likes to talk big—run his mouth."

"That's the truth," Gelf said, folding his arms.

"I'm standing right here," the agent piped up.

"The point is, it's an empty threat."

"No Max, the point is that he works for the vecking GAC and you're letting him run you. He's trying to run me!"

"It's an idle threat." He turned to Glintock. "Tell her it was an idle threat."

"No, I *can* run her in on a dozen different warrants. Her attitude needs an adjustment. I don't expect her to like me, I get that, but I do demand respect."

"I don't owe you anything, Glintock," Alesha said.

"I think you owe me for letting your boyfriend here warn you about a serial killer gunning for you."

"I don't need any help. I've been surviving on my own my whole life." She stalked away from Max and Glintock.

He held his hand out to the agent. "This is why I wanted to be alone with her. Alesha doesn't do well with authority figures. Just…follow along behind us."

Glintock looked ready to protest, but relented. "Fine."

"And stop being a dickhead—you're fucking this up for me." He caught up to Alesha, nearly having to push through the surrounding crowd, but she shrugged off his touch as he tried to comfort her.

"Don't touch me."

"Hey, I'm not the bad guy here."

"Aren't you? You brought these people into my life, disrupting everything. You killed Carfen."

That last remark cut him. "I came here to help you, to save you."

"When have I ever needed saving?"

He stopped walking. "Then why did you even come?" She wasn't stopping. "Turn around and talk to me, damn it!" He grabbed her arm, which she wrenched away violently.

Her eyes were wide, jaw set. He'd seen that look before—she was ready for a fight. Even her fists rose into a defensive position. Some nearby aliens looked in their direction, probably not seeking to help.

He raised his hands in surrender. "I just want to talk. Help me understand what's wrong."

She hesitated—so long he thought she might really hit him. Finally, she lowered her hands. "I'm angry, Max. About everything. Kalen killing Carfen. This Glintock guy. *You*, for screwing up my life. But at the same time, I *am* glad to see you. I've got a lot of weird feelings churning up inside."

He stepped closer to her. "I feel the same way."

Alesha held up her hand, stopping him in his tracks. "No. No, you don't."

"What do you mean?"

Her eyes softened like she didn't want to hurt him, but knew she was about to anyway. "You think that us going on this little adventure together is going to put things back the way they were and that's not going to happen. You don't...fit in my life anymore. I care for you and I don't want to be the one to hurt you, especially after what you've been through. Then I remember what you put *me* through and I think, maybe I *do* want to hurt you, just a little bit. But then I catch you looking at me a certain way and it destroys me all over again."

Her revelation hung between them. For once, he didn't have a ready quip.

She sighed. "I'm here to catch Kalen, because I quite like living and I owe him for Carfen. I'm not here to rekindle anything with you and I'm certainly not here because of some vague threats from Agent Asshole over there."

"I heard that," Glintock called over to them.

"I've got a good thing going right now, Max, and I don't need you or anyone else vecking that up for me."

"Romantic sentiment." He wasn't sure how he felt about this *new and improved* Alesha.

"Back at the house, I did appreciate you saying you needed me. That was sweet."

"But…"

"But, you ran off with Sierra and got yourself thrown in prison. What was I supposed to do—hang around and wait for you? I did what I've always done—moved on and survived. My crew is good and we're doing well."

Max winced. That was clearly code for: *Better than I was doing with you.*

"Once this is done, I'm going back to what I was doing. I hope you weren't expecting more than that."

That was the thing about Alesha—she was always direct. "Apparently, it doesn't matter if I was." He paused, unable to look at her for what he had to say next. "I *did* think about you every day in prison."

"I can imagine—not a lot of women to look at in there, I'd guess. Did you think of that horvorka too?"

"I thought about you both. I—"

"*What?* That's not really scoring points with me, Max."

"You didn't let me finish. I thought about you in different ways. Sierra was murdered right in front of me. That kind of thing tends to stick with people. But you…all I thought about—*dreamed* about—was getting out of there and coming home to you. Prison forced me to think about how I couldn't lose you, but it looks like I already have."

A half-smile twitched across her lips, but that was about it.

Better than her slugging me in the face, I guess.

"I'm sorry about Carfen. I'll never forgive myself for getting her involved."

She winced. "I…I didn't mean it when I said you killed her."

"Yes you did."

She squinted and clenched her teeth. "Yeah, yeah, I did—at first. That's my grief talking. I know you never wanted that to happen. We've all chosen dangerous lives and Carfen had a lot of enemies." She drew a quivering breath. "She knew the risks."

"I'll never stop trying to make it up to you."

"And then you say things like that and I can't help but love you for it."

He wanted to take her in his arms, but stood his ground, not sure if she was ready for that. They turned to face Glintock and Gelf as they walked over. Alesha wore an annoyed expression.

"Sorry to interrupt," Glintock said, "but it doesn't look like she's going to murder you anymore, so we should probably get a move on."

Max looked to Alesha. "Are we square?"

"Square?"

"It means, are we good?"

Her lip twisted. "We're getting there." She shot Glintock a glare. "I don't like you."

"So I gathered from my excellent hearing."

She then glared at Gelf. "And I don't trust you."

"Fabulous," Gelf said. "I'm so thrilled that I was forced to come on this errand and forfeit the things I had to get done. Are we doing this or not?"

The four of them continued into Low City. Peak City was the postcard that the Apex Tourist Bureau sent out to the galaxy, while Low City was the grimy underbelly where all the behind the scenes deals got done. Without Low City, there would be no Peak City and without the GAC there wouldn't be an Apex at all. For centuries, a hotly-contested city by the three nations surrounding it, Apex was the logical capital choice when it came time to establish Modan's world-government for GAC membership. Solely governed by GAC laws, the sprawling, bi-level city had become a symbol of cooperation between the three rival nations that shared it.

Low City's streets had a thin layer of muck, which Max was convinced was only there so big guys could rub little guys' faces in it. It wouldn't have taken much to clean it. The *civic leaders* wanted it that way. It enhanced the seedy, depraved image the area put out. There was a lot of scum in Low City, but some of it was exaggerated. Sure, city corruption was normal in a metropolis as big as Apex, but if Low City was as bad as advertised, no way would the residents of Peak City leave their gleaming towers to set foot in the area.

Max started. A beautiful woman passed by, flashing him a lusty look. Looking at her head on, she didn't look like Sierra, but when he'd seen her out of the corner of his eye, he was convinced it had been her. He shook his head. Was he constantly going to see her around every corner? Was it guilt or had the rimi finally cracked his mind open? He tried to shake the fear from his mind and pressed on.

After about fifteen minutes, the group finally arrived at their destination—according to the blinking dot on Max's communicator. He looked up at the signage outside the building.

"Of course. Perfect."

Glintock read the sign. *"Hermes' Laugh Palace?"*

"It's a comedy club," Max explained.

"I gathered that, but why is it perfect?"

"You'll see. Come on."

The bouncer tried to charge them a cover, until Glintock started waving around his credentials. The place was like most of the rest of Low City—dark and dank. There was a decent crowd sitting in front of a tiny stage. A tattered, sickly yellow curtain hid any backstage shenanigans. Max didn't see Roeger anywhere.

A very human-looking android served as hostess and seated them at a small table toward the back of the club. Max admired the pretty bot's considerable curves, but the plastic sheen of her synthetic skin as well as the seams running up the backs of her legs were dead giveaways. With her design, she was more than likely a pleasure bot, or had been one in the past. Androids were just as likely to be rescued from the sex trade as any flesh and blood beings.

"May I provide you with any refreshment?" she asked them in a sweet voice. No hint of digitization—she was a pretty high-end model.

"Tickto Ale, darlin'," Gelf said as he practically drooled over the bot.

"Neja Spirits for me," Alesha said.

"Nothing for me, thank you," was Glintock's response.

"Just water, thanks," Max said.

"Very well. If you need anything, my name is Lana." The bot sauntered off to fill their order.

Alesha touched Max's hand. "My precious Earth Boy and his crippling water habit." The nickname tugged at his heart.

"What does that mean?" Glintock asked.

"He doesn't drink. Well, *rarely*."

"Really? That kind of destroys the hard-living spacefarer image."

Max shrugged. "I never understood the drinking mentality. I like to be in control."

Glintock arched his eyebrow, glancing at Gelf. "Really? That doesn't…mesh with what I've come to know."

Max glanced at Alesha, who appeared confused. "Look, I—"

"Here are your drinks," Lana interrupted. "One Neja Spirits, one Tickto Ale, one water, and one…nothing." She paused, blinking once at Glintock. "Is there anything else I can get you?"

"No thanks, Lana," Max said, sending her on her way.

"I gotta say, that bot would make me go synthetic in a heartbeat," Gelf said as his gaze lingered on the departing Lana. He took a pull from his ale.

Alesha turned up her nose at Gelf before taking a sip of her drink. "It's all right, Agent, if Max's water unnerves you that much, you can watch me drink this delicious concoction that will surely get me drunk by the end of the night." The purple drink looked like cough syrup.

Alesha had clearly decided to ignore Glintock's allusion to Max's drug use. As she and the agent discussed the pros and cons of Neja Spirits, Max fidgeted under the table with a sliver of rimi. He thought back to his possible hallucinations of Sierra and wondered if he shouldn't take a break from the drug. However, he felt himself getting shaky and knew he needed to be at the top of his game. He slipped the small piece into his mouth.

Once they'd gotten off of Aval, it hadn't taken Gelf long to score some more rimi from a supplier. He figured that was where the little guy had been headed before Glintock corralled him into the Roeger expedition. Glintock had his suspicions, but Max trusted Gelf. More than that, he trusted the gnarled brown tab to make him feel infinitely better. He just couldn't let Alesha see him taking it. If she knew he was taking it…that was a fight he didn't want to have.

"Hello? Excuse me?"

Max smiled, turning toward the kind, digitized voice coming from the stage. It was Roeger. The sight of his box-shaped head and gangly limbs filled Max with relief. He was safe. Sure, Max had the tracer, but with Kalen on the loose, the device could have been leading them to pieces of Roeger. A small lump formed in Max's throat at the sight of Roeger's wide, blank, sad-looking eyes. He'd missed the old bot.

Max had been twelve years old when he'd stumbled onto Roeger at his parents' home. A noise had woken him in the middle of the night, a noise caused by Roeger. Seeing only the bot's glowing yellow eyes in the darkness had been more than a little unsettling, but when Max made that discovery, his father's secret life and what he *really* did for a living came to light.

"Welcome to a night of mirth and laughter," Roeger said to zero reaction at all from the audience. Someone coughed. "Um, yes. I am your host for the evening, Rocking Roeger."

No response.

"That's your bot, Boss?" Gelf mumbled. "No offense, but he doesn't look like much."

Alesha shot him a dirty look.

Roeger's head moved slightly from left to right, as if he had a nervous tic. "Has anyone seen the traffic in Peak City? It gives new meaning to the word downtrodden here in Low City."

Again, no response and again, Roeger's head made its nervous movement. Every word out of his vocalizer was delivered in the same gentle, digitized voice. If he'd had a collar, Max was sure he'd be pulling on it. "Let me tell you about my girlfriend. She is an older model pleasure bot and always looking to be serviced."

While nary a chuckle escaped from any of the other audience members, Max let out a loud laugh that echoed through the small club.

Roeger's head turned in his direction. "Maxim?" The metal flaps above his eyes moved up and down like eyebrows before he cleaned his photoreceptors with a blink. All of those doo-dads were designed to give Roeger's line of bots expressive faces to go with their emotion and personality programming. The plate covering the bottom half of his face, though, made it look like he was perpetually frowning. He was a much older series, though, so he looked more like a robot than a model like Lana.

Roeger seemed to stand a little straighter as he delivered his next quip. "My last boss' girlfriend was so beautiful, when I looked at her, I felt like I had lights in my eyes."

Again, Max laughed. He looked over at Alesha, who smiled warmly. Glintock looked confused. Gelf appeared bored.

"Shut down, bot! Bring on the talent!" a burly Thorjin shouted.

"Ah, um…." Poor Roeger looked completely flustered—at least as flustered as he *could* look. He attempted to soldier on. "Has anyone here been out to the rings of Vestrun? Let me tell y—"

"Aooooooooow," the Thorjin bellowed. "Aooooooooow."

"Uh, yes."

"Now see," Gelf whispered, "that's not nice. Bot's trying his best."

Alesha tapped Max's arm. "We should do something."

"Don't look at me—I'm a wanted fugitive." He looked at the emerald-skinned Thorjin, who appeared happy with himself. "And that guy is *big*."

Her eyes narrowed. Pushing herself away from the table, she wove her way through the other tightly-grouped tables toward the heckler.

Glintock leaned close. "Am I going to have to haul her in?"

"Yeah, good luck with that."

Alesha sidled up to the Thorjin, who was still howling at Roeger. Without warning, she hit him with a chop to his throat that instantly doubled him over. She then kicked his chair out from under him, cracking his head on the floor, knocking him out cold. As she returned to their table, her self-satisfied smirk bloomed into a full smile once the audience broke into applause.

Max smiled at her broadly. *God, I love this woman.*

Up on stage, Roeger blinked twice. "Thank you. Here is our first performer…."

Once the show had ended and the unconscious Thorjin had been removed from the premises, Roeger approached the table. Max rose to greet him, pulling the bot into a warm embrace, which Roeger returned tentatively.

"It is good to see you, Maxim. I am happy that you have been released from prison."

"It's good to see you too, buddy. Good job up there tonight." Roeger was an awful comedian, but no sense in making him feel bad.

"You are too kind. The audience did not laugh."

"*I* laughed."

"It is not the same, Maxim, and you know it. And Alesha, I am surprised to see you here, considering all the expletives you screamed when Maxim left."

She smiled sheepishly, but didn't miss a beat. "I had some more for him when he turned up at my door, but he made a compelling argument as to why I should come along."

"How is your new endeavor going?"

"It's going great, Roeger, thank you." She smiled like a kid on Christmas morning. "I'm so excited for you! Your big break."

"Thank you. It took quite some doing, but I finally landed this slot after Lana put in a good word for me with Mr. Thomkin. She has been a great help to me."

Max and Alesha exchanged raised eyebrows.

"How's it goin', bot? I'm Gelf, Max's prison buddy."

"Delighted." Max could tell from his tone that Roeger was anything but. Roeger turned his attention to Glintock. "And who is this?"

"GAC Agent Matthias Glintock. Pleased to make your acquaintance."

Roeger jerked his head toward Max. "The authorities, Maxim?"

He shrugged. "Price of doing business, Roeger. Sit down, we need to talk."

Roeger tilted his head slightly before taking a seat. "What would you like to discuss? This feels like more than simple catching up."

"You're right about that, buddy. Kalen's on the loose and Agent Glintock here thinks that he's going to be gunning for all of us."

Roeger blinked. "But why would he come after me? I had nothing to do with him after your defection."

Roeger's nonchalant delivery stung a little. "That's true, but Kalen isn't exactly the most tightly-wound individual. He may *think* you know something and try to beat it out of you."

"You of all people should know, Maxim, that I cannot feel pain. Well, physical pain at least."

Another subtle dig. He must have taken passive-aggressive lessons from Alesha. "Well, that's true too, but he could pluck your brain out of your head and see what makes you tick."

"Hm. An excellent point. However, the odds of Kalen even findi—"

"He's completely capable, Roeger," Glintock said. "Trust me." Max was grateful to him for stepping in—Alesha looked quite uncomfortable with all the Kalen talk.

Roeger looked at the agent for a moment. "Well, thank you for the warning." He moved to get up from the table.

"Wait, Roeger, wait," Max said. "That's not all I came to say. Sit down, please."

He paused for a moment before finally sitting back down. "Yes, Maxim?"

"What's your hurry? I mean, I haven't seen you in two and a half years."

"Three years, four months, and twenty-one days to be more exact, but that is not my doing, Maxim. *You* left *us*."

Even Alesha winced at that, but Max put on a brave face. "You're right and I'm sorry about that, but I left to protect you guys."

"And yet, here you are, warning me of danger from the same parties you tried to protect us from before."

Hoo boy. This is not going well. Everything Roeger said was true, but what frustrated Max the most was his matter-of-fact tone. Sometimes it was tough arguing with a robot.

"That's a good point, Roeger. That's why I'm helping Agent Glintock out and trying to track Kalen down before he can hurt anyone. That's why I'm putting the crew back together—so we can protect each other."

"You do not need to speak to me as though I am a basic program, Maxim."

He gritted his teeth. "What does that mean?"

"I mean, you are talking to me as you would a child. Softening your tone will not change my mind. I will not be joining you. I may not be successful at what I am doing right now, but I am enjoying myself. I will always be grateful to your father for what he did for me, but now I am pursuing what I want. And, as I have already mentioned, it was *you* who walked out on *us*."

"Jesus fuck," Max groaned. "Look, Roeger, I made a lot of mistakes. I know that and I'm sorry. I should have never taken the job with Sierra, but everything I did after that was to shield you guys. You've got to believe that. We've known each other since I was twelve. You've always claimed that you woke me up by accident that night, but I think you did it on purpose because you were lonely and needed a friend. Dad kept you around, but you were always more my friend than a member of his crew. We're family, Roeger. Hell, we're practically like brothers. It wouldn't be the same without you and I need you, buddy."

Roeger gave no indication of what was going on in his CPU. After a few moments of appearing to stare blankly at Max, he turned his head to Alesha. "Do you believe him?"

Max gave her his most convincing smile.

She rolled her eyes. "He seems sincere, yes. He really is sorry—or so he says." She took a deep breath. "I believe him. He is right though, it *wouldn't* be the same without you, Roeger."

Again, Roeger paused, looking at Max.

Glintock jumped in. "Keep in mind, Roeger, you'll be much safer with us than on your own."

"That is most certainly true, Agent Glintock. However, unlike you three, I can be repaired following any catastrophic damage. That fact, combined with my overall level of happiness, far outweighs the need to sail around the galaxy and possibly get disassembled anyway."

Max's heart sank.

Then, Roeger's left eyebrow raised. "Unless…."

A glimmer of hope, but Max suspected a trap. "Unless?"

"Unless you allow me two weeks per a standard Earth month in order to pursue my comedy."

"Two weeks a month? Did someone torch your wiri—?" Alesha kicked him under the table. "*One* week."

Roeger put on his patient death gaze again before finally speaking. "Very well, I agree to your terms because they were the true terms I was seeking to establish in the first place, so thank you."

"You sneaky…"

"I will not come back to the crew as a slave, Maxim."

"When have I *ever* called you a slave?"

After a moment's pause, Max's own voice emanated from Roeger's vocalizer. "*You are my slave…bitch!*" He then switched back to his normal voice. "I rest my case."

Gelf busted out laughing.

Max's face went hot. "I was joking! That was a joke. Why do you still have that? It's from, like, over ten years ago!"

"Regardless, I will not be treated like a servant on the ship. Are we clear?"

Max paused for effect. "*Yes.*"

"Excellent. Then, I am happy to be back on the team." He rose from the table, heading over to a grizzled man in a sharp suit.

Gelf continued laughing. "Hoo boy, Boss, that bot took you for a ride."

Max turned to Alesha, consternation all over his face.

"He did, but I'm proud of you." She reached for his hand, but stopped herself. "Roeger needed to hear those things."

Maybe she is coming around.

Glintock had a wide smile on his face.

"What are you so happy about?" Max asked.

"This went much better than the last one."

Alesha's face said, *How nice for you.* "Don't expect smooth sailing on the *Galactic Dream*," she said, chuckling at her pun. "No way Robbie abandons that gig."

"Let me worry about that," Max said, wondering how he'd extricate his pilot and friend from his stable, well-paying job. As they moved to the exit, he overheard Roeger's nervous conversation with the man in the suit.

"Mr. Thomkin, I am, um, afraid that I must—ahem—end my full-time employment here at *Hermes' Laugh Palace*. I would like to come back on a more part-time basis, but unfortunately, my friends need my assistance with a rather urgent matter. It embarrasses me to no end that I am leaving you without suitable notice, but this really is an emergency, so I must apologize for that."

Thomkin stared at Roeger, blank faced, until finally responding. "Yeah, okay fine. I'll just get Lana to do it...or whatever. Thanks."

"Very good. Thank you for the opportunity." He walked away from Thomkin over to Max.

"Are you okay, buddy?"

"I am fine, Maxim. That was an astonishingly good exit interview."

As Roeger headed toward the exit, Max marveled at his resiliency.

I love that bot.

Trouble appeared around the corner as Lana marched up to the departing Roeger.

"Is it true you are leaving?" she asked with an edge of hurt in her voice.

"Lana, ah, I was just looking for you. Yes, I am afraid so. I will back though...someday."

"This hurts me more than you know, Roeger."

Gelf leaned into Max. "She's really his girlfriend? She's a sex bot."

He shrugged. "Well, he can't bang her—might as well let somebody do it."

"Charming, Max," Alesha said. "Really romantic."

"*What?*"

"Maxim?" Roeger stood right in his face. "Can you all wait for me outside? Lana and I need some privacy."

"Sure, Roeger. Sure."

Twenty minutes later, they were still waiting for him on the dodgy Low City streets. Even though it was late, the walkways were packed. Finally, Roeger emerged from the comedy club. He looked a little wobbly on his feet. If Max hadn't known better, he'd have said Roeger looked drunk.

He stumbled out to the group, reaching out for Max's arm to steady himself. "All right. I am ready to go now."

"You sure about that?" Max asked. "You don't look so good."

"On the contrary, Maxim, I have never felt better. Lana just...erm...overloaded my pleasure center...a bit."

"All right, Roeger!" Gelf blurted.

"How? You don't ha   "

"*Max*," Alesha interrupted. "Does it really matter? Was she all right with you leaving, Roeger?"

"It is safe to say that she is now, Alesha."

"Lucky petch," Gelf muttered, shaking his head.

"Forget what I said earlier. This has definitely been a stranger trip than Marina," Glintock said.

"Before we head back to the *Sequel*, Roeger, I have to ask—do you still have Christi with you?" Max asked. The ship could run without Christi, but it ran far more efficiently *with* her.

"Of course she is, Maxim. She has always been here with me," Roeger said. His reverent tone made it clear who was number one in his cybernetic heart. Standing up straight, he unlocked his chest plate. As the plate opened, it revealed another metal casing that contained Roeger's inner workings. Above that casing was an open space where a small, translucent blue disc, barely the size of a poker chip, hung suspended in two crisscrossing beams of white light.

Roeger's chest closed up and he turned his palm upward. A hologram projected out of his hand of a six-inch Christi, who looked more like a *Playboy* model than a regular woman. Max always played off her looks to the others, but he knew the truth. His computer had been hooked into the ship's mainframe one night and after a snooping session, Christi picked a look from his hard drive she thought he'd like. He never thought he'd hear the end of it from Alesha.

Gelf looked gobsmacked. "Boss, you've been holdin' out on me."

Christi glanced around as if she'd just woken up. Her eyes settled on Max and she started. "Maxim! I am delighted to see you again!" she said in her flirty voice.

Max smiled. Alesha heaved a sigh. "Hi Christi!" he said. "Has Roeger been taking care of you?"

"Oh yes, Maxim. He's been my knight in shining armor since you've been gone. How are you back?" She balked at Glintock for a moment. "Why is a GAC agent with you?"

"We'll discuss all that once we get you back onto the *Sequel*."

"As you wish, Maxim. I look forward to it." With that, she disappeared from sight.

"Thanks Roeger, good work."

"Of course, Maxim. Shall we go?"

As he nodded, he caught Alesha glaring at Roeger's now empty hand.

"Hussy."

CHAPTER 10

It was getting late as Max and his crew headed back toward the spaceport. Just thinking that word *crew* made him smile. Glintock he could still do without, but he had Alesha and Roeger back and they were all on their way to secure Robert. Even if it wasn't perfect he foresaw more growing pains trying to integrate Gelf— he felt better than he had prior to arriving on Modan. He was free and back with his friends. Sure it was under threat of murder from Kalen, but again, it wasn't perfect.

"Once we get back to your ship, we'll take it up and dock with the *Galactic Dream*," Glintock said, laying out the plan going forward. "I'm working on securing us passage."

"You don't foresee any problems?" Max asked as they turned a corner.

"What do you mean?"

"Glintock, we shot our way off of Aval. Somebody's got to be keeping an eye on you. What about that guy who called you? Brontin?"

"I can handle Brontin," Glintock replied sharply. "And you don't know everything you think you do, Ultra. I have other ways to get around Brontin if he tries to shut me down." As if on cue, Glintock's communicator beeped incessantly. He arched his eyebrow at Max and then looked at the device's screen. His eyes widened.

Max started feeling sick. "That's *not* Brontin. Is it?"

Glintock only shook his head. "Another murder matching Kalen's hallmarks. It's in Peak City."

Alesha tried to grab at Glintock's communicator. "Where in Peak City?"

"What are you doing?" Max asked.

"He's here!" Alesha cried. "We can end him now!"

"What about Robbie?"

"If we stop Kalen, we don't have to worry about Robbie!"

"Where should we start looking? Traipse all over Apex? Meanwhile, Kalen goes on board that ship and slits our friend's throat? No, we stick to the plan."

"What if he kills again?" Alesha countered. "It's okay as long as it's someone we don't know?"

"We know Kalen's coming for us. That way, we can direct him."

"Right, because you did such a great job controlling him before."

Max gripped her shoulders. "Look, I know you want revenge for Carfen, but this is the best way. You'll have your chance." He didn't like indulging her need for vengeance, but couldn't see any other way out of the argument.

"Yeah, sister," Gelf said. "Don't be in such a hurry to die."

She closed her eyes and sighed. "I just want this over."

Max nodded, distracted. His head jerked to the side, a sinking feeling settling in on him. Something felt off. Peering around, he tried to place the source of his discomfort.

Alesha's eyes narrowed when he caught her gaze. She too looked around.

The street they were on was as brightly-lit as any other in Low City and equally filthy. It was different in one way—it was deserted, and *no* street in Apex was *ever* deserted.

"We have to get off this street," Max said, his eyes darting around for an escape route.

"What? The spaceport is just a few more blocks," Glintock said, pointing for emphasis.

"Take a look arou—" Max stopped as his eyes locked in at the end of the street.

A lone man stood roughly fifty yards ahead of them, a man that Max recognized just from his stance.

"Merthane."

"I hope you've had your fun, Maxim," Merthane's electronically-amplified voice echoed up the street. "Because you're coming back with me to Aval."

Max said nothing, letting Merthane's words flow around him. His blood went hot. Here was the man who'd put him in prison, ready to haul him right back. What punishment was suitable for Merthane? Choking? Eye-gouging? A crippling blow to the spine? Max's mind swirled with choices.

The street was empty, which could only have meant Merthane wanted it that way. No need to rush into what was certainly a trap. Despite his rapid pulse and trembling hands, Max waited. If Merthane wanted him badly enough, he could come and get him.

Unfortunately, Glintock wasn't as patient. Whipping out his credentials, he started toward Merthane.

"Glintock, no," Max said.

"I don't have time for this nakra," Glintock called back over his shoulder as he kept walking. "Mr. Merthane, as an agent of the

Galactic Authority Commission, I'm going to have to ask you to cease and desist. Mr. Ultra is in my custody." He'd cut the gap between him and Merthane in half.

"You're Glintock, right?" Merthane asked with that perpetual half-smile he always wore.

"I am, and you are obstr—"

"Good. I'm here for you too." Merthane hit a trigger on his belt and four pitons attached to high-tensile cords launched from both sides of the street. The cords wrapped Glintock up, pinning his limbs to his body. Merthane's hidden launchers ratcheted up the cords, suspending Glintock in the air. He cried out as the launchers tightened once more.

Max didn't have time to worry about his chaperone. He pulled his pistol from his holster and snapped off two laser bolts at Merthane, who deflected them easily with a body-sized energy shield that sprang from his wrist.

As Max fired, Alesha scrambled to the left to try and flank the hunter. Her laser fire was no more effective than Max's. The good news was, both their attacks prevented Merthane from going on the offensive himself.

"Roeger!" Max called to his friend. "You and Gelf head for the spaceport. Alesha and I will keep Merthane occupied."

"But Maxim, should I not—"

"No time to debate, Roeger! *Go!*"

With a nearly imperceptible shrug, Roeger set off toward the spaceport with tentative steps. He hadn't gotten fifteen feet before he was swept off his feet by a magnetic snare. His body flipped into the air, latching itself to one of the buildings lining the street.

"Uh, Maxim...."

"Hang tight, pal!" He winced at the unintentional pun.

Gelf looked up at Roeger and Glintock, spared Max a glance, and then took off back the way they'd come, turning down a side street.

Thanks, buddy. Max's stomach twisted. Had Glintock been right about Gelf? He didn't want to think that, but running out on a friend was a pretty shitty thing to do. *I'll deal with it later.* Focusing on the problem at hand, Max pressed forward, keeping his laser fire steady, not allowing Merthane to move. As he passed Glintock, he heard a click under his foot.

Fuck.

An explosion of pink light illuminated the area. Max tripped down the street, head spinning. When he could see at all, his vision was blurred. He heard an explosion to his left and hit the ground, covering his head. Keeping his eyes shut for a moment, he hoped his vision would clear. No dice. Everything was doubled. Shaking his head to loosen the cobwebs and quiet the ringing in his ears, Max could just make out Alesha lying face-down in the street. It didn't look like she was moving.

"No!" he cried as he reached out to her. His muffled shout sounded like he was underwater.

Pushing himself up, he staggered to his feet. Through the blur, Merthane charged at Max, leading with his knee. The strike doubled Max over. Merthane hit him with two punches to his midsection and a shot to his head that dropped him back to the ground.

"Stay down, son. I have other jobs to tend to."

Max's head swam. His brain felt like it was short-circuiting as his limbs wouldn't respond to his commands. Maybe his body agreed with Merthane. As his vision cleared, he had trouble keeping his eyes off the motionless Alesha. Shuddering, he considered the fact that Merthane may have taken yet another person away from him. The fear coursing through him quickly twisted into rage.

"I'm sure the other prisoners will be more than happy to see you back on Aval," Merthane said as he tried to handcuff him.

Max kicked out, hard.

The strike knocked Merthane back and the handcuffs skittered across the concrete. "Hah! All right, let's make this a fight, then."

Max struggled to his feet, looking over at Alesha. Knowing Merthane would make him pay for any attempt to check on her, he kept his focus where it needed to be.

"You've got to be careful who you trust in this life Maxim," Merthane said.

"I guess I'm like my father in that regard." His jaw was on fire as he pushed the words out, but he took satisfaction in Merthane's eye twitch telling him his verbal jab had hit home.

"Your GAC buddy has some powerful enemies."

He has to mean Brontin. Who else? He glanced at Alesha. *She's still not moving.*

"Let's finish this quick," Merthane said with his own look at Alesha. "I want to see what she looks like under those tight clothes of hers."

Max lunged with a haymaker.

Merthane easily knocked his fists away. "Come on, boy! Show me what you learned in prison."

Max feinted left, but came back with a right hook. Merthane blocked the punch and then hooked Max's arm, wrenching it behind his back before shoving him to the ground.

Max skidded across the asphalt, scraping his knees and palms. Grimacing, he moved to get back up, but Merthane picked him up by his jacket, dragging him to his feet. Max tried to turn and swing at him, but Merthane held him fast. He pulled Max backwards until his hot breath was in his ear.

"I've missed kicking your ass," Merthane said.

Turning him away from Alesha, Merthane threw him back to the ground. Before Max could completely register the waves of pain shooting through his body, Merthane delivered a savage kick to his chest and one to his stomach for good measure. Max rolled over weakly, gasping for breath. Exposing his back to Merthane was a mistake. The hunter kicked him square in the spine. Max jerked away from the source of his pain and rolled away. Each rotation felt like rolling over broken glass.

"Honestly, I was expecting a better fight than this, considering where you've been for the last few years," Merthane said, pressing his boot into Max's back.

Max yelped in pain. The small bit of rimi he'd taken helped, but apparently didn't cover severe beatings. He'd need more to really be effective. He didn't think Merthane would give him a moment to take the drug. He looked back over his shoulder, eyes widening.

Merthane took a shock bar from his belt and fit it onto his gloved hand. It was like a Taser and brass knuckles in one strip.

Max could only groan and writhe on the ground, unable to escape as Merthane buried the shock bar in his back. He howled, his body convulsing uncontrollably as the electricity coursed through him. Shitting his pants was a definite possibility.

The pain stopped ever so briefly as Merthane pulled the torture device away. Max's relief was fleeting, though, as Merthane again plunged the shock bar into his back.

Max tried to reach out and grab Merthane, but his limbs were unresponsive. He hoped the tears streaming down his face weren't his eyes leaking out of his head.

Merthane pulled the bar away again. All Max could hear was his own panting.

"Oh, just look at her," Merthane said. "I just can't stop killing your girlfriends, Maxim."

God, no. A spike of terror went through his hammering heart. His eyes shot to Alesha. Images of Sierra's cold, dead eyes flashed through his mind, only to have Alesha take her place. Several breathless moments passed before she finally stirred, but she still didn't get up.

"Well, I guess we can't always get what we want," Merthane said. "No matter. I'm sure I've got some open contracts with her name on them. *Somebody* probably wants her dead."

Max's jaw set. *I'm done with this asshole.* Adrenaline flooded his body in a cool rush and he swung his left fist up in a wide arc, cuffing Merthane in the head. As his opponent reeled back, Max got up off the asphalt. It felt like a thousand needles in his torso, but he pushed the pain from his mind.

They circled each other. Max limped around, making his injuries look worse than they were. He definitely hurt like hell, but nowhere near as bad as what Elkeith had put him through while on Aval.

Merthane threw a couple of jabs at him. They were designed to keep him off balance, but they'd done this dance before. Merthane led with his left before his right sped toward Max's head.

Max caught his fist and delivered a shot to his opponent's face, knocking him back a few steps.

The punch bloodied the older man's nose, but he just smiled, spitting on the ground. "So, you did learn a thing or two on Aval!"

Max kept his mouth shut. Engaging in pointless, tough-guy banter was not in the cards. Instead, his eyes perused Merthane's gray fatigues, but more specifically, his utility belt and bandolier. He half-smiled when he found what he wanted.

Apparently, Merthane didn't like the look on Max's face, because he took a wild swing that left him open to a gut punch. When Merthane doubled over, Max brought both his fists down on his back, knocking him to the ground. Max kicked him in the head before delivering another kick to his midsection. He felt himself losing control.

He attempted another kick, but Merthane recovered enough to catch his foot, flipping Max onto the ground. The fall stunned him, leaving him barely able to move. As he attempted to roll over, Merthane was already taking the opportunity to get back to his feet.

"You know what I can't recall?" Merthane asked. "When did you stop calling me *Uncle Talon*?"

"I never…called you that," Max panted, trying to find his third or fourth wind.

"You were probably too young to remember. Your father and I were thick as thieves once. You probably don't remember that either."

Max managed to get to his knees. "What is this? A walk down memory lane? Is this what you came here to do?" His eyes flicked over to Alesha, still prone on the ground.

"You remind me so much of him. Just one of the reasons why I love making your life miserable."

Max dodged Merthane's kick, which narrowly missed his head. He grabbed the bounty hunter's leg, using it to pull himself up. Then he struck Merthane in the face with his palm, pushing him back. Merthane tried to follow up with his shock bar, but Max blocked the attack, grabbing Merthane's fatigues to hold him fast.

He delivered a shot to Merthane's midsection and kept going from there, delivering punch after punch to the man's body and a few to his face. As he pummeled Merthane, images of Sierra, dead on the streets of Tonicen, flashed through his mind again. He thought about the prison on Aval and the daily beatings he'd endured there. The fear he'd experienced every night that caused him to wake in a cold sweat coursed through his system and out through his fists as they drove into Merthane. He screamed as he unleashed all the rage and pain he'd endured the last two and a half years on the man who'd put him there. With a final strike to Merthane's throat, Max hit the hand-sized disc on Merthane's belt and then pushed him away, letting the device do its work.

Similar to the trap that had ensnared Glintock, four metal cords shot out of the disc and wrapped around Merthane, locking down his arms and legs. Unable to walk, he crashed to the asphalt in a heap.

With Merthane suitably neutralized, Max collapsed to his knees, chest heaving, exhausted. His face was wet and his bruised and bloody hands shook as he tried to calm himself. His mind instantly shifted across the street to Alesha.

He struggled to his feet, practically tripping over them as he rushed as best he could to her side. Kneeling beside her, he saw she was breathing. A wave of relief crashed inside him. Gently, he cradled her head in his lap.

She stirred for a moment before her eyes finally fluttered open, looking around frantically. Then, her eyes met his and she stopped, smiling up at him with something that might have been relief. "Hi, Earth Boy."

The affection in her voice made his heart swell. He took her hand in his, brushing her hair back with his other. "Hi, Sleepy. Are you okay?"

She nodded, closing her eyes for a few moments. "He hit me with a concussion grenade. I must have whacked my head on the street."

"So…it really was a *concussion* grenade?"

She chuckled and winced at the same time. "Ow. Shut up. I hurt all over."

"You've got nothing on me, sister."

She touched his face. "Were you crying?"

He winced, more because of his physical pain. "Merthane and I had a heart-to-heart," he replied, wiping his face.

"You know," Glintock called over from his suspended state. "This doesn't feel very good."

Max laughed. "I bet it doesn't. We'll get you down in a minute. I'm just catching my breath." He turned back to Alesha. "You're sure you're okay?"

"Yes," she replied, slowly pulling her hand from his. "Thank you."

"You're welcome." He could feel the walls going up between them again.

"Go check on the others," she said. "I'll be over in a minute."

"Okay." He kissed her forehead before gingerly placing her head back on the ground. He tried not to groan as he stood up. His body was a tangle of misfiring nerves—pain clusters erupting all over. He made his way over to the squirming Merthane and knelt beside him.

"No tears? Alesha must have made it. Damn," Merthane said through fewer teeth than he'd had at the start of the night.

"Shut up," Max replied curtly as his hands searched his enemy's body for the trap release control that would free Roeger and Glintock.

"Do you think this changes anything?" Merthane asked.

"Of course not, but you lost today and you need to shut the fuck up before I shove a dirty sock in your mouth." He found the trap release and yanked it off of Merthane's belt.

"You're just like your father. It makes me sick. Eventually, I'll have you in cuffs, dragging you kicking and screaming back to Aval."

Max gave him a hard look. "I'm never going back to Aval."

Merthane snorted. "Like I told you in Tonicen," he pushed a button on his belt that flashed blue, "there's more than one way to get someone." The trap ensnaring Merthane released.

Before Max could register what was happening, Merthane rolled away from him and tossed a disc onto the ground that exploded in light. Once Max's vision cleared, Merthane was gone.

"My friends in Apex law enforcement are on their way," Merthane's voice echoed all around them. "See you around, Maxim."

Shit. He fumbled with the controls for Roeger and Glintock's traps as Alesha walked over, rubbing her neck. Precious seconds ticked by as he scanned the device and disarmed the traps. Roeger fell to the street with a crash, while Glintock landed deftly on his feet.

"The cops are on their way," Max said as he dropped the trap control and smashed it with his boot. "Bring Roeger over here, quick."

"There's no hurry, Ultra," Glintock said. "I'm GAC. We'll be fine."

"Do you really think that's going to mean a damn thing to corrupt cops? Merthane's paid up with the right people, Agent. That's why he was able to pull all this off. Our best bet is to get as far away from here as possible."

Glintock nodded as Alesha helped Roeger up the street.

"Are you hurt, Roeger?" Max asked.

"I should be fine, Maxim. I just have a joint out from the fall."

Back the way they'd come, blue lights flashed from around a corner.

"Damn it," Max said. With his crew looking like the walking wounded, they'd never escape cops in vehicles. He heard the distinctive whine of a hover car approaching and tensed for another fight.

From around a nearby corner, a cherry red hover car convertible bolted out and spun to a stop in front of the crew. "Come on, get in!" Gelf called from the driver's seat.

"You beautiful son of a bitch!" Max said with a laugh as he ushered the others to the waiting car.

"This isn't a stolen vehicle, is it, Gelf?" Glintock asked with a stern glare.

"Borrowed, my good agent. Borrowed!"

"Whatever," Max said with a sigh. "Just get us out of here, buddy. And thanks for coming back."

"Of course! You didn't think I'd abandon my sidekick in the heat of battle, did you?"

Max levelled his gaze at Glintock, who met the stare evenly. "No, of course I didn't."

"Then, we're off!" Gelf chuckled as he spun the car around and sped off down a side street on a path that would eventually deliver them to the spaceport and the waiting *Sequel*.

CHAPTER II

The *Sequel*'s elevator touched down on the *Galactic Dream*'s hangar deck with a gentle bump. True to his word, Glintock had secured all of them passage on the ship. While Max's primary goal was to try and bring Robert back into the fold, he planned to take full advantage of the cruise ship's amenities—probably starting with a long massage. After prison and recently serving as Merthane's punching bag, he felt he'd earned a little break. Besides, as the captain of a glamorous cruise ship, Robbie was probably the safest one of all from Kalen. So, his odds of survival were probably fifty-fifty.

The crew gathered beneath the *Sequel* with their meager luggage. Max winced as he limped off the elevator before sending it back up. Turning to face the others, he grimaced and caught a flash of concern from Alesha. He reassured her with a nod.

"All right people, we're all set," Glintock said as he passed room keys out to each of them. He moved a little gingerly himself. "Unfortunately, this ship is pretty packed, so we'll have to pair off. Gelf and Gerry are in one room."

"Fantastic," Gelf said before turning to Gerry. "You don't leave a trail behind you, do you?"

The Glutob's eyes narrowed. "Not that I'm aware of, no."

"Great," Max said as he shuffled over to Glintock. "Alesha and I will share a room."

"Nice try, Ultra. You're with me," Glintock said. "Being that she's the only female here, Ms. Cabal will bunk with Roeger."

"That's considerate of you, Agent," Alesha said, taking the card from Glintock. "I'm going to the room now. Wake me when Robbie turns you down."

"I'll walk you up," Max said, grabbing his own passkey.

Glintock cleared his throat. "Actually, I was hoping we could map out our strategy for after your friend accepts or declines."

"We can figure that out after the banquet tonight," Max said as he took Alesha's hand, which she promptly pulled back. "Everybody take a breather and we'll meet in the banquet hall."

Glintock gave a humorless laugh. "No, I think we should stick to—"

"Maxim," Gerry interrupted. "Might it be possible for me to tour the galley?"

"I'll check on that for you, buddy. See you later." He moved his hand to Alesha's back, steering her away from the group.

"Where do you think you're going? We still have fugitives on the loose," a practically apoplectic Glintock called after them.

"Can't hear you, too loud down here—bye!" Max called over his shoulder.

"What about our bags?" Alesha asked as he guided her out of the hangar into a glass-encased lift.

"The porters will get them." He slumped against the gold railing that ran along the cylinder with a sigh, hoping that would ease his throbbing body.

"Well, while I appreciate the sweet gesture, I'm perfectly capable of finding my own room."

"It's a big ship," he replied with a shrug. "You could get lost."

She folded her arms. "Glintock sent us schematics of the entire vessel. Try again."

Clearly, she wanted him to come right out and say it. "Is it so wrong that I want to spend some time with you? Especially considering what we just went through with Merthane?"

She shook her head gently as the lift let them off on the Luxury Deck at the top of the massive vessel. "That's sweet, Max, but I'm fine—just a headache. What we should be doing is marching straight to the Captain's Quarters to see Robbie and then getting the hell out of here. I told you, I have obligations I have to get back to."

He paused, but not because he didn't know what to say. "Robert's not returning my calls. I've tried multiple times since we left Marina."

"Wonderful. So he doesn't even know we're here?"

"He should, but we'll see him tonight at dinner regardless. The captain always dines with the passengers the first night on these big lavish cruise ships. I'll ambush him there."

He ignored her disapproving look, focusing instead on the Luxury Deck's design. The star field above them, complete with Modan's sun, provided the perfect setup for sunbathers. A protective, domed force field covered the deck with built-in radiation filters. Three swimming pools populated the deck, two of which hovered above them, slowly rotating through the air. The clear bottoms allowed Max to see that not all the passengers adhered to the ship's swimwear rules. The crowds made it difficult to take a casual stroll, but everyone seemed to be enjoying themselves. He wished he could do that—just let go and lose his cares.

"And when Robbie says no?" Alesha asked, getting him back on track. "Because, he's most definitely going to turn you down."

"I'll remind him that he wouldn't even have this cushy job if it wasn't for me."

She snorted. "How do you figure that?"

"'Lesha, if I hadn't brought him up here, he'd still be flying dinky commuter flights back on Earth."

"Because his life's been totally perfect since that happened, right?"

His grimace wasn't just for the spike of pain that shot up his leg as he walked. He knew what she was getting at. Robert wasn't exactly a teetotaler and space living had given him much more freedom to explore his wild side. Max knew his friend had to have straightened out, or else the cruise line wouldn't have hired him. His lip twisted, guilt gnawing at his guts.

"What's wrong?" Alesha asked.

"You're right, as usual. I just...I'm beginning to think this wasn't a good idea."

"What, coming on the ship?"

"No, rounding you guys up. Everyone seems so much better off with me out of the picture."

She tried to stammer out an explanation. "That-that's not true, Max."

"You don't have to deny it. I can see the writing on the wall."

Another long pause.

It's worse than I thought.

"I'm not going to lie," she said. "I'm really happy with my life right now."

Thanks for sugar-coating it, sweetheart. "Tell me about it."

Her wide smile told him everything he needed to know, but she elaborated anyway. "I *love* running my own ship. My crew is like a well-oiled machine at this point, it runs so efficiently."

Her happiness made him glad, but every word was a dagger in his gut. *I should have just stayed in prison.*

"I have my pick of jobs and choose the ones that are best for me. It's great. Working for myself has been, quite possibly, the most rewarding experience of my life."

Well, that's that.

Another lift took them down to the main deck. This section of the ship was like an elegantly decorated shopping mall concourse, but with lower lighting to create a night-on-the-town feel. In the spaces where there were no stores or eateries, there were spectacular views through massive port and starboard windows. Alesha stopped by one of these, gazing out into space.

"All that being said," her brief silence gave him a flicker of hope. "There always feels like there's something missing, and that's you, Max."

A ball of happiness bounced around in his chest. Her sentiment surprised him, touching him more than he could say.

"Neither situation's perfect, of course," she continued. "Running my own ship opens up a whole host of problems I didn't have to deal with when I was running with you. I wouldn't know how to handle any of them if it weren't for you, though."

"Glad I could help."

"Don't be like that."

"Like what?"

"Sarcastic. Cynical."

"What? I'm glad you're happy."

She looked out the window again, resting her head against the force field with an electronic hum and a tiny flash of blue light.

"I'm not trying to make you feel bad, Max. I really learned a lot on the *Sequel*—enough to do what I'm doing now. And I'm grateful. It's amazing to me now, since all I ever felt on that ship was useless."

"Why would you say that? You were an integral part of the crew."

"No, I was an integral part of your life."

"You still are."

She blushed with a warm smile. "Regardless, I never felt like an equal member of the team. I always felt like your girlfriend tagging along for the ride."

"Did I ever make you feel that way?"

"No, it wasn't anything you did. These are all *my* insecurities. But believe me, I definitely worried about you—a lot."

That cheered him a bit. "And the others?"

"I think it's obvious that Roeger was thrilled to see you. Sure, he was happy doing his comedy, but he was clearly missing you."

"And Robert?"

She expelled a long breath. "He'll be tougher to crack. Robbie was really angry when you left. We all felt betrayed, but he took it particularly hard. Probably because you brought him out here in the first place.

"As far as all of us doing better without you, I think there's merit in that. We're all survivors, Max—we had to be. It's like I said on Modan, we weren't just going to sit around and wait for you. You were supposed to be gone a good long time, possibly forever. We had to get on with our lives. If you have a problem with that, then I don't know what to tell you. I think that's beyond selfish if that's the case."

He couldn't argue with that. "I didn't think your lives would stop, but mine did. Time kind of…froze. I just didn't expect you all to be getting along so well without me. That's not to say I thought you'd fall apart, but it's…it's a blow to the ego to say the least." He sighed. "I think when I got out, I wanted things to go back to the way they were for all of us. That's *still* what I want."

She shook her head. "That's impossible. We can't go backwards, Max. No one can. We can only reconcile our mistakes and push forward, get on with our lives."

She was right, of course. Things would never be the same again and he was a fool for expecting that they might. The future scared him, especially a future without Alesha, and he'd had enough of being scared. He tried to hold onto the fact that the future, the unknown, could also be exciting, and there was so much more he wanted to know about her.

As he gazed out at the glowing blue orb below that was Modan, Alesha touched his arm gently. Focusing on her eyes, he caught something in his peripheral vision. He looked away from Alesha immediately, a rush of panic flooding through him.

Sierra. Again.

She vanished, lost in the crowd of passengers, if she'd been there at all. Scanning every face, he looked for a clue. This was different from when he thought he'd seen her in Marina and Apex. Those could have been similar looking women, but this time he was sure he'd seen her. But, could he be sure? The fight with Merthane had left him a pulsating nerve. The pain combined with his general rustiness could have had his senses deceiving him. Why now? Why here? Was it guilt at reconciling with Alesha? Naturally, he tried to ignore the nagging possibility that it was the rimi driving him insane. His body broke out in a cold sweat as fear prickled through him.

"Hey," Alesha's voice sounded far away, but it pulled him back. "Are you okay? You zoned out there for a minute."

"I...." He couldn't tell her the truth. She'd absolutely *freak*. Partial truths were the order of the day. "I thought I saw someone I knew. No one you know, though."

Her eyebrow crooked as she placed her hands on her hips. "I'm pretty sure I know everyone you do out here, unless one of your old girlfriends joined Earth's space agency."

He'd forgotten how sharp she was, even though it was one of the things he loved about her. "Haven't you ever looked around and thought you saw people you recognized?"

Her lopsided smile rapidly became a frown. "Only if they were already on my mind. So, who are you thinking about while you're walking around with me?"

"*No one.* I'm not thinking of anyone but you, darling. Get off my back." He started to turn, but the movement sent a spike of pain through his body, causing him to wince. The pain washed Sierra—and his rimi fears—to the back of his mind.

"I'm just playing, Max. But speaking of your back, you look like hell. I don't think you could support my weight."

"Thanks a lot. I'm managing."

"Not well. Why didn't you take care of that in prison? You had plenty of time to hea—"

"It was sorted, but tussles with lifelong enemies tend to leave me hurting."

"So, it's *not* fixed."

"Did you see what Merthane did to me down there? I'm like a walking bruise."

She pointed to the knot on her head. "No, I must have missed that while I was knocked unconscious."

He decided to stop thinking only of himself and touched her face tenderly.

She flinched at his gesture, but didn't pull away.

"I thought I'd lost you, 'Lesha."

Her eyes closed and he felt her lean into his hand for a moment. *Then* she drew away from his touch. "Well as much as I want to get back to my life, you can't get rid of me that easily." She said it with a smile, but all he wanted was to know what was going on behind her dark eyes. She'd never felt so elusive to him.

Shaking his head, he grimaced as he turned his attention back out the window. With all the years he'd been cruising the stars, it was easy to forget just how beautiful the universe was. A distant nebula grabbed his attention, blue and violet against the black of space. He glanced over at Alesha, an internal struggle playing out on her face.

She caught him looking and gave him an uncomfortable smile.

Although all he really wanted to do was take some rimi, crash into his bed and sleep, he held his arm out. "Care to tour the rest of the ship on the way to your room?"

She took his arm with a dazzling smile. "Of course. We still need to swing by the shops so I can pick up a dress for tonight."

He smiled broadly at her, but as they hobbled on their way, he kept a wary eye out for any more hallucinations that might be trying to kill him.

CHAPTER 12

Matthias clenched his teeth as he watched Ultra and Cabal leave to gallivant around the ship.

It is impossible to keep this kid in line.

Looking around to the rest of the crew, he watched Gelf heading for the hangar exit. "Going to get settled in your room?" he called after him.

"Yeah, something like that," Gelf said over his shoulder, never breaking stride. Despite his most recent heroics, Gelf was once again attempting to skulk off by himself with no explanation. There was no real release agreement with Gelf, since Matthias really only needed Ultra, but as he was the one who got Gelf out of prison, a little gratitude would have been nice. He didn't like it.

"Actually, Agent, Glutobs by nature are curious beings, so I am off to tour the ship as well. I will see you both later," the Glutob said as he slinked off.

"Good luck," Matthias replied, his eyes never leaving Gelf's back.

"And you, Agent," the bot said. "Where are you off to?"

"Since your captain ran off, I was going to get some work done in my room, but suddenly I'm far more interested in where our friend Gelf is going."

"His arrival after Merthane escaped was quite fortuitous, but still, I do not trust him."

Matthias raised his eyebrows. "Really? What makes you…ah, feel, that way?" Bots with emotions—he wasn't a big supporter.

The bot blinked at him once. "He was very secretive on the *Sequel*, always poking around in areas that should not have concerned him."

"Really…" He kept his eyes on Gelf. The little man began blending into the crowd. "Let's follow him."

"E-excuse me?"

"Let's get after him—see what he's up to. You said it yourself—you don't trust him."

"Yes, but he is Maxim's friend."

He took the bot's arm and started after Gelf. "Well, Maxim's judgment is a little impaired when it comes to Gelf."

"What do you mean?"

Matthias curbed his usual bluntness. Normally he would have told Roeger exactly what he meant, but the concern and sincerity in the bot's voice…. He hadn't dealt with emotional robots, or emotes, for some time. That was by design. "Prison buddies have a different kind of connection than normal people. Maxim's opinion of Gelf is probably a little clouded by that."

"You mean he will not be objective."

"Exactly. It may all turn out to be nothing, but we can at least put our minds at ease about Gelf."

The bot appeared to be considering it even as he followed Matthias. "Then let us pursue him if not to help Maxim."

Not exactly my goal, but that works. "Sounds good."

Gelf had a good lead on them. His height made it especially difficult to keep him in view amongst the other passengers milling around the ship. Matthias noted how the little man avoided the elevators, sticking to the large banks of escalators that ferried the passengers between decks. Gelf appeared to be oblivious that he was being followed. He checked his mobile communicator every so often, but otherwise looked completely at ease, like a man on vacation.

Maybe he is *just heading to his room.* Matthias couldn't believe that, though. Gelf had been acting too suspicious on Ultra's ship—always off by himself, not interacting with anyone really, except for Ultra of course. *Maybe he's just shy.* It was true that Gelf had been incarcerated for some time. That was sure to make a person far more skittish around others, but Matthias couldn't shake the feeling that he was up to something more. He chalked it up to his instincts as an investigator. Also, all Gelf could talk about when he and Ultra were alone together in Marina was escaping. It was thin, but as an investigator, he was compelled to dig a little deeper.

"What exactly did you see him doing on the ship that made you suspicious?" he asked the bot.

"It is as I said, Agent, he was exploring areas of the ship that should not have concerned him. He seemed particularly interested in the main computer—always looking at it. He never touched it to my knowledge. I think Christi would have alerted me to something like that. Far be it from me to suggest that he should have been confined to his quarters, but what would he need in the cargo areas of the ship? He went down there a lot as well."

Cargo.... Was it possible Gelf and Ultra were going into business together? Maybe they'd struck some sort of deal for Ultra to run narcotics for him? Matthias sincerely hoped that wasn't how Ultra planned to spend his newfound freedom.

"Mostly though," the bot continued, "I just have a bad feeling about the man."

"I see…." It took everything Matthias had not to roll his eyes. How did a robot have a gut feeling? Where did he feel it—in his wiring?

"I sense, Agent Glintock, you are not totally at ease with emotes. Am I correct?"

Matthias couldn't resist. "I don't know, what does your *gut* tell you?"

"I suspected as much. Your history with emotes makes your passive-aggressiveness entirely explainable."

"How did yo—"

"I researched you back on the *Sequel*, Agent. I am very sorry for your loss."

"You had no right," Matthias choked out. He wasn't about to discuss his past with a bot.

"Of course I did, Agent. I did it to protect Maxim. I do not know you. For all I know, you are a corrupt GAC agent looking to use Maxim to your own ends. I was happy to find that you have an exemplary record."

"Thank you," he replied emotionlessly. *Typical bot—does something he shouldn't have, but manages to compliment an organic anyway.* However, there was something endearing about Roeger's looking out for Ultra. Matthias wasn't ready to embrace the bot, but maybe his personal experience wasn't the best jumping off point in dealing with *this* bot in particular. It didn't make him miss Fiona any less.

"I am sorry if I brought up a painful memory, Agent. It is as I said, I was only looking out for my friend."

Matthias nodded. "It's all right, I understand. And I *do* have a thing about bots. It's nothing personal, believe m—"

"You are essentially questioning my existence. I can do nothing else *but* take it personally."

He's got me there. "Look, understand, I've been around a lot longer than I look."

"Correct. You are a Prebrue—basically, a very long-lived human."

"More or less, yes." The bot's definition wasn't exactly precise, but Matthias guessed that was a product of his emotion programming. "The point is, I'm kind of old fashioned, if you haven't guessed already. To me, robots are tools—machines to help organics get work accomplished. That's what I mean by nothing personal—I feel that way about all robots."

Roeger blinked at him. Matthias could almost see a thoughtful expression on the bot's face. "No harm done, Agent. You old-timers just need to open your minds a bit before the robotic holocaust becomes reality."

Matthias' eyes widened.

"That was a joke, Agent."

He shook his head. "Very funny."

"Well, comedy was my previous profession."

"How did all that come about anyway?"

"It is a long story, Agent, and it appears our quarry is pulling away from us."

Gelf was definitely becoming harder to pick out from the crowd. "Come on." Picking up the pace, he heard Roeger's joints whirring behind him. He pushed past some passengers directly in front of him, receiving a few dirty looks in the process. His communicator chimed. It was difficult to hear in the din of voices filling the ship, even with his earpiece. Pulling the device from his belt, he stopped in his tracks long enough for Roeger to pass him.

The screen flashed red. An alert was coming through. Like the others he'd already received, this one was more bad news.

Roeger turned back. "Agent Glintock? He is getting away."

Matthias scanned the alert for the third time, nodded, and then put his communicator back on his belt. "Let him go. Something else has come up."

Ten minutes later, Matthias and Roeger stood with a member of the ship's security in one of the passenger cabins. A young woman with orange skin and lavender hair lay naked on the bed, her throat slit. A medical officer sat in the corner with a similar-looking woman, consoling her.

"It was a good thing you were onboard, Agent. How did you get down here so fast?" the security officer asked. Despite his large, barrel-chested stature and gray, craggy skin, the officer looked a little green and kept his eyes averted from the body. His skin pigmentation immediately reminded Matthias of his thief. No fur on the security officer, though—the grainy surveillance footage recovered from the destroyed facility had shown the thief had fur on his hands.

"I'm investigating another case. This...this is my bot. May we inspect the scene?"

"Be my guest. We would greatly appreciate the help of you and your automaton," the officer replied, looking relieved to walk away from the bed.

"Thanks." Matthias stepped closer to the victim with a grumbling Roeger. "What's the problem?"

"That...*gentleman* called me an automaton," the bot replied in a digitized whisper. Matthias didn't even know bots *could* whisper. "That is an insult to a synthetic life form of my programming. I've never been called an automaton in my entire lifespan."

Matthias sighed. "Do you have a sensor sweep you can run?" he asked the bot under his breath.

"Perhaps not what you are looking for, but I can make it appear convincing."

He nodded at the bot and a green laser shot out of one of Roeger's fingers, illuminating the room in an emerald glow. While the bot scanned the victim, Matthias leaned close to her. The deep wound on her neck had drenched the once-white bedsheets in blood.

"Bruising on her wrists," he said more to himself than to anyone else. Without a proper medical exam, he couldn't be positive, but more than likely, a sexual assault had occurred. "Who found her?"

"Her travelling companion over there in the corner," the security officer replied. "Passengers heard her screams up and down the corridor."

"Are these rooms sound-proofed?"

The security officer almost looked embarrassed. "Yes. Some of the guests get a little rowdy."

"That explains why no one heard the victim's screams."

"My scan is complete," Roeger reported as his laser cut off.

"Cross-reference the scene here with known crimes of Kalen Vandeir." Matthias could have used his handheld to get the information, but he'd forgotten just how efficient working with a bot could be. Plus, he wanted to make everything look good for the security officers. With Merthane, Brontin proved he wasn't fooling around, but as far as Matthias knew, the bosses still weren't taking the man seriously. That could change, though, and if it did, they would revoke his status. So, he had to play the role of the diligent agent as best he could and hope that no one scanned his credentials.

The bot's head twitched a few times. "I have completed my investigation."

"Well?"

"Yes. This crime scene is consistent with Kalen's previous murders."

"I thought so." He turned to the security officer and flashed Vandeir's picture on his handheld. "Put out an alert for this man, Kalen Vandeir. His picture should already be circulating, so I'm shocked he even got on board." He didn't bother hiding the contempt in his voice, feeling like he was dealing with rank amateurs. "Has the captain been notified?"

"We are keeping him apprised with updates. He is pre-occupied with the run of the ship. Pre-flight and post-takeoff are the busiest times for cruise ship vessels."

Another security officer, this one a human, entered the room. "We've got a crowd forming out here."

Matthias looked out the open doorway. Sure enough, a small gathering built outside the room. As his eyes passed over the faces, he did a double-take, but tried to not make it obvious. *Vandeir.* He couldn't believe it, but standing off to the side, smirking, was Kalen Vandeir, apparently back to admire his handiwork.

Matthias chanced another look, but Vandeir had locked onto him. He was no longer smirking.

Vandeir bolted.

"*Stop that man!*" Matthias shouted as he ran through the door to pursue the murderer. "Come on, Roeger!" Once they pushed their way through the crowd camped out at the door, Matthias saw Vandeir dash around a corner. "Get some vecking security down here!" He didn't wait to see if the security officers were complying with his order as he led Roeger down the corridor after Vandeir.

Matthias turned the corner to find another empty corridor. He continued down the hall at top speed. There was only one way Vandeir could have gone and that was around another corner at the end of the passage. Matthias came around the next corner, pistol drawn, and stopped.

"*Veck.*"

The path ended in a waiting area for a bank of six different transport tubes, all going in different directions. A security camera rotated above, scanning the area.

The bot arrived on the scene as a plan formulated in Matthias' mind. "I apologize, Agent Glintock, I am not designed for high-speed pursuit. Who were we pursuing again?"

"It was Vandeir. I need you to do something for me."

"Yes Agent?"

Glancing up at the camera, Matthias kept his voice low. "See who's in those elevators."

"I am sure that I do not have to remind you, Agent, that a course of action like that is highly illegal."

"We have to find Vandeir now!" Matthias hissed. This was *not* the time for the bot's ethics programming to kick in.

"Can the ship's security not handle it?"

"You saw those guys down there—they can't handle a criminal like this." He stopped himself and took a new tack. "Let me ask you this, how many illegal acts have you committed with Ultra?"

"I am not at liberty to say for fear that my answer will most certainly incriminate me."

"Access the panel, Roeger, find out who's in those elevators. Do it for Maxim, because Vandeir is surely looking for him. And don't forget, I'm a high-ranking GAC Agent."

"On a highly suspect pursuit," Roeger mumbled. He approached the control panel for the elevators, off to the side of the lifts. "Can you at least block the camera with your body?"

"I'll do my best," Matthias replied, repositioning himself.

Roeger stood in front of the glass panel, its soft blue lights reflecting off his body. A jack extended from his index finger. He plugged it into the panel's port, nodding as he did so.

"Why are you nodding?"

"To make it appear as though we are having a conversation for the camera."

"So, *how many* times have you done something like this for Ultra?"

Roeger didn't answer. His attention remained fixed on the panel. He blinked his eyes three times before unplugging. "One elevator is headed to deck seven, two to deck twenty-eight, another to deck thirty-six, one to deck thirty-nine, and the last to deck forty-three."

"Yes, but which car is Vandeir in?"

"I could not ascertain that information."

"Dammit."

"The ship has quite a sophisticated security system. This panel could only provide access to information about these specific elevators, but no access to the cameras inside. Are you sure you saw Kalen? I did not see him at all."

"It was him, dammit. I'm sure of it. I really don't want to, but I think we should split up. The lower levels are generally for operations and storage. He could have gone down there to hide or wreak havoc."

"Unless he went to the upper decks to blend with the other passengers. Or worse—seek out another victim."

Matthias clenched his teeth. Time was running out. "You have better eyes than me. You check the upper decks as fast as you can. I'll go to deck seven."

"Very well, Agent."

As Matthias rode the elevator down, he wondered if the bot had been right. *Was* the man he saw Vandeir? He didn't believe his mind would play tricks on him like that, but it wasn't unheard of for a dogged investigator like himself to see his suspect when he wasn't there.

But, if it wasn't Vandeir, why did the guy run? He heaved a frustrated sigh. *Because, I was investigating a murder and looked at him like he was guilty.* The multiple alerts had made him jumpy. He had to admit that he couldn't totally be sure it had been Vandeir.

The elevator delivered him to deck seven, and Matthias figured he might as well investigate to be sure. Exiting the lift, he found himself in one of the ship's cargo holds. Dimly lit and filled with towers of metal crates and plastic boxes, the hold looked more like the ship's storage deck as opposed to one for passenger cargo. The lanes between the stacks were wide, shrouded by looming shadows. Off to the side, he spotted a mobile cargo lifter. What he did not see were any crewmembers.

The situation didn't feel right. The familiar buzz at the back of his mind came with it. He drew his pistol, wincing as the sound of the weapon charging echoed through the hold.

It would be very easy for Vandeir to get the drop on me down here. Need to stay on guard. The warm then cool rush of nervous perspiration swept through him as he conducted his search. His brief doubts had vanished.

He stopped. The murmur of voices floated through the stacks. *Who the veck would Vandeir be meeting down here?*

Using the columns of cargo as cover, he wove his way through the hold to where it sounded like the voices were coming from. A hazy white light emanated from around the corner.

He froze. On the floor to the right were two uniformed crewmembers, riddled with laser scorch marks. Unless they slept with their eyes wide with horror, they were dead. To his left there were three more, piled up like slabs of meat and discarded as callously. He drew a ragged breath as he leaned against a stack of crates. It had been some time since he'd worked in the field. He'd held it together for the audience upstairs, but seeing dead bodies wasn't something he would ever get used to. However, he made sure to take a quick moment to make sure none of them were Vandeir. He couldn't turn it off—always on the job.

Could Vandeir have worked this fast? If not him, who?

"Listen up!" A sharp voice cut through the undertone.

Keeping to the shadows, Matthias moved toward the voice, making sure to stay at least one aisle away. Positioned behind a stack of crates, he took several deep breaths to calm his nerves. He leaned out slightly to see around his cover.

A man with a thick thatch of white hair and matching beard stood in front of fifteen or so masked humanoids. They carried laser rifles, with spare energy magazines strapped to their belts and chests. Two portable lamps bathed the area in harsh white light. They all wore black military fatigues.

"The target is onboard. We believe the item is here as well. The Revash who stole it has also been sighted by our reconnaissance teams."

Matthias' eyes widened. The strands of his case began to tie together. *A Revash, of course. The thief's description makes sense now. He's on board?* One mystery solved, but if the thief wasn't the target, who were these people looking for—Vandeir? Were they some kind of GAC special operations team that was above his clearance?

He turned at the scuff of a boot behind him just in time to see a rifle butt speeding toward his head.

CHAPTER 13

Litning's booming laughter filled the small recreation area shared by the crew members in his sector of the *Galactic Dream*. He sat at a table with three of his crewmates playing a game of *Kuffnan*. He was winning. His crewmates were not happy about that.

"*Veck!* That's four hands in a row!" Neron cried, slamming both his cards and his pale orange hands down on the table. His bald head shone in the room's harsh lighting.

"I am sorry, my friend. I suppose I just have a natural aptitude for the game."

He played the part of the jovial winner well—too well. As he took another swig from the bottle placed in front of him, he could feel the demons he had struggled with in Apex tugging at his nepast. However, while he felt he could easily succumb to the temptations around him, he told himself he indulged in order to blend in with his crewmates.

Ever since he had stepped aboard the *Galactic Dream*, he could not shake the feeling that eyes were on him at all times, despite requesting work assignments away from the passengers. It was a feeling similar to hunting on the plains of Revjekt, when something far more dangerous than his prey spotted him, turning the tables of any hunt.

It could have just been the cruise line management keeping watch on their employees, but the feeling of unease went deeper than that. He engaged with his crewmembers to gauge their interest—not only in him, but in Memta as well. As he had done in Apex, he kept Memta in a drawstring bag, this time strapped to his back. He feared leaving it with his belongings in the quarters that he shared with two other individuals.

Aside from his current streak of luck in Kuffnan, nothing was really going right for him. He was still no closer to figuring out how to get to Revjekt and keeping a constant eye on Memta created stress he did not need. His stomach roiled constantly. Sleep did not come easily either. The only way he felt he could get any decent rest was if he drank himself into a stupor. However, he had to keep himself alert enough to defend Memta from any potential thieves. It was exhausting.

"How is it this is the first time you've played Kuffnan?" Neron asked as he shuffled the deck.

"Maybe he's lying," another crewmember, Bijin said. His yellow eyes settled on Litning, filled with suspicion. His blue, scaled skin seemed to darken as he glared.

"Revashes are quick to adapt, my friend. I promise you, there is no deception at hand here." Though what he said was true, he knew that disgruntled gamblers like his crewmates would not accept it as such.

"Funny, I've never seen a Revash before," said Omdil, the third crewmember and only human at the table. "Generally, Kuffnan is only played in the gambling dens of the big cities. So, you can understand our confusion over how well you're doing, considering you're probably new to the outside galaxy."

On the surface, Omdil's comments sounded positively curious, but his tone was filled with a quiet menace that Litning found unsettling. The possible threat, combined with the alcohol pumping through his system, blunted his good-natured attitude considerably.

"Perhaps I play well because money holds no allure for me." Another truth that he predicted his opponents would not take well.

"No allure?" Bijin spat. "Then why do you even play?"

"For the camaraderie of my crewmates as well as the challenge. There is more to life than simple wealth, my friend."

"There's nothing simple about a pauper's life," Neron said.

"Agreed," Bijin said with a nod. "If you do not want our money, why not give it back?"

Litning chuckled. "Just because money has no hold on me does not mean that I do not need it to survive in this galaxy." Almost at once, his opponents' eyes narrowed. They did not share his good nature. Whatever he was drinking, it was good and strong.

"I can see why you would feel that way, my Revash friend," Omdil said. "The money holds no personal value for you, so you play with abandon. The consequences of losing have no impact, but perhaps it's because you're betting the wrong thing."

His brow creased. "What are you getting at?"

"What's in the bag?"

"It is none of your concern. Are we playing or not?"

"You said yourself that you play for the challenge, but what kind of challenge is it if you aren't playing for the same stakes as us?"

"You had no idea of my approach to the game until just now. As far as I know, you were playing your best and I defeated you."

"Or maybe we were going easy on you to keep you interested," Omdil said with a smile. "See, you can't tell. But we know you weren't playing for any real stakes, so where is the challenge for you? How can it be a fair contest when you're playing for nothing?"

He eyed Omdil closely. Was he one of the people watching him? Why was he so interested in the contents of the bag? Did he want Memta? How could he even know about her? His mind drifted to the main concourse of the ship and the escape pods housed there.

"Well, Mr. Revash, what do you say?"

"What is in my bag is far more valuable than any paltry currency you could throw on this table—more dangerous as well."

"Well, now you *have* to show it to us," Neron said like a child excited to be receiving a present.

What was the harm in letting them look at the statue? Why should he deny them Memta's beauty? If they wanted to touch it, they were in for a surprise. He made no move to open the bag, though.

"I say, you are full of nakra," Bijin said. His eyes became slits as his clawed hand raked across the table.

Litning snarled at him. It was clear he could trust no one but himself.

Omdil raised his hands to the rest of them. "Gentlemen please, there is no need to make this unpleasant. We're just four hired hands having a friendly game. If our Revash friend doesn't want to share his good fortune with us—if he is too *afraid*—then who are we to judge him?"

"I fear nothing, human."

"Then show us what's in the bag. You are double the size of all of us—how could we take it from you?"

"You could not."

"Exactly. Then what's the problem?" Omdil sighed. "If money means so little to you, as you claim, you should have no issue showing us this bauble. Unless, of course, my friend Bijin here is correct and you *are* full of nakra."

Litning growled, but stifled it.

A crowd had gathered around the table. Several of his crewmates watched him with expectant looks. Perhaps showing them all the statue would buy him some friends he could count on in the future. It was still a long way to Revjekt. Their eyes burned into him like branding irons. If he left the table now, as his nepast told him to do, he would only invite their scorn and possible betrayal if his identity became known.

"Very well." He unstrapped the bag from his back and placed it on the card table. Gripping the base of the statue through the bag, he slid the top down to reveal Memta in all her glory. There was a hushed awe from the crowd gathered around the table, but at least one spectator was unimpressed.

"That is it? A slab of carved rock? Seems like a lot of buildup to nothing," Bijin said with a bored expression.

"Oh I don't know, Bijin," Omdil said. "It seems your lack of refinery prevents you from truly appreciating such a treasure." He began to reach for the statue. "May I?"

Litning quickly scooped the statue back inside the bag with a snarl, drawing looks of alarm. "No one touches the statue." The looks of alarm slowly became expressions of distrust.

Omdil raised his eyebrows. "Very well, no harm done." He pushed away from the table. "I think that's all the excitement I can handle for tonight. Early start tomorrow—I need to get some sleep."

Neron and Bijin also rose. Bijin's eyes lingered on the bag clutched in Litning's hands a little too long before he headed for his bunk. The crowd around the table broke up as well, snippets of low conversation drifted into Litning's highly-tuned ears.

"Strange."

"That growling can't be good."

"Don't get too close to that one."

"Probably stole the damn thing."

His eyes darted around the emptying room. Little did they know, he had just saved Omdil's life. Or had he? It no longer mattered. They did not trust him, but could he really blame them? If he had not been under scrutiny before, he was now. He felt even less safe than he had before.

I have to get off this ship.

CHAPTER 14

Aval. Talon Merthane hadn't intended on arriving there empty-handed, but Maxim Ultra had had other ideas. The boy had done a real number on him. The med bay on his ship had healed most of the damage, but he still had some bruising that would take a while to go away. The metallic taste of blood was ever-present in his mouth as his ship, the *Claw,* entered the planet's atmosphere, and his teeth were an absolute mess. He'd lost several in the fight and would have to get some prosthetics as soon as possible. By admission, Talon had been cocky not going with the rimi. He sneered at the memory of what Maxim had done to him. It would sustain him until their next meeting. In the meantime, Talon needed some more firepower.

He wasn't keen on seeking help, but facts were facts. He'd effectively subdued Maxim's comrades and the boy still bested him. Talon had thrown multiple taunts at Maxim, but secretly, he'd been impressed with how the boy handled himself. There was something different about him. Prison had hardened him. There was a determination there that Talon wouldn't underestimate again. If that new element to Maxim's personality had been forged in the crucible of Aval, what better place to seek help?

His communicator trilled in his ear again. He looked at the caller information on the *Claw's* pop-up display and rolled his eyes. It was Brontin—again. The man had been calling him nearly non-stop since the debacle on Modan. Once again, he chose to ignore the call, but only because the dispatcher from the prison was contacting him.

"*Unidentified ship, please transmit your Ident Code.*" The detached dispatcher's voice filled the *Claw's* cockpit.

Talon punched his code into the digital keyboard, keeping the ship on course.

A smokier—*female*—voice responded over the comm system. "*Merthane, welcome back.*"

"Dayna—good to hear someone I recognize." He would have been concerned if it *hadn't* been her. They had already set up the details of his visit, keeping their current conversation mundane for anyone else listening. "Where can I set down?"

She paused briefly, then returned, speaking barely above a whisper. "*You've been flagged by the GAC. It could be a problem.*"

Brontin, you impatient veck. "Dayna, give me a docking assignment. I can place a call to make this all disappear."

"*I could get into trouble for that.*"

"I can make it worth your while."

She chuckled. "*Like you did the last time we crossed paths?*"

"Perhaps." They always kept their conversation professional over the open channel, but if the prison's warden knew just *how* close they were, Dayna would have lost her job a long time ago.

"*You can put the* Claw *down on Docking Pad Twelve.*" Her tone didn't scream reluctance—more like resignation.

Perfect.

"I'll go ahead and place that call." He clicked off the ship's comm unit and programmed the computer to fly him to Docking Pad Twelve. Then he heaved a calming sigh before keying his communicator. *I hate dealing with idiots.*

Brontin answered immediately. "*I figured flagging you at every spaceport in the galaxy would get your attention. Why has it taken you this long to contact me? I hear about explosions and gunplay in Lower Apex and* now *you call me? Only* now?"

"Shut up, Brontin, and don't forget who you're talking to. I could be there in two days, sticking a knife in your ear and you wouldn't even know what was happening until your head hit your desk."

Brontin remained silent for a moment, as if processing Talon's threat. "*How dare you? Threatening a GAC agent? This is how you do business? I can see now that it was a mist—*"

"Just shut up and listen to me. Things didn't go as I had planned on Modan, so I'm on Aval."

"*What in Great Torva's name are you doing there?*"

"I need reinforcements." Though loath to admit it, he needed Brontin's help to make his plan work.

Talon could almost hear the wheels turning in Brontin's tiny brain as he paused again. "*Wait, are you going to one of the cities, or…*"

"Brontin, don't be stupid."

Another pause as his feeble mind processed the details. "*Wai— no. No.*"

"This is the only way, Brontin, and I need you to sign off on it."

"*Let me see if I understand this. You're faltering in your old age and now you want me to commit the same exact infraction I'm trying to charge Glintock with? You must be going senile too.*"

Talon said nothing, trying to quell his rage at the spineless bureaucrat. "You wanted me on this job, Brontin, and I intend to complete it. What you fail to understand is that you're not in charge here. You are merely a cog to facilitate my completion of the contract."

"*Who do you think you are? You work for* me."

"I work for myself. If I feel it benefits me more for you to be deceased, I'll make it happen. Maybe I'll find Ultra's old friend Kalen Vandeir and point *him* in your direction. Just one of the hundreds of scenarios I've thought up since we started this conversation." He'd actually only thought of, maybe, five scenarios, but he'd always had a flair for the dramatic.

"*I could have GAC agents hound you from one end of the galaxy to the other.*"

Talon arched an eyebrow. Maybe Brontin had a little backbone after all. In any case, it was a hollow threat. "Brontin, if you think I haven't dealt with my share of GAC agents over the years, you've got a lot to learn. Go ahead and put that in motion. You'll be dead within a week."

There was no answer on the other end of the connection.

"Then it sounds like we understand each other," Talon said, not waiting another moment for Brontin to object. "You will facilitate a prisoner release. These prisoners will be signed over to my custody and then you will butt out of it. Are we clear?"

Brontin said nothing for several moments. "*How can I sign off on this when I don't even know who you're releasing?*"

"I'm transmitting the list to you now. I went through Ultra's prison records on the way here and you can rest assured, I'm only recruiting some of his *very* best friends."

"*I-I can't do this. My career—*"

"Will be the least of your concerns if you *don't* do this. Relax, Brontin, it's not like I'm going to take these convicts to a field and set them free. If they get unruly, then they'll be killed in the crossfire, so to speak."

The *Claw* began its final descent onto Docking Pad Twelve. Brontin still hadn't said anything.

"Make it happen, Brontin. If I have to end up shooting my way out of here, my next stop will be to wherever you are." Talon clicked off his communicator and headed for the boarding ramp. As it lowered, the first thing he saw was Dayna waiting for him. Her dark blonde hair was pulled back in a tight bun and she had a pleasant smile for Talon, which contrasted with her severe military-style uniform.

As he stepped onto the docking pad, she walked up to him, giving him a chaste kiss on the lips. Considering their time apart, he'd hoped for a little more than that. Their situation wasn't exactly normal, considering his work kept him mobile most of the time, but they'd built a simple life together. How they'd managed to keep it a relative secret was incredible to him. They were just very, very careful. So, her brief kiss was the right play to make, but it just made him want more.

"I missed you," she said, her voice low.

"Same here." He didn't want to get all into their feelings, not while he was working.

"You look like hell," she said.

"Complements of my boy, Maxim Ultra. I looked a lot worse before hitting the med bay."

She nodded solemnly, gently touching his face. "How's our girl?"

He smiled tightly at Dayna's mention of Alexis. "Impatient. I left her back on Vale to do some more training."

"You're going to have to let her off that planet some time, Talon."

"When she's ready." He handed her a credit chip. Just because they were together didn't mean she shouldn't be compensated for bending the rules for him. "Is everything set?"

"Yes indeed. We have to make this quick, though. The alert for you is still active and I don't know how long I can keep the warden in the dark. What happened to that magical call you were going to make?"

Vecking Brontin. "My contact is a little slow on the uptake. He should come around by the time I'm done inspecting the troops."

"Will the three we discussed earlier be enough?"

"I'm sure they will be."

Dayna led him inside the tower's hangar bay. He received curious looks from the mechanics there. As he looked around, he spotted scorch marks on some of the walls.

"Quite a mess in here," he commented.

"That's what happens when Maxim Ultra blasts his way out of our hangar."

Not bad, kid. Not bad, he thought with a grim nod.

They were about to enter the prisoner processing center when the warden and two prison guards burst through the doors.

"Out. I want you out of here," the warden said, wagging his finger at Talon. "There's a GAC alert out for you, Mr. Merthane, and I'll not have you bringing this facility under greater scrutiny." He looked to Dayna. "You, Miss Suander, are terminated—effective immediately."

"*What?*" Dayna's incredulous expression couldn't hide the hurt in her eyes.

"Yes. We all heard you two lovebirds conspiring over the radio. I had no idea it was in a bid to make an unauthorized prisoner release."

"Warden," Talon began as he slid in-between Dayna and the perturbed man. He brought his voice low. "You heard the call. It was just me taking advantage of Ms. Suander's affections." He didn't mind looking like a sleaze—he *needed* Dayna where she was. "I take full responsibility. Perhaps you can see your way to lifting this silly termination order."

"Nice try, Mr. Merthane. We know all about your *professional relationship* with Miss Suander."

Behind pursed lips, Talon gritted his teeth. "Very well then, I can assure you that the GAC alert is just a misunderstanding. If you allow me to contact Agent Brynden Brontin at the GAC, he can clear all this up."

"Agent Brontin is the one who put out the alert!"

Talon stretched his neck, patience ebbing. "Well, what if I told you that Agent Brontin was about to provide me with a signed prisoner release for these gentlemen?" He looked at his data pad and smiled—Brontin had finally come through with the authorization. "In fact, here it is now."

"We already fell for that one recently, Mr. Merthane, and we won't be doing it again. I'm having the guards return the prisoners to their cells. As for the two of you, I have more guards on the way if need be, but you can show yourselves out."

"But the release has been approved by the GAC," Talon said. Through the narrow windows set into the doors, he could see two more guards attempting to lead his three prisoners away, but the convicts weren't making it easy for them.

"Mr. Merthane, despite the unsavory nature of your profession, you're well-respected here by much of the staff. Please don't make a scene and be on your way."

The guards flanking the warden were armed with shock sticks—nothing Talon couldn't handle, but he wasn't interested in a fight. "You're going to ignore the GAC order?"

"This is not a GAC facility. We accommodate, but we don't kneel."

"What if I made it worth your while?"

The warden arched his eyebrow, but the discomforted look that passed between his guards said that this wasn't the first time he'd been offered a bribe in their presence. "I'm listening."

"Twenty thousand. You fulfill Brontin's order and bring Dayna back onto the payroll."

"Talon...." Dayna didn't sound keen on that plan.

The warden wore a smug smile. "Twenty-five." He turned his gaze to Dayna. "I just deplore insubordination."

"Done." He frowned at Dayna's disappointed expression. "I need you here."

"That's one of us." She looked to the warden. "I vecking quit."

"Dayna!" Talon couldn't believe it.

"You're the idiot who offered him more money. I didn't ask for that."

He wasn't pleased, but her independent streak was one of the reasons he loved her.

The warden held his hand out. "Deal is a deal, Mr. Merthane."

Talon sized up the guards one more time. He was exhausted and still hurting from Apex. Shrugging, he ejected a chip from his wrist pad and placed it in the warden's hand. "Nice doing business with you."

"Ye—"

Dayna punched the warden square in the face, cutting off his response and knocking him out. The guards made no move to arrest them, so Talon passed the warden's chip to them. He and Dayna stepped over the warden's unconscious body and into the processing center.

Just as she'd promised, Dayna had three of the ugliest vecks he'd ever seen lined up and covered by the other two guards. He was sure they were getting a cut of Dayna's payment—probably all of it now since she'd be leaving with him. Each of the prisoners' hands were bound together by carbon steel chains. Dayna had sent him their files to read on his journey to Aval, so he knew the basics of their crimes and incarcerations. What he really wanted to know, though, was how they felt about Maxim Ultra.

There was a four-armed alien with crimson skin called Crag— at least, that was his prison name. He also wore some kind of brace on his knee. Talon looked to Dayna as he pointed at the brace.

"Ultra," she whispered with a nod.

Another alien named Zeor had orange skin with sharp teeth. From the file, he knew that Zeor's brother hadn't been as lucky in his encounter with Maxim as Crag had been.

"Sorry for your loss," he said.

Zeor responded with a gurgling growl.

At the end of the lineup was the crown jewel of the group, a beefy Inwain called Elkeith. The stink coming off of the fat veck was repulsive, but he looked strong and from what it said in his file, he could definitely handle himself in a fight.

"Gentlemen," Talon began, pulling a data pad from one of his vest pouches, "you have been selected to participate in a little game hunting. My name is Talon Merthane." He let that settle on the group for a moment. Once he received looks of recognition, he continued. "You have been chosen by me personally to bring in a fugitive that you are all familiar with—one Maxim Ultra."

CHAPTER 15

Max ran his hand over the back of his neck several times, enjoying the feel of his new haircut. After he and Alesha parted ways, he'd found the ship's barber and had him shear off the majority of the mop that had been on his head as well as his beard. With the shave and haircut, things felt like they were actually getting back to normal.

He stood outside the *Galactic Dream*'s banquet hall, waiting for Alesha to turn up. While she had bought a gown for the evening—a gown he hadn't seen yet—he'd brought a suit down from the *Sequel* that he always had on hand in case things got fancy. Well, fancy by Earth standards. Nothing in his paltry wardrobe could compete with the outlandish alien fashions parading through the archway to the massive dining room.

His was a simple black suit that hung loosely on him thanks to his stay on Aval. He'd toyed with the idea of rolling up in a t-shirt and jeans. *Because, fuck Robert, that's why*. He could understand his friend's reluctance to meet with him, but to shut him out completely? That was shitty.

He gazed into the banquet hall. Passengers milled about, mingling before the Captain graced them with his presence. All the banquet tables hovered above the floor, anchored in place by small metal moorings built into the deck. Max had seen similar setups in other fancy dining establishments. Each table had elaborate settings including holographic centerpieces depicting interpretive dancers performing in another part of the ship.

Massive windows lined the wall, revealing the shifting colors of the Cardon Tunnel outside. Discovered millennia ago by the Cardon family, the Tunnels were interstellar pathways through the galaxy left behind by an unknown alien race. The Cardons had stumbled upon them by accident and charged spacefarers a fee to use them. Travelers could tour the stars without the tunnels, of course, but they'd probably end up dead before reaching their destination. Sci-fi movies back on Earth made it look so easy. Little did they know that there was just as much traffic in the Cardon Lanes as there was on I-95.

What a scam.

The *Galactic Dream*, though, seemed to be on a special, private lane that would give its passengers a delay-free voyage. The soothing rainbow of swirling colors was punctuated by stray arcs of lightning. He thought he'd never see them again. It was easy to get hypnotized while flying through the tunnels, so it was usually best to let the computer take over at that point, because if you nodded off and hit the "rumble strip," you were probably already dead. Max had seen ships careen off into the tunnel walls in the past—it wasn't a pretty end, though the explosions did contrast nicely with the colors. It seemed Baron Zeth really had spared no expense when it came to his flagship—at least, that's what all the promo materials plastered with his face said.

Max didn't know much about Zeth—Glintock and Alesha filled him in on most of it. The guy was apparently some rich muckety-muck who'd made his name initially in rare mineral mining. His sister, Sestra, was a wealthy recluse, while Zeth had his hands into everything with his luxury cruise line being just the tip of the iceberg. Glintock told him Zeth might even be making a play to buy into the Cardon Lanes. It wouldn't have surprised him—rich assholes like Zeth had a need to control everything and then stamp their name on it.

A redhead passed into his field of vision. His head snapped around to get a good look at her. Normally, it wouldn't be an issue to give a woman a second glance, but ever since he started seeing Sierra, he found himself scrutinizing every woman he came into contact with. Just thinking about what his hallucinations could mean caused his palms to moisten.

It's impossible. She's dead. Sure, I'm still having nightmares about her, but it's been awhile since I've seen her all over the place. I hope I'm not going crazy—should probably talk to someone about it.

Ignoring his fears, he patted his pocket. The case holding Gelf's candies felt too light for his taste. They'd have to figure something out.

"Good evening, Maxim."

He almost jumped out of his suit at the sound of Roeger's voice just behind him. He'd been so consumed with his Sierra terrors he hadn't heard the quiet whirring of Roeger's joints. Taking a moment to straighten his tie, he regained his cool.

"How's it going, Roeger?"

"I am fine. Why, should I not be?"

He sounded overly defensive. Maybe he needed a diagnostic check. "Just making conversation, buddy. You need to relax."

"*You* need to relax. Why do *I* need to relax?" He looked around with jerky motions. Was it possible for bots to be high on drugs?

"Is everything okay? You seem, I don't know, a little out of sorts."

Roeger glanced around once more before looking back at Max. "I am fine, Maxim. Where is Agent Glintock? Is he not joining us for dinner?"

Max shrugged. "Who knows? He didn't come back to the room. I figured he was moping around the ship."

Again, Roeger's head twitched back and forth. He held his hands in front of him, fingers clacking together. He looked like a nervous Homer Simpson.

"Roeger, is there something you need to te—"

"Evening gents," Gelf said as he sidled up beside Roeger, who jumped back a step from him, glancing between Gelf and Max. "I'm surprised you're joining us for dinner, Roeger. What exactly do you eat?"

"I-ah, I am mainly here to see Robert."

"Oh, Mr. Big Shot Captain, huh? I thought you'd be exploring the ship or something." He looked squarely at the bot. "That seems like something you'd do. Speaking of big shots, where's Glintock? Did he get flushed out an airlock? I mean, with his personality, he couldn't have gotten lucky or anything."

Roeger emitted a high pitched whine before heading off into the dining hall at a speedy pace.

Max was thoroughly confused. "Do you know what that was all about?"

Gelf wore a tight smile. "Possibly. Your pal, Glintock, really does *not* trust me."

"*I* trust you. That's all that matters. Any idea where our taskmaster got off to?"

"Boss, I have no ide—" Turning to face Max, he paused with a stupefied look. "Oh, mama," was all that escaped Gelf's gaping mouth.

Max turned. His chest seized, unable to draw breath.

Alesha sauntered toward them in a tight, midnight blue gown with a keyhole cutout showing off her cleavage. She wore her hair up, held in place with a diamond clip. That didn't take anything away from the glittering jewels dangling from her ears. She was, in a word, stunning.

Gelf patted Max on the arm as he headed into the banquet hall. "Good luck with that, Boss."

Alesha stopped in front of him, striking a pose. "What d'you think, Earth Boy?"

"I think I'm curious about where you picked up those earrings, seeing as they were *not* in the shops we visited earlier," he said with a wink. They were blue like sapphires, but with dark tendrils of liquid moving and shifting inside them. They had a name he couldn't pronounce and were very highly valued on the black market.

She flashed an innocent look. "Oh these old things? I scored them on a job. Guess I forgot to tell the client about them. I have to say, I'm kind of disappointed you're only interested in the earrings."

"I did that on purpose. You know you look absolutely gorgeous."

"Yes I know, but sometimes a woman likes to hear compliments."

"And you're so modest too." He held his arm out for her.

She shot him a withering look before finally taking his arm. "Well, I'll say that you're looking nice tonight, though that suit's seen better days."

"No, it's me who has." He shrugged. "They didn't exactly feed me all that well on Aval."

"I don't imagine they did, but you could tighten it up a bit."

She was teasing him, but her critique opened the door to a very real problem for him. "They don't pay you for being in prison either."

"You know you can always come to me for money if you need it, Max."

"No thanks. That's a debt I never want to owe."

"Why, because I'm a woman and you're an ignorant Earthling?"

"No, because I'd never hear the end of it."

Her lip twisted, but she stayed quiet.

She knows I'm right.

They entered the banquet hall, descending the wide staircase slowly. He glanced over at her and couldn't help smiling. She was easily the most beautiful woman in the room and she was on his arm. It may have been a shallow source of pride, but it *was* quite the ego boost.

"You really do look beautiful tonight."

She smiled confidently. "I know."

They moved across the room to the large round table where Gelf had already set up shop. Roeger remained standing, still appearing jittery and looking around the room like he was waiting for something or someone.

As Max and Alesha approached the table, an older humanoid couple with light green skin stood up and hustled away. Gelf wore a self-satisfied smile.

"All right, what did you say to them?" Max asked as he pulled Alesha's chair out for her.

"Hey Boss, it's not my fault they can't take a joke." Gelf barked a nasty laugh as he looked after the offended party. Other passengers at nearby tables gawked at him with uncomfortable expressions.

As Alesha sat down, she glanced at Gelf and passed Max an annoyed look. Then she searched the table. "Wait, where's your babysitter?"

"Probably following up a phantom lead," Gelf said with a laugh.

Max's brow crinkled as he looked at his friend.

"Maxim," Roeger butt in, "may I speak with you about something?"

"Sure, what's up Roeg—?"

A drum roll blared through the hall. Above them, multiple holo-screens lit up, showing a black man with a neatly-trimmed moustache and closely-cropped afro in a white uniform entering the hall. He smiled and waved to the passengers. It was Robert.

He looked to be in his element as he basked in the warm ovation from the gathered passengers. As the floating camera followed Robert, Max noted that he paid particular attention to the prettier women. Some things never changed.

Max took a seat beside Alesha, eyes glued to the screen.

"Does he look fat to you?" she asked.

"Well, the camera adds ten pounds—or so they say."

"They who?"

"Uh…everyone."

"Well, he must be using a big camera, because he's fat."

He rolled his eyes. She sounded like a mean girl from Earth. Sure, Robert had put on a few pounds—that was to be expected in such a cushy job—but, it didn't seem to be hindering his effect on the ladies. Then he looked at the strained buttons on his uniform and the stiffness with which Robert walked. The uniform was so tight, it looked as if he couldn't bend.

He might split his pants.

"You'd better go talk to him now before he splits his pants." It felt like the old days. Alesha knew exactly what he was thinking.

"I *am* going to talk to him, but I want to at least eat first—I'm starving."

"Maxim?" Roeger tried to interject.

"And I think you should talk to him now," Alesha said. "Do it before he's waist deep in women. You know how Robert is."

"*Waist deep in women?* He's not a rock star, 'Lesha. He's a cruise ship captain."

"Yes and he's also the man responsible for their safety and getting them to their destination alive. You take star-hopping for granted, Max. Not everyone gets to see what we see on a regular basis. For some of these women, this will be the only time they travel to other planets. It's very romantic, so why not bed the guy who's driving the boat?"

She had a point—he'd never really looked at it that way. His travels with his father had definitely made space travel more commonplace. However, there was one thing Alesha had totally wrong.

"After where I've been, don't ever think I take any of this for granted."

She gave him a half-smile. "I'm sorry. Just falling into old habits, I guess."

"You mean stating things like they're facts?"

"I guess you've got me there." She paused. "For a minute there, it started to feel like—"

"Old times?"

Her smile was slow to emerge, just teasing the corners of her mouth before finally revealing itself. "Yeah."

"Vecking lovebirds," Gelf groaned. "Just take her back to the room and veck her, Boss. Let me and the bot eat in peace." He got up and moved to another table, prompting a few of his new tablemates to find a different place to eat.

"Maxim? I really need to—"

"It can wait, Roeger," he replied, focusing his full attention on Alesha. "It can wait."

Again, Roeger emitted a high-pitched whine. "I think I will attempt to find Agent Glintock." He sped away from the table, leaving Max and Alesha alone.

Alesha watched him go, a tiny V forming between her brows. "What if Glintock's in trouble?"

"What kind of trouble could he have gotten into? We're on a cruise ship."

Their conversation was interrupted by the sound of Robert's voice filling the banquet hall. "Thank you, one and all for sailing with us on the *Galactic Dream*. I'm your captain, Robvere Langua."

As a smattering of applause broke out through the room, Max and Alesha shared a look.

"*Robvere?*" she asked.

"You're sailing the stars on one of the most advanced pleasure vessels in the galaxy. Every passenger need has been thought of in the design of both the ship itself and the amenities we provide. If something isn't up to your level of satisfaction, seek me out and I'll do everything in my power to help make your voyage more enjoyable."

Max noted an attractive woman in uniform standing near Robert with a digital pad. She had flowing blonde hair and a petite figure. "Who's that, his assistant?"

"I bet he's vecking her," Alesha said.

"Rob was always more of a brunette kind of guy."

She rolled her eyes. "Please. If she's his assistant, she's there, so he's vecking her."

"For now," Robert continued. "Please get comfortable and let our stellar chefs take you on a tour of cuisines from all the planets we'll be visiting on our travels. Thank you for sailing with us. It is my pleasure to be your captain."

A much more enthused response broke out, probably because there was mention of food, and the holo-screens powered down. From their table, Max could see Robert taking his seat. Of course, the table was loaded with lovely ladies, but there was one empty chair.

"If you ask me," Alesha said. "You should stick your ass in that seat and talk to Robert. If he's been dodging you, better to put him on the defensive. If you approach him in front of all his honeys, he'll have to acknowledge you at least. Then we can get off this ship and get on with it."

"Right. All business." Again, his alone time with Alesha dissolved into disappointment. "Look, I'm going to talk to him, but I don't want to make a scene and get thrown in the brig—or worse, out the airlock."

"He's not going to do anything like that."

"I don't know. Success changes people."

It was a pointed remark that sent daggers shooting out of her eyes. "I'm not having this argument again, Max. We're here for a reason—get to it."

A waiter arrived with the first course of their meal—a leafy salad with blue lettuce. What he thought were noodles turned out to be worms of some kind as they moved through the foliage.

"A Jhozan Blue dish from Mintar," the waiter announced as he set the plates in front of them. "Enjoy."

Max was hungry, but not *that* hungry. "I'll go talk to Robert."

"Thank you, sweetie," Alesha called after him mockingly with a wave.

He ignored her tone as he crossed the room. Why was he so hesitant? Was it the grandeur of the whole thing, or the fact that Robert was now in a real position of power? They'd known each other as kids, but had lost contact after high school. Max went to the stars and Robert went into the Air Force Academy. When Max had reconnected with him years later, Robert was flying commercial jetliners and sifting through the wreckage of his failed marriage. Max came to him offering an escape, no matter how crazy it might have sounded. Why would Robert want to escape from *this* cushy reality? It would be an uphill climb—tougher than convincing any of the others, even Alesha. At least *she* was talking to him.

Stopping his approach for a brief moment, he took a deep breath to steel his nerves. Then he put his fifty-thousand-watt smile in place and moved to the empty chair, following the lead of the ladies at the table as they chuckled at something Robert had said.

"Oh Robvere, you're hilarious," Max said as he plopped down in the seat.

Robert's eyes bulged so much, Max was sure they were set to pop out of his head. "I'm sorry sir, I believe that seat is taken."

Sir? "Robvere, come now, don't tell me you don't remember your old friend, Maxim Ultra."

Robert's gaze narrowed. "Vaguely."

"Then let me refresh your memory. You see ladies, Robvere here has been a talented pilot all his life. When I had need of a co-pilot, I went to fetch him on a dreadful, backwater planet. Robvere was in a sad, sad state I'm afraid. You see, he and his wi—"

The table jumped a bit as Robert hopped up from his chair. His expression quickly shifted from embarrassed to jolly. "Of course, Maxim Ultra! How long has it been? At least three years since you got yourself in that nasty legal entanglement?"

He had to admit, Robert could spar with the best of them. It didn't matter to Max what was said in front of the women, though—he wasn't the one trying to impress them. "Oh, that's all cleared up now, old friend."

"Well, what brings you on board the *Galactic Dream?* Getting away from it all now that you've gotten away with it all?"

Asshole. "Not quite. I'm actually here just to see you, if you have a minute?"

"Not really, Maxim. As you can see, I'm entertaining guests."

Pausing for a moment, Max nodded deliberately before turning to the woman sitting to his right. "Has the Captain regaled you with the time he was stranded on the planet Birvack? You see, he and I were on the hunt for a very rare item when we got separated and Robvere ran afoul of the local villagers."

The woman, who had vibrant violet eyes, gazed at Max with anticipation. "What happened?"

"Well, the chieftain's daughter had caught old Robvere's eye and her father decided to punish him by st—"

"Actually Mr. Ultra, if you wouldn't mind, I think I do have a moment for us to speak privately. If you'd step over here, please."

Max winked at the women. "Ladies, if you'll excuse me, the Captain and I need to discuss some business. Won't be a moment."

He pushed away from the table, walking over to Robert, who spoke with his assistant.

"Offer all of them my apologies and a tour of the bridge. This will only take a few minutes," Robert said softly.

"Yes, sir," the blonde said with a scathing look at Max.

"Hello, beautiful," he replied to her expression. *Kill 'em with kindness.*

She rolled her eyes before shifting back to all smiles for the women at Robert's table. The Captain grabbed Max's arm and dragged him over to the staircase, somehow managing to make it look like he was casually ushering Max away from the table.

"What do you want, Max?" he said once they were finally alone.

"Nice to see you too, buddy. *Robvere Langua?* What happened to Robert Land?"

"Keep it down, will you? I had to jazz up my name a little bit for the passengers. Make it a little more exotic. We're selling fantasy here after all." He paused for a moment. "When did you get out?"

"You should know, I've been trying to contact you."

"I know. I was just being polite. I've been ignoring you."

"Wow, you're really pissed, aren't you?"

"Of course I am, Max. Let me paint the picture for you. I was a pilot, on Earth, happy."

"You were miserable and you know it. Your marriage had fallen apart and you were just drifting through life, drinking too much, screwing anything with a pulse."

"How did that change when you brought me up here? Hm?"

"It didn't, but I gave you a purpose. I showed you how to live again."

Robert laughed harshly. "You are so full of shit. You actually believe that, don't you?"

Actually, he did, to a degree. Maybe he'd laid it on a bit thick. "Look, you were wallowing back on Earth, I—"

"Yes, but I was *on Earth*, Max. You brought me up here and then abandoned me when you ran off with Sierra. Alesha was fine, she grew up in this craziness, but I was lost, completely out of my depth. We were friends and you dumped me in order to follow that floozy around."

"I was trying to protect you guys. I knew the job was going to be dicey. I didn't want you involved. And don't make it sound like I plucked you off of Earth and then just let you drift in space. We had a few good years before Sierra came along."

"The crew was the only life I knew up here, Max. And when you left, it was gone."

Max looked him up and down. "You seem to be doing all right now."

"Exactly. Get the hell off my ship."

"What? We're paying customers."

"We?"

"Alesha's here with me, Roeger too. We're getting the band back together." He knew that wasn't exactly the truth, but he had to sell it. Robert was way angrier than he thought he'd be. Max had to make it right and he was doing a lousy job.

"Hah! Yeah right. Did you even listen to anything I just said to you? I have a great job now. I get to see the galaxy and *not* have bounty hunters shooting at me. After what I'd seen, I couldn't possibly go back to Earth and be happy, so I had to make do. No way am I leaving this gig—especially not to help you out, asshole."

Max paused. How was he screwing this up so badly? He hadn't truly considered how Robert would react to seeing him again, thinking it would have been a simple matter of convincing him to leave his sweet job. There was too much bad blood there, though. No way was he going to come back to the *Sequel*. Max did the only thing he could—probably what he should have done as soon as he'd sat down at Robert's table.

"I'm sorry, Rob. I didn't know my leaving affected you like that. I thought, even with all your problems, you'd land on your feet. Of course, I wasn't planning on heading off to prison either. I'm glad you're doing well, but think about this: would you be doing this well if I hadn't taken you off of Earth? Where would you be now if our paths had never crossed again?"

"It's all hypothetical, Max. I only deal with what is and what has been."

"Then deal with this: Kalen Vandeir is on the loose and he's looking for anyone who might have information about the job I pulled with him and Sierra. That includes everyone on the *Sequel*. I'm rounding the team up so we can protect each other."

That revelation seemed to give Robert a moment of pause, but not for long. "Thank you for your concern, but we have an excellent security force onboard the *Galactic Dream*." Robert turned on his heel and walked back toward his table.

Max reached for his old friend, but Robert was already gone. *Some wounds never heal, I guess.* Dejected, he shook his head and walked back to his table. He'd failed to bring Robert back into the fold, but what upset Max the most was that his friend hated him.

"That looks like it went about as well as I thought it would," Alesha said with a smirk.

"Not now, 'Lesha. Not now." He landed in his seat in a heap. All interest in eating had vanished.

Her expression softened. "What happened?"

"He hates my guts."

"Well, honey, what did you expect?"

"I was hoping that you'd all understand that I was trying to protect you. I wasn't running out on you, not really. I just didn't want anyone to get hurt. In the process, though, I hurt everybody. I don't know how to make it right."

Her hand moved to his head, but hesitated before she started ruffling his hair. "You might not be able to."

He was sure she was just talking about Robert, but he couldn't help his voice catching in his throat when he spoke. "Do you really think that?"

"Baby, it's like I said, things will never be the way they were. That's just life. If Robbie doesn't come along, it's not the end of the universe, is it? I mean, we've survived worse situations."

He grimaced, knowing to what she was referring. They didn't talk about Swann Nestive much, because neither of them was proud of the places their shared rimi addiction had taken them. Ultimately, though, the experience had brought them closer together.

Now he was using again. He'd been deliberately keeping Alesha out of his mind when it came to the rimi, because he didn't want to imagine what would happen if she found out the truth. Whatever had been developing between them would be over. His head hung a little lower.

Her fingers ran through his hair with a little more vigor. "That doesn't mean, though, that things won't be…better."

Max jerked his head up to meet Alesha's gaze. She was looking at him differently than she had since he'd come back. There was something familiar there, something he wanted to grab hold of. "Thanks."

She pulled her hand away with a sigh. "You know, I've got a pounding headache. Walk me back to my room?"

Even as a thrill went through his chest, his eyes narrowed. "Okay...."

"There's nothing sinister here, Max. I highly doubt you want to sit here and eat this crap by yourself. So because my head is throbbing, be a gentleman, walk me to my room, and then go to your cabin and order room service or something."

He stood up and held his arm out to her. "Right. Sorry."

"Thank you."

As he escorted her out of the dining hall, he made sure to pass within glaring distance of Robert's table. Robert's bimbos ensured he never noticed.

As they boarded a glass elevator on the concourse, Max leaned against the railing running along the back wall. Alesha stood in the center of the car for a moment before joining him. He didn't look up. She sidled up to him and nudged him.

"Don't beat yourself up over Robbie. He was probably shocked to see you and it all just came out of him like that. Plus, he's got this posh job now and I'm sure he doesn't want his ex-convict friend vecking it up for him."

That made him chuckle.

She laughed with him, but then put her hand to her head. "Ow, I shouldn't have done that."

He put his arm around her shoulders. The rimi in his jacket would ease her pain, but that clearly wasn't an option. He kissed her forehead instead. "I'd better round the crew up—tell them we're shoving off."

She patted his arm. "Don't do that just yet. We're not going anywhere until we reach the next port. Let them enjoy themselves."

The elevator deposited them on one of the residence decks and he walked her down to her room. She keyed the door open and turned back to him.

"Do you want to come in?"

He got that funny flutter in his stomach. "Are you sure?"

"You're absolutely miserable. Come inside and keep me company."

"I don't want to be a pity fuck, Alesha."

"*Pity fuck?* Who says that's happening? I have a headache, remember?" She walked into the room, taking her heels off as she did so, disappearing around a corner.

The dimly-lit entrance yawned in front of him. He wondered if Alesha's knock on the head in Apex was affecting her decision-making. If she was compromised, he didn't want to take advantage of her. He wasn't that guy. If she *was* feeling okay, he *really* didn't want this to be a pity fuck.

She moved back into view. "Are you coming in or not?"

The door snapped shut behind him as he passed through the archway.

She turned her back to him. "I can't reach the thing in the back. Unhook me?"

"Uh, sure?"

She heaved a sigh. "Max, I'm not going to parade around in the nude, but it's nothing you haven't seen anyway. Don't make me have to call Roeger in here to help me."

"All right, all right." Maybe she *did* just want some company.

Apparently in space, no one had ever heard of zippers. The garment closed in the back by some kind of smart-seal that was activated and released by a button built into the fabric. As he stepped up behind her, he had to resist the urge to run his hands all over her naked back. Her new perfume was intoxicating. Reaching for the release on her dress, he inhaled deeply.

"You smell amazing."

"I thought you'd like that."

"What is it?"

"Randulian Mist, taken from the flowers in the Randulian Mountains of Modan."

"It smells great."

The bottom of her dress opened near the small of her back. "Thank you. Make yourself comfortable. I have to get a compress for my head."

"Okay."

The rooms weren't the closet-sized holes in the wall he'd expected. What he'd found instead were still small rooms, but designed more like hotel rooms.

As he collapsed into a chair set against the wall, his stomach reminded him that he had indeed missed dinner. He reached for a data pad stamped with the ship's logo, hoping to find some kind of room service menu. He looked up at the opening of the bathroom door.

Alesha stood in the doorway wearing nothing but a white towel. She'd let her hair down and tucked a few strands behind her ear as she stepped back into the room. She held a damp washcloth in her hand.

"Sorry if this is a little too comfortable. I was planning on going to bed soon," she said as she sat on the bed. She laid down, placing the compress over her eyes and reaching out to him. "Come sit with me." She patted the edge of the bed.

"What is this? Are you *trying* to torture me?"

She smiled. "No, if I wanted to torture you, I'd tell you to stay over there and I'd do a lot of this." She opened and closed her legs with a giggle, giving him an unimpeded view.

"Are you sure you're feeling okay? You hit your head pretty hard in Apex." He had to ask.

"You think I'm making impaired decisions?" She chuckled. "I'm still waiting for you."

He moved to sit beside her on the bed, wanting nothing more than to snake his hand up her leg.

"You want me right now, don't you?"

"You know I do. But after where I've been, if Roeger had a body like yours, I'd probably want to bang him too."

She sat up, the compress falling into her lap. That mischievous smile he remembered from his dreams played on her face. "Can I tell you a secret?"

"Sure." *God, she is beautiful.*

Her head shook slowly. "I don't have a headache."

"I figured as much. Why tell me that, then?"

Her hand moved to his face. "I didn't want you to think it was going to be that easy." She moved her fingers through his hair, stroking the back of his scalp with her nails. "I like this look," she whispered. "This is the Max I remember."

He smiled. "I thought we couldn't live in the past."

She inched closer to him. "Then this is the Max I want to go forward with."

Her breath was hot on his lips. Desire coursed through his veins like a drug. He wanted her more than anything, but he had to hear her say it. He had to know she wasn't doing this just to make him feel better.

"I missed you."

He pressed his lips to hers. All the fear, frustration, and desire he'd felt over the last two and a half years flowed into the kiss. She pulled him closer to her, giving as good as she got.

His lips moved down to her neck, making her sigh like she always used to. He kissed her again as he worked getting his clothes off as fast as possible. Lucky her, she only had to whip off her towel, revealing the body she'd teased him with at the house on Modan.

Once he'd finally gotten the last of his clothing off, he fell back into bed with her, moving his lips to anyplace on her body she'd let him go. Her hands ran up and down his back, pausing longer with each pass. Her body jumped as she sat up.

"Baby, what happened to you?"

She'd found the scars—mementoes of his time on Aval and all the *friends* he'd made there. "Occupational hazard." They weren't something he liked to dwell on.

Alesha's fingers traced the damage lightly, her touch gentle and loving. "I-I had no idea."

He sat up beside her, feeling the mood dying. "Aval…wasn't a fun time."

She touched his face gently before pulling him in for another kiss and back onto the bed.

Under the covers they frolicked—actually *frolicked*—as their hands and mouths explored each other's bodies. Muscle memory drew Max back to the places he knew would stimulate her as it all came back to him. He gently pushed her legs apart.

She pulled him closer, silently begging him. He was poised to enter her.

The ship rumbled violently in tandem with the dull roar of an explosion.

"You have *got* to be kidding me!" Max exclaimed.

"What *was* that?"

"Oh, just somebody shitting all over my triumphant return." He paused. Screams sounded in the hallway. "Get dressed. We've got to get to the *Sequel*."

CHAPTER 16

Matthias heard voices on the edge of his consciousness—echoing voices mixed with clomping boots. He eased his eyes open. Lifeless eyes belonging to a man with a hole in his forehead stared back at him. Despite all he'd seen in his career, waking up face-to-face with a corpse was still a horrific reality. An uncontrollable shiver worked through him.

Full consciousness brought a return of his senses and an easing of his disorientation. A pulsing pain radiated from the knot on his head. Though the room spun, he could see he was prone on the deck. He figured he'd been moved from the cargo hold, but to where? The area was bathed in red light, but that didn't mask the dark pool of blood congealing beneath the dead man's head.

Boots approached from down the hall. Matthias snapped his eyes shut, relieved to be free of looking at the dead man for a few moments. The boots squeaked to a stop near his head.

"Can't believe we had to haul this vecker down here," a man's voice said. It was a young voice—the voice of inexperience. He was also practically on top of Matthias.

"Gondal's orders—don't question 'em." The new voice was gruffer. Matthias envisioned a crusty space veteran. Gondal must have been the man with the white beard from earlier.

How long have I been unconscious?

"I guess what I'm saying is, why not just kill him? No witnesses, right? I mean, we killed this other guy here with no problem."

"Normally, yeah, but this guy's GAC. He's way more valuable than ship's security. Who knows what secrets he's got rolling around in his head? We'll finish setting these charges and then slap him around a little to see what he knows. Two hours should be plenty of time to get him to talk. He may be able to help us find what we're looking for."

"What if he doesn't give us any information?" the kid asked.

"That's easy," the older man said as they grunted and proceeded back down the hall with slow steps. "We blow the vecker up." Their laughter wormed into Matthias and settled in his stomach like a block of ice.

He risked peeking out from half-closed eyelids to see the men lugging a large container between them. Were they planning on blowing up the ship? The older man echoed Gondal's words from earlier. They had to be looking for the statue. But he still wasn't sure who else they were looking for or who they were themselves. If he wanted more information, he'd have to follow them. Once he was sure the two men had left the immediate area, he opened his eyes fully. His hands were bound at the wrists in front of him, so after some doing, he was able to get his feet.

The corridor extended a long way in both directions with no clues as to where he'd been moved. Nothing in sight looked to be a suitable weapon. The metal cuffs on his wrists were large and bulky, covering most of his forearms. They would have to do.

As he crept down the hallway, he attempted to pat his pockets, despite the bonds on his arms. He couldn't feel whether he still had his credentials or not.

I've got to get these damn cuffs off.

It was slow going as he tried to block out his throbbing headache. The corridor sloped downward into a large room that held three medium-sized escape pods as well as stacks of smaller containers. The two men set explosive charges around the room— programmable mines with a switch detonator secured to one of the saboteurs' belts.

But why blow up these escape pods? Why not the engines?

He studied how the men arranged the bombs. No matter how many they stowed in this compartment, the explosion wouldn't destroy the vessel—it probably wouldn't kill any passengers, either. The emergency fail safes installed on all cruise ships would contain the explosion with blast doors to mitigate the damage. He closed his eyes, nodding in understanding.

They're not trying to destroy the ship—they're trying to strand it.

The explosion would definitely blow a hole in the ship's hull, which would instantly dump the ship out of its Cardon Tunnel as an emergency precaution. Considering the men were on a timetable—if Crusty's mention of two hours meant anything— Matthias surmised that someone would intercept the ship at the pre-arranged coordinates. The armed men would probably take the ship hostage until they turned up the statue and the crew would be helpless, unable to get back into the Cardon Tunnels until repairs were made. It was a decent plan—one that would probably work if he didn't stop them.

He was about to spring into action when he heard footsteps behind him.

Nakra.

Matthias swung his arms around in a wide arc, hoping to connect with his cuffs, but the woman standing behind him caught his arms. She tossed him into a pile of crates.

Pain cropped up all over his body, but his pride was just as injured. No one should be able to sneak up on him. *I* have *been out of the field a long time.*

"What's goin' on over there?" Crusty called out.

"What's happening," the woman replied harshly. "Is that you idiots didn't make sure the prisoner was unconscious like I told you to." At least a head taller than Matthias, the woman had an athletic, muscular build. Her husky voice belied a strikingly beautiful face with deep green eyes.

"Don't veck him up too much," the old man told her. "We may need to pump him for information."

"That's right," Matthias said. "And if I don't cooperate, you'll just blow me up with the rest of this room."

"Veck!" the younger man said. "This bastard heard us!"

"Son, I've been at this a long time. Are we doing this or not? I'd like to get these cuffs off sooner than later."

The woman smirked. "You sound very sure of yourself."

"I'm always sure of myself."

She moved toward him with an eager, hungry expression.

Crusty didn't seem interested. "I'm too old for this nakra. You two take care of him while I set the rest of the charges."

The younger man didn't need to be told twice. He drew a laser dagger from his belt as he rushed at Matthias. The blade glowed with a bright yellow light—very easy to see in the dimly lit room. He slashed at Matthias, who blocked the attack with his bonds. The dagger burned a dark furrow into the manacles.

The woman lunged at Matthias, but he ducked her grabbing arms, delivering a shot to her solar plexus. The plates of armor beneath her black uniform blunted most of the strike, but it at least got her to back off for a moment, allowing him to defend against the man's next attack. This time the dagger glanced off the side of his bonds, but it still sheared a thin ribbon of metal off the cuffs.

Matthias' eyes darted between his two attackers. Neither carried a sidearm. That meant his best chance at defeating them was to get the laser dagger away from the young hot head. Matthias *was* always sure of himself, but defeating two opponents while shackled might have been too much.

The woman glanced at the kid. "A concerted attack, Yevin." She moved to one side of Matthias while Yevin circled from the opposite side.

"You're going to let this horvorka boss you around, son?"

"She's my superior—it's understood."

All right, so he's not as hot headed as I'd hoped and they are *some kind of paramilitary outfit. How the veck am I getting out of this?*

"Strike!" the woman cried.

Yevin slashed at Matthias' head while the woman leveled a kick at his legs.

Matthias ducked under the blade, launching himself into Yevin's mid-section, side-stepping the woman and creating distance between the pair. As Yevin brought the blade down in an arc, Matthias bashed his manacles into the kid's elbow and then into his forearm, dislodging the dagger. As the weapon clattered to the deck, Matthias punched his arms outward, clocking Yevin in the head with the heavy metal cuffs.

The strike knocked a visibly woozy Yevin back as Matthias spun around to deal with the man's superior. The woman's fist was already speeding toward his head. Landing on his jaw, her punch sent a jarring bolt of pain through his skull. He staggered back, but the woman kept coming. Her speed was formidable. He wondered if she'd been enhanced in some way.

A defensive move put his metal cuffs in the path of her fist. As she connected, he felt the vibration run up his arm. She yanked her hand away with a grunt, anger streaking her face. Matthias took his opportunity, dropping to the floor and kicking out at her knee with all his strength. He caught her just the right way, bending her knee unnaturally. She screamed, crumpling to the ground.

Matthias' victory lasted a split-second as his side erupted in searing pain. With a howl, he spun away to see a surprised Yevin, his dagger sticking out of Matthias' flank. Matthias swung his metal-encased arms to keep the kid at bay. Sweat broke out over his body as the dagger burned him from the inside. He pulled the laser blade out slowly, the heat cauterizing the wound as he did so. Staggering, he turned to face Yevin, brandishing the dagger, but the kid decided to double-down and charge at him. Matthias didn't even feel much resistance as the dagger sunk into Yevin's belly. He jerked the blade upwards, slicing through Yevin's internals, and delivered a blow to the kid's head for good measure.

Yevin sank to the floor, dead.

Matthias winced as he turned to see the woman struggling to drag herself toward the exit. He moved to intercept her when he heard movement behind him.

"That's far enough, Agent," Crusty's voice echoed.

Pain throbbed from Matthias' wound as he turned back around. Crusty had a laser pistol leveled at him.

"Damn sorry about that gash in your side." He looked down at Yevin. "Stupid kid. Taking a wound like that probably means you won't crack under questioning."

"Probably not. How about you? Who do you work for?"

The man shrugged. "You're in no position to as—"

Matthias threw the laser dagger, embedding it in the man's throat. His last words were lost in a gurgling that bubbled out of his mouth in a bloody froth as he fell to the floor.

"I have other ways to find out."

"We'll tell you nothing!" the woman shrieked as she dragged herself across the deck.

Matthias limped over to her. She clawed at his legs as if trying to pull herself to her feet. He swatted her hands away before clubbing her in the head with his cuffs. As her head bounced off the floor, he eased himself to the ground.

"What a vecking mess."

Several minutes later, Matthias crouched beside his bound, but breathing captive. Since the dagger had cauterized his own wound, he wasn't afraid of bleeding to death, but he still moved gingerly. He'd found a cache of weapons in addition to the laser dagger and pistol. A rifle, complete with a scope, was strapped to his back, while he clipped the detonator to his belt. Thankfully, he also found the release key for his cuffs.

He had about ninety minutes until the mystery soldiers had been set to blow the explosives. The sooner he could put a stop to their plan, the better, but he needed information first. He smacked the woman in the face lightly. When she didn't respond, he gave her a good whack.

Her eyes blinked open slowly.

"There she is. Your friends are dead, so you might as well cooperate. What was the plan here? Why were you trying to blow a hole in this ship?"

"I'll tell you nothing."

"I have my suspicions, but I want to hear it from you. What was your target?"

The woman set her jaw, but said nothing.

"More importantly, who *are* you people? What's your outfit?"

"You'll get nothing from me, GAC scum."

He cocked his head. "See, that tells me something right there. What are you, some kind of radicals? An insurgent army of some kind?"

She remained stubbornly silent.

"I know you're after the statue. Do you know where it is on the ship?"

Again, nothing. She was good at keeping her mouth shut. Somehow, he had to get this woman to talk. Her organization, whoever they were, unnerved him more than he let on. They were well-funded and in her case, well-trained. He didn't like wildcards—he had to know the truth.

His fingers stroked the hilt of the dagger absent-mindedly. There was one thing he could do to get her to talk. It had been a long time. Back at the start of his career, there had been moments he'd had to use more than punches to get some people to talk. His skills had dulled in the intervening years, but the defiance in the woman's eyes stoked a desire in him to sharpen them.

He drew the laser dagger from his belt. "How about I pluck out one of your eyeballs and we'll see if that gets you talking." He moved over to her, placing the dagger near her face. The heat from the blade caused her skin to perspire. He swallowed hard, fighting back bile. "Last chance."

"I do not fear death, you GAC tool. Dead or alive, my reward is in what comes next. The question for you is, can you do what must be done to defeat us?"

"I don't know. Who are you?"

She spat at him, the globule of saliva splashing against his cheek.

White hot rage flashed through him. He bared his teeth and pressed the dagger against her face. The skin beside her eye sizzled. The tip of the dagger was millimeters from her eyeball.

She didn't flinch. Not once.

He pulled the dagger away, sheathing it, eyes narrowing at the sear mark he'd left on her face.

"I knew you were a coward." She wore a smug smile like a badge of honor.

Reaching for the dagger again, he suppressed the urge to draw it with a trembling hand. Standing, he took a step back from her to quell his fury. He wasn't that person anymore. That demon had been long buried and he had no interest in resurrecting it. He had no problem killing these people—they'd done their share of killing already—but torture was a line he didn't want to cross. "How do you see this ending? Me tucking you into one of those escape pods and letting you walk away? No, let me tell you how this is going to go. Your friends are expecting these charges to go off in just under ninety minutes. I'm going to walk out of here and set them off now, with you still in this room."

That got her attention. Her eyes widened. "Why would you set them off?"

"Do you really think I'm going to hang around here? You're a well-equipped unit. I'm sure you've missed some kind of check-in while playing around with me. It's not my desire to fend off who knows how many of you by myself. If I leave you tied up here instead, someone will come along and free you, sure, but then your plan goes off without a hitch. I don't know who you are, but you're clearly an enemy of the GAC and I can't let you win this one. The statue is too important. So, I blow the charges now, ahead of your timetable, and see what develops. I've already got a ride off this ship. Maybe I flush out the thief or maybe I flush out one of your more talkative operatives. Either way, I win and get to blame you for the explosion and damage to the ship because, let's be honest, who's going to believe that a decorated GAC agent willingly blew a hole in a civilian ship?"

"You could destroy the ship if you do that. Send it careening into the Cardon Lane." She didn't seem afraid, almost as if she were testing him. Maybe she *was* a zealot.

"Come on. We both know how the failsafe works. You were just planning on setting it off later—and not being caught in the blast, of course. The passengers will get a little roughed up, but nothing too serious."

"Perhaps we'll kill all the passengers. That would certainly put a crimp in your plan."

"That's true, it would. *You* won't be killing anybody, though." Did he want to take that chance? *No, can't second-guess myself here. The statue is much more dangerous than whatever these people can do on this one ship.* "Last chance—who are you people?"

She shook her head, defiant to the last.

He shrugged. "Suit yourself. See you in the next life."

"Perhaps you do have sufficient fortitude. You should be working with us, Glintock—working with us to cleanse this galaxy."

Now she sounds exactly *like a zealot.* "No thanks. I have a job." He started to walk away.

"Wait, come back! Glintock!"

Fat chance, there are probably a dozen of you bastards on the way down here. As he walked up the hallway, he unclipped the detonator from his belt. The digital display flashed green. *Oh look at that, it tells me when I'm a safe distance away. That's keen.* Reaching for the nearest handhold on the corridor wall, he double-checked that the ship had the requisite blast doors in place behind him. *This* might *be the dumbest thing I've ever done.* He clicked the detonator's trigger.

The deck lurched beneath his feet as his eardrums thrummed from the deafening explosion. A surge of heat nipped at his back, but was instantly replaced by a loud *whoosh* as the ship's hull cracked open. The blast door slammed shut three feet away, protecting him from both the explosion and the harsh elements of space. He heard a loud clanging on the other side of the door. The deck lurched again as the ship dropped out of the Cardon Tunnel and jerked to a stop. He hung from the wall, gripping the handhold with all his might.

Once the ship finally stabilized, he dropped back to the deck. He whipped out his communicator with the ship's schematics and started on his way toward the main deck and the escape pods found there.

If my man bolts, I'll find him there. I hope.

CHAPTER 17

A thousand drums went off in Litning's ears a split-second before pain whipped through him as his body smacked against the cold, hard deck. Everything was awash in red light as he looked around, his mind trying to process what had happened. He was still in his room on the *Galactic Dream*, but somehow he had fallen off his cot. His bunkmate Neron was also on the floor, his neck twisted queerly.

A siren sliced through his mind like a scythe. He remembered the sound from his orientation. The ship had unexpectedly dropped out of the Cardon Tunnel. Several things could have caused that, but in light of the deafening roar that had woken him, it could have been an explosion.

He heard the supervisor out in the common area. "All right you lugs, this is where you earn your pay! We need you out there—it's chaos!"

Chaos. Passengers would be heading for the escape pods whether the ship was lost or not. Fear did that to people. In the confusion, he could slip away. They were not near Revjekt at all, but he could at least throw off those who were watching him.

The statue. Where is the statue? Disoriented by the noise and red light, he searched the floor like an addict looking for a cache of pills, tossing displaced items all over the small room.

A shadow fell across him. Bijin stood in the doorway as his crewmates scrambled out into the common area.

"It looks like my friends started the party a little early, but no matter. The objective is the same. Give me the statue," Bijin said.

"I would die first."

"My friend, that has always been the plan."

The lizard-man was a blur as he leaped into the room. Instantly, he was on Litning, clawing and hissing. He was so fast, Litning had trouble defending himself. His effort was not helped by the fact that he was starting on the floor and still groping around for the statue at the same time. He managed to grip Bijin's neck and throw him across the small room, but like a spring, the attacker bounced right back.

Litning delivered a gut-punch to the charging Bijin, but the blow did not seem to faze him. No matter how much punishment Litning doled out, Bijin just kept coming. The lizard-man's yellow eyes were wide and crazed as he slashed at Litning with his talon-like nails.

After Litning rebuffed another attack, Bijin drew a nasty, jagged dagger from his belt. He took several swipes, glancing off Litning's arm with at least one of the strikes, drawing blood. Another slash cut into his shoulder. He recoiled, but managed to catch Bijin's wrist as he went in for another strike. Twisting the lizard-man's arm, he forced the dagger free, but within moments of fruitless grappling, Bijin had his hands around Litning's throat. The reptile had a strength that was belied by his slight frame. He had abnormally large hands that allowed him to slowly crush the life from Litning's body.

"You stupid fool," Bijin hissed. "You were bandying that statue around as if no one else would know what it truly is."

Litning's vision dimmed. His chest heaved. Panic blocked the red haze from taking over, keeping him from becoming the killing machine he abhorred, but needed to be in order to prevent his own demise. He slapped at Bijin's hands weakly. How could this spindly alien have overpowered him? His breathing came in wheezing gasps.

Bijin tightened his grip. "Goodbye my Revash frie—"

The jagged blade burst through Bijin's frontal lobe from behind, interrupting his farewell. His grip relaxed as his body slumped forward.

Litning regained his breath in a violent coughing fit as he shoved the lifeless Bijin off him. As the fog in his mind dissipated, he realized Omdil was standing over him, holding the bag with the statue.

"Give that back to me," Litning managed to gasp in between hacking coughs.

"Not a very appreciative tone considering I just saved your life. Of course, if you hadn't thrown your communicator away, I could have warned you about Bijin and his friends before you even stepped on this vessel."

Litning's blood went cold. Only one person would have said such a thing to him—Mondo. It was entirely possible Omdil had disguised his voice whenever he communicated as Mondo, but what about the man Litning met with at the start of the job? Who was he—a surrogate?

"You look confused, Litning."

"How?"

Mondo smiled. "Isn't modern technology a wonder?" He pulled up his sleeve to reveal an electronic device strapped to his forearm. "This little doodad creates an illusory field around me that can make me look like anyone of my choosing. Very handy in my line of work."

"I am sure it is." Litning's eyes locked onto the nylon bag. *I could take it from him, easily.*

Mondo drew a pistol with his free hand. "Don't even think about it."

"The statue does not belong to you."

"Nor to you."

"I have more claim to it than you or your client ever will—whoever he is."

"Really?" Mondo asked. "An exile from your own people?"

Litning arched an eyebrow.

"Don't look so surprised, Litning. It pays for me to be informed. Apparently, that's not one of *your* priorities, though. You don't even know my real name."

Litning bared his teeth, but Mondo was right. He had been so eager to repair the damage with his people, he had not done his due diligence—the price he paid being new to the thievery business.

"No, I think I'm exactly the right person to have Memta." A faraway look took hold in Mondo's eyes. "Can you hear it, Revash? Can you hear her song?" Whoever Mondo really was, he was clearly deranged.

"So, you have the statue. Why not kill me and leave?"

After a moment, Mondo snapped out of his trance. "Because I still have need of you. You see, Bijin's comrades aren't only looking for the statue—they're looking for me too."

"But you can disguise yourself."

"Very true. However, there are quite a lot of Bijin's friends onboard and, well, I can't shoot *all* of them. Having you along as extra security or at least as a blunt object would be helpful—it'll be a riot down by the escape pods on the main concourse."

"Truly? What do I get out of all this?" Litning was not interested in helping him escape with Memta.

"For one thing, you'll get off this ship. For another, I can still get you paid for the work you've done—at least you'll walk away with something."

"These men will be looking for me as well. Why not give me the device so I can disguise myself? Surely you can come up with something else for yourself."

Mondo gave him a knowing smile. "Nice try. You're right though, they're coming to kill you anyway. With me, you have a chance to escape and not walk away empty-handed."

I could take Memta back in the confusion, so no, I will not be walking away empty-handed. "I am not sure how much help I can be when I had such difficulty with a weakling like Bijin."

Mondo waved off the comment. "Don't take that into account. He was completely hopped up on rimi."

Litning had heard of the substance. From what he knew of it, it could have definitely given Bijin the strength and reflexes needed to best him in combat. He did not feel any better about his stark defeat, but he at least had a reason for why it had happened. "Who are these people after the statue?"

Mondo's lip twisted. "Disgruntled clients. Very well-funded, and very impatient. The sooner we get off this ship and away from them, the better."

Litning nodded. Mondo downplayed his clients' reach, but they were clearly resourceful. Perhaps there was some way he could recover Memta and give Mondo to his clients—that would certainly make Litning's life easier.

Mondo strapped the bag to his back. "Do we have a deal? Or am I shooting you dead right here?"

Litning stood up. "We have a deal." *For now.*

CHAPTER 18

"Watch it! Get down!" Max called out, forcing Alesha to duck so he could fire his pistol over her. His laser blast sailed over the shoulder of a masked humanoid in black military fatigues carrying a laser rifle. A second laser bolt from the crouching Alesha caught the guy in the chest. The attacker slumped to the floor, a hole burned through his armored chest plate.

Max helped Alesha back to her feet as they huddled in a hallway connected to the main concourse. "Sorry for pushing you—I needed a clear shot."

"And you did so well with that opportunity," she mocked. "Your aim didn't improve while you were away."

"Marksmanship wasn't offered as an elective."

"Honestly Max, what would you do without me?"

"I'm sure I'll find some way to manage."

Her irritated glare showed what she thought of his comment. What did she want? He was busy fighting for his life while dealing with crippling sexual frustration. *Just another day at the office for Maxim Ultra.*

Pandemonium reigned on the main concourse as the terrorists stormed into the throng of panicked passengers, who scrambled for either cover or the escape pods. Max didn't know if they were *officially* terrorists, but anyone firing into a crowd of people qualified for him. They weren't firing indiscriminately, though. They kept their shots precisely aimed, shooting to kill, but they seemed to only target the ship's security. It didn't matter. The laser fire was enough to terrorize the fleeing passengers.

Max and Alesha had rustled up the others in order to make it back to the *Sequel*. He still had no idea where Glintock was. For all he knew, the man had been caught up in the explosion. The ship's announcement system blared a general evacuation order. It was an automated female voice, so Max wasn't even sure what Robert's status was. Though he worried about them both, he had more pressing concerns. He had to get Alesha and the others to safety before he could even think about setting out to find Glintock or Robert.

"Boss," Gelf called through a stream of screaming passengers. He stood on the other side of the hallway, a recovered laser rifle propped up on his hip. "How are we going to get through this mess?"

"I am afraid I must echo Gelf's question, Maxim," Roeger replied, sporting a laser rifle of his own. The crew had run into more of the commandos than Max would have liked. "I have calculated the different paths we could take through this crowd, but the variables are constantly shifting." He looked out at the throng of people and then back to Max. "I am afraid we may have to simply run for it."

"What else is new?" Max muttered.

Gerry hugged the opposite wall with a wide grimace.

"You okay over there, Gerry? Are you going to be able to help us out here?"

"I may not have been able to fend off a beast like Elkeith, Maxim, but I should be able to hold my own against this rabble."

Pretty confident for a guy I had to protect in prison.

"Who *are* these people?" Alesha asked, gesturing to the commandos.

"Disgruntled passengers?" Max quipped. "How should I know?" *Why aren't they heading for the bridge? They're just standing here, creating a panic.*

Passengers flooded the main concourse from every entry point. The soldiers in black kept them perpetually scattered with their constant laser fire. An observation platform encircled the area and the commandos fired up there as well, killing the armed security officers taking up positions. Their efficiency was startling. More security agents surged onto the main concourse, but their weapons were no match for the commandos, who had cut off access to both the pods and the hangar.

"Okay," Max said. "Here's how this is going to work. Alesha and I will go first, covering you three so you can get to the *Sequel*. Once you're there, get it ready to get us out of here."

"But Maxim," Roeger said. "What about Agent Glintock?"

He grimaced. "My first priority is getting you guys on the ship. I haven't forgotten him, Roeger. One thing at a time."

The sweep of laser fire had died down near Max's hallway. *It's now or never.* He waved his team out of the hallway and into the chaos of the main concourse. He and Alesha moved out first, back-to-back and constantly rotating, watching for danger. It was tight quarters with panicked passengers pushing and shoving as they tried to escape. Max kept his pistol ready, shrugging off the vacationers bumping into him.

He nodded to his friends waiting in the hallway. Roeger and Gerry moved out tentatively, but Gelf raced out onto the concourse, swinging his rifle around erratically. He looked prepared for both anything and nothing. A terrorist lined the crew up in his sights, but Max caught him with a laser blast, dropping him to the floor.

"Nice shot," Alesha said.

"See, I can make them when they count."

The group moved through the crowd as fast as they could. It felt like the hangar entrance was a thousand miles away. After a good thirty feet with little incident, the gunmen in black all seemed to look their way.

"This doesn't look good," Alesha said.

"Yeah," Max replied. "They seem pretty interested in us."

"Well, we *are* the only ones really defending ourselves," Gelf said.

"No…" Max groped in his mind for an answer. "This isn't right. Keep moving."

The crew moved closer to the hangar, but some of the commandos turned their weapons toward Max and the others. As soon as one broke through the crowd, Max snapped off two laser bolts at him. The attacker fell to the floor.

"Better," Alesha remarked as she shot another of the soldiers.

Max ignored her comment, his eyes scanning around for the next threat. Shooting two of their ranks appeared to make the other approaching soldiers a bit more gun shy.

"Why aren't they charging us?" he asked aloud before catching movement out of the corner of his eye. "Gerry, watch out!"

A soldier loomed out of the hallway with what looked like a shock baton. Thanks to his amorphous form, Gerry pulled his right side into himself. The baton whiffed. Gerry slipped behind the man with a quick sidestep. With one tendril, he gripped the man's wrist, cracking it.

The soldier howled in pain as the shock weapon fell from his hand. Another tendril wrapped around the man's throat. The soldier's free hand flew to his neck, slapping at Gerry with wet smacking sounds. Gerry freed the wounded arm to rip the man's mask off, while forming an appendage out of his lower half to fend off another attacker charging at him from his right. His moves left Max slack-jawed.

Alesha took aim at the newcomer and blasted him in the face, only to have a laser bolt whiz past her head from Gelf's rifle. The seemingly errant laser struck an encroaching commando behind her.

"You've gotta watch yourself, sister," Gelf said with a wink. "Might not be around to save your hide next time."

"Not the most gracious of saviors, is he?" she muttered.

"Starting to like him?" Max asked.

"*Maybe*."

Max wasn't sure if she was embarrassed that she'd missed the guy behind her or that it was Gelf who saved her ass. "Roeger! Take a picture of our friend over there." He gestured to the soldier Gerry slowly strangled.

Roeger turned and faced the captive, following Max's order before walking over to loot the soldier's equipment.

"What's that for?" Alesha asked.

"I want his face on file. We may be able to find out who these guys are."

"Does it matter?" she asked.

"They're too organized to be pirates and too disciplined to be terrorists. Something's up."

He quickly ducked as a laser bolt struck from above. Behind them another commando met his end. Max looked for where the shot had come from. His communicator trilled in his ear.

"*Did you miss me, Ultra?*" Glintock's voice was more of a relief than Max wanted to admit.

"Where did you disappear to?" he asked as he fired on another solider.

"*Our black-suited friends here wanted to make me their special guest. I blew a hole in the ship to derail their plan and this chaos is what I got in return.*"

"You'll have to explain that later. Get down here, we're making a run for the ship." Max heard Glintock's rifle discharge again over the communicator.

"*What, you were going to leave without me?*"

"Just trying to get the others to safety. That's the whole point of this, remember?"

Alesha and Gelf stood back-to-back in front of him while Roeger and Gerry covered his rear. At that moment, it looked more like they were getting Max to safety. His eyes scanned around for any viable targets, but the crowd was thick.

"*No, the point of all this is to stop Vandeir and secure that statue,*" Glintock said. "*That's why our friends are here—they believe the thief is on board with the statue.*"

"Is it possible they're working with someone within the GAC?"

Glintock's pause was disconcerting. Max heard the rifle discharge again. "*It's possible, but these people didn't just turn up here. They were prepared for this. I have no idea who they are. The ones I questioned didn't give me anything useful.*"

Max's eyes scanned the concourse. "Who am I looking for?"

"*A Revash.*"

Max's eyes bulged. "A *Revash?* Okay, big and hairy. Got it." He was familiar with the reclusive race, but had never seen one in the flesh.

"*I had a hunch he might take this opportunity to make his getaway,*" Glintock said.

"I'll keep my eyes peeled."

"*Good. One more thing: I think Vandeir is on board.*"

Max's blood went cold. His pulse quickened as his eyes darted around. "I-I'll keep an eye out for him too."

Their adversaries were still playing coy. Some would emerge from the crowd, but didn't make any serious bids to harm any of the crew. Their weapons were stun devices. They wanted them alive.

What's their game?

"Maxim, I see Agent Glintock," Roeger said, his eyes directed at the observation deck. "He looks to be in trouble."

He followed Roeger's line of sight. Sure enough, Glintock was dealing with a surge of commandos coming his way. Glintock's shots were precise. One foe after another fell, but in a numbers game, he was sure to lose.

"Give him some help, Roeger," Max said.

Roeger turned his laser rifle toward Glintock's position and fired. His pinpoint accuracy wounded the oncoming soldiers, but did not kill them. Max was sure Glintock loved that. Roeger wasn't a pacifist, but killing made him squeamish. Max expected he'd have to comfort the bot's guilty conscience later.

As the crew kept moving toward the hangar, the mass of panicking passengers clogged up the concourse, keeping the other soldiers at bay. Using the passengers as cover made him feel dirty, but it was a question of survival—plain and simple. Upon leaving the ship, he intended on being vertical.

A clear path opened through the crowd.

"This is our chance," Gelf said. "Run for it!"

"Wait!" Before Max could get the word out of his mouth, Gelf had taken off for the hangar at full speed. "God dammit."

"Though he has proven himself helpful, Gelf is still far from a good teammate," Roeger said.

"All right, you guys head for the *Sequel*. I'm going to stay here and give Glintock a hand," Max said, taking the laser rifle from Roeger.

"The hell you are," Alesha said. "If you think I'm leaving you out here by yourse—"

"Alesha, I'm trying to keep you guys safe. I can't do that if you're right here in the thick of it with me."

"And I'm telling you, I don't need protection." She punctuated her statement with a laser blast to an approaching soldier's head.

"Glintock thinks Kalen's on board."

Her eyes widened before a steely look took hold. "Then I'm *definitely* staying."

There was no point in arguing with her. "Fine. Roeger, you and Gerry get back to the ship—get her ready. We're out of here as soon as I've got Glintock in hand."

"Of course, Maxim," Roeger answered as he and Gerry headed after their diminutive crewmate.

Max pulled Alesha close to him. "Stick tight. We have to push through this shit."

"What are we doing? Clearing a path for Glintock?"

"No, he also thinks the thief is on board and making a run for it. Keep your eyes open for a Revash."

"I see a lot of big aliens here. Big and slimy, big and craggy, but no big and hairy."

She was right—plenty of alien life around, but no one fitting a Revash's description. In all honesty, he was more on the lookout for wiry humans possibly carrying knives. Kalen frightened him more than any Revash.

Harsh shouting cut through the general din.

"If the Revash is trying to lay low, he might have on a…disguise." Max's eyes followed the shouting and locked onto a scuffle going on several yards away.

A large figure dressed in a cloak that hid his facial features was getting into it with a human male. They struggled over a red bag. It wasn't going well for the human.

"There," Max said as he steered Alesha toward the fight.

As they pushed through the crowd, Max kept his sights on the struggling pair. The big guy gave a final tug on the bag, tearing it open. A stone statue fell out and Max's heart skipped a beat. The creature caught the statue in one gloved hand, gripping the human's wrist in the other.

"Come on!" he called to Alesha. "He's got it!"

They were close, about fifteen feet away, when there was a blinding flash. Spots danced in front of Max's eyes, but he could see the burly thief barreling toward him. The thief was indeed a Revash and the look on his face said he wasn't coming along quietly. Alesha stood to Max's left as they tried to bar the Revash's escape, but it was hopeless. As he bowled them over, the statue gripped in the Revash's hand brushed against Alesha's bare arm. A bright turquoise flash propelled her through the crowd and to the ground.

The Revash knocked Max over with a bear-like hand. He crashed to the floor as the thief cut a swath through the passengers to the escape pods. Max's head was fuzzy. His rifle had escaped from him in the fall, while his pistol had skittered out of its holster. All he could see were the legs of the fleeing passengers.

One set of legs stayed stationary in front of him—female legs. *Familiar* legs. He looked up and couldn't breathe.

It was Sierra.

CHAPTER 19

Max's head spun. Serving as a Revash roadblock wasn't the brightest idea and he was convinced that the bump on his head was making him see things. How was Sierra alive?

"H-how?"

"How what? How am I alive after Talon Merthane shot me in the back and you let him cart me off? Is that what you're asking?"

Her appearance didn't make sense. Had he seen her earlier on the ship? Was that real? Was she even real now? It felt like his mind was short-circuiting.

"Was it some kind of drug?"

"Mmm…getting warmer." As her eyes darted around, her body tensed for action. She was going to bolt.

Where's my gun?

His mind flashed to their encounter in Tonicen. Merthane had shot and collected her, leaving Max to the tender mercies of the Tonicen police. Merthane wasn't one to bring his targets in alive unless the contract specifically called for it. But clearly, Sierra was alive when he'd captured her. That meant….

"You were working with him."

"And it only took you about three years to figure it out! He wasn't very happy when I left him in the lurch later. I *am* sorry you had to spend some time in prison after that, but it was for the best."

"*For the best?*" Rage flooded his mind. Blood pounded in his ears. He could have sworn it was the pounding of footsteps. On the edge of his hearing, he heard shouts and commands as the men in black looked their way.

"I'm so sorry to cut this short, Max. This really isn't how I wanted this to go, but I have a ship to catch. I'll see you soon!"

"No!"

She dashed away. He scrambled around on the floor for one of his weapons, but they were getting kicked about by the crowd around him. As he struggled to his feet, his eyes fell on Alesha, still unconscious on the floor. He took a single step toward her.

WHACK.

His jaw exploded in pain as he reeled back from the fist that had connected with it. He shook his head. Once his vision cleared, his eyes focused in on his assailant—Kalen Vandeir.

Je-sus fuck.

"Hello, Ultra. Happy to see me? Because I know I'm delighted to see you," Kalen said, his hungry gaze passing over Alesha as she began to stir.

"Of course I'm happy to see you, Kalen. Maybe you heard, we've been looking all over for you." He glanced up at the observation deck. Glintock wasn't there, or at least, he wasn't standing. A pang of panic shot through Max. Angling his body away from Kalen, he keyed his communicator to open a channel to Glintock. *Please don't be dead.* He took a step toward Alesha.

Kalen's arm shot out. "Not so fast, Ultra."

"I'm just going to check on her." He was also planning on looking for a gun in order to blow this asshole away.

"What difference does it make?" A thin smile formed on Kalen's face. "I'm going to kill you both."

"What for? I mean, I know we weren't the best of friends, but murdering us sounds a little extreme." Much of the laser fire had died down. A few of the mystery men in black still populated the concourse, but the majority of them had vanished. Maybe they'd gotten the memo that the statue had departed.

"You know why, Ultra. You're the only one that *could* know."

Max squinted. "Not sure what you mean there."

Kalen snorted before charging at Max. He slid on the deck, his foot stretched out, and connected with Max's shin, tripping him up. As Max stumbled away from his attacker, Kalen was back on his feet delivering a kick to Max's back that sent him sprawling to the floor. He was as fast as ever.

"You're a joke, Ultra. What Sierra ever saw in you, I'll never know."

Max coughed, wincing in pain. "She liked…she liked being with a guy who didn't have to fuck her with his hands around her throat." *Why am I antagonizing this guy?*

Kalen's nostrils flared. His eyes widened. He brought his foot back, but before he could deliver another kick, Alesha wrapped a cord around his neck from behind, pulling him away from Max.

That's my girl.

"This is for Carfen, you sick veck!" Alesha gave Kalen all he could handle as she rode on his back. She gritted her teeth, the tendons in her neck popping as she pulled on the cord. Kalen turned purple, but his face exuded unnatural calm. He gripped Alesha's wrists and flipped her off of his back. She landed on her feet, but Kalen hit her square in the stomach with a kick, knocking her to the deck.

Max moved to tackle Kalen, who stopped him with a shot to the throat. Max staggered back, but Kalen pressed his advantage. He threw a punch at Max, but came up short as Alesha delivered a kick to his midsection. As Kalen recovered, Max and Alesha moved around him in tandem.

They both hit him with a series of attacks, but Kalen was too quick, defeating all their best attempts. A flash of silver Max hoped was his pistol drew his eye for a split second. He instantly regretted it. Kalen struck him hard in the chest, knocking him back down.

Max took a couple of moments before lurching back to his feet. His chest burned like an inferno.

Alesha delivered a flurry of punches to Kalen, which he easily blocked and parried. When she followed up with a kick, he caught her leg and swung her into Max, sending them both back to the deck. Though trying their best to hold their own, Max and Alesha were hopelessly outclassed. Kalen wasn't even playing the same game.

Figuring all the rimi in his system would protect him—and wishing he'd taken more of it—Max moved to shield Alesha's body with his own. Kalen stopped him with a punch and then grabbed him by the back of his jacket, hauling him back to his feet.

"Though I appreciate the workout, I'm not done with you yet, Ultra. Ever since they tossed me into that hole on Aval, I've dreamed about how I'd make you suffer for betraying us."

"*This* is what you dreamed about?" Max said through his swelling lips. "I think you need to talk to someone, Kalen."

Kalen turned Max around, swinging at him with a punch. Max got it together enough to block the attack, but was sluggish. Kalen made him pay for it with a punch to the other side of his body. Alesha interrupted Kalen's follow up with a lunging punch, but he easily kicked her back to the ground. Max launched the top of his head into Kalen's jaw. The move knocked Kalen back a few steps and Max pushed his pain down to try and press his advantage. He delivered a punch to Kalen's mid-section, following with an uppercut that sent the killer reeling.

A slight smile flickered across Max's face, but it faded when Kalen picked up a jagged piece of glass. Max knew how deadly he could be, even with such a simple weapon.

Kalen took some practice swipes, flipping the glass between his hands as he approached Max, who held his hands out in a peaceful gesture.

"Okay, you've gotten some of that rage out, Kalen. Let's just talk about this. I didn't sell you out. It was Sier—"

"*Liar!* You betrayed us and then went off to kill her," Kalen said as he took a swipe at Max. He was still too far away, but Max flinched regardless.

"If I sold you out, why did I end up in prison too?"

"You're out now, aren't you? Probably cut some sweet deal with the GAC."

"They let me out to track your crazy ass down!"

Kalen's face twisted before he slashed at Max in a series of increasingly aggressive attacks. He grazed Max's thigh with a low slash and then his arm when he reached for his wounded leg.

"Fuck! Will you stop cutting me? Sierra's alive, you stupid asshole! I didn't kill anyone!"

"More lies designed to save your skin." Kalen slashed at Max's head, nearly slicing his eyeballs.

Flinching away from the attack, Max managed to grab Kalen's wrist and elbow, holding him fast. "Listen to me. Sierra is a-live. She was on this ship!"

Kalen flipped the shard into his free hand and swiped at Max, who countered by pushing the psycho away. At that same moment,

Alesha made a bid to wrap up Kalen's arm from behind. Kalen grabbed her and positioned her in front of him, the glass shard at her throat. The tip pricked her neck, drawing a drop of blood.

"No!" Max cried out as he again held his hands out to Kalen.

Alesha's eyes were wild. She didn't struggle against Kalen, but Max could see her mind working. She didn't scream either—she'd never give Kalen the satisfaction.

"I'm done listening to your lies, Ultra. I'll deal with you as soon as I send Alesha to meet that witch, Carfen." He pressed the shard deeper into her neck. More blood dribbled free.

"God dammit, Kalen, will you fucking listen to me!?" The pain flaring all over Max's body became more acute as it pulsed with his hammering heart. He took one limping step toward Kalen. "Sierra was working with Talon Merthane." Kalen's eyes narrowed as he nodded. *Good. Got to keep his attention on me.* "She hid the statue and now just got someone else to dig it up for her. I think there's something much bigger than us going on here. Why were these soldiers here? What were they after? Think about it."

Kalen kept the shard to Alesha's throat. "What are you getting at?"

"I think Sierra sold us out in order to leave herself as the only one who could track down the statue."

Kalen's eyebrows knit together. "Then, she'd be able to find Dalian's Bounty."

"What?"

"The Bounty. The statue was the final clue." His tone was cold. It got like that when he was ready to kill.

Max's eyes darted between Kalen and Alesha, his mind grasping for words that wouldn't set the killer off. Kalen was still hung up on the cover story about the statue. "Oh, right. Sorry, of course I remember. Prison messes with your head." Sierra hadn't told Kalen of the statue's true nature either. "We can't let her get away with this."

Kalen gave him a measured look. His grip appeared to relax just a bit on Alesha. "So you're saying you want to work together to bring her down?"

A laser beam knifed into Kalen's brow, blowing out the back of his head.

"*No. He's not,*" Glintock's voice sounded over Max's communicator.

Blood and brain matter splattered onto the deck like a grisly Jackson Pollock painting. As Kalen's body fell away from Alesha's the glass shard nicked her neck, but once she was clear, she sank to her knees, the small cut glistening in the concourse's lights.

Max, dazed by what had just transpired, staggered over to her. His cut wasn't bad, but as he crouched beside her, a burning pain tore through his leg. He cradled her next to him, kissing the top of her head.

He looked at the fallen Kalen, not sure how to feel. The man would have certainly killed them all, so he didn't lament his death. It had just come so suddenly. He was there and then he was gone. Max had to admit, he didn't really feel anything at all. There wasn't even a sense of relief, only a feeling of dread in the pit of his stomach.

Alesha trembled in his arms. She said nothing, as if in shock. Stroking her hair, he held her close, not knowing what to say. This was different from their fight with Merthane in Apex. He'd really almost lost her this time. Combined with Sierra turning up alive, he couldn't catch his breath.

With a gasp, she clutched at his jacket. "Max, we have to get her back! The statue, we can't let Sierra have it." She had a crazed look in her eye and a gleam of turquoise that must have come from the lights.

"We will, 'Lesha. We'll get it back." He looked back to the observation deck to see Glintock shimmying down a length of cable. Movement in the nearby lift caught his eye.

"Thank God, you guys are still here!" Robert called out as he emerged from the damaged lift. His once-pristine captain's uniform was now blackened and torn. Along with a pistol, he carried a medium-sized travel bag with him. Max had a good idea what was in it.

"Going somewhere, *Robvere*?" he asked with a wry smile.

"Max, I'm in. Whatever it is, I'm in."

He gestured to Kalen's lifeless body. "The threat's over, Robbie. No need to bail on your cushy job for us now."

"Cushy job? Look at this place!"

The concourse looked like shit. What had been a luxury cruise ship now looked like a broken down freighter thanks to the firefight. None of the terrorists were anywhere to be found, which concerned Max. He'd been pretty busy getting knocked around at the time, but he didn't remember any conspicuous mass exodus from the ship. There was still no evidence as to who the infiltrators were or what they really wanted. He'd just assumed it was the statue.

"My employers aren't going to be too keen on keeping me around when they find out my assistant was sucking my dick while all this was kicking off," Robert explained. "I'll never find work like this again!"

"What about going down with the ship?" Alesha asked with a sneer.

"You too, Alesha? Seriously? Screw that. Do you even know who Baron Zeth is? He puts out a sunny disposition for the public, but that guy does *not* fuck around. I've heard stories. This is his flagship. Once it gets out that armed terrorists boarded and the captain did *nothing* to stop them, I'm a dead man."

Max's brow knotted in confusion. "I think you're blowing that up a little bit, Robbie. No cruise liner owner is going to kill you for a terrorist action that was out of your hands."

"He certainly might," Glintock said as he rejoined them. "Your friend is right, Ultra. People like Zeth do not veck around. These were trained mercenaries and they didn't storm the ship—they were already aboard."

"A technicality my employer will ignore," Robert said. "I need to get the hell off this ship. If your offer still stands, I'll take it."

Max gave Robert a long stare. He had about a dozen quips ready for him, but they could wait. After Kalen, joking around didn't feel right. Instead, he patted Robert on the shoulder. "Welcome home, buddy."

"I'll get her prepped for takeoff." With a relieved smile, Robert shoved off toward the hangar and the waiting *Sequel*.

Max turned to Glintock, gesturing to Kalen. "Nice shot. He's dead."

"Yes he is. You've fulfilled your end of the deal as far as Kalen Vandeir is concerned." He looked off to the bank of escape pods. "You know what I'm going to ask you next?"

"Yep."

"Are you in?"

Max put his arm around Alesha's shoulders, hugging her close. She hugged him back and he looked at Glintock. "All in."

CHAPTER 20

Even in the dim blue halo of light coming from his computer terminal, Max could see his hands shaking. The computer was the only source of light in his room aboard the *Sequel*. He'd retreated there after giving Robert the order to get as far away from the listless *Galactic Dream* as fast as possible. Now that the adrenaline was wearing off, he needed to decompress—make sense of what he'd witnessed in his final moments on the cruise ship.

Sierra—alive—apparently pulling the strings all along. Max would settle up with Merthane for his role in the game, though he was sure the bounty hunter would be *delighted* to find out Sierra had played him too. Then there was Kalen. Thanks to Glintock, the psychopath was gone, but Max couldn't shake the feeling of dread haunting him. That could have just been the knowledge that Sierra was out there somewhere, plotting.

It was strange not having Kalen hanging over him like a guillotine blade. Max's only desire had been to get his team back together and keep them safe. With Kalen gone, they were. Was there any reason for them to stay now that the danger had been eliminated? The statue was still out there, though, and despite the fact that he didn't know how the damn thing blew up that research ship, Max was fairly certain that Sierra getting her hands on it would be a bad thing.

As far as Max knew, Sierra wasn't the last person with the statue, though—it was the Revash. The Revash had been fighting over it with someone before the big son of a bitch knocked Max on his ass.

"Christi," he called out to the ship's A.I. "Pull up the star maps for the immediate area surrounding the *Galactic Dream*."

A noise, not unlike a robot farting, answered instead of Christi's sweet, gentle voice.

His brow scrunched. "Christi?"

More robot farts.

"Vocal output must be damaged," he murmured. "But why isn't the information showing up anyway?" Ready to check out the problem, he stood and immediately wanted to sit back down. His whole body throbbed, despite all the rimi pumping through his system. He wondered if his shaking hands were simply due to the emotional stress. His intercom beeped. "Yeah?"

"*Maxim?*" It was Roeger, but there was a lot of yelling going on in the background. "*Maxim, I think you are needed out here. Agent Glintock is taking issue with Mr., ah, Gelf.*"

Damn it. "I'll be right out." As he moved to the door, he made a mental note to check on Christi's systems after he put out the fire between Glintock and Gelf.

The commotion in the common area smacked him in the face as soon as he cracked open the heavy metal door. Raised voices reverberated down the hall, but Alesha's wasn't one of them. She'd been shaken by her close encounter with both Kalen and the statue. If he hadn't been so messed up himself over what had happened on the ship, he would have taken more time to see to her needs. He added her to his mental list—she should have always been at the top.

He stepped into the common area to find Gelf sitting at the table, arms folded. Glintock loomed over him, glowering, but Gelf wouldn't meet his stare. Alesha stared off into space, seemingly disinterested in what was going on. Roeger looked between Glintock and Gelf like a nervous child before giving Max a long stare, as if willing him to step in.

"What's…uh…what's going on here?" Max asked.

Gelf's eyes flicked up to meet his. He opened his mouth to say something.

Glintock didn't even let Gelf exhale. "I'll tell you what's going on, Ultra. I'm doing an investigation, trying to ascertain where our little friend Gelf ran off to after we boarded the *Galactic Dream*."

"And I keep asking, 'Why do you care so much?'" Gelf asked through clenched teeth. His folded arms tightened around his chest. It looked like his head might pop off.

"Let me remind you, Gelf, you have been released into *my* custody. Any and all illegal activities fall on me."

"I guess that's why you and the bot were following me all over the ship, then?"

Glintock didn't respond, but he didn't have to. The whirring of Roeger's servos cutting through the silence as he threw nervous glances at Glintock was answer enough.

"That's right, Mr. Hot-Shot-Agent, I knew you two dopes were following me the whole time. That's why I led you through every corridor I could." Gelf's mouth drew up into a smug smile.

If Glintock was thrown, he didn't show it. "Yes and how convenient that after following you, I got ambushed by those mercs in black."

"You left out the part about stumbling onto Kalen's murder scene. I told you, I don't know who those guys were. Why would I have anything to do with th—veck, I shot a bunch of them making our escape!"

"Are we sure your weapon wasn't set to stun? Besides, killing some of the shock troops doesn't mean you weren't in collusion with their leadership."

Gelf slammed his hand down on the table, but looked to Max. "Do I really have to put up with this nakra?"

"Yeah, Glintock," Max said. "What's with the third degree?"

"I already explained that. I'm responsible for the three of you. Any infr—"

"But he hasn't done anything," Max said. "He's just exploring freedom for the fir—"

Glintock stopped him with a condescending look. "If you really believe that, I feel sorry for you."

"You just don't trust him," Alesha said, continuing to stare off to the side.

"Oh, and you do now?"

She turned her head slowly toward Gelf, who wore an expectant look. "He saved my life—more than once. That's all I need."

"He did the same for me in prison," Max added.

"Just an eternal con man making sure his interests are covered. People don't change, Mr. Ultra. You've been defending him since day one."

"And you've been persecuting him. I think I made it clear, he helped me in prison."

"Yes, I think we all know how he *helped* you."

Max's eyes narrowed. "That's enough, Glintock."

"His record is longer than the length of this ship, Ultra, yet you put your trust in him. And we all know how well putting your faith in the criminal element worked for you the last time."

Max grimaced, but said nothing. What *could* he say? Everything Glintock said was true. Max wasn't going to get into an impassioned discussion about why it was important that people *could* change. By dredging up the whole Sierra thing again, Glintock was breaking down everything Max had built up since his release.

"It crossed my mind, Ultra, that Gelf might be using your ship to smuggle contraband. You wouldn't happen to know anything about that, would you?"

"*What?*"

"Fine!" Gelf exploded. "You know where I was on the *Dream?* Where I was trying to go in Apex?"

"Gelf, don't," Max said, his stomach lurching.

"No, sorry, Boss, I'm not taking this vecking *petch's* constant needling anymore." He reached into a large pouch on his belt and threw a quart-sized pack of rimi onto the table. "There! *That's* where I was—supporting Max's little habit."

In Max's ears, the pack hit the table like a cannonball. A good few seconds of silence followed. "Thanks, pal. Really, thank you." He didn't want to make a scene, so he simply glared at Gelf, satisfied that the little bastard squirmed in his seat. His heart sank when he caught Alesha's eye.

"*Rimi?* How *could* you?"

"'Lesha...."

She pushed away from the table, stalking off to the living quarters. "I can't believe you," she muttered as she brushed past him.

His gaze remained on the deck as he took a deep, calming breath. All the progress the two of them had made—gone. When he looked up, only he and Glintock remained in the common area. Roeger had probably gone off to comfort Alesha, while Gelf slinked off to who knew where. Max glared at Glintock.

The agent had a chagrined expression. "Sorry about that."

"You saved Alesha's life, so I owe you one, but seriously, fuck you."

"I deserved that."

Max looked down the corridor leading to the living quarters. "I need to fix this."

"We *need* to find the Revash."

He held up his hand. "Not now. This is more important."

Moments later, he found himself outside Alesha's room. He hit the buzzer for the third time—still no answer. He didn't want to look completely desperate and bang on the door, but he wanted to clear the air with her before moving forward with the job. He pressed the buzzer again.

She yanked the door open, fire in her eyes.

This is going to be tougher than I thought. "Can we talk?"

"Talk about what, Max? How you've been lying to me since you got back?"

Much tougher. "That's not true." He glanced up and down the corridor. "Look, can I come in? I don't want to have this conversation out in the hallway."

She stepped aside. "You may not have lied to me, Max, but whatever you're about to sell me better be closer to the truth."

He stepped inside her small cabin and she closed the door. The room wasn't much more than a guest cabin and it saddened him that she chose to coop herself up in there—alone. He guessed he understood why, though.

Just one look at her made him want to pick up where they'd left off on the *Galactic Dream*. Due to her expression, he felt the need to ease into the inevitable fight. "How is everything? With you?" She clearly wasn't herself since the run-in with the Revash on the *Galactic Dream*. Anger stood out in her eyes, but there was something else there—a haunted look that didn't fit her face.

"You're a junkie, Max."

That escalated quickly.

"I *knew* something shady was going on! You've been getting your ass handed to you left and right and bouncing back fairly easily." She turned away from him. "I am so vecking stupid."

"No. No, you're not, Alesha." That was the last thing he wanted. It wasn't her fault. "It's not as bad as you think. I'm not a junkie." Even as the words tumbled from his mouth, he wanted them back—they *were* lies. "I have...a slight addiction."

"There's no such thing and you know it. When did it start?"

He shuffled his feet. He'd been eager to get inside and clear the air, but now that the hard questions were coming, he wondered why he hadn't passed her room by entirely.

She folded her arms. "Please don't tell me I'm so blind that you've been hiding this from me since we beat this together. Was that even real?"

"Yes. I mean, this started long after that. Sierra really hurt me."

Alesha's eyes narrowed, her mouth pulled into a tight line. "*What?*"

He shook his head. "*Physically*. We fought before they hauled me off to Aval. She really messed me up." *This isn't going well.*

"And Gelf kindly got you what you needed to sort you out, huh? We've been through this before and I *won't* do it again." She closed her eyes for a moment. "What happened to you?"

"Prison, sweetheart. Prison happened to me."

"So, Sierra gave you some boo-boos and your solution was to turn to the drugs that we beat, *together?*"

"It's a little more complicated than that."

"Really? Why don't you tell me how complicated it was to take the most important thing we'd ever done together and throw it all away? Tell me!"

He turned away from her. Shame filled him and the ache in his body seemed to intensify. "You don't understand. I was supposed to be in that prison *for life*. There was no hope—nothing to look forward to. So, when Gelf said he could get me rimi to alleviate my pain, I knew I could also use it to escape my reality." Her incredulous expression told him that his excuse was lacking. "What did I have to lose? I was there for the rest of my life."

"Even if it drove you insane? You do remember that's a one of the possible side effects, yes?"

"'Lesha, I was already losing my mind a little bit every day in there *without* rimi. But…."

"But?"

"I think there was a part of me that dared to believe that I might someday get out of there. So I used, but tried not to abuse it. It was tough with all the scrapes I got into there."

The disappointment came off her in waves. No matter what kind of justification he came up with, she was right. The two of them had been through hell together and come out the other side. That ordeal had brought them closer together than anything else ever had. Petty squabbles always cropped up between them—it was the push and pull of their relationship—but that bond always remained intact. When he'd pushed Alesha away to join up with Sierra, he'd violated that trust. Now, the revelation of his drug problem made it that much worse.

He heaved a sigh. "I'm managing it."

"No, you're not. I can see you shaking from here."

"You should talk." It was a cheap shot, but he was tired of being her punching bag. Her silence told him that the statue had affected her even more than she'd let on. Shaking his head, he felt guilty, realizing that he'd been feeling sorry for himself now that his secret was out in the open. "We never talked about what happened with you and the statue on the *Galactic Dream*."

"I'm like you—I'm managing it."

"Not sure what you mea—"

"We're not talking about me here. We're talking about you and your problem. I'm actually impressed *and* furious that you've been able to hide it from me for this long. Congratulations."

"I got really good at hiding it on Aval." It was nothing to be proud of. His stomach turned, but was it because he'd been lying to her or because his secret was out? "I'm sorry."

"Look, I know you're hoping for some kind of future for us after this "

"You've already made it clear you're leaving when this is all done. I'm actually surprised you haven't left already, now that Kalen's out of the way."

A faraway look took hold in her eyes. "No, I'm in this until the end now. I've got a few choice words for that horvorka, Sierra." The same distant stare crept back.

"You were talking about the future?"

She blinked. "Yes. I'll see this through, but I can't be with you in any capacity if you're going to keep using."

"What are you saying?"

"I'm saying, that after this job, if you ever want to see me again, you'll stop taking that nakra. I can't be around it, Max. It was hard enough quitting it the last time."

Her ultimatum put everything into stark contrast. If he wanted any kind of future with Alesha, he'd have to ditch the rimi. *Easy decision.* The increased trembling in his hand suggested otherwise. "I don't know if I can do that on my own."

"Then you should have thought of that before you started using again."

He winced at the edge in her voice. She was serious. *I really fucked this up.* "Well, whatever solution I come up with for that will also have to wait until after the job."

She gave him a disapproving look.

"'Lesha, I can't go into this with the shakes."

She looked away from him.

"You've gotta meet me halfway here."

"It's an imperfect compromise at best, Max."

He nodded. "Yeah, but it's the best we've got right now."

Her mouth remained frozen in a tight line.

"*Maxim?*" Roeger's voice crackled over the intercom.

He gazed at her for another moment. "Yeah?"

"*Agent Glintock wanted me to inform you that he is looking for you.*"

"Thanks pal, I'll be up in a minute."

"Sounds like duty calls," she said.

"He wanted my help tracking the Revash down. I thought this was more important."

Her eyes lit up. "Then I'd better get ready for when you find him."

"Are you sure?"

Her incredulous expression felt a little forced to him. "Of course I'm sure. Why wouldn't I be?"

He touched her arm. "That statue really did a number on you on the *Galactic Dream*. I didn't know you'd be so gung ho to get back after it."

"That's why we're here, right? I mean, now that Kalen's gone, that's why we're here." She was holding back.

"What's wrong? Talk to me."

She pulled away. "I'm fine."

"Alesha, this has to go both ways. You can't rattle off everything that's wrong with me and then pretend you've got everything under control. Tell me."

Her jaw set. "I'm fine."

"You're *not* fine."

She held her defiant stare for another moment, but then let out a long breath and looked away. "When the statue touched me, it-it wasn't a simple shock, Max." Her body shook, her voice tremulous.

He took her hands and led her over to sit on the bed. "What happened?"

Her eyes fixed on an invisible point, but they were wide, feverish. "I can't explain it. I'm drawn to it. It's like...she's whispering to me."

"*She?*"

"There's a...presence in the statue. Beautiful. Frightening. She...it tried to force its way into my mind."

"You're still Alesha though, right? You fought it off?"

She turned her head away from him. "Yes." She wasn't telling him something.

"But...?"

After a moment, she looked into his eyes. When she did, shame streaked her face. "Part of me wanted it, Max. There was...a power there—something I'd never felt before."

He wasn't sure what to tell her. An alien presence tried to force its way into her mind and she welcomed it? That didn't sound like the Alesha he knew—the woman who always wanted to be in control. "Maybe you should sit this one out," he said.

"No!" Her eyes flashed with manic energy before returning to their subdued look. "No, you need me. I may be able to lead you to it."

He couldn't argue with that. The Revash could be anywhere. If Alesha had some connection with the statue or whatever it was, they might be able to use that. Plus, he wanted her nearby. "Okay."

Roeger interrupted again over the intercom. "*Maxim?*"

"I'm on my way." He turned back to Alesha. She had an almost anguished look. "I'll call you when we're ready."

Her face relaxed. "Thank you."

He exited the cabin into the main corridor of the ship, taking a moment to collect himself outside her door. He wasn't sure how to process everything she'd told him. Though he'd promised to include her on the hunt, he couldn't be positive that was the right move. If she could indeed feel the statue, though, to not take her would be stupid. He had rimi, but it looked like Alesha had found herself a new drug. He'd have to keep a close eye on her, but he couldn't have her tweaking while they were on the job.

The irony wasn't lost on him.

CHAPTER 21

Max returned to the *Sequel*'s common area to find Glintock sitting at the table by himself. The agent's knee bounced as he stared at the tabletop. He heaved a sigh and then looked up at Max.

"How did everything go with Ms. Cabal?" Glintock asked as he averted his eyes from Max's.

"It could have gone a lot better. Thanks for asking."

Glintock winced. "I have to apologize again. I'm at a loss with these terrorists, Ultra. I don't trust Gelf and I hoped he'd have some answers. It was a longshot. I didn't mean for my interrogation to make things difficult for you with Ms. Cabal."

"Oh, you mean she was supposed to be okay with you accusing me of smuggling illegal goods with Gelf? That was supposed to endear me to her?" Just because Glintock was contrite didn't mean Max was going to let him off the hook easily.

"I'm sorry. When I'm after something, I get a bit...tenacious."

"*That's* a word for it."

They looked at each other for a moment. "I don't trust him, Mr. Ultra."

"I gathered that. My only question is, so what? Gelf isn't a threat to anyone."

"I know he's your friend, Maxim, but I also know what I'm talking about. He's a bad guy."

"And I think my saving his ass a few times in prison turned him around. People aren't always how they appear on paper."

"In my experience, they are."

"Then what made you come to me?"

Glintock paused. "Call that a gut feeling. And who in the galaxy uses paper?"

"It's an expressi—never mind." He looked over his shoulder making sure no one else was around. "You don't really think Gelf is mixed up with those guys in black, do you?"

"Probably not, but who can say? We know next to nothing about them."

"Roeger ran that picture we took on the *Dream*."

"And?"

"Nothing. Not even a name." Max paused for a moment and then looked at Glintock. "Even when they had you tied up? You didn't get anything?"

"They only said enough for me to sort out their plan on the cruise ship—not why they were there. I'm speculating they were after the statue. Of course, if the Revash stole something else they wanted…."

"How likely is that?" Max asked. "We need to find him before Sierra does. I don't know what that thing did to Alesha, but I don't think we want Sierra getting her hands on it."

Again, Glintock appeared to hold his tongue. "No. We don't."

Max gave him a quick look. It felt like Glintock wanted to say something else, but didn't. He shook his head. There were enough mysteries to deal with without the agent being cryptic. "Why would the Revash want it?"

"Aren't you the expert in these matters?" Glintock asked back.

"I do research when someone needs me to hunt down an item for them, but I'm no good with something I know nothing about. It was hard enough finding it for Sierra. Carfen knew *where* it was, but not *what* it was. What did your researchers find out?"

"Precious little. They seemed to be more interested in figuring out what it did as opposed to where it came from. What are you thinking?"

Max shrugged. "Revashes aren't very common outside Revjekt...."

"They're more common than you probably think, but yes, rarer than most."

"He seemed to be fighting with someone over the statue. It *could* have been Sierra in disguise, but if so, it was a hell of a disguise. Knowing her like I do, I'd say she hired him to steal the statue and he double-crossed her, but that doesn't jibe with what little I know of Revashes. Aren't they supposed to be peaceful? This doesn't sound like a peaceful guy."

"It's not unheard of," Glintock said. "Not all Revashes are the same."

"Neither are all criminals."

Glintock's lip twisted. "Nice try."

"Keep it in mind anyway." Max moved over to the ship's main computer console. A gnawing hunger built inside of him as he kept one eye on the pack of rimi Gelf had left behind. He told himself he was only interested in it because of the beatings he'd taken recently. The fresh sweat on his brow told a different story. Feeling Glintock's stare, he turned to face the agent.

Glintock had the same mix of disappointment and pity on his face Max imagined his father would have had. He surprised Max by waving his hand. "Take it. I'd prefer you didn't, but I also can't have you curled up in agony in the corner."

With a speed that shamed him, Max swiped the pack off the table. He glanced at the bag. Was he really choosing it over Alesha? Over his self-respect? Focusing on the glass panel that served as his computer screen, he kept his eyes diverted from Glintock. He at least did the man the service of not scarfing down the rimi right in front of him, even though his body screamed for it.

He activated the terminal. "Christi?"

Once again, the robot farts from earlier sounded from the speakers.

"I take it she's *not* supposed to sound like that?" Glintock asked.

"No, there's something wrong with her interface. Roeger!" he called into the ship's intercom. "She seemed to be working fine earlier...."

"If your computer is malfunctioning, how is the ship still flying?"

"Christi isn't the computer, she's the A.I. that augments the computer. The ship can still function without her, but with her in the driver's seat, it operates faster, more smoothly. She's also in charge of some of the secondary functions. Roeger!"

"I am right here, Maxim," Roeger said as he entered the common area. "There is no need to yell."

"Christi's malfunctioning. Are you sure her disc wasn't damaged?"

"Perhaps it is a mechanical issue," Roeger offered.

Max shook his head. "The ship was dormant for the last few years and was working fine before that."

Roeger turned his head at an angle, indicating correctly that Max was stretching the truth.

"All right, it was close to fine, but the point is, no one has touched the *Sequel* since I went to prison. All systems should be good." He sighed. "I don't think we have time for all this right now."

"But Maxim—"

"Put it on the to-do list. I'll just make do for now."

As Roeger shrugged and headed back down the hall, Max waved his hands in front of the terminal. A holographic keyboard appeared. His fingers danced across the solid light keys, opening windows all over the screen.

"What are you thinking here?" Glintock asked. "Monitor law enforcement channels? See if our friend gets into trouble?"

"No, you're thinking like a cop. I'm trying to understand him We don't know anything about the statue, but what do we know about Revashes?"

"I thought we'd covered that?"

"No, we know how they *are*, but what do we know about them as a *people*?"

"Not much, I'm afraid. They're not exactly welcoming of outsiders."

A smile crossed Max's face. "When I was a kid, and my dad took me into space for the first time, he was really big on preparing me for anything. He gave me this set of…call them educational videos: *The Races of the*—"

"*Galaxy*. Yes, I'm familiar with them."

"They reminded me of these old-timey filmstrips on Earth that they would show to kids in school. There was the cheesy narrator and information that was decades out of date."

"What are you getting at, Mr. Ultra?"

"I vaguely remember there was one about Revashes. The guy who produced the videos...."

"Yes, Dr. Spulgag—I'm familiar with him too."

"He would embed himself on these alien worlds to learn about them. I know he went to Revjekt."

"I don't recall one about Revashes—they're terribly insular."

"I remember it, and I have an excellent memory."

"You're very modest too."

Max ignored the barb. "The Revash people, from what I can recall, are, like you said, very insular, but they're also very spiritual."

"Go on..."

"So, you have a spiritual people who mainly keep to themselves, but here we have one who has broken into a GAC facility to steal a statue of immense power and double-crossed the person he was probably working for."

"Right...."

The screen filled with stars and a rendering of the *Galactic Dream* going down. Hundreds of lines branched off the crippled ship. Max shook his head at the jumbled image. "I need a bigger canvas." A few keystrokes later, a prismatic beam of light shot out of his terminal, creating a larger replica of his screen image hanging in midair.

"The *Galactic Dream*," Glintock said as he stepped back from the large hologram.

"And these lines represent the escape pods," Max said. "Most of them clustered close to the ship, more than likely hoping that would help them get rescued faster."

"The others?" Glintock referred to the outliers moving away from the crippled ship. There were at least a hundred of them.

"Those trying to escape." His eyes roved the image. With a motion of his hands, the holographic keyboard came away from the terminal, so he could focus on the projection. A few more keystrokes changed the image again, isolating only the ships fleeing the *Galactic Dream*.

"Those are all escape pods? What about the ships that were docked like ours?" Glintock asked. "Do we know where Sierra got to?"

"One thing at a time, Agent," Max said, his eyes glued to the screen. He hadn't forgotten about Sierra, but he was serious when he said their first priority had to be finding the Revash and the statue. *Of course*, he argued in his mind, *knowing where Sierra went might just help us with that*. Maybe he didn't *want* to know where she'd gone.

He tapped a few more keys. Images of planets replaced the graphic of the escape pods. "These are the planets within range of the escape pods' engines and fuel capacities." Rising from his chair, he manipulated the image with his hands, sweeping all the planets away, save one. "This planet is the closest, and from the flight trajectories, it looks like most of the survivors are headed there."

"Most, but not all?"

Max didn't answer. Instead, he moved the image again to reveal a turquoise gem in the blackness of space. "One ship was headed this way." He looked at Glintock. "Ask me what other planet is found along this trajectory?"

Glintock's brow furrowed for a moment before smoothing with a grin. "Revjekt."

"Exactly. He's going home."

CHAPTER 22

Litning staggered away from the crashed escape pod. The vehicle left a deep furrow in the field in which he found himself, with the ground still steaming and alight with flames. His breathing was labored, but not due to the crash—all safety features had deployed properly. It also was not due the wounds he had received from Bijin. The cuts had not been deep and had ceased bleeding. The problem was the air, almost as if there was not enough oxygen. The teal clouds cast everything in a soft hue, making it look like he was underwater. That sensation made him gulp more air.

He had not caught the name of the planet he had landed on, but he knew it was the closest the pod could get him to Revjekt. Not very smart to head to a planet with no idea whether he could breathe the air or not, but he figured the pod would not take him somewhere unsafe. It was a lifeboat, after all. In reality, though, nowhere was safe for Litning, not with the item in his possession.

His leather glove tightened as he clutched the statue. As he gazed down at it, the details of his escape from the *Galactic Dream* came rushing back. He had not planned on meeting Mondo on board the ship, nor did he expect a woman in disguise. It was a worthy ruse—she had certainly fooled him—but he wondered how many others had been taken in by her duplicitous nature.

The wind rushed though the tall grass and he snapped his head around, looking for a threat. The mystery men in black aboard the *Galactic Dream* had certainly left an impression. He had not the slightest idea who they were, but they wanted the statue and that made them a threat. There was also Mondo to consider. She was surely on her way after him. The one thing they could all trace to find him was the smoking escape pod lying dormant a few meters away. *Probably wise to get far, far away from it.*

On the horizon, the spires of the nearest city reached for the overcast sky. Powerful spotlights illuminated ships heading off-world. It would take him a day at least to reach the city on foot, but it would take much less time to arrive at the small settlement along the way. He dared to hope he might find some kind of transport there to the city and from there, Revjekt. He just had no idea how he would pay for passage.

A small shuttle passed overhead, prodding him on. For all he knew, it was Mondo, returned to claim her prize. He weighed the statue in his hand before trudging off toward the settlement, fragile hope stirring in his nepast.

CHAPTER 23

Every ounce of Max's being told him to get some rest on the journey to Ventu—the planet on which he believed the Revash had landed—but all he could do was sit on his bed and stare at the pack of rimi tablets on his nightstand. He'd been eager to snatch up the bag in the common area, but now that he'd had hours of contemplation, he truly considered Alesha's words. Rimi had become such an essential piece of his life, he wasn't totally sure he could give it up, even for Alesha.

That was the part that gnawed at his gut. While in prison, he would have done anything to leave Aval and return to Alesha, but now that he knew exactly what he had to do to simply keep her in his life, he didn't believe he was up to the task. He loved Alesha, but did he love the rush of rimi more?

"*Max*," Robert's voice came over the intercom.

"Yeah, Robbie?"

"*We're approaching Ventu.*"

He stared at the pack for another moment. "I'm on my way up."

A few minutes later, he found Roeger in the common area running a diagnostic on the computer station, trying to find out what was wrong with Christi. His chest plate was open, a connection cord jacking him into the system. His head twitched back and forth just slightly enough to make it look like he had a tic, but Max knew it was a result of Roeger scanning lines and lines of code.

"What have we got, buddy?" Max asked.

There was a brief pause as Roeger brought his interactive systems back up. "Nothing as of yet, Maxim. I have only begun the scan."

"Well, thanks for doing it. Wouldn't be able to run the ship without you."

"I am well aware."

Despite Roeger's emotional programming, he could still pull off the cold and detached thing perfectly. "Well, keep up the good work."

"I intend to."

Max turned to leave, but Roeger stopped him.

"Maxim, the air on Ventu is not what you are used to. I would recommend inhalers for all who are going to the surface."

Wincing, he realized he hadn't even considered that. *Still rusty.* "Thanks again, Roeger. I'll grab them on the way out."

"You are most welcome, Maxim."

As he made his way to the cockpit, he felt the ship shudder under his feet. They were landing. He found Robert focused in the pilot's seat, Glintock seated beside him. "How're we doing, Robbie?"

"Scanners are locked in on the escape pod and I'm beginning landing procedures."

"Where is it?"

"Just outside a small settlement, but it's nearby a large city."

"That's what I figured," Max said.

"Are you afraid he's going to run again?" Glintock asked.

"Wouldn't you? His pod's out of fuel and he knows Sierra's out there. My first order of business would be to find the nearest spaceport." He gazed at the control console. "Do we have any idea how long ago he landed?"

"No," Glintock said. "Based on your theory, I'd say no more than a few hours."

"I'd better get the rover ready, then," Max said as he left the cockpit. Winding his way through the ship's corridors, he worked down to the cargo hold. Stacks of metal crates were sporadically spaced along the walls of the hold. They were all empty, for the most part. Max was sure Gerry had some of the foodstuffs stashed there, but a ship that had been in dry dock for almost three years wasn't going to have much in the way of cargo. It was a fact he meant to change as soon as possible.

The center of the hold was dominated by the rover—a four-person hovercraft that looked like a '70s Chevy Nova with no roof or wheels. However it appeared, it helped Max get from point A to point B planet-side. The craft was fastened to the deck, covered in a thick layer of dust. Another reminder of how long he'd been away and all he had to do to get back to normal.

"Reminiscing?" Glintock's voice echoed through the hangar.

He jumped a bit at the sound. "A little, yeah. Just wondering if I'm ever going to get it back."

"What's that?"

"My life."

"It'll come, Mr. Ultra." Glintock crossed the hangar, his eyes checking out the room. "This wreck is going to get you around down there?"

"Wreck? This is a fine piece of hovercraft technology."

Glintock chuckled. "If you say so."

"And why are you implying I'll be down there on my own? You're not coming with me?"

"No, I need to stay here."

"What for?" Before the question had left his lips, he had the answer. "Oh, Gelf?"

"Yes."

"I think you're developing an unhealthy obsession."

"I've been a law enforcement agent longer than you've been alive—I know when a hunch is right."

"Well, as much as I hate to admit it, I need you down there. Alesha's a little wonky after what happened on the *Galactic Dream*. She insists on coming with me, but I could use a more reliable backup, someone to help keep an eye on her."

Glintock smiled tightly. "What about your buddy Gelf?"

"Gelf is good at getting his shots in during a melee, but on a hunt like this, with an opponent like the Revash, I don't think he'll be much help."

"And I don't believe leaving him alone on this ship is an option."

"He won't be alone," Max said.

Glintock cocked an eyebrow.

"Roeger will be on board."

"I'm floating in a sea of relief."

Max smiled. "Robert will be here and so will Gerry. We've got it covered."

Again, Glintock gave him a disbelieving look.

"Trust me."

"You're sure we can't get Ms. Cabal to stay here and babysit?"

"Veck no," Alesha's voice carried from the front of the hold. She stepped into view, dressed in all black leather, looking more than a little dangerous. "At this point, I'm better at this than Max. I'm going." Her eyes flicked between the two of them. "We *are* going, right?"

Max and Glintock exchanged a look.

Soon, the three of them were skimming over the surface of Ventu. The sun was going down, but it was only marked by a dim light hidden behind the teal-colored clouds. The combination of the clouds and hidden sun bathed the landscape in perpetual twilight. It would have been quite beautiful, if they were only there to take in the scenery. It seemed Roeger had been right about the atmosphere. Even cruising around in the rover, Max could feel the thickness of the air. It was heavy and humid, making him sweat in his leather jacket. It was tough to dress right for interplanetary travel.

As they closed in on the escape pod's beacon, Max eased back on the throttle. He spotted the small ship's final resting place and brought the rover to a stop nearby. The pod had created a great rut in the earth, but all around them, long grass swayed in the backwash of the rover's engines. The Revash could have been lying in wait for them.

The trio disembarked and Max waved for them to spread out as they approached the pod. Flames licked the ground in the wake of the pod's crash-landing, but they were dying down. The air was too damn thick. Breathing wasn't a problem—yet—but any prolonged exertion could *make* it a problem.

He held Glintock and Alesha out on the flanks as he headed up the middle, pistol drawn. The pod's hatch was open, the craft appearing empty. His eyes locked in on the nearby settlement and the swath of parted grass that led toward it. He glanced through the open hatch to double check. Empty.

"Looks like he went this way," he said as Glintock and Alesha joined him at the pod.

"As you suspected," Glintock said.

Max shrugged. "It was logical."

"Don't put yourself down like that," Alesha said. "You pieced it together."

"Yeah well, now comes the hard part." He was fairly certain the Revash wouldn't come quietly. The dull ache that had been with him since fighting Merthane on Modan got a little stronger. He took a deep breath. "Let's take the rover—we're losing time and we may need to hightail it out of there."

"Agreed," Glintock said. As they moved back to the hovercraft, he put a hand on Max's arm. "Dead or alive, Mr. Ultra."

He drew back slightly. "Really? We don't want to hear his story first?"

"He killed several security officers when he stole that statue. Are you condoning murder now?"

"No, of course not. I'm just saying, he might be able to give us a little insight into the statue. Maybe he knows something we don't."

Glintock paused. "Perhaps. Murder is unacceptable. This is a society. A loose society, yes, but a society nonetheless."

"Oh, I think I see him waving to us on that spaceship leaving the planet," Alesha interjected. Max and Glintock looked over at her. She was trembling, eyes darting nervously. "Can we settle it later and nab this guy?"

Max gave her a hard stare. "Are you all right? You're shaking."

"I felt a chill, that's all."

"If you're sick, we should probably take you back to the ship." He knew she wasn't sick. The statue was working its voodoo on her.

She ran a hand across her eyes. "I just want to get this over with."

"She's right," Glintock said. "Let's get going."

Max kept the throttle on the rover low, not wanting to tip off the Revash by making a huge racket. His sidelong glance at Alesha went unnoticed as they crept up on the small settlement. Chewing her lip, she had that feverish, wide-eyed look again. Letting her tag along might not have been such a hot idea.

Bringing the rover to a stop several yards from the outermost building, Max got out. He drew his pistol, leading the trio toward the darkened settlement. It looked as though the collected one-story buildings were empty.

Like they had at the escape pod, the group fanned out. Keeping track of the others wouldn't be easy with the buildings cutting off his view. There didn't seem to be any rhyme or reason to the layout of the structures. It looked to be some kind of outpost town— maybe a waystation for travelers on their way to the city. The shadows stretched out along the landscape like dark fingers grasping for the light.

Max moved as silently as he could. The clinking of all the equipment in his belt sounded as loud as a rock concert to him on the quiet plains. He'd lost track of Alesha, but Glintock was a few yards behind him.

Damn it, Glintock, I said keep an eye on her!

As he moved deeper into the confines of the settlement, he began to see low orange lights glowing from inside some of the structures. It didn't mean anyone was home, though. Maybe the residents left the lights on to discourage thieves while they hit the town. There was a smattering of beat-up, one-person, land-based vehicles littered around the village, but there didn't appear to be any kind of central area where the townsfolk could gather. Some of the buildings were in dilapidated condition with cracks and holes in the walls, but the deeper Max moved into the settlement, the better the structures looked. Maybe it was a commuter's town, with all the nightlife being in the city. Then he heard harsh laughter coming from one of the buildings.

Ducking into the shadows, he waved at Glintock to do the same. He hoped Alesha took precautions, but still didn't have eyes on her. One of the buildings had a tough-looking humanoid standing outside the entrance dressed in patchwork clothing with bits of metal armor here and there. Thanks to the shadows, Max couldn't place the alien's species, but he seemed to be standing guard. There were much nicer vehicles lined up outside the building—hover bikes.

Shit. A biker gang? Really?

He wasn't afraid that the three of them couldn't handle a gang of thugs if necessary, but it complicated things. For all he knew, they had already beset the Revash and taken the statue. They might have some useful information, but he wasn't sure how willing they'd be to give it up.

Glintock sidled up next to him. "What do you think?" the agent whispered before taking a hit from his inhaler.

Not so perfect after all. "I think we have two options: go inside and see if these guys know anything or sneak around and keep looking."

"Do you even know what they are?" Glintock asked.

"No, it's too dark to tell."

"Could make communicating with them difficult."

"Yep. Hey, by the way, thanks for keeping an eye on Alesha like I asked."

"I don't need to remind you, Mr. Ultra, that you are in my custody."

"And yet, you were fully prepared to let me come down here by myself."

"I could have monitored you from the ship."

"You two are worse than a married couple," Alesha said, emerging from the shadows.

"Jesus, woman!" Max hissed, jumping back a step.

"Told you I was better at this than you now."

"Did you find anything?"

"Some tracks. He's definitely been here."

"What are you getting from your, uh, statue ESP?"

"What?" Glintock asked. "What's he talking about?"

Alesha ignored the question, but even in the deepening darkness, Max could see her discomfort. "It's close."

"Why didn't anyone tell me about this?" Glintock asked with an edge in his voice. He clearly didn't like being in the dark.

"Okay," Max said, "then we keep looking."

"What about those guys?" she asked with a nod to the biker hangout.

"Tread lightly."

"She can talk to the statue?" Glintock asked.

"Can we discuss this later? We've got a job to do here," Max said.

More harsh laughter erupted from the hangout and the door opened, revealing two more of the humanoids. In the light spilling out of the doorway, Max could see that the two bikers were furry with animal-like faces, minus the snouts. Acrid smoke billowed out of the building carrying with it the smell of alcohol. Apparently, there was a nice little party going on in there. Was it possible the Revash was inside with them?

"What are we waiting for?" Glintock asked.

Max turned to face the other two. "I'm sure I'm going to regret bringing this up, but it's possible he's in there with them." They had to cover all their bases. "You two stay here and keep an eye out. I'm going to sneak around the side of their hangout and take a peek inside."

"I think we've established that I'm the stealthier one here," Alesha said.

She was right, but he wasn't about to put her in harm's way, especially with how twitchy she was getting. "No, I'll handle this. Stay out of sight. I'll let you know when we can move out."

"But—"

"'Lesha, don't make me have Glintock arrest you." He moved to circle around.

Sticking to the shadows, he hugged the building walls as he made his way back to the biker hangout. The haphazard layout of the buildings actually worked to his advantage as he was able to bypass the bikers standing outside. As he crept closer, he felt more and more exposed due to the light cascading from the windows.

Staying low to the ground, he peeked into one of the windows. The biker gang members were all dressed in the same hodgepodge of mismatched armor and dark colors. The interior of the building was decorated with banners and various pieces of furniture. Max wondered if the town was the gang's hideout or if they had driven the original residents off like raiders.

They all seemed to be part of the same race of people, but there was no sign of the Revash. They were certainly celebrating something as drink and some kind of drugs made the rounds. Two females were stripped down to nothing and cavorting on a large banquet table, drawing the majority of the other members' attention.

"Weird," Max muttered as a shadow fell over him. "'Lesha, I told you I'd come and get y—" He stopped when he heard heavy breathing and caught the musty scent of animal hair.

He didn't have a chance to turn his head before a giant clawed hand grabbed him by the shoulder and hoisted him off the ground, jerking his pistol from his hand. For better or worse, he'd found the Revash.

"You were on the *Galactic Dream!*" the Revash hissed. "Why are you following me? Did *she* send you?"

"H-hey buddy, let's talk about this." He eased his hand to a pouch on his belt.

The Revash wasn't having any of that. He hurled Max to the ground, the lush grass doing little to lessen the impact for his already weary body. Before he could even respond, the alien cuffed his head with the back of his furry hand, knocking his earpiece into the grass.

His head swam, but it felt like it could have been much worse, like the Revash was holding back or something. With his claws, he could have eviscerated Max without a thought. *He's going easy on me, but why?* The one-sided fight had brought the biker party to a screeching halt. He could hear raised voices in the clubhouse.

Nothing felt broken, but if the Revash kept up the assault, he could pulverize Max's bones. Max's breathing was labored, thanks to the shitty atmosphere. He didn't exactly have time to take a break, though. With no idea where his pistol was, he reached into his belt for a flash capsule. He tossed the palm-sized device at the Revash, who knocked it away toward the clubhouse effortlessly. The capsule discharged its payload—the flash of a thousand cameras, basically—and the bikers let out a string of foreign words that definitely sounded like curses, but Max could barely hear them over the Revash's roar.

He dragged himself across the ground away from his adversary. "Over here!" His voice was a mere croak. "Glintock! He's over here!" Without his communicator, it was the best he could do. In this case, his best would probably get him killed.

He'd pulled himself a measly five yards away from the Revash as the alien recovered from the paparazzi-like attack. Before the Revash could lumber after him again, a laser bolt sizzled through the air between them.

"Stop right there!" Max had never thought he'd be so happy to hear Glintock's baritone. The agent stood there like he owned the town, pistol trained on the Revash. Alesha stood beside him, but she didn't even look in Max's direction. Her eyes darted around the area, looking for something. "By order of the GAC, you are under arrest!"

"An organization that I do not acknowledge," the Revash said with an arrogant tone. "You are not with Mondo and you have delayed me enough." With one fluid motion, the Revash reached up to the nearest rooftop and vaulted up onto it, scampering away from Max and his friends. Glintock fired a couple of errant shots at him before he disappeared.

"*No!*" Alesha cried out as she raced after the Revash on the ground.

"No, that's okay 'Lesha, I'm fine," Max muttered as he struggled to sit up. His breathing wasn't getting any easier from the heavy air. He pulled his inhaler from his belt and took a pull of oxygen as he groped around for his earpiece, which wasn't too far away.

At least Glintock cared enough to come over and check on him. "Can you stand?"

"Working on it," he groaned as he took Glintock's proffered hand. "He didn't have the statue. That's why Alesha ran off after him. She can feel it."

"As I've pointed out, it would have helped to have known that *before* we came down here. I told you, dead or alive."

"I'm not going to give that guy any awards, but he could have killed me in an instant and didn't. There's more going on here than we know, Glintock."

"Right you are, little man." The voice came from one of several bikers. Standing in a group, they appeared out for blood, blocking the way Glintock and Alesha had come. "You vecked up our little party and I heard this one say he's GAC. That's not—"

"Really?" Max said. "You guys show up *now*? You missed the big monster tossing me around like a rag doll?" His eyes searched the ground for his lost pistol.

The biker at the front of the gaggle looked positively confused. "What monster?"

A booming roar echoed through the buildings.

"That monster." He took another flash capsule from his belt and tossed it on the ground in front of the bikers, pulling Glintock around the corner to shield them. The capsule went off, followed by several more foreign curses. He peeked around the corner and saw that the bikers were not handling the flash capsule's effects well at all. "Come on, we've got to help Alesha."

Glintock led the way as Max limped off in pursuit. They came to a more open area and found Alesha facing off with the Revash. She danced around the alien, a knife in each hand. Max had never seen her move the way she did. Her attacks were graceful— beautiful, even. In the growing darkness, he could see the dark wetness on the Revash's arms. She nicked him again and the Revash bellowed.

"Woman, you know not what you are dealing with," he said as he lunged at her in an unsuccessful grab.

"The vessel is mine, beast. Memta will be free once more!"

What the hell is she talking about?

Max's eyes scanned the shadows. The Revash must have stashed the statue nearby. He tapped Glintock on the shoulder. "Get in there and help her. I'll hobble around and try to find it."

"With the things she's saying, I'm not sure *who* I should stop."

"Wait, you know what it means?"

The two of them were split apart by a knife slicing through the air between them.

"What the fuck?"

The Revash labored for breath on the ground, while Alesha glared at the two of them with a sinister stare.

"'Lesha?" Max said as he took a step toward her.

She brandished her remaining knife. "Come no closer, mortal."

"Mortal? What's gotten into you? What's wrong?"

Her sinister sneer cracked. The knife in her hand wavered. She blinked and her eyes darted around. Her appearance wasn't unlike a frightened doe. "Max...I can hear her in my head! The vessel is so close." This last part was a whisper. She sounded like a woman losing her mind.

He reached out to her. "I know, sweetheart, I know. Just come over here and we'll look for it together."

She closed her eyes tightly and pressed her hands to her ears, but threatened with the knife again when Max took a step toward her. "It's like she's devouring me! Her voice is so loud in my mind. I have to find the statue—set her free...."

"How long did she hold the statue?" Glintock murmured.

"It brushed her arm," Max replied, no shortage of confusion in his voice.

She took a halting step toward a ruined building behind her.

"No! Alesha, let's-let's look together. We can find it together."

Her face relaxed and she smiled at him. "Together?"

Relief pulsed through him. "Yeah, we can beat this together."

She closed her eyes with a warm smile, but then her face twitched and her expression shifted to pure malice. "*Like we beat the rimi?*"

Fuck.

Before Max could stop her, she broke into a run toward the ruined building. She reached into an alcove and let out a throat-shredding scream.

"ALESHA!"

Turquoise flame spread up her arm until her entire body was wreathed in the blue fire. Pulling her hand from the alcove, she revealed the statue clutched in her hand. Her expression shifted from shock to pain, but as she tossed her head back and forth, she almost didn't even look like herself. She convulsed, as if wracked by an invisible blow and screamed again.

"Give me your gun!" Max said as he grabbed at Glintock.

"I've read your file—I'm a better shot." The agent took aim and fired a shot at the statue that was deflected by the blue energy enveloping Alesha.

A powerful wind blasted into the area, whipping her hair around as she slowly rose into the air. Once she reached about ten feet, the statue fell from her hand, thudding harmlessly on the ground. Her eyes opened—blank and glowing blue.

"I *LIVE!*" Blue light streaked away from her into the evening sky, a look of absolute ecstasy on her face.

Leaning on Glintock, Max looked up at her forlornly. "Je-sus fuck."

CHAPTER 24

"The heavens will weep and the universe will tremble, for Memta has arisen!" Though the words came from Alesha's mouth, they were not hers. Her voice was still clearly feminine, but deeper as if it had been processed through both a synthesizer and an amplifier. "The payment of souls will begin here, on this world."

"This is definitely a problem," Max muttered to Glintock as the agent dragged him behind a broken wall for cover.

"Your talent for understatement is astounding."

"If I don't say anything, I'll collapse in a screaming heap." His eyes flicked over to the Revash, who shielded his face from both the light and wind of Memta's rebirth. "We need to huddle up with the Revash and figure this out. Maybe he can tell us what a Memta is and how we can get it out of my girlfriend."

Glintock let out a long sigh and Max had a feeling that he wasn't going to like whatever the lawman said next.

"What aren't you telling me?" Max asked.

"That this turn of events is not entirely surprising."

"I've a growing urge to punch you in the face, but keep going."

"Believe me when I say, I didn't want this to happen to Alesha."

"But...."

"I wasn't completely honest about what happened on the research ship." Glintock gave Max an uneasy look. "One of the scientists, a female scientist, touched the statue with her bare hands and *she* destroyed herself and the ship."

The sobering revelation left Max speechless. He looked at Glintock with glazed eyes, like he couldn't really register the agent's face. Across the clearing, the Revash had wisely sought cover too, but Alesha arrested Max's gaze. The smile on her face could only be described as one of malicious joy. Her expression was both her and completely alien. She seemed to be getting brighter as jets of blue plasma spilled out of her aura, igniting the buildings they struck with blue flame.

If she controls that shit, this could get messy fast. Reaching into his jacket, he produced a pair of leather gloves. As he pulled them on, he started to stand up.

"Where do you think you're going?" Glintock asked.

"I'm going to circle around and meet up with the Revash. He may know something we don't."

"You mean the same Revash that beat you so badly you've been limping around ever since?"

Max squinted at him. "I can't tell if you're joking or just being an asshole."

"Half and half. I don't know if approaching him is a good idea. What if she sees you? She may be just as inclined to fry you as hug you."

"Well I can't sit here and do nothing!" The dam was breaking inside him. His chest tightened as his stomach twisted in knots. A lump formed in his throat. *Keep it together, Max. For her*. "I'm not letting her go out like this, Matthias. The Revash has to know something and I'm going to find out what."

As he rose up again, he immediately ducked back down. The biker gang had arrived on the scene. He cautiously peered over the top of the wall to see how their interaction with Alesha would play out.

The bikers stared up at her with mouths agape. They looked ready for a fight with knives, clubs, and blunt metal objects clutched in their furry hands. As they fanned out around the clearing, he could see that some of them carried laser rifles strapped to their backs. Alesha's expression was cool, almost detached, curiosity.

"I think we just got our diversion," Max whispered.

"Ah," Alesha, or Memta said, "fresh souls for me to play with."

"Oh, you want to play, honey?" the lead biker called out to her. "We can definitely play. Those are our homes you're destroying there!"

"Like you, they are but dust motes amongst the stars— insignificant."

The biker spat on the ground and pointed at Memta. "Show 'er how we play, boys!"

Every biker with a gun took aim at Memta. Max's heart thudded in his chest, but then he remembered how successful Glintock had been with his pistol. The bikers opened fire.

"Apparently, these guys see women spouting combustible blue energy every day," Max said. "Let's go. Something tells me this won't last long."

Keeping low and behind cover, Max and Glintock moved back around toward the other side of the clearing. Every so often, Max glanced over the wall to see what was going on with the bikers and Alesha. The screams were not a good sign.

Predictably, the laser fire did nothing to Memta and she reciprocated with jets of what could only be described as blue magma shooting from her hands. The grass in the clearing ignited, as did the flesh of the bikers unfortunate enough to get caught in her sights. The smell of burning fur filled the air and Max had to fight back his heaving stomach. Memta's attack didn't kill instantly and those struck by her outburst ran around screaming, engulfed in flames. She torched her hopelessly outmatched opponents without remorse. Her mouth pulled back in a sinister grin as she lashed out with her power.

The bikers' screams were knives in Max's heart. *She is not that thing. We can get her back.*

His battered body didn't agree with running while crouching, and he grabbed for his lower back as it locked up on him. He sank down to the ground.

Glintock sat beside him. "Are you all right?"

He nodded. "Just need a minute to unknot my back."

Glintock nudged him and pointed. "Looks like you were right."

He followed Glintock's finger. The two of them were angled on the Revash, so they could see him safely huddled behind a building that wasn't on fire. The alien looked utterly defeated.

"He looks like he could use a friend," Max said.

"I still think this is a bad idea, but there's no way we can beat her as she is now."

Nodding, Max said nothing. He didn't want to acknowledge that Alesha and Memta were the same—he couldn't. Only the Revash could help, he was certain—unless there was more Glintock wasn't telling him. The agent had seemed remorseful about holding back earlier, so Max was sure he wasn't keeping anything else from him. The floating woman wrapped in blue flame reminded him he couldn't be sure of anything, though.

The bikers' screams pulled him out of his doubt-filled reverie. He set his jaw. "All right, let's do this." It felt like claws scraping against his weary body as he worked himself into a crouching position, but he gritted his teeth, trying to push the pain from his mind. He had another way to fix it, but he had to be strong for Alesha.

The two of them moved behind a sturdier building, allowing them to stand upright. Stretching out his muscles gave him some blessed relief, but not much—pain still flared all over his body. Smoke hung lazily throughout the area along with sweltering heat from Memta's fires. The screams had died down, thankfully, but that only meant those who had been screaming were dead.

He peered around the corner to keep eyes on the Revash. The hulking alien sat on the ground, making no obvious move to escape. Max began to doubt the despondent Revash would have any answers. Maybe the guy just caved under stress.

Memta hung in the air over the clearing, a look of ecstasy on her face. She appeared to be totally unaware of Max and Glintock.

Motioning for Glintock to follow him, Max moved as quickly as he could across the expanse, plopping himself right beside the Revash. The alien jumped, but soon bowed his head again. Glintock sat on the other side of him.

Max held his hand out to the Revash. "Maxim Ultra. Nice to meet you." The alien ignored him. "You don't seem nearly as rambunctious as before."

"Be gone, human. Let me mourn my failure in peace before Memta takes my life," the Revash said with a growl.

"That's a pretty defeatist attitude."

"Can you not see her power? There is no hope. I have failed her as well as my people."

"All I see is my girlfriend having a complete meltdown." He hoped his pun masked the fear in his voice. "What was in the statue that's got her all riled up?"

The Revash gave him a bemused look. "Memta, of course."

"Right, but what is Memta?"

"You do not know? Then why have you been pursuing me? Why should I help you?"

"Because if you don't," Glintock said pointedly. "You'll be going up for murdering those security officers when you stole the statue."

The Revash bowed his head. "Regrettable actions, I can assure you. There was no other way."

"Somehow, I doubt that."

The Revash nodded, but flinched as another building on the other side of the clearing exploded. "My name is Litning. The person who hired me to steal the artifact, I only knew as Mondo."

"Was that the guy you were fighting with on the *Galactic Dream*?" Max asked, though he was sure he knew the truth.

"It turned out *he* was a *she*," Litning responded.

"Sierra," Max said.

"She positioned me to take all the blame, but I had other ideas for the statue. I planned to return it to my home world of Revjekt."

"Called it," Max blurted, drawing a glare from Glintock.

"I had hoped to buy my way back into my tribe by recovering the statue."

"Why were you separated?" Glintock asked.

"I was exiled for killing another."

"No surprises there," Glintock said.

"Do not speak as if you know me...."

"Glintock. Agent Glintock, actually. All evidence points to you being a violent offender, so...."

Another explosion and a fresh chorus of screams interrupted Glintock. Max couldn't bring himself to see what was going on as Alesha's once-pleasant laughter turned into a cutting cackle that echoed all around them.

"Okay, right now, I don't give a fat crap who did what, but I've got to get this Memta thing out of her. Is there any way to do that?"

"Perhaps. You must understand, Maxim, Memta is a Revash goddess. She will not free your mate easily."

"Wait, did you say a *goddess*?"

"Imprisoned eons ago by Revash spell casters, Memta is known by my people as the Goddess of Fire. The elders at the time were able to trick Memta and secure her in the statue, or so the legend goes. The statue was stolen hundreds of years ago from Revjekt, lost until Mon—Sierra rediscovered it."

Max slumped back against the wall. "With help from yours truly." He looked at Glintock. "Did you know this?"

Glintock shrugged. "Only what I've already told you."

"So how do we stop her?"

"We need to get the statue back," Litning said.

"That could prove to be difficult," Glintock said as he peeked out at the clearing.

"What's the statue going to do?"

"We can use it to imprison Memta again."

"And how do you propose we do that?" Glintock asked.

Litning's shoulders sagged as he looked at them with tired eyes. "The legends speak of an ancient Revash incantation that should work."

"*Should* work?" Max asked. "That sounds pretty suspect."

"No one has had to use it in thousands of years."

Max wasn't brimming with confidence. "Well, getting the statue won't be easy—maybe we can do an end run on her or something—but the rest doesn't sound so bad. I'm guessing you do the incantation?"

Litning looked at him blankly and Max got a sinking feeling that he was missing something. The Revash clarified things for him. "You do not understand, the statue must be in contact with her skin while the incantation is recited, if the legends are correct."

That *complicates things*. He kept his face neutral, but in his mind, he was screaming like a man with his hair on fire. "Tell me this, is Alesha still in there?"

Litning's lengthy pause wasn't encouraging. "I do not know. She may be completely consumed by Memta."

"Then cramming your god back into that statue won't necessarily bring her back."

"No. But Memta must be stopped."

Blood thudded in Max's ears. The hopelessness of the situation collapsed in on him, like he was being buried alive. He'd gotten her involved in this and then let her come along to catch Litning, knowing that she wasn't completely up to the task. He might have lost Alesha forever and it was all his fault.

"Litning's right, Maxim," Glintock said, his words managing to slice through Max's panic. "We have to stop her." It was the truth, but Max wouldn't accept it. There had to be another way.

He closed his eyes, focusing to find a way out for all of them. In his mind's eye, he could only see Alesha and her dazzling smile. She was laughing at something, but before he could figure out what it was, her smile was perverted into the malevolent grin of Memta.

Shaking his head, he tried to dislodge the image from his mind. *How could this have happened? How did this thing corrupt her so fast? Alesha's the strongest woman I know.*

His head shot up as an idea struck him. "We don't have to do this alone."

Glintock's brow knitted. "What do you mean? Call the ship?"

"No. You two try to grab the statue and get ready to corral her or whatever."

"What are you going to do?" Glintock asked in a tone that said he already didn't like the plan.

"I'm going to have a talk with my girlfriend."

"*Ex*-girlfriend, and I don't think she's in a talking mood," Glintock countered.

"I'm the diversion, Matthias. You were in this to stop a killer and secure the statue. I'm in this to get my life back and I don't have much of a life without her." He stood up gingerly.

"Maxim, this might not be the best plan," Glintock said.

"Look what she's doing, Matthias. If you think the three of us are going to be able to sneak up and tackle her or something, we're going to have to discuss you going into my rimi stash. You're the one with the authority and Litning here is the only one who can get the statue back where it belongs. I'm expendable. If Alesha's still in there, she won't kill me."

"You can't depend on that."

"It's all I've got." He started to leave, but Litning stopped him.

"How should the two of us approach this?"

"What, I have to think of everything?"

He moved out from behind the building and limped into the clearing to face probable death. *I am a dumb shit.*

Memta still hung in the air, her blue glow lighting the area. She held one of the bikers by the throat, his neck already snapped.

That's not Alesha. That's not Alesha.

"So many ways to take a mortal's life, but this way is almost...beautiful."

Dammit, she definitely sounds *like Alesha.*

She turned her head toward him, flashing Alesha's smile. "Hello, Maxim."

It was a knife in his gut. "You know who I am?"

"Of course, you are very prominent in this host's mind."

"Can I speak with her?"

Memta looked back at the lifeless body in her hand. She casually released the corpse, letting it hit the ground with a crunch. "No."

"Can I ask why? Letting me talk with her isn't going to impact your standing, right?"

The goddess' eyes narrowed. "I see what you are doing."

Oh shit, can she read my mind?

"I can feel her, just below the surface, struggling to get out. I like this host. She's strong...sensual. I'm positive I could get any man—or woman—to do my bidding."

Looking around the scorched clearing, he didn't doubt she was right. Buildings blown apart, brush still ablaze, but the cool blue glow from her body made it all less hellish. "Why are you telling me this?"

The wicked grin returned to her face. "Because I wanted to give you a modicum of hope before I steal your life!" She whipped her arm out and a blue beam of light shot toward him.

He had no hope of avoiding the strike. In the split second before the blast hit him, he resigned himself to a quick death. It left the sour taste of failure in his mouth.

The beam struck, but instead of flash-frying him, it hit him like a wave—a wave of bricks. As he tumbled across the clearing, he afforded himself the hope that Memta had taunted him with. *Maybe Alesha's still in there after all.*

The blast packed a wallop, reminding him of past injuries he thought he'd left behind. At least he wasn't engulfed in flames—

the charred corpse beside him hadn't been so lucky. As he struggled to his knees, his body groaned in protest.

I am not *going to look like I'm kneeling.*

"*How?*" Memta cried. "You should be a cinder!"

"Sorry to disappoint, sister."

Her eyes blazed, but her confused expression slowly became a smile. "Oh, I *do* love this host. She is indeed a strong one. I will bend her to my will and to do that, I will destroy *you!*"

Again, Memta unleashed a cone of blue energy at him, but it simply knocked him flat on his back. It didn't feel good by any stretch, but he knew he was getting off easy. *Thanks, sweetheart.*

The screech that erupted from Memta also pleased him to no end.

Slowly but surely, Max pushed his way to his feet. With every twitch of his body, he had to resist crying out in pain. He stood up straight, his gaze locked on Memta, save for the quick flick of his eyes to check on Litning and Glintock. Apparently, they had set the slapdash plan in motion. He had to get Memta near the statue.

She ruined everything by floating closer to him.

God damn it.

"Why do you struggle, Maxim?" she asked, her voice actually becoming some form of soothing. "Clearly you are in agony. Why not let me send you to the next world, free of pain and the shackles of responsibility?"

"That sounds nice, but I've got too much to do here. The most important thing I have to do is talk to Alesha. Can we make that happen?"

"Am I not a worthy companion? I am the best incarnation of Alesha."

That's debatable.

She floated closer and lower, so that he wasn't constantly looking up at her.

"I just want to make sure she's all right in there. No offense, I'm sure you're a lovely lady, but you're a bit too aggressive for me."

She smiled. It looked like a genuine Alesha smile—the kind she gave him when she liked something he said, but didn't want to admit to it by laughing. Memta drew closer and his mind flashed to the biker with the broken neck.

Fuck.

He tried to block her grab, but she was inhumanly fast. Her hand wrapped around his throat and he grasped at her wrist. When she lifted him off the ground, he started to panic.

"Is this the aggression to which you were referring?"

His voice was a gurgled mess as he fought for air. "Yeah...that's it."

"I offer you the companionship of a goddess and you *rebuke me?*" The blue glow around her intensified as they rose off the ground.

He slapped at her arm, but to no avail—she wasn't releasing him. "A...Al..."

"What?" Her grip eased enough for him to catch his breath, but he was more afraid of gravity as they went higher.

"Alesha."

She laughed. "You are persistent, mortal, I will grant you that." She pulled him closer until they were nose to nose. "I do not know how much clearer I can make it, but this body is *mine* now. Your precious Alesha no longer lives here."

She's lying. There was one simple reason how he knew Alesha still existed, but he had to draw her out before Memta started choking the life out of him again. "I know you're still in there, Alesha, and I hope you can hear me. I'm sorry."

Memta flinched, but snarled. "Quiet."

"I'm sorry about all of this. When I came to you on Modan, it was to protect you from Kalen, but more than that, I wanted you near me."

She gritted her teeth, but her grip only tightened slightly. "*Silence!*" With Max still in tow, she dive-bombed the ground, but pulled up at the last moment, floating much lower than they had been.

"You're all I've ever wanted in this life, from the moment we met. I lost sight of that and I'm sorry."

Her grip tightened. Breathing became more difficult.

"I hope I'll have the chance to make it up to you."

Memta closed her eyes tightly with a growl. There was clearly some internal conflict going on inside her.

"But if I've really lost you forever, then I hope Memta makes it quick, because I don't want any part of a life without you." He felt lighter. Two and a half years of baggage, unloaded in a few moments. He wished he had told her that any of the numerous times they'd been alone over the last several days. Hopefully, some of it got through.

His heart sank when he was greeted with Memta's wicked grin. "I told you, she is gone—*forever*."

Last card to play—it better work. "Then why haven't you killed me yet?"

Memta's face twisted in a snarl before her scream pierced his eardrums. Her grip tightened on his throat again, but it was followed by a sharp increase in his body temperature. She was slowly doing to him what she had done instantly to the bikers—she was going to cook him.

"Don't…let…her…do this, 'Lesha. Love…you."

The heat cut off and for a moment, Memta's eyes changed from blank blue orbs to Alesha's dark brown eyes.

"'Lesha?"

"Max!" She sounded like Alesha again.

Before they had a chance to say anything else, she threw him away from her.

"NO!" The scream sounded like Memta again. His speech had definitely triggered something.

He plummeted several feet before landing in Litning's waiting arms.

"Thanks, Fuzzy."

"I do not like this name, *Fuzzy*."

Another Earth-shattering scream from Memta split the air. The goddess clutched her head and rose even higher. Litning deposited Max on the ground as Glintock joined them, statue in hand.

"How is he holding that?" Max asked.

"With Memta free, it is just a statue," Litning explained.

"How do we get her back in here?" Glintock asked. "It'll be impossible to get her down."

"Give it a minute," Max said, his gaze to the sky. "I think the two of them are working out some issues."

Memta's aura had turned violent, going from a luminous glow to something resembling fireworks shooting off her. If it hadn't filled Max with so much dread, he might have called it beautiful.

A basketball-sized probe from the *Sequel* floated into the area and caught his attention. It looked like the crew had gotten concerned and wanted to check the scene out. He waved at the little robot, letting the others know they were all right. Alesha probably wouldn't be happy they were recording her at her lowest, but she'd get over it, if she actually came back to them.

The goddess hurled her trademarked blue magma down into the clearing, pummeling the ground and buildings she'd already destroyed. To add insult to injury, she destroyed the probe as well.

"We've got to get out of here!" Glintock bellowed over the exploding projectiles.

"No wait!" Max surveyed the area quickly to confirm. "She's missing us on purpose."

It definitely looked that way. The three of them were grouped together, easy targets if Memta were really trying. It was Alesha fighting back, he was sure of it.

Memta, or possibly Alesha, screamed as she hurled more bolts out into the air. Her screams came in two distinct voices and Max recalled what Glintock had said about the scientist on the research ship.

"Come on, Alesha," he whispered. "Come on! You can beat her!"

On the horizon, the *Sequel* sped toward the clearing. If Robert suspected Alesha was a danger to all of them, he might fire on her. In her current conflicted condition, Max wasn't sure what that would mean for her. Would Memta save Alesha or let her die, hoping to score another host?

She clutched her head as she floated even closer to the ground. The glow surrounding her ignited the nearest grass she hadn't already torched. Her body twisted and contorted as she continued crying out.

"Max!" she called out in Alesha's voice. "Help me!"

His heart broke for her. He didn't know how Alesha could expel the goddess from her body. Then he looked at her hands. They were bare. He whipped off his leather jacket. "Glintock, give me the statue!"

"What? Why?"

"Give it to me!"

Glintock tossed the statue to Max, who in turn, passed his jacket to Litning.

"What is this for?" the Revash asked.

"To protect you when you tackle her. Now, Fuzzy!"

Max and Litning sprang into action with the Revash wrapping Max's jacket around Memta as he drove her into the ground. Max took the inert statue in his gloved hands and pressed it to Alesha's forehead.

She screamed as soon as the stone touched her skin and her aura dimmed for a moment before it flared. The expression on her face shifted rapidly from ecstasy to fear to anger and everything in-between. It felt like watching a person with multiple personalities physically transform into all their personas. It was nothing compared to the blue beams of energy that shot out of her eyes and mouth.

Her screams grated on Max's soul, but he kept the statue pressed to her head. He could feel it warming beneath his gloves and his stomach lurched as he wondered if instead of freeing Alesha, he'd actually accelerated her demise.

His breath caught in his throat as he realized something. "We forgot the goddamned incantation!"

"There is no guarantee it will work!" Litning hollered over Alesha's screams and the roaring in Max's ears.

"She needs all the help she can get!"

A wind rushed through the clearing—the engine backwash of the *Sequel* landing just outside the settlement. Max didn't take his eyes off of Alesha.

"You can do it, baby," he muttered. "I know you can do this."

A look of pain gripped her face as she gritted her teeth and screamed. "*Get out of me, you bitch!*"

The aura imploded on Alesha. A shockwave blew Max and Litning back, tumbling across the scorched grass. The smoking statue shot into the air before embedding itself in the soil, while Alesha appeared to pass out. Max rushed over to her, cradling her in his arms. Her eyes were closed, skin pale and clammy, but she was breathing.

Brushing her hair back from her face, he kissed her forehead, rocking her back and forth. He refused to let the worst possible scenario into his thinking, instead putting his lips close to her ear. "Come on, baby, wake up! Don't let this all be for nothing. The ship's here—didn't even have to call them. We can leave and get our lives back to normal, but I just need you to wake up!"

Her eyes shot open and she inhaled sharply as if she'd just awoken from a nightmare. She looked around frantically for a moment before her gaze settled on Max. Her look of desperation melted into a relieved smile. She touched his face. "Thank you," she croaked.

"For what?"

"Believing in me."

"Always."

She embraced him and he held her tight.

The sound of slow clapping interrupted their reunion.

"Bravo, Mr. Hero. Bra-vo."

The voice sent a shiver up Max's spine. He didn't have to look up to see who it was, but he did and was shocked anyway.

Standing there like she owned the town was Sierra. Beside her, a timid-looking Gelf.

"Je-sus fuck."

Glintock leaned closer to him. "I told you my hunches were usually right."

CHAPTER 25

It was a shitty situation. A smirking Sierra stood about fifteen feet from Max and his friends, holding them at gunpoint. Her no longer silent partner, Gelf, stood to her left, his own pistol trained on Max. Gelf's face was streaked with shame.

"Sorry Boss, it's nothing personal," Gelf said.

"It feels pretty personal, Gelf." Max wasn't sure if he was about to spit with rage or break down in tears.

"You shoulda listened to Glintock. He almost had me a few times, but you being my biggest defender helped in keeping my cover, so thanks."

"Fuck you," Max said with as much venom as he could muster.

"Now Max," Sierra said, "don't be a sore loser."

His glare turned in her direction. Her aim was less trained on him than it was floating amongst the group, lingering on Litning longer than the others. Why she and Gelf weren't gunning them all down was a mystery to him. Maybe he was missing something.

"Do you like my new style?" Sierra asked, tousling her hair.

"What?"

"I did it for you." Her stare turned to Alesha and Max realized that she *was* kind of wearing her hair like Alesha did before. The color was black with blue highlights. He figured she'd changed it to avoid detection, but now she just sounded insane.

"What happened to Roeger, Gerry, and Robert?"

Gelf chuckled, seemingly getting over his guilt. "Oh, they got what was coming to them." A toothy grin broke across his face. "Especially that nosy, vecking robot."

Max's body tensed. Though it would most certainly end up in his getting killed, he wanted to charge Gelf and beat him to death. He didn't want to think about what the little shit had done to Roeger.

"You needn't worry about them, Max," Sierra said. "You've got bigger problems right now—your *former* crew being the least of them."

Now I want to beat her *to death*.

"The Glutob in particular was quite easy to handle. I thought he'd be tougher to take out after what Gelf told me about his performance on the *Galactic Dream*."

"Yes, how *did* you escape the *Galactic Dream*, anyway?" As soon as Max asked, the answer clicked. "You stowed aboard the *Sequel*."

"Of course. Once you'd inadvertently helped Litning get away from me, there was only one place I *could* go." She looked at Litning. "If anyone could track this vecking turncoat, it was you, Max."

"I was never going to give you Memta, witch," Litning spat. "My path was set. Neither you, nor your masters can ever hope to contr—"

"Don't pretend you were being an altruist in all this, Litning. I know what your plan was—*was* being the operative word." She fired her pistol and a thin red laser struck Litning in the side as he turned to try and avoid it.

With a sharp cry, the Revash crashed to the ground, unmoving.

"No!" Max blurted. Though he hadn't been sure if he could completely trust Litning, he'd helped them bring Alesha back and Max had a feeling they'd need his help with Sierra—if they lived that long.

"Sorry," Sierra said. "I don't speak well in front of large groups. Now, if you're interested in preserving the lives of friends both old and new, Max, you'll join me for a little chat. I think you owe me that much for keeping you alive in prison."

His brow furrowed. *What is she talking about?*

Gelf cleared it up for him. "You're the whole reason I was on Aval. You're welcome."

"My rimi addiction thanks you." He found it odd that the comment came so easily to him when only hours earlier, Alesha had to practically beat it out of him. He just wanted to stick it to Gelf somehow. "I trusted you, Gelf—vouched for you every step of the way."

"And I thank you for that." His smile faded. "Don't try and guilt trip me, Max—it won't work."

Sierra cleared her throat loudly. "Come here, Max. My trigger finger's getting itchy."

He didn't have a choice. It was a small thing, but once again, Sierra was getting what she wanted. If Alesha and Glintock had any hope of surviving the ordeal, he had to comply with Sierra's orders. He glanced over at Glintock, who nodded at him. Max suspected the agent had experience with these types of situations. He looked into Alesha's eyes, hoping it wouldn't be the last time he'd ever gaze into them. All he wished for was more time. They kissed, slowly and deeply.

The sound of a laser bolt cut through the air.

"That's enough of that," Sierra said, her pistol pointing into the sky.

Is that jealousy? I might be able to use that. He stood up slowly, unwilling to let go of Alesha.

"Be careful," she said, eyes locked on Sierra.

"Always."

"Oh, one thing before you come talk to me," Sierra said as she produced a folded up velvet bag from her belt. Unraveled, it looked big enough to hold the statue. She tossed it to Max. "Be a dear and bring Memta to me."

The bag landed in the grass near the statue, which sat embedded in the ground near Glintock. Max looked at the bag to Sierra and back again.

"Is there something wrong, Max?"

"You think I'm just going to bag it up and hand it to you?"

A short laugh erupted from her mouth. "Bag *her* up. *Her*," she muttered. "Take a look around, lover. I have your ship and your crew under gunpoint. Me walking away with Memta is an inevitability, whether I kill all of you and pick her up myself or not. I'm sure you'd like to avoid that particular fate."

She clearly wanted to rub her victory in his face, but she also had the same fevered look in her eyes he'd seen in Alesha's. Was Memta talking to Sierra too? As Max tightened his gloves and trudged over to the statue, he had to wonder: *Why is she dragging this out? Why keep us alive?*

Though he had his gloves on, he touched the statue gingerly. After what happened to Alesha, the artifact needed to be treated with *respect*.

Gelf didn't see it that way. "Stop being such a *flaza* and pick it up."

Max's eyes jumped to Gelf, who didn't flinch from his gaze. *Fucking worm.* "Maybe I'll drill it at your head and we'll see how well you can catch before Memta turns you inside out."

"You try that, and I'll perforate your entire body." Gelf's vivid threat shook Max.

"I thought we were friends, Gelf."

"We were, Max. This is business. It's just a job, that's all." There appeared to be a hint of sorrow in Gelf's eyes.

"I told you not to trust him, Mr. Ultra. He's nothing but a lowlife piece of nakr—"

Gelf cuffed Glintock across the head with his pistol. "Shut up!"

The strike bloodied Glintock, opening a welt above his eye. Once he'd righted himself, he locked on Gelf with a defiant stare.

Gelf didn't spare Glintock another glance. Instead, he swung his pistol back in Max's direction. "Now stop vecking around and pick up the vecking statue." His detached tone chilled Max's blood.

"Thank you, Gelf," Sierra said. "I was afraid I was going to have to shoot Alesha in order to speed things along here."

"You can try, you vecking hor—"

"*Alesha*," Max cut her off. "Not now." He ignored her steely look. She didn't know Sierra like he did. Alesha was a tough, independent woman, but Sierra was a straight up killer—something she'd already proved with Litning. He wasn't going to lose Alesha because she needed the last word.

"Why so hostile, Alesha?" Sierra asked. "Especially with all we shared the last time we saw each other?"

"We didn't share anything, you vecking petch!"

"Now, now, I don't believe you. That's not what you said after our hot and sweaty girls' night."

"You couldn't get me hot if you tried, you lying sack of—"

"*Alesha!*" Max glared at her. "*Enough.*" Didn't she know Sierra was pointing a gun at her? He tried to communicate with his eyes. *I've got this.*

Alesha's confused expression said he had to work on his silent communication.

"It's all right, Alesha," Sierra said with a sultry smile. "Your secret's safe with me."

With a sigh, Max put the statue into the bag, pulling the drawstring tight. He got to his feet and walked the prize over to Sierra, her eyes hungry.

"There, was that so hard?" she asked, snatching the bag from him. She flashed him that smile that had once gotten him to do a lot of regretful things—now it just turned his stomach. However, he couldn't tell if she was smiling at him or the bag. "I knew you were the best when I hired you to help me rescue Memta in the first place."

"I'm honored." He slathered his words in sarcasm.

Again, the smile. "Walk with me."

"Why? We can't talk right here?" He glanced over at his friends, his eyes lingering on Litning. He could have sworn he saw the Revash move.

"I told you, I don't like an audience. Besides, it's a nice night and is it so unbelievable that I want to relive a bit of the old days?"

"Right now? Yes, that's unbelievable."

She looked down at a gray box clipped to her belt. "I've got time to kill. Come." She led him around the clearing, away from the others.

"Where are we going? I'm not leaving my friends with that fucking snake."

"You're acting like Gelf betrayed you, Max," she said. "He was only doing the job I paid him to do first. I would have thought that the time you spent with me would have altered your quaint views of how the universe works. It's not all good versus evil. Speaking of which, thanks for taking care of Kalen for me. That was one loose end I was *not* looking forward to tying off." As she cradled the bag in her arm, she stroked it with her fingers. She seemed to be in a talkative mood, giddy, like a teenager unable to keep a secret in any longer.

He decided to play along. "Don't mention it. I'm assuming you were behind his unsanctioned release?"

She smiled broadly. "See? You catch on pretty quick. My buyers actually helped put that together. I needed something to keep the GAC busy while I had Litning procuring the statue."

"Well, I'm sure all the people he killed while trying to find me are grateful. And of course, he was only looking for me because he thought I betrayed him, so thanks again."

"Technically you *did* betray him, but not in the way he thought. And that's not my fault. How was I to know that Captain Justice over there was going to think outside the box?"

"His name is Glint—"

"I know who he is. He's actually one of the least corrupt members of that decaying carcass. I wanted you in prison so that you'd be spared from all this. Sure, Kalen might have killed your girlfriend there and some of your friends—and maybe I even wanted him to—but I didn't want him to kill *you*."

"What did I do to deserve such charity?"

Her incredulous look told him he was missing something big. "Because...I love you, Max."

He arched his eyebrow. "You've got a funny way of showing it."

"You're not dead yet, are you? After you turned and started hunting me, you should be."

Her mention of death made him want to check on Litning, but he fought the urge. Instead, he focused on keeping her talking. He had to stall for time and see if a solution presented itself. "So, you had me hauled off to prison to protect me, but what were you doing all this time? It must have been hard moving around considering you were supposed to be dead."

"The universe is a big place, Max, you know that. But yes, I couldn't let word of my *resurrection* slip, because it would have seriously vecked with my plans. First thing I had to do was get away from Merthane. He was all for throwing you in a hole on Aval. Unfortunately, he also thought we were going to split the profits from selling Memta, so I had to give him the slip. He really is a horrible person, Max. The only reason I teamed with him was because I had to make *you* believe I was dead and I knew you'd believe it if Merthane pulled the trigger. I knew he'd hunt me all over the galaxy for double-crossing him, but he'd never tell anyone about it for fear of losing face. I had to stash Memta in a safe place while I kept a low profile and bounced around the galaxy and there's none safer than a GAC facility."

"So you were the anonymous tip?"

"Correct. Why think she'd be safe where I stashed her? No, Merthane would have turned over every stone he could, but mess with the GAC? He probably wouldn't risk that. Of course, leave it to the GAC to veck up a perfect thing. That space lab disaster forced me to hunt her down all over again. The one good thing that fiasco clued me into was how powerful Memta was. That, combined with Alesha's little episode here tonight, has got me rethinking things with my buyers."

"Look, that's not a great idea. That thing is bad news."

"Don't speak that way about her!" After a moment, her crazed expression melted away and she reassumed an air of calm. "Are you saying that because of what happened with Alesha? Believe me, I think I can handle Memta's little kick." Her eyes gleamed as she stared down at Alesha. "I'm ten times the woman she is and you know it."

Ten times as crazy, maybe.

"Admit it, could she have pulled off such an elaborate plan like this? Bested you in such a way?"

Looking over at Alesha, he recalled their kiss before he indulged Sierra. "No, she couldn't."

"See?"

"She couldn't because she would never have the need or desire to. You say you love me? Well, Alesha would never screw me over in order to get ahead." He turned back to Sierra. "Love starts with respect and she and I have both."

She glared at him and for the first time, he really felt like she might kill him. "Maybe I'll kill her right now and ruin your *love*."

"You won't. You know I cared for you, but if you do that, you also know there's nothing in this universe that will stop me from finding and killing you—not even your little statue there."

She opened her mouth to say more, but the flashing red light on her gray box stopped her. "Well, while I've enjoyed catching up, Max, I have to go. I have another appointment in the city."

"Who *are* your buyers, anyway?"

She clicked her tongue and checked the gray box again. When she looked back up at him, he saw sincerity in her eyes. She was much better at the silent communication game than he. "I can take you to meet them."

Wait, what? His eyes narrowed, but he kept the hint of a smile on his lips. "What's the catch?"

"The catch is that you leave these others behind, now, and you come with me."

He felt a belly laugh coming on, but stifled it, remembering that Sierra still had her pistol. "Intriguing."

"Think of it, Max. With Memta, we could reshape the universe any way we wanted. We could wipe away the old way—antiquated monoliths like the GAC. People would be free to do what they wished. Freedom would reign supreme."

"Sounds more like chaos to me."

"And what's wrong with that? Look what happened to you, Max. You had nothing to do with Kalen's crimes, but you ended up in prison anyway."

"Because you orchestrated the whole thing."

"I took advantage of the situation in order to protect you, but if we joined with Memta," she said, brandishing the bagged statue, "we wouldn't fall victim to their rules again." She drew a quivering breath. Her voice became a whisper. "I wish you could hear her song."

"I'm familiar with it."

Shaking her head slowly, her eyes took on a haunted look. "I'm barely holding on here, Max."

"Then give me the statue. Do the right thing here. Let me—"

Her face contorted in rage. "You would just give her back to the GAC—her former jailors!"

"She's already in jail. She was put in the statue because she couldn't be controlled."

Sierra gazed longingly at the bag. She blinked and the crazed look in her eyes faded. "No. My buyers would hunt me down if I lost her again."

"So your answer is to use it instead?" He grabbed her arm as she turned away from him. "Don't do this, Sierra. You don't know what you're getting into with that thing, but your buyers probably do and that scares me even more."

Wrenching her arm away, she threw him a hurt look. "My mind's made up, Max. And you've shown that your concept of the universe is still as small as it was the day you left Earth."

"No, I just don't believe in genocide or whatever it is you're planning to do with that thing—if it doesn't swallow you up first."

His words went unheeded as she moved to look past him. "Gelf!"

"Yeah, Boss?"

"Thank you, you've been such a great help to me." She didn't flinch as she fired a laser bolt into Gelf's head—a cloud of red mist escaping out his forehead.

"Gelf!" Max couldn't stop himself from calling out his former friend's name as his body crumpled to the ground. Despite his betrayal, Gelf had kept Max alive in prison. For better or worse, he owed him. He shook his head at Sierra. "Why?"

Sierra looked at Gelf's lifeless body without a hint of remorse. "Loose ends, lover. You know how this works."

"So that's it, then?" Max asked. "You've got what you want and you're going to kill all of us now?"

"It's like I told you, Max, I don't want to kill you. These other two...why not?" She leveled her pistol at Alesha.

"No, goddammit!" Max cried as he pulled Sierra's arm up, her laser bolt streaking into the sky.

They struggled for a moment, but stopped as a high-pitched whine cut through the air. Sierra looked to the horizon. "Veck."

Max squinted into the darkened sky to see landing lights approaching—fast. The pattern was familiar. His face dropped. *Merthane's ship? Here? Now?*

"Well, it looks like our mutual friend is about to drop in, so I've got to go. Hope you don't mind if I take your hovercraft into the city. I believe there's room for two in there."

He squinted at her. "In what possible dimension do you see that ever happening?"

"Because I know you, Max. You hate to lose. And I have to tell you, Memta gives me the winning hand."

She was right—he hated losing. He turned his eyes to Alesha, thinking about what he'd almost lost thanks to the statue in Sierra's hands. How could he have ever left her for the personified insanity standing in front of him? His eyes moved to Litning and then, Gelf's body. "It seems to me," he said as he looked back at Sierra. "That the cause of my losing streak is standing right in front of me."

Her mouth twisted in a wry smile. "Yes, you're probably right about that." She pulled a detonator from her belt and activated it. An explosion rocked the *Sequel*, fire and smoke shooting out of the open hatch.

"*No!*" Max cried out. "You fucking bi—"

For the first time that evening, Sierra pointed her weapon directly at Max. "Watch that tongue, Max. I said I don't want to kill you, but that doesn't mean I *won't*." She stared him down for another moment before cutting and running for the rover.

CHAPTER 26

"We've got to get that horvorka," Alesha said, struggling to her feet—anger seemingly fueling her recovery.

"No, we've got to get to the *Sequel*," Max said, his eyes fixated on Merthane's fast-approaching ship. "For more than one reason."

"Help me get him on board!" Glintock called out. He groaned under Litning's weight as he helped the Revash to his feet.

"I will be fine, Agent," Litning said. "I turned enough to avoid...any permanent damage." His shallow breathing told Max he needed much more medical attention than he let on.

He helped Glintock steady Litning and the four of them double-timed it back to the *Sequel*, with Alesha well out in front. Max prayed to every intergalactic god he knew of that the others were all right.

The whine of Merthane's engines grew louder.

"It doesn't look that bad!" Alesha yelled as she looked up from the elevator to the open hatch above. She was right, in the sense that flames were no longer visible and smoke was only trailing out instead of billowing.

No matter. It was too late. The roar of the *Claw*'s engines was right on top of them. They swayed in the engine backwash as the ship flew in low…and continued on toward the city. Merthane did not eject from the ship. He did not leave an explosive device in the clearing for them. The *Claw* simply carried on, racing toward the lights of the city on the horizon.

Max's crew looked after the ship, confusion writ on all of their faces.

"He's…after her?" Glintock asked as he looked to Max.

How? How could Merthane even know that she's ali—? Her buyers. They're going to double-cross her. "This isn't good. This isn't good."

Glintock's expression said he'd put the pieces together too. "We have to get after him. The only way that statue gets off this planet is with us."

"Then we'd better see if the ship can fly," Max said as he led them toward the elevator carriage. He had to make sure his friends were all right, but Glintock was correct—urgency was essential.

The four of them piled into the elevator and Max punched the control button. Litning groaned as the carriage rocked while beginning its ascent.

"Sorry," Max said, wincing.

Agonizing seconds passed as the lift deposited them back inside the *Sequel's* cargo hold. Soot and blast marks marred the walls. Some of Max's empty containers had been blown apart—possible homes for Sierra's bombs—but the damage didn't look nearly as bad as he'd been expecting. He helped Glintock get Litning out of the elevator carriage and propped up against a small tower of containers while Alesha scrambled to the upper levels of the ship.

"Go with her and check on your ship," Glintock said. "I have this."

Max backed away, looking at the injured Litning warily. "The medical kit is on that wall there."

Glintock glanced up at him. "Go. This is under control. If we don't get the ship up and running none of this will matter."

Max ran to one of the staircases that led to the central deck of the ship. When he arrived in the common area, he found Alesha crouching on the ground beside, "*Roeger!*"

Roeger's torso remained intact, but his arms and legs had been torn from his body and decorated the deck. His normally bright, yellow eyes were dark and gray. He looked dead, if a robot could be dead. Cold logic didn't prevent the lump forming in Max's throat.

His mind reeled back to his time with Sierra and Kalen. Max remembered her way of dealing with electronic defenses. She would make use of a kind of EMP ball to knock out any surveillance devices or robotic security measures. He didn't see a ball nearby and the ship was still running, but he did notice a disc fastened to Roeger's chest.

"Damn her," he muttered as Alesha's hands worked to remove the disc. "Leave it. I'll take care of it." His eyes widened as he continued to take in his friend's condition. His breathing quickened and sweat beaded up on his forehead and the back of his neck.

Alesha got to her feet and came to his side. She put her hand behind his head, pulling him into an embrace. "Get it together, Earth Boy. I'm going to find Robbie and Gerry. You stay here and get Roeger working again."

Max nodded, taking her place on the deck, crouching beside Roeger's deactivated body, as she left to find the others. He put his hand on Roeger's shoulder. "I'm so sorry, buddy." Finding the button under Roeger's head to reactivate him, he wondered why he uttered the sentiment while Roeger was still shut down—probably because he'd never hear the end of it from the bot. Max loved Roeger, but he didn't need to have the bot lord it over him.

Roeger's eyes slowly brightened as his systems booted up and Max worked at removing the disc. He tried pulling on it, but whatever magnet held the disc to Roeger's chest was exceptionally strong.

Once Roeger's eyes reverted back to their usual bright yellow, the bot blinked slowly as a human would after being knocked out. His head slowly turned left and right as he took in the damage to his body. His eyes eventually settled on Max. "What are you doing, Maxim?"

Max let Roeger's voice wash over him like a wave of relief, but he kept his response measured. "Good, you're awake. I'm trying to get this disc off of you."

"You will probably tear a hole in my torso first. Standby." A noise like a small generator powering up filled the cabin until the sound of a fuse blowing replaced it. The disc fell off Roeger's chest with no incident.

"How'd you—"

"I generated a charge, rendering the device's magnet ineffective." He looked at his disassembled body again. "Please do not let me die, Maxim."

Max's heart swelled in his chest at the request. "You can't die, Roeger—you're a robot."

"But, I can lose my core programming."

"Have you?"

A moment passed as Roeger's head darted around. "No."

"Then you'll be fine." He said it more to reassure himself than Roeger. "I need to get you hooked into the *Sequel* so we can find out how bad the damage is."

"I will do my best, Maxim."

"I know you will, pal." Max dragged Roeger's torso across the deck to the central computer as fast as he could. "What happened? Gelf?" He set up the computer's connecting cables to Roeger.

"Well, yes, he and Sierra ran amok."

"They got the drop on you?"

"Well, ah, no. My injury resulted when I, ah, moved in front of the device to protect Christi."

"I thought Christi was already on the fritz?" Max asked. "I'm assuming that was Gelf too."

"Yes, she was incapacitated, but I think they hoped to, ah, take her out completely."

"So you stopped them."

Roeger turned his head away from Max for a moment before looking back at him. "Yes."

Max let a smile creep across his face. He found Roeger's bashfulness adorable. "Good work, buddy. I appreciate it and I know Christi will appreciate it too, once we get her up and running again."

"It will be my first priority once you reassemble me," Roeger said. "By the way, where did Sierra and Gelf get off to?"

"She's headed to the city with the statue and Gelf...he's dead." It was still hard to fathom that his closest ally in prison had not only betrayed him, but was now no longer among the living.

"That is...unfortunate."

"It's okay, Roeger. You don't have to fake being sad on my account." He jacked Roeger into the terminal and the bot buzzed with the stream of information. While he let Roeger scan the system for the information he needed, Max set about recovering Roeger's lost limbs from around the cabin and inspecting them. His father had shown him how to repair the bot in the past, but Max never trusted his own craftsmanship and usually took Roeger to a professional for his maintenance. Considering their pressing predicament, that plan didn't make a whole lot of sense.

"May I attempt, Maxim?"

Gerry's gurgling voice scared Max out of his pants. He turned to face the Glutob, who nodded and smiled, looking eager to help. Beyond Gerry, Alesha emerged from the cockpit with Robert, who held a bloody rag to his head.

Max beamed as he let out a cleansing breath. "Thank God you guys are okay. Yes, Gerry, have a go at it. Thanks."

The Glutob wrapped his appendages around Roeger's and shuffled over to the disabled bot. "And how is the patient today?"

"Comedy is supposed to be my expertise, Gerry," Roeger said with a frown in his voice.

Deciding his friend was in capable hands, Max crossed the cabin to help Alesha ease Robert into a chair. "Are you all right?"

"I'll be fine," Robert snapped. "Your little friend Gelf cold-cocked me when I wasn't looking. Where is that little fucker?"

"He's dead," Alesha said.

Robert snorted. "Well, I guess that makes us more than even."

"Maxim?" Roeger interrupted from the computer.

"Yeah, Roeg—" Max froze as he turned to face the bot.

Roeger was standing—*standing*—beside the computer with a grinning Gerry beside him.

"Roeger...Gerry, how did you—"

"I'm very good with my, well, my hands," Gerry said with a bashful smile as he held up his tentacles.

"The damage to the ship is mainly confined to the engines, but it is fairly extensive," Roeger reported. "We could be here for some time."

"So I guess flying after Sierra and Merthane is out of the question?" Max asked.

"Merthane?" Robert looked up. "When the hell did he get involved?"

"Before we picked you up, but apparently he's after Sierra now," Max replied, his mind scrambling.

He stood rooted to deck for several moments, paralyzed with doubt. His crew was in a bad way, except for Roeger who, thanks to Gerry, looked to be in fantastic condition. His rival was jetting after his former lover, who was on the verge of unleashing a pissed off goddess with untold levels of power. On top of that, his ship was completely screwed, leaving him with no way to get after problems one and two. He looked at his ragtag crew, mentally putting them in the best positions to help get them out of the mess they were in.

Then, a solution to his travel problems shook him out of his temporary panic. "Robbie, get bandaged up and check out the engines." He paused and glanced at Gerry, who was proving to be full of surprises. "Best if you take Gerry with you. We need to be up and running ASAP."

"We can do that," Robert said. "What are you going to do?"

"I'm going after Merthane and Sierra, but I'd like to try and stall them if possible. Roeger, are the communications working?"

"No Maxim. It appears that Sierra was not interested in letting us call for help, either."

Shit.

Alesha grabbed his arm. "How are we going to get to the city?"

"Don't worry about it. You're staying here." Dashing out of the common area, he headed for his quarters, Alesha hot on his heels.

"The hell I am!"

He hit the release button for his door and scrambled over to a large trunk. Pushing the mound of clothing off the lid, he dug into the container, sifting through the items inside. "Ah, here they are." He pulled three short range radios out of the trunk, flipping them all on to make sure they still had power.

Alesha stepped into his room. "You can't take this away from me, Max. I'm invested."

"And I'm not? I need you here on the *Sequel* to help get her repaired." The holster bolted to the inside lid of the trunk held one of his pistols, which he transferred to the holster on his belt. He stood up to leave.

She scowled. "Robbie, Roeger, and Gerry can handle that. It sounds like you're sidelining me."

He shook his head. "No, I'm keeping you safe. I don't want you anywhere near that statue."

"Really? What about when you take it from her? What then?"

Her point was valid. "We'll figure that out, but Memta's in her head. I know she's going to try and use the statue and I don't know what that means for you if you're in the area. Please, do me a favor and stay here. I almost lost you once tonight. I can't go through that again."

"That's sweet and I love you for it, but I keep telling you, you *don't* need to protect me."

"That wasn't the case earlier tonight." The response was harsher than he'd wanted, but he had to show her he was serious.

"That's not fair and you know it."

"We don't have time for this." Every second they wasted, the threat of Memta increased. He stepped around her and out the door. She followed.

"You're not blowing me off that easily, Max."

They stalked through the common area on the way down to the cargo hold. "I'm not blowing you off. I'm trying to get after them."

"So am I! You're not hearing me. You know what she can do with that statue. Do you know what'll happen if Memta gets her claws into someone who's a *willing* host?"

They reached the cargo hold. Glintock crouched near Litning, tending to the Revash's wounds. Max turned to face Alesha.

"You didn't see yourself when we were in that village looking for Litning. You were practically foaming at the mouth. I know you got Memta out of you, but you looked pretty willing at first."

Her eyebrows knit together as she began flailing at him with punches. Most landed on his arms, while one cuffed him across his head. He did his best to protect himself, but he'd clearly touched a nerve.

"You vecker! How dare you accuse me of being out of control when you had Gelf scouring the galaxy for rimi!"

"My addiction can't destroy a city, 'Lesha," he replied as she stopped swinging at him. Both were out of breath.

"No, but it can certainly destroy you." She let that hang in the air for a moment before heading over to an undamaged locker for a medium-sized laser rifle. "I'm coming with you. Nobody here knows that thing better than me."

"She has a point, Mr. Ultra," Glintock said as he crossed over to them.

"Thanks for the support." Max nodded over to Litning, who had his eyes closed, but was breathing. "How's the patient?"

Glintock literally had blood on his hands. The med kit was a mess on the deck with bloody bandages and compresses littered about. "Stable. But I really think he should stay here. He's not exactly in any shape to fight, if that's what you're thinking."

"You know that I can hear you, yes?" Litning's deep voice rumbled. "Rest assured, Mr. Ultra, I will be ready to assist when needed, as long as it results in returning Memta to my people."

"This ends with that statue buried in a GAC vault," Glintock said with a stern glare.

"Because that worked out so great the last time?" Max asked.

"Don't forget, I have Litning cold on several homicides. Both he and the statue are coming with me."

Litning opened his eyes and stared Glintock down. "I respect you, Agent Glintock, but I do not recognize your authority. The statue comes with me to Revjekt. After that, the gods will decide my fate."

Max glanced between Glintock and Litning. "I hate to interrupt this scintillating debate, but we're wasting time here. I'm all for a trip to Revjekt after we sort things out here and since I own the ship, my word is pretty much the law."

"I could commandeer your ship on behalf of the GAC—if it were working, of course." Glintock turned to Max. "I'm within my rights to do that."

After all they'd been through, Max couldn't believe their argument was a real thing, but he also knew he had the upper hand. "Yeah, you could do that, but you'd have to get past the rest of us and we both know that's not going to happen."

Glintock's glare intensified. "You'd better know what you're doing."

I guess that counts as a win. He tossed Glintock one of the radios and clipped a second to his belt. The third radio weighed heavy in his hand. His eyes moved to Alesha, who stood away from him, looking wounded. He'd meant what he said to her—he didn't want her anywhere near Memta. By the same token, she was right in that out of all of them, she had the most experience dealing with the statue. With a sigh, he held the radio out to her, a hopeful look on his face.

She offered him a wispy smile as she sauntered over and took the radio from him.

"Sierra's not getting off this planet," Max said. "Not with the statue anyway."

"So, what's the plan?" Alesha asked.

"Yes, Mr. Ultra, how do you intend to get us into the city without your ship?" Glintock asked.

Max gave them both a half-smile. "I have an idea about that."

CHAPTER 27

"Haven't ridden one of these in ten vecking years," Max muttered as the hover-bike he "borrowed" from the now-dead bikers wobbled wildly beneath him—for the fifth time.

"You're also on an open channel," Alesha said over the short wave radio.

He could hear the smile in her voice. It was possible their argument about her coming along was fading into the background. Not likely, but possible.

A shiver went up his back and he realized that despite the wind whipping his face, he was sweating. He'd kept his word to Alesha, but hoped that the dull ache spreading across his body wasn't the precursor to feeling like an exposed nerve. Though he'd taken some non-addictive painkillers from one of the med kits on the *Sequel*, he also stashed some rimi in his belt just in case things got hairy.

The four of them sped over the plains of Ventu toward the dazzling city on the horizon. As he struggled to maintain his balance on the bike, he looked at his communicator, which he'd slipped into a handy pocket welded to the bike's frame. His screen displayed a crude map with a blinking red dot nestled in the city. The dot represented his stolen rover, but he hadn't a clue as to how long ago Sierra had stopped.

"The rover's stationary. Sierra might already be gone," he reported over the radio.

"*Hopefully Merthane caught up to her and did us a favor*," Alesha responded.

"*That doesn't mean we stop*," Glintock said. "*We have to get that statue back.*"

Even speeding across the plains, Max could hear Litning's harsh laugh cut through the dull roar. He could have guessed at what the Revash said to Glintock about the statue on their shared bike.

"*What do we do if we even find her?*" Alesha asked.

"Arrest her and secure the statue," Max said, thinking it obvious.

"*I think we need a more permanent solution for her*," she said.

"No," Max replied a little too quickly. "No killing. We take her alive. If she lets us. Glintock, back me up on this."

A long pause preceded Glintock's response. "*She may not leave us a choice if the statue takes control of her.*"

"Like I said, if she lets us."

Alesha snorted, her words oozing with disgust. "*I can't believe it. You still have a thing for her.*"

This is why I wanted her to stay behind—partially. "Hardly. No one has more cause to kill Sierra than me, but given our history, I don't think I can do it. I thought you'd appreciate honesty."

"*I'd appreciate it more if she was dead.*"

"*All right, that's enough, you two*," Glintock cut in. "*We understand, Ultra. Just don't let Sierra use that sentiment to get the best of you.*"

"Come on Glintock, I'm not an idiot."

"*That's debatable*," Alesha mumbled.

Glintock chuckled. "*Glad you brought her along?*"

Max ignored them as they passed into the city. The lack of a teeming population reminded him that he'd lost all sense of time since they'd begun their Ventu expedition. His communicator pointed them toward the outskirts of town. *Why is it always the outskirts? Outskirts are only good for ambushes.*

He throttled back on the accelerator, seeing his rover parked in front of an industrial warehouse attached to a towering office building. However, his attention was more drawn to the two ships docked at the top of the structure—one was the *Claw*.

"Shit," he muttered.

"Are you sure she is still here?" Litning asked, following Max's skyward gaze.

"I'd say that's an affirmative."

"Who are those others?" Glintock asked.

"Her buyers, probably."

"But how?" Glintock asked again. "How was she able to even set up a meet?"

Max shook his head. "She had plenty of time. She was stowed away on the ship and once she learned where we were headed, she probably contacted them. Or Merthane told them—if he's even working for them. He had to have been tracking the *Sequel*."

"Let's go ask them," Alesha said.

"Right. Let's get up there before they hustle her out of here," Max said. "Oh, and keep a sharp eye out. This place is probably wired to blow."

"What makes you say that?" Litning asked.

"Experience." Entering through the building's simple two-door entrance felt too easy, but they didn't have time to futz with side doors or climbing through windows. They had to find Sierra and end it, preferably without getting caught in a crossfire with Merthane and the mystery party. They'd have to be careful when time for care wasn't available to them.

As he eased the doors open, a clanging sound washed over the group. A small unmanned receiving desk sat in the corner of the dimly lit lobby beside a set of doors that led into the building proper. Laying on the desk was a small magnetic explosive device.

"Boy," Alesha said. "You sure do know her."

"If she had the time, she probably spread them around," Max replied.

"I thought she *didn't* want to kill you?" Glintock asked.

"She may not, but she doesn't want us getting the statue either. Or she left presents for Merthane." He shook his head. "We've gotta get up there."

As he led them through the second set of doors, a wave of suffocating heat punched him in the face. The four found themselves on a wide ledge that looked out onto the bustling floor of a smelting factory. If the furry inhabitants of Ventu weren't ready to shave off all their fur due to the humid conditions outside, they *had* to be considering it if they worked in the hellishly hot factory. Dozens of the Ventu people walked the floor on the night shift and as Max peered at some of the support beams, he saw remote controlled explosives, which he pointed out to Glintock.

The agent's mouth pulled into a tight line. "We need to get these people out of here."

Max turned to Alesha. "I don't suppose I could convince you—"

"Not on your life," she replied as she led the way to a long catwalk that extended from their ledge over to another ledge across the factory floor.

"If you want to get these people out of here, Glintock, you'll have to stay behind," Max said as he followed Alesha.

After a moment's hesitation, the agent sighed, falling into line. Apparently, his desire to capture Sierra and figure out her buyers' identities outweighed his need to get the innocent bystanders to safety.

"Who knows? Maybe we'll wrap this up real quick and there won't be a need to get these people out of here," Max offered.

Litning snorted. "Unlikely."

"Let's get this over with," Glintock grumbled.

Alesha led them across the catwalk at a quick clip. They whipped around the corner to find two elevators, one on the top floor and the other sitting a few floors up, waiting for them to make a decision.

"This could be a trap," Glintock said.

"Yeah, or we could be the four luckiest sons of bitches to ever walk into this place," Max replied, hitting the elevator call button.

"Which seems more likely?" Litning asked.

Alesha beat Max to the punch. "Trap."

He looked for a stairwell, but didn't see one nearby. "This looks to be the only way up."

"And we know Merthane's waiting upstairs," Alesha pointed out.

"For all we know, he's tied up with her buyers or with Sierra herself," Max said, trying to make their infiltration a little less hopeless.

"Or, we're about to run into a bunch of those guys from the *Galactic Dream*," Alesha said.

He gave her a look. "Don't help."

"Then what's your plan?" Glintock asked.

"We take this lift up and snoop around before making a move," Max said.

The four of them piled into the elevator and Max punched the button for the forty-seventh floor. He ignored his growing fear that there would be dozens of armed men waiting to drill them full of holes as soon as the doors opened. To be safe, he inched over to the elevator wall so that he received a modicum of cover from the control panel. He noticed Alesha lining up behind him.

"What are you two doing?" Litning asked.

"Hedging our bets," the two of them replied simultaneously.

Glintock and Litning shared a look and then followed suit, taking up positions on the opposite wall.

The elevator ride was uncomfortably silent. Usually, Max would have cracked a joke or two, but he just couldn't muster humor at that moment. His pain intensified, but he tried to ignore it. Drawing his pistol with his right hand, he felt Alesha's hand sneak into his left. They shared a warm smile as he squeezed her hand. After a long moment, he turned to Litning. "You'll probably need a gun."

"My strength is my weapon."

Max made a face. "That's corny."

"You are not the first to say so, Maxim Ultra."

The lift came to a stop and the doors opened with a loud *ding*. *Sure, tell everybody we're here.*

Making sure to keep behind cover, Max peered out. The elevator opened onto a small vestibule. A glass door appeared to lead to a set of offices. The floor was darkened, the only illumination coming from the city lights outside the windows.

"There are some strange scents in the air," Litning growled. "Definitely a few humans, but the others are...alien."

"Stay alert," Max said as he led the way through the glass door to find another receiving desk and a metal door that led deeper into the building. The metal door was ajar. Tightening the grip on his pistol, Max eased the door open to find a wide open area that had a couple of branching hallways off to the right and a few closed doors that presumably led into offices. The first hallway was about twenty feet away. Max figured that was as good a place as any to start the investigation. As the group followed him into the large area, he marveled at how light Litning was on his feet. He'd expected to hear the Revash thumping around, making a ton of noise. An excited grin spread across his face as they approached the hallway. *We might actually be able to pull this off.*

"Maxim!" Litning called out.

The Revash had barely gotten out the first syllable when Max was clobbered by a massive fist that knocked him across the polished wooden floor.

"Merthane told us to be patient," a familiar voice said. "Looks like that paid off well."

"Fuck my life," Max muttered, shaking the cobwebs out of his head.

Standing before him, larger than life, was Elkeith. His associates, Orange Zombie and Four Arms stepped out from the other hallway, both holding laser rifles. From behind Elkeith, a beautiful blonde carrying a laser pistol emerged.

"Your roles in this game are finished, Mr. Ultra," the blonde said as she looked over to Alesha and the others.

"And you are? I recognize these degenerates, but you're a mystery." He made sure to keep his pistol hidden under his body as he repositioned himself on the floor.

"I'm Dayna. Now, Talon is willing to let you walk away, but you have to do just that. Walk away."

"Merthane, let him walk away?" Alesha asked. "That sounds like a load of nakra."

"It's true. He's about to have Ms. Numani in his possession and our business here will be concluded."

"And who's in the other ship? Not *these* losers?" Max asked.

"I'm not at liberty to disclose that."

"Because you don't know or because you think you can't tell us?" Glintock asked. "I'm GAC, I think my authority carries a little more weight."

"Not when you're outgunned, Agent Glintock," Dayna replied. "You lost. Just walk out the door and leave."

"Enough talking!" Elkeith roared. "This wasn't part of the deal! Merthane promised me Ultra's blood!"

"The situation has changed, Elkeith. He still secured your release. That should be sufficient for yo—"

Elkeith lashed out at Dayna, grabbing her by the throat. "I will have what was promised to me." He threw her clear across the room toward Max. The impact of her head with the window left a crack and she crumpled to the floor. Elkeith then turned to Max and drew a wicked-looking dagger from his belt. "Where were we?"

"Now!" Max yelled as he drew his pistol and shot at Orange Zombie and Four Arms. He wanted to eliminate their weapons, but they didn't seem to know what to do with them as they didn't get a shot off before being riddled by laser bolts from Alesha and Glintock. The attack left them both smoking heaps on the floor.

Elkeith's dismayed expression was all he left behind as he dashed back down his hallway, taking cover in one of the offices.

Max groaned as he got to his feet. The others joined him beside the unconscious Dayna.

"What do we do with her?" Alesha asked.

"I'm just trying to figure out who she is," Max replied. "Did she work at the prison on Aval?"

"She looks vaguely familiar. It's possible," Glintock said.

"Is she this Merthane's mate?" Litning asked.

"I don't know." Amazingly, Max realized that there was quite a lot about Merthane he didn't know. He shook his head before looking down the hallway. "We're losing time. She said Merthane didn't have Sierra yet, so there's a chance she's hiding around here. Then there's Elkeith."

"He is close," Litning said. "It will be weeks before I get his stench out of my nose."

"I hate to do this, but we should probably split up," Max said. "Alesha and Litning sniff out Elkeith and put him down. Glintock and I will find Merthane or Sierra or both."

"I'm going to have to veto that plan," Alesha said.

"We don't have the time to argue. I don't want you near that statue and Elkeith has to be dealt with. This is how it's going to be, so let's get to it."

Alesha glowered, but headed off with Litning down the first hallway. Max and Glintock moved into the second.

"She really wants to play a part in this," Glintock said.

"She is. We can't let Elkeith out of here. He's a menace."

"That's not what I mean, and you know it."

"I know what you mean, I jus—"

Elkeith crashed through the wall to their right, filling the hallway with dust and debris, as he knocked them both to the floor. "You always talked too much, Ultra. I could hear you through the wall!" The Inwain breathed foulness in Max's face as he reached for him. "I knew you'd be too much of a coward to come after me directly." His powerful hand wrapped around Max's throat.

"I guess...I just got tired of...kicking your ass," Max gasped.

Elkeith roared and slammed Max to the ground before turning to Glintock. "Anything to say, Agent?"

Glintock coughed. "You're under arrest."

Elkeith let out a bellowing laugh. "That's very funny. I'll kill you quickly." He stabbed Glintock in the shoulder with his dagger, pinning the screaming agent to the floor. Elkeith then turned back to Max. "After I murder my friend Ultra, of course." He dragged Max to a standing position.

Max wavered on his feet, his eyes scanning the floor for his gun amongst the pieces of wall strewn about. He also glanced at Glintock to see his condition. It didn't look good. Blood seeped from his wound. He appeared ready to pass out. A woman's scream sounded from behind Max. Thinking it might be Alesha, he turned his head.

Elkeith rewarded him with a punch in the gut. "Come now, Ultra. Don't tell me you're not going to even participate?"

Max fell to one knee, trying to catch his breath. Still he looked behind him down the hall. *What danger could Alesha be in? She's with Litning.*

"If you're so interested with what's down there," Elkeith said as he picked Max up off the ground. "Join them!" He threw Max down the hall and into another open area.

Max landed hard on the wood floor and slid a few more feet. Groggy, he raised his head to see Merthane dragging Sierra out of one of the offices that ringed the space. He reached out uselessly. "Stop!"

Merthane didn't even pause in what he was doing as he hustled the bound Sierra away.

Got to be taking her to the roof. Max struggled to get to his feet, feeling like he'd forgotten something major. The powerful kick in his back reminded him. *Oh yeah, Elkeith.*

Elkeith sat on Max's back and grabbed him by the head, exposing his neck. "I wanted to drag this out, Ultra, but I don't think I'll be able to fight *all* of your friends, so...."

Max's stomach clenched at the sound of another blade sliding from its scabbard. Closing his eyes, he tensed for the inevitable.

Pounding footsteps and a snarl were followed by the weight being removed from Max's back and his neck remaining conspicuously *un*bloodied. He turned on his side to witness Litning atop Elkeith, ravaging him with his claws. The Inwain's screams were music to Max's ears.

Alesha rushed to his side. "Are you okay?"

He pointed. "Help Glintock. He's hurt bad."

She gave him a stern look.

"I'll be okay. I'm just shaken up." As she headed over to help Glintock, Max noticed that Elkeith's screams had become gurgling.

Litning rose to his feet, his hands dripping with Elkeith's blood. He crossed over to Max, who had difficulty sitting up.

"How would you like a job?" Max asked with a lopsided grin.

"I am afraid not," Litning said, favoring his bandaged side. "You know why I need the statue."

"Right. Well, keep us in mind." The Revash helped Max to his feet. "Thanks for the save."

"Thank you for coming to my aid against Memta and Sierra."

"Hey, we've got to stick together, right?"

Alesha approached, supporting the injured Glintock, who held a torn piece of cloth to his wound. She handed Max his pistol. "Sorry it took so long for us to get in the game. We tried to find Merthane and Sierra while you dealt with ugly over there."

Max nodded as he took his pistol from her. "How are you holding up, Glintock?"

"I'm not. Your girlfriend is doing that for me." Glintock chuckled until a coughing spasm hit him. "I should be all right."

"Good." Max trudged over toward Elkeith, who was a bloody mess. Long, deep scratches cut into his flesh. His face was awash in blood. Bubbles formed around his mouth, the only sign that he was still breathing. "Will he live?"

"I only meant to subdue him," Litning said. "I...lost control."

"But he'll live?"

Litning shrugged. "I do not see why not."

"So long, fuck face." Max shot Elkeith in the head.

"That was not an invitation to kill him, Maxim," Litning said, his face darkening.

"It was my decision, Litning. You're in the clear on this. Merthane is headed to the roof with Sierra. I'm going after him."

"And I'm going with you." Alesha's tone said she wouldn't take no for an answer.

He gazed at her for a moment. He wanted her as far away from the statue as possible, but also knew he needed help. "You're right. You *are* coming with me." He turned to Litning. "I need you to get Glintock and all those people downstairs out of this building."

"I will get him out."

Max raised his eyebrows in surprise at Litning's matter-of-fact statement.

The Revash qualified it with a shrug. "I owe him for treating my wounds."

"Thank you for caring," Glintock muttered.

"You are threatening me with imprisonment," Litning said as he picked Glintock up. "I am being as generous as I can."

Alesha jerked her thumb back toward the entrance. "What about Blondie back there?"

"Leave her," Max said. "If she wakes up, good for her. If not, she knew what she was signing up for." He took Glintock's radio and gave it to Litning. "Take this. I may need your help with the statue."

"We did not need the incantation for Alesha."

"Yeah, but everyone who might use the statue up there actually *wants* the damn thing. We had Alesha fighting back."

Glintock grabbed Max's collar, pulling him close. "Get the statue—it's everything!" His eyes were wild with purpose. "And try to find out who her buyers are. If they're the same people from the *Galactic Dream*, I can't have an unknown like that running around the galaxy."

Max looked at Alesha, who nodded back at him. "We'll do our best."

Glintock groaned. "Go!"

Though he felt he was abandoning his companions, Max led Alesha after Merthane and Sierra, confident Glintock was in good, bloody hands.

CHAPTER 28

Max limped behind Alesha as she raced down the hallway after Merthane and Sierra.

"Slow down, god dammit!" he called to her. "We need a plan!"

"No, we need to stop Merthane before he gives her to those people!" She reached for the door at the end of the hall, but Max fired a laser bolt over her head, scorching the wall. "Are you vecking crazy?!"

"I don't know," he said, finally catching up to her. "Are you?"

She pulled away from him. "What are you talking about?"

"Which *her* are you afraid of losing?"

"Are we seriously doing this now?"

"No, but until you can start referring to that statue as *it* again, stay behind me." Easing the stairwell door open, he realized that if she *really* wanted the statue, she could easily stab him in the back. *Wonderful*.

They moved into the stairwell, Max listening intently for any sound that wasn't them. Nothing. Aside from the scraping of their boots on the metal staircase, there was nothing. He didn't know whether to be relieved or concerned.

"What are we waiting for?" Alesha asked, making like she wanted to run up the steps.

Max grabbed her arm. "*Quietly.*"

"You're no fun anymore," she replied with a lopsided grin.

He led the way up the staircase, wincing as his footsteps clanged on the metal stairs, the sound echoing up and down the stairwell. After several nerve-wracking moments, they reached the roof access door. Max took hold of the handle and eased the door open. A cool breeze actually cut through the dense Ventu air, ruffling his hair. He poked his head out, straining to hear over the persistent hum of the cluster of transformers outside that powered the building.

Max was about to step out onto the roof when he caught movement out of the corner of his eye. He pushed Alesha back into the stairwell, pulling the door closed to only a crack.

"Max! What are y—?"

"Shh!" he snapped before peering out through the slight opening. "Those guys from the *Galactic Dream* are out there. Armed to the teeth, it looks like."

A moment of tense silence passed. Max watched through the crack of space as one of the black-clad soldiers strolled past with an easy stride. His rifle was perched across his forearm, but he didn't seem aware of their presence or of the door being ajar.

Max felt Alesha fidgeting beside him. He glanced over at her and her wide, feverish eyes. "Are you okay?"

After a moment, she furrowed her brow and glanced up at him. "I'm fine."

"Mm-hm. Maybe you should w—"

"Maxim Ultra, if you say, 'Wait here,' I may shoot you."

He considered her threat for a beat and then turned to once again peer outside. "I think the patrol's passed. Let's go."

Easing the door open, he waved her through onto the roof before closing the door behind them and taking cover amongst the transformers. The loud electric hum of the large black boxes created a disorienting effect, making it difficult to hear anyone approaching. However, the units were tall enough that it was easy to find cover and stay out of sight. The hum might not have been loud enough to drown out a laser blast, though, so avoiding the enemy was the order of the day.

Alesha got that faraway look again. Her eyes pointed toward where Max thought Sierra's buyers had their ship. With a comforting smile, he gripped her forearm. She patted his hand with a strained smile of her own.

He waited another beat before leading her to the next transformer. Time was not on their side. The units were arranged in parallel rows, but ahead of them, it looked like the layout changed so that the next set of units ran perpendicular to the former. He couldn't tell where the whole thing ended. For all he knew, they could turn a corner and fall off the damn roof.

Peeking around the corner, he saw another soldier patrolling the area, but facing away from them. He stared at the soldier's back intently, silently willing him to not turn around. He motioned for Alesha to cross the aisle and quickly followed, exhaling as they crouched behind the next unit.

After what felt like an eternity traversing the maze, the two of them huddled behind a transformer at the edge of the field in a final row of units. On the other side of the box was an open area of rooftop. A medium-sized troop transport loomed above it.

Max tried to steal glances without getting spotted. "Four more of these mercenaries guarding the area. Two fancy-looking guys with them—one's green, the other's got slicked hair."

"Where is sh—" Alesha stopped, gritting her teeth. "Where's the statue?"

He masked his worried look, but at least she tried to catch herself. "Merthane's there with Sierra. I can't see where he's got it from here."

Her eyes widened. "He might have given it to them!"

"Without Sierra? No way. They're going to want to stick it to her along with taking the statue."

Alesha climbed over him, poking her head out for a peek. "It's definitely here. I can feel it."

He put his arm around her and gently pulled her back behind the transformer before taking another look. "They're talking, but I can't hear what they're saying."

"Then let's go have a listen," a harsh voice said from behind.

Max spun around, only to come face-to-face with a laser rifle barrel and the soldier that carried it. "Shit."

"Way to go, *hero*," Alesha remarked as she dropped her pistol and threw her hands up.

"How is this *my* fault? You were supposed to be lookout!"

"Shut up!" the soldier barked. "On your feet!"

For a split second, Max considered fighting the guy, but that was high-risk-low-reward. If discovered, the four soldiers on the other side of the transformer would most assuredly kill them. He relinquished his pistol and the soldier marched them over toward Merthane and the others.

Indeed, the statue hung from one side of Merthane's belt, while on the other he wore what looked like a handheld detonator—that had probably belonged to Sierra too.

Merthane shook his head as he turned to face them. "Maxim, my boy, why didn't you accept my offer from Dayna and walk away?" His eyes narrowed and his demeanor turned icy. "Where is she?"

"Sleeping it off downstairs," Max replied as the soldier pushed him in the back.

Though it didn't seem possible, Merthane's frown deepened.

"Hey, I'm not the one who thought bringing Elkeith along would be a good idea. We didn't touch her."

"Elkeith, hm? I'll kill the scum myself."

"Way ahead of you," Max said with an irritated glance at the soldier behind him.

"Oh ho! Broadening our horizons, are we?"

"If you're both quite finished?" Slick asked with a sneer. "Mr. Merthane, I believe we were concluding our business?"

"Wait," Max said. "Why did you hire Merthane if Sierra was already bringing you the statue?"

Slick got a funny smile on his face. "I'm sorry, Mr. Ultra, I had believed that you were acquainted quite intimately with Miss Numani. Surely you know that duplicity is practically her second nature? Mr. Merthane was our...insurance policy, so to speak."

"Now shut the veck up," Greenie said. "We'll deal with you shortly."

"Now then, Mr. Merthane, I believe the agreement was for Miss Numani *and* the artifact?" Slick asked.

"Are you two running these mercenaries?" Max asked.

"Shut *up*," Greenie said with a glower and a nod.

One of the soldiers struck Max in the back with the butt of his rifle. Max stumbled forward before his attacker grabbed his shoulder roughly, pulling him back into place.

"I'll take that as a yes," Max said with a wince. He glanced over at Alesha, who stared intently at the Memta bag. The fresh sheen of sweat on her forehead worried him.

Sierra didn't look much better. Her face kept twitching and she had that faraway, haunted look in her eyes as she gazed into space. Her mouth moved wordlessly, as if in prayer.

"So, Mr. Merthane, if there are no further interruptions?" Slick asked.

"Where's my money?"

"Once we take possession of Miss Numani and the artifact, the funds will be transferred to your account," Slick explained.

Glancing around at the soldiers covering the rooftop, Max didn't buy it. Merthane's steely look said he didn't either.

"Who's to say I give you both and you don't have these mercs kill all of us? What guarantee do I have?"

Greenie's mouth turned up in a nasty grin. "None."

"Forgive my associate's theatrical nature," Slick said. "You're just going to have to take that chance, Mr. Merthane. I can assure you, though, that if you fail to hold up your end of our bargain, the scenario you detailed will most certainly play out." With a nod from Slick, some of the soldiers put themselves in positions to surround the group.

"Well, that's not very friendly," Merthane said, casually glancing around at the developing situation. He nodded at Max. "What are you going to do with the kid?"

"We were considering giving him to you," Slick said. "If you're well-behaved, of course. I'm sure they're missing him on Aval."

"And the girl?"

Slick took a long look at Alesha. "Miss Cabal is a fascinating specimen. We'll be taking her with us."

Merthane arched his eyebrow. "She's definitely a looker, but that's a really odd way to put it."

Clearly, Merthane had no idea what the statue was capable of. Max's palms started to sweat as his eyes darted around, looking for any means of escape. Alesha didn't appear to have registered what Slick said. She kept staring at the bag, almost as if in a haze.

Yeah, bringing her along was a great *idea.*

"Now, Mr. Merthane, if that sates your curiosity, let us complete this transaction," Slick said, holding his hand out.

"Merthane," Max said, "don't do this. You don't know what that statue is. Do what you want with Sierra, but do *not* give them that statue."

Greenie pulled his pistol and drilled a laser bolt into Max's leg. "That's enough out of you!"

"God dammit!" Max cried, dropping to one knee. Wincing, he forced himself to inspect his leg. His jeans were charred and though the wound had cauterized, it wasn't a pretty sight. One look at his blistering, exposed skin turned his stomach. He breathed in gulps, hoping he wouldn't go into shock.

"Max!" The attack shook Alesha out of Memta's trance. She crouched beside him.

Merthane pulled his own sidearm on Greenie. "What the *veck* are you doing?"

The soldiers all took aim.

Greenie's aim switched to Merthane. "So, he shows up on Aval with a limp. What's the vecking problem?"

"The problem, you little *petch*, is that he belongs to me," Merthane said. "The less work for me, the better. I don't feel like lugging him around."

Slick held out his hands. "Let's all calm down. Everybody lower their weapons and we can finish this. There's no need for any more violence."

The roof door slammed open. All attention and weapons turned that way as Dayna rushed out onto the roof.

"Who the *veck* is this?" Greenie asked, his pistol shifting between Merthane and Dayna.

"No! She's with me!" Merthane cried. "She's with me!"

"And that's supposed to put us at *ease?*" Slick asked.

Max put his arm around Alesha in an attempt to sneak away to safety amidst the chaos, but out of the corner of his eye, he saw Sierra lunge for the bag on Merthane's belt. "*Shit.*"

A brilliant blue flash blinded him as a concussive force flattened everyone. A roaring, powerful wind buffeted the roof, but cutting through all of it was Sierra's ragged scream.

He reached out and grabbed Alesha's hand. In return, she clenched his. Together, they struggled to their feet, taking cover behind a transformer.

"Are you okay?!" he yelled over the howling wind.

She nodded, but her eyes stared over his shoulder, wide with fear.

He touched her face gently, turning her gaze to focus on him. "Are you okay?"

Her fearful expression softened. It looked like she was seeing him for the first time in a while. She threw her arms around him. They held each other tightly. "Max," she whispered in his ear, "what are we going to do?"

"I *LIVE!*" came a familiar voice from the other side of the transformer. Memta's voice was similar to before, but slightly different due to the new host.

The wind ceased and the rooftop went deathly silent. The hum of the transformers remained, but to Max, it felt like the atmosphere had shifted. He released Alesha, but put his hand on her shoulder to keep her back. Turning, he peered around the transformer to get the lay of the land.

Sure enough, Sierra had transformed into Memta. Her hair swirled around her head as if moving of its own volition. A blue aura wreathed her body, while her blank eyes burned with turquoise light. She surveyed the scene like a conquering general, her face a picture of cool detachment.

The mercs struggled to get to their feet, while Merthane stayed on his back, gawking at Memta. Max couldn't see what had become of Dayna.

Slick and Greenie were a different story. Greenie kept his pistol handy, a wary look on his face. Slick, on the other hand, looked like he'd been prepared for this eventuality. He got on his knees and gazed up at the hovering death merchant, arms raised in reverence—or was it surrender?

"Oh, great Memta! Allow these humble servants to shepherd you away to safety, so we might discuss the future course of the galaxy!" Slick called out before bowing.

A smile flickered across Memta's face. "Just what I wanted to see upon my return—willing sacrifices."

Slick and Greenie didn't have a moment to react before a stream of glowing blue magma shot from Memta's outstretched arm, engulfing them. The smell of burning flesh filled the air as their guttural screams gurgled to a stop.

Memta's smile stayed firmly in place as she turned in midair toward Max and Alesha's position. He pulled his head back behind the transformer, hoping she hadn't seen him.

"Maxim," she called in a sing-song voice. "Where are you? Do not force me to incinerate this entire structure just to find you."

He glanced over at Alesha. "We're totally screwed."

CHAPTER 29

Max winced as Memta's cackling laughter danced on his ragged nerves. He and Alesha remained huddled behind the paltry cover afforded them by the transformer unit as the goddess rose higher in the air. Eventually, she'd spot them.

The whine of a ship's engines encouraged Max to get the lay of the land. The brief hope that the *Sequel* had arrived disintegrated as he watched the *Claw* pull away from the building and head to parts unknown. Max ducked back behind the transformer.

"Merthane's leaving," he said.

"What?"

"I guess he found his girlfriend and bugged out."

"That doesn't sound like him," Alesha said.

"No, it doesn't." Max eked his head out as much as he dared, watching Memta rotate in the air. As soon as her back was turned, he grabbed Alesha and pulled her behind the next row of transformers. They were still closer than he wanted to be, but he felt slightly safer.

That modicum of relief vanished when Merthane plopped down beside them, scaring the hell out of Max. "How are you still here?"

"Don't tell me you don't have the *Sequel* on remote. I don't like my ship being around things I don't understand. So, stop gawking and tell me what happened."

Alesha grabbed Merthane's collar. "The *statue* happened, you horvorka's son!"

Merthane caught her wrist. "Watch it, sweetheart."

Though the fire remained in her eyes, Alesha deliberately released her hold on Merthane. His glare remained on her for another couple of moments.

"How do we get off this rooftop?" Merthane asked.

"We can't leave. She won't let us," Max said. "You and your pals wanted to dick around, so now we're fucked."

"I think the correct response is, she won't let *you* leave. I believe Dayna and I will be just fine."

"Right," Alesha said, "because you and Sierra have such a warm and friendly relationship."

Merthane grimaced. "Is that even her anymore?"

"Clearly, your clients didn't tell you jack about that statue. Who were they, Merthane? Were Slick and Greenie the only ones? What were they after?"

Merthane stared at him for a long moment. "I don't know *who* they were. It was an anonymous call and a figure. That's it. This was the first time I'd met them. If it helped me veck Sierra over, so much the better." Something else lived in his eyes. Was it fear?

He's holding back. What person or persons in the galaxy could scare Talon Merthane into silence? "I need information, Merthane. Whoever they were, they wanted to unleash *that* on the galaxy. I need to know if there are more of them."

"I think your buddy Glintock is the one who really wants to know." Merthane's defiant mask was back in place. "I don't know what to tell you, Maxim. Maybe ask them." He nodded over to the black-clad soldiers that had managed to pull themselves together enough to shoot at Memta.

"That's not going to end well," Alesha said.

"No. It. Is. Not," Max said as he pulled Alesha closer and more behind the transformer.

"What are you afraid of?" Merthane asked with a smirk. "They've got her dead to rights!"

"Just...wait a second," Max said.

It actually took about three seconds, but the soldiers' screams were no less agonizing as they echoed among the transformers. A wave of heat rippled across the roof as Memta melted her opponents with her blue magma. Then she spun in the air, shooting another jet of the destructive substance at Slick and Greenie's docked ship. The molten lava burned through the ship's hull effortlessly. The vehicle pitched and teetered before finally plummeting down to the city streets below.

"No escape, Maxim. We're alone now," Memta taunted as she floated down closer to the roof.

Merthane's mouth dropped open. "Torva...I-I've never...."

"Now you know what she's capable of. That's not all she can do. If she wanted, she could destroy this entire building—probably the whole city."

Merthane only shook his head. "We can't let her get off this planet."

Max and Alesha shared a surprised look. "Not in her current condition, no," he said.

A nearby transformer exploded in a blue flash. "Where are you, Maxim? Soon enough, I'll stop asking nicely."

Merthane's horrified gaze fixated on the blue fire. When he spoke, it seemed as though he wasn't even talking to Max and Alesha. "I have to find Dayna. I-I have to find her."

Alesha and Max exchanged another concerned look before she reached out and touched Merthane's arm. "Get it together, Merthane. We can't have you drifting away when we actually need you."

Merthane turned to face her. His expression made it seem like it was the first time he'd seen her.

Max sighed, grabbing Merthane by the shoulders. "Snap out of it. This isn't the weirdest thing you've seen."

One look at Max was all it seemed to take. Merthane's brow furrowed and he jerked away from him.

"Okay, there he is," Max said. "Listen, Alesha will go find your girlfriend, while you and I keep Memta occupied."

"You mean Sierra," Merthane said with a questioning look.

"Not anymore, pal. 'Lesha, go find Blondie so we can wrap this up." Max's outward confidence hid the terror taking root in the pit of his flip-flopping stomach.

At the precise moment Memta turned away, Max tapped Alesha on the back. She bolted out into the transformer farm and Max took a small explosive from his belt, tossing it in Memta's general direction.

"Run. *Run*," he said, pulling Merthane to his feet.

As the device detonated, Max limped with Merthane behind some cover farther away from the crazed goddess. Memta reacted as Max thought she would, tossing a blue fireball at their previous position. Max crouched behind another transformer, bracing for the subsequent explosion.

"Stop toying with me, Maxim," Memta said as the transformer erupted. "You are annoying me."

"For the record," Merthane said, "this plan is terrible."

"Well, it wouldn't be the first time."

"Like your plan in Apex."

"Hey, we *won* that fight."

"Hah. Just barely. The point is, we may be working together on this, but it doesn't change anything between us."

Max glared at the older man. "Really? *Now* is when you want to do this?" He tossed another explosive charge and hustled Merthane behind fresh cover. "Look, the most important thing right now is that we get that statue. After we shut Memta down, we can go back to our thing." *If Memta happens to kill him in the process, I won't shed any tears.* He glanced at Merthane. *He's probably thinking the same thing about me.*

He winced as another transformer went up, this one much closer than the last.

"This is getting tiresome, Maxim," Memta said.

"Why doesn't she just incinerate the roof?" Merthane asked.

"She...likes to play with her food, so to speak." Just saying it forced Max to repress a shudder.

"Wonderful. What's your plan?"

A boot scraped the concrete behind Max. He spun around, pistol drawn, to find Alesha with Dayna in tow. He pulled his weapon back, a wave of relief washing over him.

She smiled at him. "Yeah, Earth Boy, what's your plan?"

Before Max could reply, Merthane gripped Dayna's shoulder. "Are you all right?"

"I'm fine, Talon," Dayna replied. She turned to Max. "Thanks for sending Alesha."

"Don't mention it." He looked up at the sound of small arms fire. Peeking out from behind the transformer, he saw that some more soldiers had shown up and stupidly fired on a rising Memta.

Max's attention shifted back to his comrades. "Okay, these guys aren't going to be able to hold her for long. We need to get that statue, get her on the ground, and then push that fucker into her face until we suck Memta out of her."

Merthane's glare narrowed. "And that'll work?"

Max's uneasy glance shifted to Alesha. "It's worked before."

The small arms fire intensified. Then a fresh chorus of terrified screams erupted from the soldiers as Memta retaliated.

"We're running out of time!" Max cried, attempting to block out the screaming.

"Yes, but you're not running anywhere with that leg, Maxim," Dayna replied. "One of us will get the statue."

Max gave her a patient smile. "No offense, Blondie, but your payday is out the window. I'm not letting you or Merthane anywhere near that thing."

Dayna shrugged. "Alesha, then."

Alesha's eyes lit with what could only be called hope, but just as quickly, she looked away in shame. "I-I can't handle the statue."

"Yeah," Max added. "That's out of the question."

"Then it has to be one of us," Dayna said. "Pick one."

Another transformer detonated. The gunfire ceased.

"I'm telling you—"

"You're hobbled, Maxim," Dayna said. "I'll do it."

He opened his mouth to argue, but couldn't. She was right. With his injured leg, he'd have major difficulty maneuvering around Memta and getting the drop on her. He didn't trust Merthane in the least, but maybe Dayna could get the job done. An eerie quiet descended on the rooftop.

"You'll need gloves. Without them, Memta may just jump right into you."

Dayna looked at Merthane, who hesitated before handing her a pair of gloves. She pulled them on and then kissed him deeply. "Be careful."

"I should be saying that to you," Merthane said in a husky voice. Max had never seen him in such a human moment.

"You know me. I'm always careful." She kissed Merthane one more time. "Get her on the ground." Then she dashed off, disappearing around the corner.

Max clapped Merthane's shoulder. "Let's go."

The trio ventured into the transformer farm. The nauseating odor of burning flesh slapped Max in the face. In the unsettling quiet, the sizzling of the smoldering soldiers set his nerves on edge. His eyes searched frantically for any sign of Memta. Turquoise flame burned wherever he looked and a permanent cloud of smoke had taken hold of the rooftop. They needed to find her and strike fast. Giving her any opportunity to figure out their plan would spell doom.

"Call her," Merthane said.

"What?"

"Call her. You said she wants to play. She clearly wants to play with you, so call her."

Max looked to Alesha, who nodded. "It's the only real way to draw her out, Max."

"We'll take cover and use you as bait," Merthane explained.

"Uh...I'm not the biggest fan of this idea."

"Do it," Merthane said as he and Alesha took positions on opposite sides of the aisle, disappearing into the haze.

Max suddenly felt very exposed. The result of stopping Memta wasn't for him to end up dead. But, they'd all been in agreement—Memta couldn't be allowed to leave the planet. If he had to give his life to prevent that *and* he could keep Alesha safe? That would be worth his life.

He straightened his posture with a fresh surge of courage. "Hey, Memta! Where'd you go?" He walked down the aisle a bit, leaving Alesha and Merthane behind him. He passed another set of transformers to find the smoking bodies of Memta's most recent victims, but that was about all he could see in front of him.

A plasma bolt fired, followed by a wail.

I couldn't be so lucky that she killed Merthane. He tried to assure himself that the cry had definitely been a man's. His insides trembled and he threw himself behind a transformer, as if that would help him. With each passing second, Memta came closer to finding Alesha. She was all that made him find his voice again. "Come on, Memta! You talk a big game, but where are you now? You're disappointing me!"

He turned his head to look down the connecting aisle and the blue glow settled in on him.

"Hello again, Maxim," Memta said with a tight smile.

Before Max could respond, she picked him up and threw him toward the edge of the roof. Instinctively, he reached out to break his fall. He went over the ledge, but before plunging to his death, he grabbed the tiny parapet, which wasn't much bigger than a tall curb. The small concrete bumper had saved his life. As he hauled himself back up, his heart hammered in his chest. He felt on the verge of hyperventilating, but couldn't resist peering down the side of the building. His stomach lurched as he considered the structure's height.

That was too *close.*

Memta sailed over, landing about fifteen feet away. "As much as I enjoyed her, I have to thank you for helping me escape Alesha, Maxim. This host is so much more welcoming."

Sweat poured down his face as he groaned and got back to his feet. "Glad I could help." Scraped and bruised, the worst of his injuries remained his wounded leg. He scanned the rooftop for the statue. His heart leaped into his throat.

Beyond Memta, behind one of the nearby transformers, Dayna huddled on the ground, the statue cradled in her arms. He averted his eyes, not wanting to tip Memta off. In his peripheral vision, he saw Dayna get to her feet, while Merthane and Alesha charged toward Memta from another aisle. Dayna cleared the transformer field by two steps before Memta spun around and unleashed the blue magma with both outstretched hands.

"*NO!*" Max cried out.

Dayna didn't even get the opportunity to scream as Memta immolated her. The magma hit her body and she instantly burst into flames, frozen in mid-stride.

"*DAYNA!*" The anguish in Merthane's voice cut Max to his core. Even though Merthane was a son of a bitch, Max wasn't immune to his pain.

Instantly, Merthane unloaded his twin pistols at Memta. Despite the lasers' uselessness, Memta tossed two fireballs at Alesha and Merthane, who both ducked down an aisle to avoid being incinerated.

Max's eyes widened as Dayna's remains crumbled to dust. Then they narrowed as he saw that the statue had survived Memta's attack, just as it had survived the research ship explosion. His eyes flicked to the goddess and he balked when he saw her staring at him.

"That cursed statue," she said with malevolence in her voice. "What do I have to do to erase it from existence?" With outstretched arms, she turned and created a wall of blue flame that separated them from the statue. She faced him with a proud smile. "That should provide us with some privacy."

"If I didn't know any better, I'd say you're starting to like me."

"Of course I like you, Maxim. It seems that every host I touch has some romantic connection to you. Would you prefer I melt the flesh from your bones?"

"I'd prefer you stop all of it."

Her mouth twisted. "I can hear the tone in your voice—you will not be coaxing me out of *this* body."

"Fair enough, but let's be honest—what happened last time was more of an eviction by the host."

Memta's eyes darkened. Her hair started to blow about like it did when she was ready to go off. "You tempt fate, mortal. Do not test me. This host will not reject me like the last and the longer I dwell, the more control I gain." She tossed multiple plasma bolts at him, setting the roof ablaze. She definitely missed him on purpose, though—her demonstrated aim told him that much. It was like when Alesha had been possessed, but with far more potential for accidental death.

Maybe Sierra doesn't love me as much as she claimed. He flinched at the flames, but once he sorted out her approach, he stood tall.

"You seem rather confident for a man about to be burned to ash."

He shrugged. "It seems Sierra has a little more control than you let on."

She turned her head away with a distasteful expression. It was the same face Sierra would make when she had to tell the truth. "She is like quicksilver—both drawn to me and frightened by my power."

He glanced over at the flames and the statue beyond them.

"You can get that thought out of your head, Maxim," she said as she faced him again. "I am never returning to that vessel."

"Well," Max said, "never say never. Now!"

From the other side of the flame wall, Alesha hurled the statue to Max before leaping through the fire to deliver a kick to Memta's mid-section.

"Alesha, don't!" Max called out in frustration as he bobbled the statue into his arms. Gripping the artifact, he looked over at the ladies, wondering why Memta hadn't yet scorched Alesha.

Alesha threw punches and kicks at the goddess, who easily batted them away. Judging from the expression on her face, Memta enjoyed the interaction, like she was playing with Alesha.

Max stayed on the sidelines, looking for his opportunity to strike with the statue. However, he knew that Alesha needed to face Memta.

"Come on, Sierra," Alesha said as a few more of her punches were rebuffed. "We need you to shake this off now."

"Alesha, so good to see you again," Memta said. "I missed you."

"Shut up," Alesha said through gritted teeth. "I want to talk to Sierra."

"You know how this works, Alesha. She's mine. Only I reside here now."

"Is that how I rejected you? Because I wasn't there anymore? Come on out, Sierra!"

Again, Memta rebuffed her attack. "What were you hoping, Alesha? That you could lure Sierra out by recounting the night of bliss you shared so long ago?" A wicked smile formed on her lips. "I *know* you think about it."

Alesha appeared to be thrown off, but it didn't show in her response. "I do. Any chance I can get her out here to reminisce?"

"A valiant attempt, but I have been inside your mind, Alesha. Despite the obvious physical delights you took away from your time with her, I know that you loathe Sierra and were quite happy when you thought that she had already met her demise."

Max felt Alesha had distracted Memta enough for him to finally make his move. Trying to stay out of her line of sight, he limped around to get behind her. His heart pounded in his ears as Alesha kept her busy with ineffective attacks, allowing him to creep closer. In moments, Memta loomed before him. He raised the statue. *Her scalp is skin; I'll just bean h—*

Memta spun around and grabbed him by the throat. "Did you think you could sneak up on me, Maxim? I am a *goddess* and I tire of this little game." Her hand flared.

He tried to scream as his neck began to sizzle, but her grip was too tight. She held Alesha off with her other hand, ringed in blue flame. Pain and the lack of oxygen made him dizzy. In desperation, he swung the statue forward, smashing it into her head.

As soon as the statue connected with her skin, Memta let out an ear-splitting scream. Her hands moved to protect herself as she staggered backwards.

He fell away from her, taking deep, gulping breaths and touching his burned neck gingerly. As Memta attempted to gather herself, Alesha planted a kick firmly in her back, knocking the goddess off balance.

Max lunged at her with the statue.

Memta grabbed his wrist. The heat radiated through his jacket sleeve, but at a lower intensity from her previous attacks.

He gritted his teeth against the pain and moved the statue toward her. In her weakened state, he was able to overpower her and press the statue against her face again.

"Maxim, please! This will destroy me!"

Was that Memta or Sierra? Her voice definitely sounded more human. Despite everything Sierra had put him through, he hesitated for a split second, letting up in his attack.

She responded to his indecision with a vicious backhand that knocked him to the ground, a bloody welt across his cheek.

The shock jarred the statue from his hand. It bounced on the rooftop and rolled to a stop at Alesha's boot. She snapped it up and held it threateningly over Memta, who held her hands up.

"Alesha, no! You cannot do this!"

"Watch me," Alesha said as she pushed the statue closer.

Memta grabbed her wrists. "I know your desires, Alesha. Join with me again and I can make them all reality."

Alesha pulled back. "What?"

"Alesha…don't listen to her!" Max called as he struggled to his feet. The force of Memta's attack had left him a little groggy.

"That's what you want, is it not?" Memta asked. "To join with me again? You have but to ask and take my hands."

Alesha had that faraway look in her eyes. "I…I…." She looked lost as she stepped away from Memta, the statue cradled limply in her hands.

Memta rose to her feet. "Yes, Alesha. Throw the statue over the roof's edge and we can be one again."

Alesha looked out over the roof.

Memta turned to face Max, who had finally gotten to his feet. She leveled her arm at him with a triumphant smile. "Goodbye, Maxim."

"*NO!*" Alesha cried as she swung the statue into Memta's head, knocking her back to the ground.

As Memta fell, the plasma beam she'd intended for Max slammed into another nearby building, setting it aflame. Alesha tossed Max the statue as he scrambled over to Memta, careful to avoid the still-pulsing plasma stream. Catching the artifact, he hit the ground and slammed the statue against Memta's head. *Maybe this'll knock some sense into her.*

The stream cut off and Memta grappled with Max, who held the statue tight against her face.

The statue flared bright blue in his hand. Memta screamed at the top of her lungs for several moments until her voice gave out. Everything went quiet on the roof, even the incessant humming of the transformer field. Then in an explosion of light and energy, Max and the statue were blown across the roof.

His eyes snapped open after feeling like he'd passed out. Willing his weary body to move, he found the statue cradled in his arms. Alesha appeared to be unconscious off to the right. Complete exhaustion swept over him. *What a fucking day.*

Sierra lay on the ground several yards away, looking at him with longing. "Give it to me, Max. I need it."

He snorted. "You're out of your mind."

"You don't know what it was like, Max. The universe was open to me."

"But she shunted you to the side, sweetheart. It was a lie."

The sound of heavy footsteps interrupted their heart-to-heart. Max was able to raise his head to see a grim Merthane walking toward them with purpose.

"Kudos, my boy. Kudos."

Max rested his head back on the ground. *This isn't going to end well.*

CHAPTER 30

As Max tried to gather his strength for the inevitable confrontation, Merthane crossed to Dayna's final resting place. He knelt by her ashes, bowing his head solemnly. His lips moved, but Max couldn't hear what he said.

Merthane rose and moved closer. "You've both made my life incredibly more difficult."

Max squinted. "*Both?* What are you talking about?"

"It was your plan, Maxim. You put her in harm's way. You shoulder the blame," Merthane said as he sauntered over to Sierra, who thrashed on the ground like a junkie going through withdrawal.

Usually when Merthane made Max's life a living hell, he had a playful quality to his demeanor, especially when he had the upper hand. This Merthane, though, was different. Max hadn't seen him like this since Gage. He was cold, detached, frightening.

"You can't seriously blame me for the actions of, literally, a possessed person," Max reasoned. "Hell, Dayna volunteered!"

"But only because you conveniently couldn't execute your own plan. And why couldn't Alesha handle it?" Merthane asked as he looked over at the unconscious Alesha. "Were you afraid she'd turn into this Memta?"

Max's mouth opened, but no sound came out. The answer was plain on his face.

"And what did you think would happen to Dayna? Did you even care?" Merthane asked. He didn't wait for an answer. "No, you knew exactly what you were doing here, putting her in danger to spare your girlfriend." Again, Merthane's gaze wandered over to Alesha.

Max's stomach dropped. "Look, Talon, I know you're in pain. I feel for you, I do, but don't do anything we'll both regret."

Merthane didn't even seem to hear him as his attention drifted to Sierra. "And this one." He walked closer to her. "You may have put Dayna in danger, Maxim, but this one is the real person to blame." He delivered a savage kick to Sierra's stomach. "Whatever pain I could deliver to you here would never be adequate." He kicked her again.

Sierra coughed and spat onto the ground, letting out a harsh laugh. "You vecking petch! You have no idea the forces you're playing with—either of you. Memta killed your girlfriend. Not me."

Merthane lunged at her. "How convenient for you." He punched her before drawing his pistol. Max was surprised when Merthane turned it on him. "I'll be taking that statue now, Maxim."

Max sighed. "You motherfucker. I fucking hate you."

"The feeling is mutual."

Max gripped the statue tighter.

"All right." Merthane said as he holstered his pistol and stalked over to the still unconscious Alesha.

"What are you doing, Merthane?"

"You're leaving me with few options and I'm losing my patience." He grabbed Alesha by her throat. She writhed in his grip. "Not as helpless as you let on, hm?" Dragging her to the edge of the rooftop, he dangled her over it as she kicked and slapped at his hands. "Don't squirm too much, Alesha. I might drop you."

Max struggled to sit up. "Stop! Stop! Here!" He tossed the statue toward Merthane, arcing his throw to keep it away from Sierra.

Merthane looked at Max in disappointment. "Always the quitter." He pulled Alesha back onto the roof, throwing her to the ground. His foot pressed down on her throat. "Be good, Alesha, or you'll end up like Sierra over there."

"What a big vecking man you are, Merthane," Alesha said, rubbing her neck as Merthane turned away from her. "Is threatening violence how you got Dayna to veck you?"

Merthane stopped and turned on his heel. He towered over Alesha, who sat on the ground.

Max's heart raced. He knew Merthane would probably shoot him if he tried to intervene.

Sierra apparently hadn't considered that option and lunged for the statue.

Merthane whipped out his pistol and hit Sierra square in the chest, dropping her to the ground in a heap. He then turned the pistol on Alesha. "Consider yourself warned, Alesha." He backed away from her toward the statue. As he picked the stone artifact up with a gloved hand, he holstered his pistol. Cradling the statue in his hands, Merthane turned his eyes back to Dayna's ashes. "She's going to be devastated."

"Who?" Max asked as scenarios of how he might wrest the statue back from Merthane ran through his mind.

"Someone I'd hoped to introduce you to one day, but since you're probably going to die here, I guess that's not going to happen."

"You sound pretty confident about that. Why don't you take Sierra and leave the statue? We can secure it so it never hurts anyone again."

"Hah! Where's that? Another GAC facility? No, Sierra here will be joining you in eternity, while I take this and find a potential buyer."

"I thought your clients were incinerated?" Max knew there had to be more to the story. Maybe in his grief, Merthane would slip up.

"For all I know, they were. But maybe there was somebody behind them, somebody who clearly wants *this* more than they want *her*. So, I'll hold onto it until they contact me."

"And if they don't?"

Merthane faced him, his gaze lethal. "Well, I don't think you're going to need to worry about that, Maxim." He unclipped Sierra's detonator from his belt.

"So that's where that got to. Why not just shoot us?" With as wasted as Max's body felt, he half-meant it.

Merthane walked back to the edge of the roof, giving Alesha a wide berth. "Because I have a flair for the dramatic and if you manage to actually survive, I get to keep making your life miserable." He nodded at the unmoving Sierra. "Her, I hope she rots. So long, Maxim. Alesha." He clicked the detonator, but his face dropped when he saw a screaming Sierra charging at him.

The building shuddered. Max fought to get to his feet.

Merthane dropped the detonator and fumbled for his pistol. Sierra collided with him, dislodging the statue from his grip as he defended himself against her wild attack. In an instant, the two of them went over the edge—gone.

Max looked at Alesha, stupefied. He didn't have much time to ponder their fates as the statue hit the roof with a single bounce before settling in-between the two of them. *See, good things happen to good people.*

The building rumbled and a transformer went up in flames.

Or...maybe not. The fight with Memta had left his injured leg feeling like it had been ripped open. He was so drained, the thought of moving made his body tremble. However, Glintock's words echoed in his mind: *Get the statue. It's everything.*

Then he saw Alesha staring at the statue with a hungry look.

Oh God, no.

In his hurry to beat Alesha to the artifact, he pushed off on his bad leg and ended up flat on his face. Pain shot through him, but all he cared about was what Alesha was doing. He looked up helplessly as she strode over to the statue and scooped it up like a baby.

"Fight it, sweetheart," he said. *I can't lose her.*

Her breathing quickened. "I can hear her calling to me, Max. She's in my head!"

"You're stronger than her, 'Lesha! You don't need her!"

"But...I can use her to help us escape." As if the building understood her, the entrance to the stairwell at the other end of the roof collapsed in on itself.

Shit. "Come on, baby. Throw me the statue." He struggled to his feet, wincing the whole time. "We just need to get it back to Litning's people."

Her eyes closed and she held the statue up to her head, but didn't make contact with her skin. She seemed completely oblivious to the building disintegrating around them. "She's speaking to me—telling me how to join with her to save us."

"It's a lie, Alesha. She doesn't want to help us. She just wants a body. You know this."

Alesha's face twisted into a mask of hatred. "Silence, human! You will be the first to die!" Then her mask fell. Fear filled her eyes. She looked at the statue, as if seeing it for the first time, and hurled it away.

The statue hit the roof behind Max, skittering to a stop. He knew he had to secure it, but his only concern at that moment was Alesha. She rushed over to him. They embraced tightly.

"Max, I'm sorry! I don't know what came over me!" She kissed him and touched his forehead to hers. "What's happening to me? Why can't I shake her?" Her voice was barely above a whisper.

"It's okay, sweetheart. We'll beat it. But, do me a favor?"

"Anything."

"Don't fucking touch that thing again."

The roar of several transformers tumbling into the fiery hole created by the collapsing roof interrupted their moment. However, the sound was quickly overtaken by a familiar whine on the wind.

"The *Sequel*," he said with a wide grin.

Cresting over the roof's ledge was indeed the *Sequel*. The back end of the ship leading into the cargo hold was open. Litning stood on the edge as Roeger rigged him up in a harness. The ship turned so that the open hatch rested on the edge of the roof. Litning motioned for the two of them to board.

Max put his hands on Alesha's shoulders. "You go on ahead. I need to get the statue."

"But you're hurt!"

He shook his head. "That doesn't matter. We have to secure it." He kissed her. "I'll see you soon. I love you."

"You'd better." She stepped onto the hatch and Litning inched out to pull her to safety.

Max turned and zeroed in on the statue. He took a few painful steps toward the artifact. The *Sequel* dropped sharply as the portion of roof on which it was docked fell away and flames shot up into the air. Max blinked at the distressing development and waved the ship off. Their safety was more important than his. All he had to do was get that statue and hold on tight.

The *Sequel* peeled off as more flames leaped toward the ship. Max could hear Alesha screaming as the ship moved to safety. He took another few steps toward the statue when his section of roof buckled and cracked, breaking on an angle. The shift wasn't so serious that Max slid down the incline uncontrollably, but it put the statue in a precarious position. Gripping the roof, he did his best Spider-Man impersonation as the artifact teetered on the rift in the concrete, threatening to tumble into the flames below. They were not Memta's blue flames, but very real, burn-you-alive-flames.

The building shook again. The statue seesawed on the broken ledge.

With his last ounce of strength, Max lunged up for the statue, intercepting it right as it teetered the wrong way. He hugged the stone to his chest as another transformer exploded and his section of roof slid a bit more into the abyss. There was no escape.

I'm strangely okay with this. The band is back together and none of them seem to totally hate me anymore. Kalen's dead and Sierra...well, if she and Merthane are dead, then all the better. They'll find the statue with me and hopefully Glintock will let Litning take it back to his people. Just wish I'd had more time with Alesha. At least I got to say goodbye—more or less.

The roof slid deeper into the hole. A briar patch of flame yawned below him. After his encounters with Memta, it almost appeared as though the flames reached for him. He closed his eyes, tightening his grip on the statue, resigned to his fate.

Across from his position, the roof crumbled some more, tossing a transformer into the flames. The resulting explosion caused Max's island of concrete to slide sharply, jolting him out of his malaise.

Keeping the statue tightly secured under his right arm, he reached out with his left hand to try and stop his slide. Apparently, he wasn't *completely* ready to die. He flopped onto his stomach, attempting to drag himself back up the collapsing section of rooftop. As he clawed his way up, he was greeted by two boots landing on the building's ledge.

It was his girl, Alesha. The *Sequel* had swooped in over the flames and hovered above with Litning standing by at the winch to haul her back in. As usual, her lopsided grin was firmly in place. "This reminds me of the day we met."

He grunted, pulling himself closer to her. "Different circumstances."

She shook her head. "I'm always saving your ass, Earth Boy."

"It's Earth Man, god dammit."

The roof shifted again and Max slid a good two feet away from her.

Her eyes widened and she waved the ship lower before crawling out onto the unstable concrete. "We'll argue about it later. Give me your hand."

While he planted his left fingers firmly in a crack in the roof, Max worked the statue from his armpit into his hand. He thrust the artifact toward Alesha. "We can't lose this."

That faraway look took hold in her eyes and she swiped the statue from his hand with a quickness that frightened him. Cradling the artifact in her gloved hands, she gazed at it deeply, swallowing hard.

Come on, Alesha. You can beat her. He felt himself losing his grip as the building rumbled again.

Alesha's brow furrowed. With a fluid motion, she threw the statue through the open hatch, into the cargo bay, and then extended her hand to Max. "Take my hand, baby."

With a surge of adrenaline, he pulled himself up and grabbed her hand as the roof fell away beneath him, into the imploding building. His body swung wide, but Alesha held on tight. The flames surged, licking his boots as he swung himself in a position to grab her other hand.

Litning worked the winch, propelling them rapidly up into the thick Ventu air. Within a few hair-raising moments, Litning and Roeger hauled them on board the ship. Alesha unhooked her harness and sat on the deck beside him.

"I knew you could do it," he said. "Thank you."

Brushing his hair back, she wore a wide, relieved smile. "Shut up and kiss me, Earth Boy."

This time, he didn't argue with her.

CHAPTER 31

Litning bowed his head as he stood before the Meshmark and what looked to be nearly half the population of his settlement, Rejaan. At last, he was home.

After proving to the guards at the gate that he did indeed carry Memta with him, Litning was granted an audience with the Meshmark. Although, if he was honest with himself, it was to be more of a trial. He silently wished the guards had simply turned him away.

He stood in the center of the Great Chamber. Four guards armed with spears formed a square around him, each Revash serving as a vertex. To further isolate him, six stone pylons rose up from the floor to waist-level, hemming him in place.

Litning raised his eyes enough to survey the room. His new allies stood off to the right side of the gallery. Maxim and Alesha wore concerned expressions, while the pilot, Robert, craned his head around as if trying to take in every last detail of the chamber. Glintock, on the other hand, displayed a steely gaze that betrayed nothing of his inner thoughts.

Of the many Revashes that packed the chamber, only Avala had any empathy in her eyes. As Litning had been hustled through the settlement, Avala pushed past the guards, allowing the two of them to share an all-too-brief moment before his trial. That moment had been worth the journey to Revjekt.

The rest of Litning's people glared at him, silently screaming their accusations. No one knew the truth about his exile, save Avala and the Meshmark, and it was clear that no one had the desire to uncover what had really happened. However, could they all still be considered his people, after he had been gone so long?

A dais sat at the front of the chamber with a long stone block atop it. Behind the block sat the Meshmark. Vorkoth sat at the center of the three council members, his golden headdress glittering in the light that poured in from a hole in the ceiling. The old Revash held Litning in his stony gaze, his face inscrutable.

Vorkoth banged a large rock against the stone bench. "I would call for silence," he said in his gravelly voice. At his command, the gallery fell silent. His eyes shifted over the crowd for a moment. He gestured to Maxim and his crew. "For the benefit of our visitors from the outside, we will speak in the general tongue." He looked to Litning. "Garnath Tokcha, you were exiled from this settlement two-hundred-forty-moons ago, yet you appear before us now when your exile status has not been lifted."

"Meshmark and people of Rejaan, I have traveled the galaxy seeking atonement for my transgressions against the settl—"

Barjaan, the judge sitting to Litning's right, balked. "You mean murder of one of our citizens? *That* is merely a *transgression*?"

Out of the corner of his eye, Litning saw Glintock react to the revelation.

"No!" Avala cried out. "That is not how it happened!"

"Silence!" Vorkoth called. "Silence!"

After a few moments, Litning spoke. "May I be allowed to continue?"

"Yes," Huna, the lone female judge said. "I am curious as to the veracity of the claims you have made today. They are, after all, the only reason we granted you admittance."

"Yes, you and your outsider...rabble." The words oozed out of Barjaan's mouth as he turned his head toward Maxim's crew. The rest of the spectators followed Barjaan's eyes.

"H'lo," Maxim said with a nervous wave.

"You mean, have I truly returned Memta to her resting place here in Rejaan?" Litning asked. "You tell me."

"Show us," Vorkoth demanded. "Show us what you have brought."

Without a word, Litning reached his gloved hand into the bag and brought Memta into the open, holding her over his head. A murmur rippled through the gallery, but there was surprisingly little fanfare for the reveal.

At Vorkoth's gesture, one of the guards surrounding Litning moved to take Memta. Litning looked the guard over, making sure he wore gloves, before handing her over. The guard mounted the dais and set Memta in front of Vorkoth. Barjaan and Huna leaned in for a closer look.

"It certainly looks like Memta," Barjaan sniffed. "But, could easily be a forgery."

Huna faced Litning. "How can we confirm your claims?"

Litning smiled tightly. "You can touch the stone, but I would not advise it."

Alesha took a step forward. "I can vouch that it's real."

"We all can," Maxim added.

Barjaan glared straight ahead, refusing to look at them. "You are not permitted to speak, outsi—"

Vorkoth held up his hand. "You may speak, young woman."

Alesha glanced around nervously. She took a few steps toward the dais, each one becoming more confident. When she stopped, she looked at each member of the Meshmark. "The statue possessed me."

Another murmur rolled through the assembled spectators.

"Silence," Vorkoth bellowed, his voice echoing over the crowd. Once he had quiet, his gaze swept the room before focusing on Alesha. "You may continue."

"It initially touched me by accident, but once it did, I craved its power. I touched it again and nearly killed my friends." She closed her eyes with a shiver. "I can still hear her calling to me now."

Vorkoth's eyes widened, while Huna kept a neutral expression. Barjaan, predictably, was apoplectic.

"Of course she's lying to help Tokcha!"

Alesha's back went up and Maxim stepped up behind her, putting his hands on her shoulders. She reached up and gripped one of his hands. Litning could only wish to touch Avala like that.

Barjaan continued his tirade. "How did you free yourself from Memta's hold, pray tell?"

"She rejected the goddess' power and forcibly exorcised her from her body," Max said. "Another touched the statue and I had to hold it to her skin to re-imprison Memta. It's real."

Glintock stepped forward. "Ladies and gentlemen, my name is Matthias Glintock. I am an agent of the Galactic Authority Commission. That statue destroyed a research ship before Lit—er, Mr. Tokcha recovered it. I can attest to its authenticity."

"We respect your station, Matthias Glintock, though we do not recognize your agency's authority. Thank you for your testimony," Vorkoth said.

"How did Memta come into your possession, Tokcha?" Barjaan asked.

Litning bristled against the question. Nervousness gripped his stomach. "I...liberated it from a GAC facility."

Barjaan continued grilling him. "How did you learn it was there?"

"From an associate—an outsider."

"Is that person here now?" Huna asked.

"No. I do not know where she is now."

Vorkoth leveled his gaze at Litning. "Is she the other woman who touched the statue?"

Litning bowed his head. "Yes." He could barely get the word out.

"Can we assume you were procuring Memta for this woman?" Barjaan asked.

Litning raised his head. "That was her understanding, yes, but I—"

"Betrayed her trust?" Barjaan interrupted.

"I had always intended on bringing her back here," Litning finished through gritted teeth.

The tone of Barjaan's questions became almost airy, as though the answers were a certainty. "And you hoped to buy your way back into Rejaan? Tell us this, did those at the GAC facility allow you to simply walk in and take Memta?"

Litning could not repress an edge of anger creeping into his voice. "Not exactly, no."

"Matthias Glintock," Barjaan said with practical delight. "As a representative of the GAC, can you tell us *exactly* what happened?"

Glintock stared at the Meshmark blankly. He turned to Litning, who met his gaze head on. Their eyes locked. After a moment, Litning's shoulders slumped and he nodded at Glintock.

"Ah, several security officers were killed in the defense of the facility."

Barjaan leaned forward. "Did Tokcha do this killing?"

Glintock's mouth opened, but no words came forth. Again, he looked to Litning, who once again prodded him to tell the truth. He would not hide behind lies. "Some. Yes."

The gallery erupted. Many of those in attendance leveled their ire directly at Litning. Avala merely bowed her head, crestfallen.

Vorkoth banged on the bench repeatedly. "Silence! *Silence!*"

"You see? *You see?*" Barjaan said as the gallery quieted down. "He learns nothing from his exile!"

"You think I should have let them kill me—that I not defend myself?" Litning asked, his defeated air evaporating in anger. "Just like with Raork?"

Several heads in the gallery turned toward Avala, who kept her eyes locked on Litning.

"You were in that facility illegally!" Barjaan argued.

"The woman I worked with would have stolen Memta with or without me. I felt securing her was more important tha—"

"But you hoped to receive something in exchange, no?" Huna asked.

Litning looked to Avala, sorrow in his eyes. "Yes." A wave of grief crashed within him. The Meshmark had not delivered their verdict, but he knew what it would be.

After a few moments of stillness, Vorkoth cleared his throat. "I have heard enough. We will deliberate briefly."

The dais sunk into the floor until the Meshmark disappeared and a trap door closed above them. A low rumble of conversation broke out in the gallery, but the guards maintained their positions around Litning, who kept his eyes on Avala. He would look at her as long as he was physically able, for he feared these would be their last moments together.

Through the swell of voices, Litning's sharp ears picked out Glintock's. "I had no choice. I'm obligated...."

Then Maxim's voice. "We know, Matthias. He does too."

Litning did not blame the agent. He had only been doing his duty. Litning's fate was his own.

A few minutes passed and the dais rose up out of the floor again. The gallery silenced itself without prompting, leaving only the sound of stone scraping against stone. The members of the Meshmark all wore grave expressions, even Barjaan.

Vorkoth glanced around the chamber before zeroing in on Litning. "Garnath Tokcha, you have our sincerest gratitude for returning Memta to us. We have heard whispers of the destruction she has wrought over the centuries and you and your companions can be rest assured that the statue will be safe here on Revjekt. That being said, Barjaan is correct—you have learned nothing from your exile. You violated our laws by killing. We do not kill—even in defense. Raork would have attacked you and been punished, but you struck first."

"To protect my life," Litning interrupted.

Vorkoth took a long pause with a stern glare. "It is not our way. Long ago, the Revash people were savages, stalking the plains, guided only by their baser instincts. We were monsters, but after centuries of self-reflection and a desire for our race to progress, we emerged a civilized people. By continuing these practices outside of Revjekt, you strip away all that we have accomplished and revert back to our monstrous past. You have killed your nepast in order to reclaim it. Your name will live on in our history as the one who returned Memta to us. But you are banished from Rejaan from this day forward, never to return. Your actions have proven you to be a threat to this settlement. I do not doubt the sincerity of your intentions to return, but I am sorry. We will now secure Memta."

"Sir," Glintock spoke up. "I know you do not recognize my organization, but I have to ask, how will the statue be secured so as to never harm the galaxy again?"

Vorkoth gave Glintock a long look. "Memta will be returned to the fire from which she was born. We will lower the vessel into the magma at the top of Mount Vustame."

"In order to complete my mission here, I would like to be present at this ceremony," Glintock said.

"No outsiders may be present."

"I must insist."

Vorkoth's eyes narrowed. "Agent, you are in no position to insist anything. Now, the guards will escort you all out of Rejaan."

The pylons around Litning lowered and the guards began hustling him along with the rest of the crew toward the exit.

"No!" Avala cried out, pushing past the guards to be at Litning's side. As when they had met outside, they pressed their foreheads together, eyes closed. Their hands clasped together briefly before the guards dragged her away.

Litning snarled. He felt the red haze threatening to consume him.

Maxim jumped to his side, putting a hand on his arm. "Litning, don't. Don't give them the satisfaction."

"I have nothing left to lose."

"Wrong. You're alive, so you keep fighting."

Litning looked at Maxim solemnly. His eyes flicked to Alesha and he thought about all Maxim had gone through to save her from Memta. Perhaps he understood the rage boiling in Litning after all. He nodded at Maxim, but the guards cut their moment short, becoming far more aggressive as they pushed the crew through

Rejaan and out the main gate. Within minutes, they were back on the frozen plains of Revjekt, outside the energy dome that protected the settlement.

Robert gaped at the closed gate. "That's it? So much for gratitude."

Litning stared forlornly at the gate, but could only see the anguished Avala in his mind's eye. The pain and despair that had festered inside Litning throughout the trial boiled to the surface in a long guttural cry as he sank to his knees. Tears stung his eyes as the magnitude of his failure pressed down on him. It had all been for nothing. Unjustly exiled and now, his only hope for redemption had been destroyed. Had he killed to liberate Memta? Yes, but how many thousands, possibly millions, of lives had he *saved* by returning her home? Should he have argued that to the Meshmark? Would it have mattered? *No, most likely not.*

He kneeled in the snow for several moments, chest heaving. His eyes closed as he took a deep, cleansing breath. Exhaling slowly, he opened his eyes again to gaze at the walls of Rejaan and the energy dome that kept him outside.

"It is as if I had never been exiled and it is all happening again for the first time." His chest seized. "Avala...." He remained in the snow like that for a few moments more before rising and turning his back on Rejaan for possibly the last time.

Now, I must forge ahead, alone.

CHAPTER 32

The walls of Max's quarters on the *Sequel* were not soundproofed, so he was fairly certain everyone on the ship could hear his and Alesha's moans as they climaxed. In fact, that had probably been the case for the entire week the *Sequel* underwent repairs on the other side of the ridge that overlooked Rejaan.

Eh, I'm the captain. They'll get over it.

Max had some repairs he had to undergo himself. Alesha had been a more than attentive nursemaid as he healed from all the injuries he'd sustained since the job started. They made it about a day before they tore each other's clothes off, giving in to their desires. Of course, they told each other, it was all in the interests of "keeping warm" due to Revjekt's harsh, freezing climate.

As Alesha let out one last long moan, a blast of turquoise light bathed the room for a few brief moments. When the light faded, Max and Alesha could only stare at each other, panic in their eyes.

"What the hell was *that*?" Max asked, wondering if he should reach for his nearby pistol.

"I don't know," Alesha said with terrified eyes. "I think it might have been a parting gift from Memta."

"Well, how do you feel?"

Alesha looked at him with unfocused eyes.

His body tensed.

Her head snapped toward him. "Human," she said in a husky voice. "I need to join with you to fuel my power."

"*Wh-what?*" He moved for his pistol, but she reached under the sheet and gripped him.

"I…hunger!" she cried as her voice cracked before breaking into laughter.

He pushed her away. "What are you *doing?*"

She fell back onto the bed, laughing, before slapping his leg. "I'm kidding!"

He looked at her with mistrust. Was she being for real, or had Memta taken control again?

Her expression softened, perhaps seeing the fear creeping into his eyes. She touched his arm. "Hey…I promise, I'm all right."

"What was that? Why aren't you scared by it?"

"I don't know *what* it was. Maybe some kind of…ethereal residue, if that makes sense. And the reason I'm not scared is simple—I don't hear her in my head anymore."

He was still leery. There wasn't any hint of Memta in her voice or appearance, but if even a scrap remained, would she still be Alesha?

She must have sensed his apprehension. Rubbing his arm, she cuddled up to him. "Max, I really mean it, I feel fine. For the first time since I touched that statue, I feel like myself."

"But, the power, do you still have it?"

"I don't think so. It could be like side effects of the possession. I'm pretty sure I'm fine." A relieved smile broke out across her face, but it quickly turned mischievous. "But…if I *do* still have Memta's powers…ooh, this could definitely come in handy." Her hand wandered beneath the covers again. "I have to say, I'm glad that Memta left your cock intact."

He gave her a tight smile. "That makes two of us."

She gave him another quick squeeze before sliding out of bed. "I have to pee." She leaned close to him. "Are you sure you'll be all right without me here to save you?"

"Fuck you," he said with a shake of his head. She'd been dining out on that one since she pulled him off the roof on Ventu.

"I expect you to." She gave him a quick kiss and then padded off to the bathroom.

As he watched her beautiful body leave his sight, he sat back in the bed, content. His day could have been much worse. In all honesty, he was lucky to be alive—they all were.

The makeshift repairs Robert and Gerry had made to the *Sequel* had been just enough to rescue Max and limp the rest of the way to Revjekt, but it needed extensive work if they were going to get home.

Home. Max wondered what it would be like when they got there. Alesha seemed adamant about rejoining her own crew and he couldn't really blame her. However, that wasn't what his heart wanted. They hadn't discussed it in the week he'd taken to recuperate, but the time felt just about right to blow up the bliss they'd been enjoying.

In between bouts of sex, Alesha nursed Max back to health, while constantly harping on the fact that she'd been the one to rescue him—again. He let her have the glory for the most part. Whatever helped heal her mind from the trauma inflicted by Memta was fine by Max, even if it came at the expense of his ego.

Unfortunately, one thing Max wasn't willing to do on the trip back was go through withdrawal pains. Though he'd stayed off the rimi when he probably should have been on it on Ventu, he'd been sneaking low doses ever since. His body already felt like shit—no reason to make it worse with fever, chills, and whatnot. He promised himself he'd deal with it back home, once all the craziness died down. It'd been tough to hide it from Alesha, but she had to know since he *wasn't* going through withdrawal. She hadn't said anything to him about it, though. He was managing it. Soon, he'd have to confront it head on.

Aside from feeling guilty about his rimi use, most everything in Max's world was right. He had his crew back for the time being and that's what he'd set out to do when Glintock sprang him from prison. However, one thing buzzed at the back of his mind—he still wasn't sure of Sierra and Merthane's fates. When the *Sequel* arrived at the factory, the *Claw* was nowhere to be found. He was sure Merthane wasn't dead—he couldn't be that lucky. Though their communications had been limited, Max felt sure he'd have heard something if his rival had perished. They'd been at odds for so long, he thought that he might somehow *feel* it if Merthane had left the physical plane.

Sierra's fate was an even bigger mystery. Wherever she was, she was more than likely with Merthane. Though, for all Max knew, Merthane had saved himself and let her fall to her death. He doubted it though. After what Sierra had done to Dayna as Memta, Merthane would want to make her suffer. For as long as Max had known him, revenge had always been a more potent motivator for Merthane than money.

Of course, the biggest mystery of all was who it was Sierra had been working for. Max and his crew had fully expected the soldiers in black to regroup and pursue them to Revjekt, but they never returned. Had they given up on the statue? Or, had they conceded the victory and instead chosen to make other plans? It definitely needled Max, but he felt it was more of Glintock's concern than his.

All thoughts of Merthane and Sierra dissolved as Alesha stepped back into the room. Their reunion had left him exhausted, but just the sight of her was enough to stir his arousal.

"Ooh Captain, I'm getting chilled again in this harsh climate," she said teasingly.

Despite her effect on him, he put up a meager defense. "Damn woman, I'm supposed to be healing."

"Stop being a baby," she said, sliding back under the covers. "You've had over a week and the meds healed you up enough."

"I'm sore as hell."

"That's probably my fault." She kissed him lightly on the lips. "Can I help that getting possessed by a goddess makes me horny?"

"No...you were plenty horny before we made Memta's acquaintance."

She kissed his chest. "Well...you can't blame me for trying." Her lips moved to his, while her hand found him beneath the covers.

He groaned at her touch.

"It looks like there's still some life in you yet," she said with a grin.

"You always knew how to get me going." Taking her in his arms, he kissed her deeply.

"I missed you, Earth Boy."

He pointed at her. "That's Earth Man." Though he wasn't interested in getting into an argument about their future, he saw his opening. "You know, there's a way that you'll never miss me again."

Alesha sighed and pulled back from him. "Way to kill the mood. We've already discussed this."

Her dismissiveness wounded him, but he suspected it might be a defense mechanism. He'd hurt her and she clearly didn't want a repeat of that. "As I recall, you made declarations and I'm supposed to accept them."

"I have to leave after this, Max. I have a whole life that I'm content with."

"All that tells me is that you weren't content with *our* life."

"I wasn't—not professionally. And *you* left! Remember?"

"I left becau—"

"You left because we were in one of our lulls and Sierra shook her ass in your direction."

He grimaced.

"Look, I'm not blaming you. I fell for her charms once too. And, I know I'm not the easiest person to live with—do *not* say a word."

Erring on the side of caution, he kept quiet.

"You have your moods too, but that's why this works. Neither of us wants to be tied down. You just need to shed your antiquated Earth beliefs about relationships."

She was right about that—no matter how long he'd been out there, he still had a lot to learn about relationships in space. Still, that didn't change the way he felt. "Look, Alesha, I get it. I do. But, we've made a ton of progress on this trip. Give me a chance to make the other side of it right. I had no idea how unhappy you were."

"Neither did I. Then you were gone and I had to make do for myself."

He winced at yet another jab about him leaving. "I never learned how to work with a partner. My dad mainly ran the ship and the crew followed his lead. The only other regular example I had was Merthane and I *know* you don't want me running things like him."

She looked away for a moment and then back. "No, definitely not."

"Give me another chance. I need you in my life."

"Max, if I go off with my crew, I won't disappear completely."

"That's a lie and you know it. You know how the life is."

She didn't seem to have a reply to that.

"Are you really going to make me say it?" he asked.

After a moment, her gaze locked squarely on him. "Yes."

He balked at her direct response. "I-I...."

She leaned into him. "I want to hear you say *why* you need me, because it's the first step you need to take in beating this."

"That's not the only reason I need you. You know that."

"No, but right now, it's the most pressing."

He stared at her for a few tense moments.

"Just say it, Max. I need to hear the words, because like I told you before, if you keep doing that garbage, you won't have me in your life at all. And I already know you're sneaking it on the side. I'm not an idiot."

"I never thought you were."

She folded her arms. "I'm still waiting."

Why couldn't he do it? He'd already said he needed her. Wasn't that enough? His eyes closed as he admitted the truth—he didn't *want* to give up the rimi. He'd beaten the worst of the side effects thus far. Who was to say he couldn't maintain that control? *But, that's not why you started taking it again. You have that reason sitting here in the flesh.* He opened his eyes. *And you'll lose her forever if you don't stop.*

Alesha's eyes had softened. She grabbed his hand.

She's literally reaching out to you, you stupid son of a bitch! "I…." His eyes shifted away from hers, even though he knew he had to meet her gaze in order for her to believe he was committed. He looked into her eyes. "I need your…help…to beat the rimi."

Her eyes welled up and her face broke into a relieved smile as she embraced him. "You've got it, Earth Boy. You've got it."

He put his arms around her and his embrace tightened as the reality of his admission sunk in. "Thank you," he whispered.

"You'll always have my heart, Max. We'll beat this again."

He took her face in his hands and kissed her tenderly. The sweet taste of her lips was tinged with her salty tears. He chuckled. "I'm taking the big bedroom back, you know."

"Oh no you're not. I'll fry you with a Memta bolt if you try." Her face tightened in concentration, but only a puff of turquoise smoke escaped from her lips.

"Yeah, I'm really scared." He pulled her toward him and they fell back beneath the covers.

A few hours later, Max sat at the head of the common area table. To his right, sat Glintock. To his left, Litning. The two had steered clear of each other over the last week, probably avoiding the conversation they knew had to take place. Max decided to force the issue, considering he'd just had a difficult discussion of his own and that ended extremely well. He hoped his good fortune might extend to others.

They'd been sitting in silence for about five minutes. *My career transition to couples' therapist isn't going well.*

Robert's voice piped in from the intercom. "*Max, all systems are go. We're ready when you are.*"

"Thanks, Robbie. I'll let you know soon." As the intercom clicked off, Max continued to stare at his passengers.

"Shouldn't you be getting into space?" Glintock asked. "I'm sure the people of Rejaan are ready for us to leave." He winced when Litning flinched. "Sorry, I didn't mean…."

"I know what you meant, Agent," Litning rumbled. "The wound is still raw."

"Of course. Again, I apologize."

"You're right," Max said. "They probably *do* want us out of their, ah, hair. The problem is, I have no idea where we're going. I mean, I know where *I'm* going, but you two are a mystery."

Litning shifted in his seat. "I also must apologize for my absence of late. I have…had much to ponder."

"Completely understandable," Max said. "In all honesty, I was pretty busy myself."

"So I have heard," Litning replied with a slight smile.

Max rolled his eyes. His face flushed in embarrassment.

"I must thank you, Maxim, for accompanying me to Rejaan. So, thank you."

"Don't mention it, Fuzzy."

Litning growled something under his breath. "You mentioned something about a job?"

"Yeah, if you're interested. We could use someone like you, Garnath," Max replied with a smile.

Litning shrugged. "I have nowhere else to go. And to outsiders, my name is Litning. I thought I could keep Litning's transgressions separate from Garnath's, but I realize now they are one in the same. In doing the right thing, I did harm and now I will never see my home again."

"You'll always have a place with us. In the short time I've known you, you've shown me more of your character than your Meshmark will ever see."

"Thank you, Maxim," Litning said, bowing his head.

"By the way, who was Raork anyway?" Max asked.

Litning did not respond right away. "He was Avala's brother."

Max and Glintock exchanged a somber look.

"Of course, my offer to Litning is contingent on your move, Matthias."

Glintock remained silent a few moments. "I was outvoted on coming to Revjekt. Despite our recent record, I wanted the statue in GAC hands. It's an artifact that can bring ruin to the galaxy and I would feel safer if we could keep our eye on it. But, if the Revash solution is to seal it away in magma, I can't really argue with that. My superiors won't be happy, but they can't argue the statue isn't safe."

He paused for a moment and his eyes fell on Litning. "All that being said, Litning is still a killer."

Max held up his hand. "Now, hold on."

"He *killed* people, Max, innocent people who were just doing their jobs. Yes, by securing the statue and bringing it back here, he's saved countless lives, but those he killed still demand justice."

Litning bowed his head again, but this time, his back went up as well. Max feared that their little meeting might get violent.

"I believe in justice," Glintock said. "I believe in giving perpetrators punishments equal to their crimes." Glintock looked directly at Litning, who met his gaze evenly. "But then I watched Litning lose everything he had fought for. He has no home, no people, and no mate. My testimony unintentionally helped in that and I ended up causing him more pain than I ever could by throwing him in prison or killing him. If I'm not mistaken, he would probably see both as release."

Litning only nodded in response.

"So, when I think of that, I think Litning is suffering enough."

"Thank you, Agent Glintock," Litning said as he rose from the table. "I will endeavor to atone for my sins."

"Just behave yourself. I don't want to hear about any more rampages."

Litning bowed his head. "I will strive to prevent that from happening. And thank you, Maxim, for offering me a place with you and the crew. You were not the family I had been looking for, but you are the one that will have me and for now, that will do just fine."

"Thanks…I think," Max replied with a perplexed smile.

"Gentlemen, I will now take my leave." Litning left the common area and headed down the hall leading to the crew's quarters.

Max held his hand up to Glintock until he heard the metal door of Litning's room slam shut. "All right, how much of that little speech did you really believe?"

"Personally? All of it. Putting him in prison now would be the worst idea ever. He would probably relish the idea of thrashing some other inmates. However, the GAC won't see it the same way. As far as they're concerned, the Revash people wouldn't let me take Litning with us. Understood?"

"Aye, aye, captain."

"I mean it, Max. I'm holding you one hundred percent responsible for him—no more violent outbursts."

"I'll do my best. So, that means I'm free to go too?" Max tried to tamp down the note of hope in his voice.

"I'll make sure everything is squared away with the GAC. Maybe...don't go to Aval anytime soon."

"Will do."

The two of them sat at the table in comfortable silence.

"Thank you for all your help, Maxim. I couldn't have done it without you."

Max smiled broadly. "*That* had to have been difficult."

Glintock's tight smile and shake of his head told Max that it had been.

"Y'know, as hellish as it was, it was all for the best. I got my crew back and the statue is where it belongs," Max said.

"We still don't know who Sierra was working for or what happened to her or Merthane."

"He'll turn up again—he can't help it," Max promised. "We'll figure it out."

Again, they fell silent and Max looked at Glintock expectantly. He still hadn't gotten any answer to where he'd begun the conversation. Glintock caught his look and began to chuckle.

"What's up?"

Glintock cleared his throat. "I can't believe I took this detail for granted, but now that you're a free man, I guess I have to ask the question: Can I get a lift back to Modan?"

Max flashed a wide grin.

"What?" Glintock asked.

"Of course. You're our first new customer."

EPILOGUE

WHAM!

The loud crash snapped Sierra back to consciousness. A dark hood secured over her head prevented her from seeing anything, though. Her foggy mind told her that Merthane had sedated her for the trip to wherever she was. The last thing she remembered was falling. She had tackled Merthane in a bid to reclaim Memta, but her enthusiasm and momentum carried them over the edge. It had been her first misstep the entire job and it had cost her.

Whoever carried her limp body tossed her into the air and she hit the floor with a hard *smack*. She suppressed the urge to groan in pain. Instead, she focused on what she could hear, hoping to learn more about her current predicament.

"Here's your prize," she heard Merthane growl. "After what she's done, you're lucky I didn't bring her in a small container, but it can still be arranged."

"Unnecessary, Mr. Merthane." The respondent was a woman with a very cultured voice. "Most guests knock before entering."

"Well, I'm not in a very friendly mood."

"Yes, I can imagine. My sincerest condolences on your loss."

"Don't even presume to understand what I've lost." Merthane's voice was husky, thick with emotion. Sierra remembered killing his girlfriend while Memta possessed her. The memory sent a pleasant tingle up her spine.

"I was not presuming anything, Mr. Merthane. Simply extending my sympathies," the woman said.

"Well, save them." He paused with a heavy sigh. "Fancy suite you've got here. I hope you can still afford to pay me."

"You should know better than that, Mr. Merthane."

"I only know what I'm paid to know. Speaking of which…."

"Yes, of course. You're as good as your reputation. The funds have been transferred to your account, as we agreed."

Merthane clicked his tongue. "Full payment, huh? Even without the statue?"

"The artifact is out of the GAC's hands, which is more important than us possessing it. Consider the payment…compensation for your troubles."

"That's a vecking insult and you know it."

"I assure you, it was not meant that way. We take care of those who work with us."

"Does that include having your men threaten me when we were supposedly on the same side?"

"Come now, Mr. Merthane. You of all people must understand the need to keep one's options open. We couldn't very well entrust you solely with the success of our designs. We had to have other agents working at cross purposes. If our soldiers had teamed with you that would have created a link in a chain that would inevitably lead back to us. If the GAC suspected we were working together, they could find you and squeeze the information out of you."

"Hah! Not very likely."

"Your bravado notwithstanding, now there is doubt in the eyes of the GAC and we accomplished what we set out to do—more or less."

"Don't underestimate Maxim Ultra. That kid's petulant, but he's got a sharp mind. It might not be good for you that he's all buddy-buddy with that Glintock guy now."

The woman sighed. "Just one of the hundreds of obstacles we're set to deal with moving forward."

Sierra heard footsteps approaching her and felt someone looming over her.

"Don't," Merthane said. "If you take that hood off and I see her face, I'm liable to kill her right here and now."

"Then I think it is time for you to take your leave, Mr. Merthane." The woman was not the one standing over Sierra.

"It's dangerous to keep her alive. I know more than anyone," Merthane said. The ache in his voice—the need to lash out at Sierra—was plain.

"Duly noted, Mr. Merthane. Ms. Numani failed us this time, but it would be a waste of good materials to dispose of her so arbitrarily."

Sierra could almost hear Merthane grinding his teeth.

"I trust you know the way out, Mr. Merthane?"

"If we ever meet again, don't bring Sierra. I'll kill all of you."

"Hopefully none of us will see that day."

Sierra heard Merthane walk away and a door close behind him.

"A hateful man," the woman said. "But in this game, a necessary evil."

The hood was ripped from Sierra's head, flooding her eyes with light. She blinked several times as she tried to get her bearings. A man in a suit—like the two she dealt with on Ventu—stood over her, holding the hood while undoing her bonds. There were a few more dressed like him sprinkled around the room. Merthane had been right—the room *was* an opulent suite. Plush red carpet covered the floor and the obsidian walls were polished to a mirror finish.

Sierra recognized the skyline outside the large tinted windows. "We're in Tonicen?"

"Very good, Miss Numani," the cultured woman said from a chair doused in shadow in the suite's living area. "Come my dear, join me over here." At a motion of the woman's hand, the lights in the living area came up to a reasonable level.

Thanks to the increased light, Sierra could see that she recognized the woman. A human, she had her graying hair pulled back in a ponytail. She wore a meticulous cream-colored suit and a pleasant smile. However, Sierra knew that the smile was far from sincere. "Certainly, Madam Zeth."

Her utterance of the name gave the woman pause. Her smile tightened, becoming more uncomfortable. "And how did you piece that together, my dear?"

Sierra shrugged. "I'm in the business of knowing the wealthiest and most powerful people in the galaxy, no matter how hard they try to conceal their identities. You never know when they might end up as clients." She paused with a look. "Or marks."

The woman's expression implied that Sierra's deduction impressed her, but she still had a disappointed air. "Very good. I am indeed Sestra Zeth and like our Mr. Merthane, you are equal to your reputation, Ms. Numani."

"Call me Sierra. I didn't know you were so central to your organization's success, though. What about Baron?"

Zeth's mouth curled in disgust. "My idiot brother. You could say that he is the face of our corporation, while I…write the script."

"Incredible you've kept it mostly quiet. I have to say, I wouldn't have pegged you as anti-GAC. It's worked well for you so far."

"Yes, it has, hasn't it? But when you get to be as powerful as I am, you get to see what goes on in the shadows and there you find that our beloved GAC is not as righteous as they advertise."

"Oh, I'm no fan of the GAC and corruption is everywhere, but knowing what you know about the statue and not wanting the GAC to have it? There's only one thing you've got to have in mind then," Sierra said as she took a seat on a burgundy couch. "Pretty bold move too, attacking your own ship."

Zeth's smile appeared a little more genuine. She shrugged slightly. "A calculated risk. What better way to deflect attention from myself and my associates than to strike against the *Galactic Dream?* You truly are as brilliant as I'd heard. I knew we made the right choice. We're not looking to overthrow the GAC, but they clearly cannot be trusted. No, I would say a cleansing would be a good start."

"Is that what you and your friends are—cleansers?"

"My friends?"

"Well, you keep mentioning 'we.'"

"Ah yes, well I wouldn't call them *friends* exactly. Let's settle on a cadre of like-minded individuals. I suppose Cleansers could be a suitable name. In all honesty, we had not thought as to what to call ourselves. I only know that we would like you to join us."

She balked. "Join you? I'm afraid not, Madam Zeth. I'm more of a free agent."

Again, that tight smile appeared. "Not to be too indelicate about it, my dear, but you *do* owe us. You are indeed a talented young woman who would be a great asset, but you *did* fail this job and were quite ready to double-cross us. I was honest when I told

Mr. Merthane that we did not see any reason to kill you." Zeth paused before fully leveling her gaze at Sierra. "However, reject this offer and our viewpoint could change considerably."

The sinister edge in her voice took Sierra aback. "So what you're saying is, I don't really have a choice in this?"

"I'm afraid not. I'd prefer you join us willingly, but I am not above pressing you into service."

Sierra nodded slowly, considering Zeth's words. She also noted that two of the suits had positioned themselves near the door, not shy about flashing their concealed pistols. *No way out of this. I might as well go along with it—for now.* "Well, when you put it that way, how can I refuse?"

"Splendid!" Zeth motioned to one of the suits, who brought over a decanter filled with lavender liquid. "Let us celebrate our new partnership. I also meant what I said about your brilliance. I am very excited to be working with you again."

"Even if the first time I didn't know it, right?" She could barely repress the sneer that threatened to reveal itself.

If Zeth knew how she really felt, she appeared clueless giving Sierra a wink while the suit poured them two glasses.

"Merthane was right about Max," Sierra said. "He won't let this go and I doubt Glintock will either."

"My dear, plans are already in motion to remove them both from play, but at the same time, two men against our organization would be like fighting against gravity," Zeth said with a thin smile as the suit handed her a glass. "What shall we drink to?"

Sierra considered it for half a second. "The future."

"Yes, to the future."

As Zeth drank from her glass, Sierra pretended to admire the wall's highly reflective surface. A wicked smile crossed her face as her eyes glimmered with turquoise light. "Yes, the future."

ACKNOWLEDGMENTS

Though I've been living with Maxim Ultra for as long as I can remember, I didn't get to the book you're holding in your hands alone. A massive thank you needs to go out to my writing group partners: Barbara Davis, Matt King, Lisa Rosen, Mitch Richmond, and Michelle Hicks. All these folks contributed in various ways to helping me find the way through Max's first adventure. Thanks also need to go out to Tara Lynne Groth and the members of Triangle Writers, who gave some great advice when I decided to finally commit and start Max's story.

And as always and most importantly, thanks to you, the reader. Thanks for taking a chance on this book. Thanks for reading!